OPENING DAY

DAN BERTALAN

Envisage Unlimited Press East Lansing, Michigan

First Printed 1994

10 9 8 7 6 5 4 3 2 1

Manufactured in the United States of America.

Library of Congress Catalog Card Number: 94-70352

ISBN 0-9623955-2-8

Envisage Unlimited Press
P.O. Box 777
East Lansing, Michigan 48826
517-834-2276

PUBLISHER'S NOTE
This is a work of fiction. Names, characters, places, and incidents either are the product of the author's imagination or are used fictitiously, and any resemblance to actual persons, living or dead, events, or locales is entirely coincidental.

ACKNOWLEDGMENTS

I am grateful to Mark Woodbury for his insight and editorial assistance. Thanks to Stan Materna, Scott Becker, and Ken Thompson for their technical guidance.

Cover art by Greg Hurley

Table of Contents

CHAPTER 1 – UNCERTAINTY

Brad Mercer eased his finger across the trigger. He swallowed. He drew in a deep breath. Okay, this is it. Don't miss. Don't screw up again.

The cross hairs in his scope wavered around the silhouette of a deer a hundred yards distant. He clenched his jaw and tightened his rigid grip on the rifle. Aiming offhand, it made the cross hairs dance even more. He tried to calm his thoughts but uncertainty came creeping. His breath became shallow and quick like a panting dog. His heartbeat became a drum roll that hammered in his throat. With a barely audible groan, he squeezed his eyes shut and jerked the trigger.

The old Model 94 Winchester bucked into his shoulder. His ears rang from the blast, his nostrils tingled from the impact and acrid smell of burnt gunpowder. Slowly, he opened his eyes. Heat swelled into his cheeks. He looked down at his feet. Crap, a gut shot. I'll never do it right. At least it was only cardboard.

He scuffed his boot into the gravel. Had it been real, Brad realized he would have wounded one of the most wonderful creatures on earth, the one animal that still added a wildness to the tamed world around him. The stray shot would have meant a long tracking job, maybe beyond the skills of a fifteen-year-old. Maybe he would have lost the whitetail and had it fall into the hands of another hunter, a man or possibly even a hungry coyote. Both hunters just the same. Both claiming his deer. The thought made his stomach churn.

He nervously glanced down the practice range at Detroit's North-Metro Sportsman's Club. I suppose they're all watching me. Nobody ever watches when you do good, only when you screw up.

Brad looked the other way at the rows of shooters squatting across the tables. None of the throng of red and blaze-orange gunners appeared to give him notice. They all seemed lost in their own world, strengthening bonds between flesh and blued steel.

A man three tables over finally looked his way. Brad lowered his eyes. A fresh heat rose into his cheeks. Yeah, he probably saw me. How many others turned away when I looked up? How many were chuckling under their breath after watching me struggle with this thing? He looked down at the rifle in his hands. Did they notice how bad I was shaking? Crap. At least they don't know why. No one knows, not even Pa.

Brad squinted down range at his target. He racked the lever action, the hiss-click of steel sharp in his ear. The spent cartridge clinked in the gravel near the four wasted shells before it. He narrowed his eyes. Okay, no wasting this one. No scattering it across the target like the rest.

He shouldered the rifle and pressed his cheek against the stock. He canted his head slightly to bring the off-center mounted scope into full view. He took a deep breath, the sweet aroma of gun oil mixing with the cool air. Just stay calm, it's only cardboard. Squeeze slowly like he taught you. He's watching. Don't let him down again. Show him you can do it, that you're ready to become one of them.

The deer silhouette came into focus as Brad centered his eye through the scope. He swung the cross hairs on the shoulder area. His finger tightened on the trigger. He began to exhale slowly. The scope clouded under the wash of his warm breath, just as it had a year ago on opening day. And as he waited for the scope to clear, the fogged shape of the target suddenly took on the image of the spikehorn that day.

The memories came flooding over him again, sweeping him back to last year's opening day.

His father had placed him on an oak ridge that day and told him to sit tight, but Brad soon became restless and began sneaking through the woods, determined he could creep up on a whitetail like the generations of deer slaying Mercers before him. By mid-morning his sneaking had turned into a steady walk. By mid-afternoon his steady walk had turned into a trot as he realized he was lost in the big woods of Michigan's Upper Peninsula — a place his grandfather said even the best of men shouldn't get turned around in.

By late in the day Brad had grown near panic. His shins were bruised from stumbling over deadfalls, his hands and knees soaked from slipping in the wet snow. Near dusk and nearly out of hope, he finally discovered the old logging trail that led back to the Mercer cabin. While trudging down the trail in the fading light, he came upon the spikehorn.

He wasn't paying much attention as he crested a rise in the trail and was shocked to see the spike standing in the road at fifty yards, staring dumbly in his direction. He shouldered the rifle and tried to take aim. He remembered looking into the black depths of the buck's eyes. After that, the rest meshed into a blur. His breath became short and pallid, gathering in a steamy cloud. His scope fogged. His heart raced in his throat. His numbed finger fumbled for the trigger. A strange weakness swept over him like a raging virus, draining the strength from his knees and quickly rising into tremors in his arms. His rifle swayed then sagged as if too heavy to hold. Quivering uncontrollably, he stood transfixed while the buck walked off into the shadows.

Brad had stood there for some time on wobbly legs, wondering what strange affliction had overcome him. By the time his legs were finally solid enough to walk, darkness had closed in around him. He plodded on toward the cabin, trying to shake free the hollow tightness in his gut. His biggest wish was to take a buck that day, yet when fate had dropped one in his lap, his nerve had crumbled like a house of cards.

The further he walked into the darkness, the more it began to sink in — buck fever, the dreaded malady of hapless deer hunters had claimed him. He had heard stories of hunters losing their senses when faced with shooting a deer. And he had snickered too; like it was an affliction that only happened to city slickers, spineless nerds who didn't belong in the woods, pretending wimps who dressed in red but weren't really hunters on the inside. But how could it ever happen to him, a deer hunting Mercer?

Walking back that evening he trembled as if gripped by an unshakable chill, realizing his buck fever reached far beyond uncontrolled excitement. It threatened all that was important; taking a buck, carrying on his hunting heritage, joining the ranks of successful deer hunters before him. But the worst part was that it had also spawned a new and unexplainable fear of the forest that night, a fear that curdled his insides to mush.

As he walked on, the woods looked different. Its once vast beauty wore an uncertain aura of veiled thickets and unknown depths. He wondered if another buck would step from the shadows, its watery eyes unraveling his nerves again, sapping his strength, turning him into a pretend hunter who couldn't manage to pull the trigger.

As he finally neared the lights of the cabin that evening, he decided to keep his buck fever and failure a secret. He had also held tight to the other thing, the unexplainable fear, burying deep the shame of that day.

Now as he waited for his scope to clear on the target down range and for the image to again become only cardboard, filaments of that buried buck fever began to rise in his throat like spider legs climbing. He tried to swallow them away. His mouth tasted like rusty iron. His arms began to tremble. His aim wavered.

"Getting a might windy for offhand shooting," a voice rattled over his shoulder. "Why don't you settle down on the bench here for your last shot, Brad? It's best you make that final one count before heading up north. What do you think, boy?"

Brad didn't reply at first. He simply lowered the gun's hammer and cradled the rifle in his arms. He nodded. That breeze isn't strong enough to make my shots wander. But thanks for the excuse, Pa, thanks for being the best shooting instructor I could ever hope for.

"I believe you're right," Brad finally said. "Maybe this darned wind is giving me fits. Besides, I'll probably be sitting when I take that buck anyway."

Trying to mask his embarrassment, Brad turned to his grandfather sitting behind the shooting table. Brad sat next to him and rubbed the lens of his scope with his handkerchief.

"Darned thing fogged on me again."

Pa nodded. Brad glanced at him, avoiding his eyes. Why lie about the scope? He's probably getting tired of that same excuse. He's glassing each shot, watching me close. He knows I'm shaking, flinching.

"Your stance is good but try lowering your cheek into the stock more," Pa offered. "That will divert your breath down plus give you a better view through the lens. Might help."

Brad nodded and kicked at the ground again. He deserves a better student than me.

"Come on, Brad. No sense getting worked up over a few stray offhand shots. Plenty of logs and trees in the woods to steady a man's gun on. It's only natural for a deer hunter to use all that nature has given him out in the wild, don't you think?"

Pa paused only long enough to spit an amber stream of chewing tobacco into the coffee can near his feet then answered his own question before Brad could reply.

"Yep, no question about it, boy, a tree standing or fallen makes a fine thing to brace your gun on."

He reached down and picked up a split section of log laying near the table and placed it in front of Brad.

"Why look," he said faking a surprised grin, "a piece of some tree has been struck down by the forces of nature, just laying here begging to help a young deer hunter steady his weapon. Why, I can almost hear that log talking."

Brad shook his head and smiled. He braced his elbows on the table and laid the gun's forearm across the log. He hunkered over the rifle, pressing his cheek on the side of the stock. Its well-oiled surface felt like a cool kiss on his face. In his grip it seemed like the handshake of an old friend.

Despite his frustration with mastering the weapon, Brad loved the old Winchester. He loved the iridescent sheen of its blued steel contrasting with the time-blackened walnut of its stock and forearm. He also loved its clean, rugged lines, and the captivating sound of its lever action. It resembled the classic rifles that had helped tame the wild west, warded off charging grizzlies in Remington paintings, and defeated overpowering odds against marauding Indians. For Brad its magic transcended time. His imagination leaped into its usual overdrive, taking him to pioneer days. While in his hands, he often traveled back in time, saving wagon trains and turning charging cougars. In his daydreams he never wavered, his bullets never missed.

The old gun was also a corridor into Brad's future. Its smells spawned dreams of hunts yet to come. The aromas of gun oil, WD-40, and Hoppee's Number 9 stirred anticipation of seasons ahead. Maybe he would face a pack of hunger-crazed wolves or get a crack at one of the fabled bucks of Deadman's Swamp? Whatever the quarry, Brad knew the gun was his key to unlocking the doors of excitement at deer camp, where the vastness of northern Michigan's woods held untold adventures.

Perhaps most of all, Brad loved the gun for its heritage; for its unbroken bond within his family. His grandfather had received it as a gift from a great uncle almost 60 years ago. After downing many a monster buck during Michigan's great deer days, the gun was passed on to Brad's father, Al Mercer, who, for the most part, followed in the deer hunting footsteps of his father. Just over a year ago, it was given to Brad. Now it was his turn to carry the weapon into his early deer hunting years, carrying on a seasonal ritual as old as man — fall's harvesting of the whitetail. As Brad leaned forward and peered into the offset scope, Pa hovered near his shoulder.

"Yep, boy, I can hear that old log whispering to you right now."

The old man edged even closer, the spicy odor of his tobacco breath warming Brad's ear.

"Why lookie here," Pa continued, in a high-pitched whisper. "It's Brad Mercer resting his grand old rifle right on top of me. Nothing I like better than helping a fine young man in the wilds, especially when he leans into me, using his weight against the fullness of my girth and the sure grip of my bark."

Brad flowed with the words, pressing his body forward. He was rewarded with a steadying of his aim as his arms grew firm against the pressure, the rough bark biting into the thick wool of his coat sleeve.

"Yep, that feels better," Pa went on. "I'm sure my brother walnut in your gun's stock, would also welcome a firmer hug, especially from such a good looking boy as you."

Brad grinned slightly as he pulled the gun tighter to his face. The cross hairs in the scope settled into a slow moving arc near the ring in the center of the vital area.

"Now if there's one thing a young guy like you can learn from an old chunk of tree like me is how to breathe. Us trees you see, we breathe real slowly. Matter of fact, in cold weather like this when we're settling into our dormant season, we hardly breath at all. It's so slow and steady it's hardly noticeable, especially when we breathe out r-e-a-l s-l-o-w."

Concentrating on his breathing, the banging and chatter of gunners at nearby tables faded from Brad's ears into a faint hum just beyond perception. His heart calmed to a steady rhythm. He slowly drew in a long breath and gently pressed his finger on the trigger. Exhaling in a steady flow, the cross hairs settled quietly in the ring. Brad didn't hear the shot, didn't feel the gun's recoil as it spit flame and the bullet streaked toward the target.

CHAPTER 2 – JOY RIDE

Sergeant Simmons held his breath and opened the small viewing port. Being a ranking corrections officer at Marquette State prison had its privileges at times, but this wasn't one of them. Nevertheless, duty called. He hesitantly peeked through the gray steel door.

There, only inches away, loomed the ruddy muzzle of Little Eli, his gaze perpetually lost on some distant horizon. Simmons met the blank stare. It seemed to pass through him. He pulled up the fleece collar of his coat to help shut out the chill creeping into his bones. It did little good.

Scars crisscrossed Little Eli's face like a road map tracking a lifetime of bucking everything that got in his way. His head sat directly on his shoulders, a few deep wrinkles near his ears and chin suggesting where most men wore necks. Tree-trunk arms hung limp at his sides, massive hands folded together over his waistline.

"Kinda looks like he's praying, don't it Sarge?"

Simmons turned to another officer who had stepped close behind him.

"Eli a saint?" Simmons said in hushed tone, "that will be the day."

His eyes flicked back to the big man's hands. Another chill crept up his shoulders. Praying? Those hands? Never. Memories flashed in Simmons' mind like pages flipped in a photo album. He shuddered. Images of those who had dared to get in Eli's way over the years appeared then faded, faceless victims with crushed larynxes or snapped neck bones. They were faceless not because Simmons didn't remember the men. He remembered them all too well. They were faceless because of Eli's trademark; rearranging the victim's features like a kindergartner squishing toy heads made of molding clay, his powerful fingers gouging out eyes, crushing cheekbones and collapsing noses with a mighty squeeze. Simmons blinked and shook off the thought.

He looked back to the hands, the massive wrists tightly shackled with not one, but two pairs of cuffs chained to a heavy belly-chain encircling Eli's torso. The folded hands waited, like the unblinking eyes and subdued hulkish frame. Only his bear-like jaws moved, flexing with their familiar rhythm.

Behind Eli in the narrow corridor, nine others shuffled restlessly, chains dangling from their cuffed feet and hands tinkling an abstract music known only too well to the residents of Cell Block F, the prison's deepest hole in maximum security. Some place to be a "resident", Simmons thought. No, these men weren't residents. That would imply that they belonged somewhere. And these guys didn't fit in anywhere. That's why they were confined here. But nowadays you couldn't call them what they were; convicts, cons, inmates — no, to be socially correct you called them residents. Besides, calling them a con would only get them pissed, and there was no need for that, not when you had to spend most of your waking day with them — and sooner or later, you had to turn your back on them.

The residents in Block F shared another bond beyond the tinkling chains; lifers with no chance of parole, losers with nothing to lose who had enrolled in the State penal system's experimental drug-testing program; long ago signing releases that occasionally made them guinea pigs for select agencies with enough governmental stroke. With Marquette's stringent security preventing even a trickle of smuggled-in drugs from reaching the dark confines of Block F, the lifers would risk anything for a controlled high in the name of science — not that any of them gave a damn about science. They simply wanted the extra money or privileges that came from participating in the testing — that, and the chance at a brief mental escape through drugs.

An electronic latch buzzed for an instant, then sharply clicked open. Simmons tensed at the noise. He swung the block door wide. The musky stench of caged bodies poured from the corridor, mingling with the crisp air drifting into the prison courtyard from Lake Superior.

Gripping his night stick, Simmons curtly motioned the residents ahead while six other guards nearby readied for any hint of an outbreak. Behind him stood the deputy warden, eyes locked on the inmates. Up on the east wall, a tower guard lowered the muzzle of his M-14 rifle toward the cons. The guard, mostly a dark silhouette on the brownstone wall, resembled a black knight atop some Medieval castle. His elongate shadow stretched across the courtyard. But the heavily clothed troop paid him little notice as they shuffled passively ahead, some grinning and winking from under their blue stocking caps as they walked toward a waiting bus.

Watching the prisoners pass, Simmons looked toward the bus. He shook his head. "I don't like this," he whispered to the deputy warden. "Controlling this bunch behind bars is bad enough. Letting them board the bus for a trip beyond the gates is lunatic's play. Someone either has brass balls or a vacant brain. Either way they're asking for trouble. It ain't right. It ain't policy."

"Policy's out the window on this one," the deputy warden said. "I know you take your job seriously, Simmons. You're one of the few who really cares about who we're guarding and who we're guarding them from. But this one's over all our heads. So don't fight it, just follow orders."

Simmons nodded and looked toward the inmates.

"Someone with stroke all the way to Washington," the deputy warden continued, "combed the files on this bunch carefully. It's as if they were looking for magnum hair-triggers daring to be pulled." His eyes followed the lead inmate. "I sure as hell hope they got all the way through Eli's file. Can't imagine anyone approving him on this thing if they knew what he did on the outside."

Simmons turned back to the deputy warden. "You mean something worse than what he's done to other residents?"

"Fraid so."

"What could be worse than that?"

The deputy warden paused for a moment, a visible shudder passing through him. "Believe me, you don't want to know. It wouldn't make your job any easier. Just drop it."

The deputy warden glanced up to the top section of windows in the administration building overlooking the courtyard. There, looking out one of the Gothic windows, stood Warden Jacobs, arms crossed, eyes narrowed.

"I'm sure the warden likes it even less than we do," he said. "He's not used to having Army brass flashing Governor's orders in his face and taking his residents beyond the walls where they don't belong."

The deputy warden stepped alongside Simmons and lowered his voice. "He didn't give them up without a fight though, as short-lived as it was. He tried to get the backing of the Director's office. All it earned him was an ass chewing from the Lieutenant Governor. The L.G's an ill-tempered fart. Must be from all his years backing the military. Anyway, by the look on the warden's face I'd say he's still plucking administrative teeth from his butt."

Across the courtyard, the inmates' shadows danced like a procession of grim reapers as they paraded toward the bus.

"Looks like Uncle Sam has his dink in this one," hissed Laragy, a homicidal child rapist in the middle of the pack. "And he wants YOU to enlist, today."

A few snickers filtered from the lumbering mass of chains and denim.

"Zip it up," snorted Simmons as he rushed from the deputy warden to keep up with the residents. "Keep it tight and quiet or you'll all be marched in an about-face." He added a stern look to the lie.

In the lead, Eli slowed and began rotating his massive head like a tank turret. Laragy shrank into his wiry frame and scuttled behind another man.

Simmons focused on Eli's every move. "Okay boys, let's keep it going," he said. "You don't want to upset your trip with the boys in green."

Flanking the prison's white bus, nicknamed the Snow Bird, two rows of National Guardsmen stood ready in full riot garb. From under visored helmets peered the jaw-locked faces of an elite squad of Riot Control Specialists. Unlike ordinary ground-pounders, the RCS were exclusively trained to squash unruly mobs. Their arsenal contained the latest in near-lethal crowd control. Unleashed, their hard-core tactics verged on malice but the results were swift and undeniable. Unwavering, they looked like Dobermans in fatigues.

Filtering past the men in green, the inmates lingered just enough to probe the visors with icy stares. Jerome Johnson, a towering black bringing up the rear, welcomed the pause with a sadistic grin. He casually stepped out of line and stooped his seven-foot frame in front of a slightly built RCS.

Simmons edged closer but loosened the grip on his stick. Typical J.J, all harmless show and no go. What a big blowhard. But I suppose that's how he survives on the inside.

Johnson looked into the clean-shaven, almost boyish face.

"Well, if this don't beat all," he said, flashing a half snarl, half smile. "Looks like they got this half-pint from the cub scouts. Now tell us true, is that right baby-face? Or did they enlist your sorry little white ass from the brownies?"

Simmons walked closer but the RCS replied before his second step hit the ground. From under the starched fatigues, wire muscles uncoiled like a switchblade. Most saw only the slight twist of the hips and heard the snap of cloth as the arm lashed out. Johnson, still wagging his face, didn't have time to blink. In a blur, a single iron thumb struck him just above the clavicle at the base of the neck. Johnson wheezed in numbing pain. His knees buckled as if they had been severed.

Before Johnson's head hit the asphalt, two other inmates managed to grab a handful of his jacket and uprighted the wincing giant. Glassy-eyed, his feet fluttered out of sync as they kept him moving.

Simmons rushed in front of the specialist. "What in hell was that for? The man was shackled. J.J. didn't mean no harm."

The young RCS ignored the question and stepped back in line, restriking his staunch pose. His face remained expressionless as if he had swatted an annoying fly.

Simmons looked back to the deputy warden who simply waved him toward the bus. Simmons' face reddened.

Leg irons tinkled against the steps as the inmates boarded the Snow Bird. Like its outside, the interior of the bus was painted bone white — as bleak as the cells in solitary. It smelled better though. It only reeked of disinfectant and diesel. They filed past the inner mesh cage into the two rows of austere seats. Watching Johnson stagger aboard, some of the inmates' pit bull features melted into the looks of worried pups.

"What's the deal?" growled one of the men who had grabbed Johnson. He spoke in a hushed tone as he moved along the seats. "We got rights. We sure as hell didn't sign up to serve as punching bags for some goons in green."

The rest began to grumble and strain against the confines of their cuffs. Like nervous show tigers snarling at their handlers and one another, they took their places. "That's right", Simmons said, as the last of them finally settled into their seats. "Let's all behave so you won't miss your little adventure today." He paused, looking out the bus window. "Whatever that might be," he finished, mostly to himself.

He moved swiftly down the aisle, locking each cuff chain to a latch on the steel arm of the seat while another prison guard in a cage at the rear of the bus watched with a readied shotgun. Simmons finished securing the chains without another word. The inmates' attention riveted to the RCS squad outside. Narrowing their eyes against the unaccustomed daylight, they stared past the windows, quickly fogging the cool glass under their breath.

"Hey, Sarge," Laragy whispered as Simmons passed. "Where these watchdogs taking us?"

"Don't know. Never seen them before. Maybe they're on some kind of special prisoner transfer training."

Simmons saw the doubt on Laragy's face. But none of them knew squat. Not even the warden had been told the details of the operation. Prison officials had been curtly instructed to turn the chosen ten over to the Army then stand clear until they returned the prisoners. Why they had selected the worst of the lot was beyond reason to Simmons. No, he didn't like breaking procedure. That's when bad things could happen, especially with this bunch. His eyes drifted toward Little Eli.

He double-checked the latched chains as he walked down the aisle to the front of the bus. Reaching the entry cage, he slammed the meshed door behind him with a resounding clank and stepped toward the outer door. He paused, glancing out at the elite squad, then looked back to the chained passengers.

"A word of advice," he said, his eyes flicking back to Johnson, "you better behave today. I don't think your friends out there will tolerate any bullcrap, so for your own good, settle back and enjoy the ride."

As Simmons left, the guard in the rear cage exited the back door, leaving the bus unguarded for a moment. A few inmates started to grumble but fell silent as two RCS entered the front cage and another entered the rear, slamming the bus doors behind them. One sat in the driver's seat and roared the diesel to life.

"Hey, you ain't prison officers," sputtered a revived Johnson, his eyes wild. "Th-th-this ain't right. You ain't supposed to be taking us nowhere. We demand to talk to the warden."

Several others joined Johnson's plea. But their words were drowned out by the grinding engine. Even the yells from near the front seemed to fall on deaf ears. The driver crammed the bus into gear, roaring the troop past the prison gates.

After leaving the prison drive, the bus swung southeast on Highway 41. Immediately, some of the inmates who had received lab-controlled drug testing at the State Clinic flashed confused faces.

"Wait!," Laragy whined, "this ain't the way to the Clinic. You jar-heads don't know where you're going. Turn around, turn around!"

The two RCS in front exchanged a brief stare then indifferently looked back to the highway.

Most of the inmates, straining at their shackles, failed to notice the two unmarked vans trailing the bus. Only Little Eli, passively watching the rearview mirror, spotted the escort. His mind however failed to make the connection. He just sat looking out the window and enjoying the ride. All the while his jaws continued to pulse in powerful rhythm.

Far to the north, gray clouds bunched along the horizon. A storm was brewing.

CHAPTER 3 – HOPE

Brad stared through the scope at the target. The recoil hadn't even made him blink, let alone flinch. Then, as if someone else had shot his target, a new hole appeared in the silhouette, neatly cutting the "X" in the center of the vital ring. Several hard slaps on his shoulder jolted him back into focus. He suddenly realized he had shot, and hit the mark.

"Heck of a shot, Buwana!" shouted Corey Stiles, as he threw himself down on the bench next to Brad and continued pounding his back. "Man you're a deadeye. If I were a buck, I'd be shaking in my hooves just at the thought of you, Man."

"Where in blazes have you been?" Brad said, pointing at the club safety officer stepping near the far end of the firing line. "It's almost your turn. This isn't soccer practice where you can go running all over the field."

"Sorry Brad, but I just had to go down and watch that dude near the end with the 7MM Weatherby. Man, you should have seen it. He's got over a grand worth of shiny gun knocking his double chin silly and he still can't hit squat. What a toad."

The lead safety officer blew a whistle and hollered. "CEASE FIRING! ALL SAFE ON THE FIRING LINE. CLEAR CHAMBERS, OPEN BOLTS, GUNS DOWN."

Clicks and clacks rang down the rows of tables. Most of the gunners stood and stretched. Another officer at the other end of the line signaled back to the lead man.

"ALL CLEAR, FIVE MINUTES TO CHANGE TARGETS."

Pa stood and picked up a new target. "I'll get this one, guys," he said picking up a staple gun and heading for the targets. "Why don't you get your gun out, Corey, while I put up this fresh buck for you."

Corey nodded and picked up his gun case from the far end of the bench. He began fumbling with a knot in the draw cord of the tattered cloth case. He paused and looked at Pa walking down range.

"You know I never thanked you for sharing your grandfather."

"You don't have to thank me, Corey. What's there to share? It's not like you get to take him home or anything."

"I mean, he's such a deer hunting legend. Man, half the guys in school who hunt would give up their babes to go hunting with him. And ever since we finished hunter's ed together, you've let me hang around like he was my grandfather too."

"You know Pa, there's plenty of him to go around. And I think he enjoys all this as much as we do." Brad paused and looked at his grandfather walking slowly in the distance. "Just remember, he doesn't hunt anymore, so don't expect too much when we get to camp. His eyes and, well, the rest of him isn't like it used to be. But he's still the greatest as a deer hunting teacher."

"Man, you're telling me. I can't wait to get up there and show him all we've learned from him. It's going to something else, being in camp with all the deer hunting Mercers."

"Yeah," Brad replied, his eyes gazing somewhere in the distance.

"Brad?"

"Yeah?"

"What about your dad? I mean don't you miss not having him be part of all this?"

Brad's eyes narrowed. "He could be part of it if he wasn't so busy with work all the time. He thinks that putting in overtime and paying bills makes him the complete father. As far as hunting goes, Pa has been more of a father to me the last couple of years, more of a friend than my dad ever could. No, I'd just as soon have Pa showing us the ropes. Besides, my dad will be so busy puckering up to Mr. Crane's fat ass in deer camp, he won't find time for us there either. And I guess that's fine by me."

Corey shrugged his shoulders and resumed yanking on the knot. "Well," he said in a hushed tone, "at least you got a dad to bitch about."

Brad's eyes snapped back to Corey then softened. Yeah, he's right. Here I've got both a dad and grandfather and all I can do is gripe. And all he's got is an overworked, underpaid mother and two bratty sisters. Maybe I should be more thankful.

"Sorry, Corey."

"Don't be. Not your fault he split. He'll be back someday once he hits pay dirt. I'm sure of it. Why else would he have left me his favorite gun?"

As Corey struggled with pudgy fingers, more color rose into his face, its pink flush setting off the rust-colored hair sticking out from under his stocking cap. He finally attacked the cord with his teeth, unraveling it and pulling the gun from the case.

"Now that's chomping at the bit," Pa said, returning to the table. "Just take your time, son. That target ain't running nowhere. Got him stapled to the braces real good, just like we do in deer camp."

Pa flashed Brad a quick wink and drew his face into a tight-lipped smile.

The safety officer yelled. "HOT ON THE FIRING LINE. COMMENCE SHOOTING WHEN READY."

"Okay, target," Corey said, as he ceremoniously withdrew shells from his pocket, "it's time to meet your maker."

Exaggerating a steely gaze toward the target, he handled the gun with the delicacy of a custom-made European rifle. But it couldn't have been further from it. The battered H&R Model 1900 single shot 12 gauge was a pulp cutter's blunderbuss, a raw-boned piece of steel and wood made for close-range spraying of pellets at small game. It was a simple starter gun at best. Certainly not a deer gun. But Corey handled it like a thing of magic. Its abused stock and faded bluing contrasted with the shiny bead and adjustable dovetail sight Corey had brazed on in shop class.

"What you're looking at men," he said in an announcer's voice, tilting his cap to one side, "is twenty-eight inches of smooth-bore, straight-shooting, slug-spitting demon. Yes sir, a genuine whitetail widow-maker in disguise. What you're about to witness is pure beauty in action."

Corey sat down on the shooting bench, straddling it with his ample rump. He flicked the breech lever then snapped the barrel open. He picked up one of the three-inch magnum slug shells on the table, slipping it into the chamber. It seated with a soft "tunk".

"Ahhhh!" Corey hissed, "What a lovely sound. Only three sound sweeter."

He flicked his wrists, snapping the barrel shut with a high-pitched "clink".

"That's the first," he said, then laid the gun gently on the table.

He pulled his cap on tight like he was about to mount a bucking bronco then spread his feet wide, digging them into the sand under the table. Corey picked up the gun and leaned over its slight frame, pressing the short stock firmly into his shoulder. He spread his elbows wide then reached up with his thumb and drew back the tarnished hammer. "Click-CLICK."

"That's number two. Oh what sweet notes."

Brad, now plugging his ears with his fingers, stood behind Corey, peering over his shoulder. Pa, apparently only half-trusting the magnum load in the old gun, scooted to the far end of the bench and leaned back, cupping a gloved hand over his ear.

Corey propped the barrel on the log and clenched his jaw like a fighter about to get hammered. There was no forewarning of the shot, no steadying of the aim, no squeezing of the eyes, no tightening of the shoulders — just instantly the unmistakable "VA-ROOM" of the magnum blast rippling across the range, echoing far into the distance.

A yellow flame belched from the barrel as the gun kicked backwards like a bee-stung pony, half knocking Corey off the bench. He righted himself, shaking his head as if trying to regain his senses.

"Wow, THAT'S number three," he said, rubbing his shoulder. "Man, this little dude's got a wallop. Those old bucks are in deep trouble if I even come close. The blast from this thing alone should be enough to scare them to death."

"Looks as if you're going to be doing a lot more than scaring them bucks, son," Pa said.

He was still looking down range through binoculars, making sure his eyes weren't deceiving him. There, just inside the vital ring, sat the unquestionable thumb-sized hole of a 12-gauge slug.

Pa spat in his can, steam rising from the trickle running down the inside. He nodded his head slowly and placed his hands on his hips.

"No question about that one, son," he said. "That's fine shooting, Corey." Pa patted Corey's shoulder. "Your dad would be mighty proud of the way you handle that gun. Mighty proud indeed. Take a look, Brad."

Pa handed Brad the glasses. Corey's lower lip quivered for a second before tightening into a smile. It continued to spread into a glow that rose into his freckled cheeks and a shine that lit up his eyes. Corey continued to smile as he broke open the gun and replayed his four favorite sounds. Again the air shook in response, and again a lethal hit registered in the target. After four shots, Corey laid the gun aside and began rubbing his shoulder.

"Whoa horsey," he moaned. "Guess I better save some of these magnums for the real thing. No sense wasting these buck-buster loads all at once. Right, Paw Mercer?"

Brad listened to the way Corey drew out the word Pa, with a sweet drawl like the southern boy in the old-time movie The Yearling; a story about a kid who raised a fawn that in turn raised hell on their small farm. He looked at Pa. No, short and silver-haired, there wasn't much resemblance to the actor Gregory Peck in the movie. But his Pa, the famed deer hunting Pa Mercer, was real and stood taller than any movie star.

"I can't believe it," Brad finally said after looking through the binoculars. "You made every shot count yet you hardly even took aim let alone squeezed your shots off slowly. How in the world can you hit anything just blasting away like that?"

"Darned if I know," Corey replied, shoulders shrugged, palms up. "I just do what feels right. I set the bead over the shoulder area then touch her off. I don't see how there's much else to it. It's pretty simple, really. Mostly I just do what Paw Mercer showed me. Besides, like I said, that gun's magic. Kind of like me, a born deer slayer."

The fresh innocence of Corey's infectious smile soon spread smiles on Brad and Pa, and even a half-dozen other gunners watching the show from nearby tables. Moments later, the range officer cleared the firing line.

"What do you cardboard killers say we wind up this show," Pa said. "I think you're both ready for whatever lies ahead. Besides, there's still plenty of packing to do before your dad gets home, Brad. Go grab your target, Corey. We'll pack up this stuff."

Brad slid his rifle into the case and zipped it up. Pa picked up the empty shell casings.

"Corey acts like he doesn't even care if his slugs hit the vitals or plow into the dirt, Pa."

Pa stuffed the casings into his coat pocket and glanced down range. Corey was trotting ahead of the other shooters toward the targets, his old coat appearing to lag one step behind.

"I think for him it's just part of the whole event," Pa said. "It all excites him; the air tainted with spent powder, the patchwork of oranges, reds, plaids, the unknown, the anticipation of opening day. Must be great to be young and full of so much piss and vinegar."

Pa gathered the targets under his arm. Brad cased Corey's gun and cradled it with his own. He sighed. Yeah, the unknown, the anticipation. Opening day, I wished I could look forward to it like

Corey. He probably wouldn't get buck fever if a moose stepped into his sights. God, I wished I was more like him in some ways.

Corey joined them as they headed toward the parking lot. He was still smiling, eyebrows bouncing as he stuck fingers through the holes in his target. The boys flanked Pa as they walked, Corey edging ahead with a bounce in his step, Brad keeping pace with Pa in a measured, almost hesitant gait.

Pa didn't seem to notice. Eyes narrowed and a new crease adding to the lines in his brow, he appeared lost in his own private thoughts.

As Pa drove the boys home from the sportsmen's club, an ashen line of clouds began moving in from the north. A damp stillness hung in the air.

"How long will it take us to get to deer camp?" Corey asked from the back seat.

Pa glanced in the rearview mirror. "Oh, I suppose Marquette's about a ten hour haul. The western U.P. is a no-man's land to most down-staters, but that's why we hunt there, less people, bigger bucks."

Corey nodded at Pa's logic.

"Pa," Brad said, looking at the skyline, "do you think we might get fresh tracking snow before opening day?"

"Normally don't make weather predictions for someplace five hundred miles north. But if my old bones are any clue, I'd say we might be in for a real dumping within the next couple of days."

He paused and rubbed his collarbone above his heart. Although intent on the sky and the prospect of snow, Brad still noticed it.

"Yep," Pa continued, putting both hands back on the wheel. "Got a feeling it might be an opening day to go down in deer hunting history. The kind of day you story tellers thrive on, Brad."

He grinned and glanced over at Brad.

"Come on, Pa," Brad said wagging his head. "You know I don't sling bull like I used to when I was a kid. Gimme a break."

"Yeah, give him a break," Corey said. "Ol' BS Mercer here is trying to clean up his name. He only BS's when he gets excited — or when his lips move."

Corey threw up his arms as Brad turned around and swatted at him with his hat.

"Okay, fine," Brad said, readjusting his cap. "Just wait until opening day. We'll see who has the best story — and the buck to prove it."

Brad looked back to the gray streaked sky in the north. Yeah, we'll see on opening day.

CHAPTER 4 – PARTY TIME

The prison bus ground down Highway 41 southeast of Marquette for a half-hour before turning on a gravel road that wound through the expanse of forest and swamps. The ten inmates caged inside appeared strangely engrossed with the foreign wilderness around them. They stared out the windows at leaf-bare aspens contrasting with black spruce and golden-needled tamaracks clustered along the low areas. Some watched the damp November sky thicken into a matting of bleak clouds threatening to rain or snow. The bus rattled on.

The inmates exchanged glances as the bus slowed and turned down a two-track leading deeper into the forest.

"This ain't right," Johnson said. "They ain't taking us back to nowhere land for our health. Somethin' bad's going down, real bad."

"Maybe if we refuse to get off we'll stand a chance," Laragy said. "Maybe if we just stick together and hold—"

He fell silent as he looked over his shoulder and noticed the RCS in the rear cage had leveled the automatic on him and was slowing shaking his head. The gesture proved enough. Laragy's gaze dropped to the floor and he turned back toward the window, his face drawn, his lips pressed. Most of the others were beginning to show cracks in their hardened shells; the darting of eyes and chewing of lips — weaknesses they couldn't afford to reveal in prison. Only Eli wore his usual granite face.

The driver slid the bus through the narrow curves, barely missing the gauntlet of trees hugging the two-track. The bus slowed as it passed an open gate, the single iron bar bannering a white sign: **WARNING! Army National Guard Training Grounds. Restricted Area From June 1 Through September 1. Open To Hunting.**

Only Little Eli managed to read part of the sign as they sped past. The three-syllable words proved too much for his mind to unravel but he caught a few of the easy ones and recognized the final word — *hunting.*

He mouthed the word. Hunting, yeah, he knew about that. Not the kind of hunting he saw in the prison library magazines showing pencil-necks with dead ducks, no not that. He meant a real man's hunting, the kind where you picked your prey: man, boy, whatever, stalked them, caught them, played with them like a cat would a mouse, seeing how much the body and mind could stand and then the rush when you finally took them out. The end was always the best part, feeling that last twitch of life under your grip as it left the body. Yeah, he liked hunting, liked it a lot.

The isolated Training Grounds sat in the center of the Marquette State Forest. The 2400-acre plot was leased from the state and used mostly for summer maneuvers. But today the National Guard had a special mission and the bus roared deeper into the woods.

After snaking along the trail for two miles, the bus wheeled to a stop at the edge of a clearing. The whining diesel coughed to silence. The inmates quietly stared as two vans trailing the bus pulled along side and stopped.

The side door of the first van sprang open and the battle-clad RCS quickly positioned themselves near the front of the bus. From the other van stepped a man bundled in civilian garb followed by an Army Colonel decked in field greens. The civilian, a stub of a man sporting a shaggy beard, spoke to the Colonel who then motioned to the driver with a quick nod.

Obeying the silent command, the driver opened the bus door, unlocked the inner cage, then stepped aside. As the squat man and Colonel climbed aboard, the specialist in the rear cage stood and leveled his assault rifle near his hip. With the inmates chained to their seats it was more a show of force than a necessary caution. Nonetheless it served its effect. The inmates didn't twitch.

"Well, good afternoon gentlemen," the civilian said softly as he paused near the front cage. "My name is Doctor Robenthral. I'll be directing today's exercise."

The stiff-necked Colonel stepped up behind him as if to add strength to the smaller man's words. The doctor paused for a second, surveying the puzzled faces. He casually drew a handkerchief from his pocket and began cleaning his glasses as he strolled past the cage door and sauntered down the aisle. Robenthral looked no more threatening than a donut, yet the inmates shrunk back as he approached — all except Eli.

"I know this operation isn't your typical lab session," he said, giving them a sterile grin. "Most of you are probably accustomed to individual tests at the Clinic. But today's session requires, well, let's say, an outside group effort. And I rather think you'll enjoy the after-effects."

"There ain't going to be no after-glow, Doc," Johnson said. "You and your goon-heads out there are up to somethin' we don't want no part of."

"Yeah," Laragy said. "Just take us back to the prison. Besides, it's too cold out for us to leave the bus."

Most of the others agreed with a chorus of head-bobbing and grunts. The Colonel moved aggressively forward but Robenthral stopped him with a wave of a hand. The doctor shrugged his shoulders innocently and spread his arms like a preacher addressing his congregation.

"I assure you," he said, "the men outside are merely here to ensure the overall integrity and success of this operation. They mean you no serious harm." His words were crisp and well-chosen, falling softly off his tongue like a soothing lullaby without the melody. He walked down the isle, patting a few of the inmates on the shoulder. "It's really going to be just fine boys. The only difference today is that our operation is better suited for an open-air, natural setting. It's a beautiful fall day. Be good sports and I promise a fun time for all."

The inmates stared at Robenthral for a moment before exchanging glances, looking for some sign of what to do. Little Eli strained to rise in his chains. The sharp click-clack of a bullet being chambered into an assault rifle sounded from the rear cage. Everyone tensed and looked at him. He wore the eager face of a kid waiting in line at the Ferris wheel. He nodded toward his hands locked to the seat.

A few of the others reluctantly followed Eli's lead, motioning to be unlocked from their seats. At a nod from Robenthral, the Colonel motioned to the specialist in the front who began moving down the isle unlocking the inmates one at a time and ordering them off the bus. A few hesitated but were quickly prodded along and shuffled off. As they stepped from the bus, waiting specialists quickly secured their leg chains to brass rings attached to a long nylon strap at four-foot intervals. With the last inmate finally tethered to the strap, they looked like an oversized stringer of bluegills ready to be led toward the skillet.

Flanked by the squad of RCS, Robenthral marched the stringer of inmates into the clearing. Reaching the center, he turned and raised a hand. The RCS rooted themselves on the spot while the inmates shuffled to a stop.

"Your role in this operation is rather simple," he stated, his tone turning as cold as the air. "All you have to do is react to any given response. Just be your disgusting selves. We'll do the rest."

He flashed the ten oversized lab rats one last clinical glance before turning back to the vans. The Colonel paused and spoke to one of the specialists wearing a remote headset and lapel microphone. He then turned and hurried after the doctor. The RCS broke their rigid guard stance, forming a loose circle around the inmates. Despite the inmates' heavy jackets and caps, most began to shiver.

Robenthral and the Colonel stepped into the van and slid the door closed. The Doctor began eyeing through a tripod mounted camcorder pointed at the side window.

"What you're about to witness, Colonel, is the eradication of riots and wars as we have known them."

The Colonel raised an eyebrow and turned toward the doctor. "Considering this is your first test on humans, you sound awfully sure of yourself."

"Humans, lab rats, chimps, whatever," Robenthral replied with a matter-of-fact air, "their adrenal systems all function basically the same under stress. I'm staking three year's worth of research on it. Everything will work all right, as long as your troops can generate the adequate fright-flight reaction."

The Doctor pressed the record button on the camcorder and nodded to the Colonel. "Show time. Give your men the order."

The Colonel spoke briefly into a hand-held radio then pressed his face to the window. Robenthral leaned close to his side.

In unison, the RCS unsheathed their arsenal of electric stun prods, riot sticks, and whip-end saps. The inmates immediately backed up until they stood huddled in a bunched mass.

"That little twirp sold us out," Johnson barked. "If I get my hands on that worm I'll —"

His words were cut short by a stinging blow to the knee from a well-directed riot stick. He bellowed a vicious curse that was quickly swallowed by the cries from the others as the RCS darted into the mass like swordsmen, jabbing and lancing the helpless inmates, their crisp blows striking groins and shins — only the most pain-sensitive areas.

"How much of this?" the Colonel asked, his features hardening at the scene before him.

"Enough to fill them with fear or anger, the same emotions experienced in riots or war. I imagine their veins are already pumping epinephrine like crazy. Epinephrine, or adrenaline as you probably know it, is a chemical synaptic accelerator secreted by the adrenal glands during stimulation of the sympathetic nervous system — like now. My discovery, once it's inhaled, directly alters the adrenaline in their bloodstream. The effect is like pumping millions of tiny resistors through an electrical circuit, restricting the power to the appliances on the other end. Quite simply it scrambles the electric impulses to the brain. Blocked from normal electrical response, the brain takes over with another response, producing its own narcotic effect from a portion of the thalamus."

"It looks like your appliances might overload from a power surge before you have a chance to try your drug."

Outside, the relentless attack had already transformed the tethered men into a snarling pack of beasts, rage slobbering from their mouths, hatred swelling their eyes.

"Give it a moment longer," Robenthral said. "The beauty of my discovery is that the more enraged they are, the stronger the secondary effects of the thalamus secretions on certain nerve pathways connecting the thalamus to portions of the cerebral hemispheres. The drug should cause an opposite reaction verging on euphoria."

The Colonel arched his eyebrows and shook his head, apparently lost in Robenthral's explanation. "Well, whatever. But it looks as if you can't get them any more agitated than this. Let me call it off. I don't have the stomach for much more of this."

"Hold your stomach a few more seconds," Robenthral said, placing his hand over the radio in the Colonel's grip. "I thought your men were trained to be ruthless."

"There's a difference between ruthless and cruel," the Colonel said, yanking his hand free.

In the clearing, the inmates who tried to strike back floundered to the ground on shackled legs, only to be struck again as they tried to stand. Like a Cape buffalo, Eli held his ground in the withering mass of inmates, taking more than his share of blows, shaking off the pain from the strikes as if they were bee stings. He strained against his cuffs to grab one of the attackers. One quick squeeze was all he needed, yet with his cuffs chained fast to the heavy chain around his waist, he was helpless to fight back. Just a few more prods from the stun sticks and the fuming mass would teeter on madness. But the final prod, a jab to Eli's groin, proved too much.

He bent under the blow but still did not go down. And when he again lifted his head, his eyes held a murderous rage. With a thunderous wail he lowered his body toward his shackles. Massive hands strained at the chains, the belly chain groaning under their force. Grasping the tether strap between his feet, Eli slowly stood, blood vessels rippling under his reddened face. Inside Eli an overdeveloped adrenal system surpassing any of Robenthral's computer models raged out of control. The tether ring holding his leg chains snapped.

"Now, Colonel. Now!"

Eli didn't hear the shrill whistle piercing the afternoon sky. Only rage echoed in his ears. Like a runaway rhino he broke from the pack, heading straight for the van, the leg chains restraining him to choppy strides. Two RCS jumped in his path wielding riot sticks. But Eli simply whipped a mountainous shoulder into each specialist, spilling them to the ground. With legs pumping wildly he picked up speed as he neared the van, then threw all of his considerable force at the side door. The steel crumpled and the window imploded in a spray of glass. Inside, Robenthral and the Colonel slammed to the floor.

Stunned from the impact, Eli staggered to his feet. He turned to the yelling inmates. What? Watch out? It took a moment for Eli's mind to recognize that the frantic shouts as warnings. He spun to meet the onslaught of more RCS. But none came. They had retreated to the edge of the clearing, their riot helmets now replaced with rubber-hooded gas masks.

Eli whirled, his eyes wild in confusion. What's that? What's happening?

A pulsating growl rose above the nearby trees. A helicopter, gray as the sky, emerged from nowhere and swung over the clearing, bearing down on him.

Inside the chopper, the gunner lowered his tracking visor and flicked on the laser-guided sight. A wavering red dot floated across the ground toward the smashed van. Following its mark, a long muzzle hummed electronically in sync from the underside of the gunship, its barrel tracking the path of the beam.

Eli stood frozen, mouth agape in apparent awe at the thing. The red dot drifted in slow motion up his leg, over his chest and settled between his eyes. The gunner's thumb slid the safety off to the side and squeezed the trigger.

From the muzzle blasted a high-pressure stream of liquid nitrogen mixed with Robenthral's drug. It shot a hundred feet from the gunship in a narrow jet before misting in the air into a yellow cloud that covered Little Eli. Immediately the chopper dipped hard and swung around toward the yelling inmates. Short bursts of the liquid followed the laser's mark, soon engulfing the enraged troop in an iridescent yellow fog.

With its brief mission complete, the gunship swung east low over the trees. The thumping roar of its rotors faded to a faint hum in the distance, leaving the clearing in an eerie calm.

Near the van, Eli sat cross-legged, making wheezing noises and rocking back and forth. His face, clothing and the ground twenty feet around were covered with a sparkling yellow dust. From the broken window, Robenthral and the Colonel stared through the goggles of gas masks they had pulled on at the last moment. Robenthral turned away long enough to upright his still-running camcorder and focus back on the clearing.

Before them, Eli's high-pitched giggles bubbled in freak contrast to the hulk they poured from. More giggling rose from the center of a large yellow swath in the clearing as the nine other inmates drifted in and out of uncontrollable fits of laughter. Like pre-schoolers, some joked about being dandelions while others rolled in the frost-dried grass like romping puppies.

After the last of the sticky dust settled, Robenthral and the Colonel removed their gas masks and approached Little Eli. The giant looked at them as tears of laughter streamed down his ruddy cheeks.

"Get up, Eli," ordered Robenthral, pausing then glancing over his shoulder at the Colonel. "You're coming with us."

Eli looked up at Robenthral as pink rose into his face. The Colonel lagged two steps behind the doctor, edging closer to Eli, ready to radio his troops for assistance.

"Whatever you say, Doc!" Eli said, standing and sputtering an embarrassed giggle. He tried to hide his reddening face by drawing up his shoulder.

"It's okay, Eli," Robenthral said, boldly patting him on the back. "No need to be embarrassed. You're supposed to be enjoying yourself today. So come along now."

Trailed by the giggling hulk, Robenthral walked across the clearing toward the playful string of inmates. At a nod from the Colonel, the RCS broke into a run from the nearby trees and quickly restruck their guard positions around the inmates, riot weapons at ready.

"Hey guys, look," Laragy shouted with a broad smile. "The boy scouts have come back to play war."

The specialists had removed their gas masks and now exchanged confused looks as the inmates cheered and jumped up and down, their rage replaced with laughter.

"You can have your men stand at ease," Robenthral said with a wave of his arm. "We won't be needing any more guard detail. I'll handle the situation from here on."

The Colonel's brow dipped and threatened to knot but finally arched high on his forehead. "I'll be damned," he said. "I'll be goddamned."

"Everyone is going to behave now," Robenthral said, smiling like a man behind a brace of pheasants. "Isn't that right boys?"

The tethered inmates, all nodded blissfully, wearing happy faces.

Mouths still gaping, the specialists stepped back as Robenthral sharply ordered the lifers to their feet and led them toward the bus. He even ordered the inmates to skip around the bus three times while singing Twinkle, Twinkle Little Star. Most intertwined the broken lyrics with laughter. Eli and Johnson, however, giggled helplessly as they licked yellow dust from their hands and jackets to heighten their high.

No one seemed to notice.

After nearly an hour of videotaping the inmates' docile behavior, Robenthral directed them to the edge of the clearing where two specialists waited with a small compressor. Again donning gas masks, the specialists quickly air-dusted the inmates clean and turned them back toward the bus.

"Okay, boys, play time's over," Robenthral said. "Afraid we have to go back to the big house now."

"Awwww, Doc," Johnson pleaded, "a little more?"

Robenthral crossed his arms and shook his head. He pointed to the bus. Johnson lowered his head and obeyed.

"I never would have believed it in a million years if I hadn't seen it for myself," the Colonel said, stepping along side Robenthral as the inmates obediently shuffled into line in front of the bus.

Several specialists unlocked the inmates from the tethered strap and ushered them aboard. Even the stiff men in green had to smile at the childish antics of the lifers boarding the Snow Bird.

"Come, Colonel. Let's ride in the rear cage on the way back. Your men in the vans can pull up the rear as escorts. I have some follow-up observations to make. And I'm sure you'll want to see the after-effects of my drug."

The Colonel nodded and climbed aboard behind him. They made their way down the aisle toward the rear protective cage. Robenthral stopped as a specialist leaned over and began shackling some of the inmate's cuff chains to their seats.

"No need for that," he said, curtly waving off the specialist.

The specialist paused and looked to the Colonel.

"Sorry, Doc, but my job is to ensure the safe return of these men. We can't take any chances."

"Chances?" Robenthral blurted. "Chances of what, Colonel? What can you possibly be afraid of? Afraid of showing the world we have just discovered how to turn hostiles into placid children? This is our moment in the sun, Colonel. Let's savor it."

The Colonel took a deep breath and paused as if searching for a hole in the doctor's logic.

"What if that stuff wears off?"

"Are you kidding?" Robenthral continued. "With the dose they received, they'll stay as peaceful as kittens until tomorrow sometime. Their hands and feet are already cuffed, plus they're locked behind these cages. I think your men up front and the rest following escort can handle things. Besides, I've never had any negative side-effects during my lab tests. Don't you want to see the look on that overwrought warden's face when he sees us march this bunch off the bus singing lullabies?"

The set in the Colonel's jaw melted into a grin at the doctor's final notion.

"Well, of course my men can handle these monkeys. Okay, I'll go along with it. But I'll also order them locked to their seats at the first sign of trouble." The Colonel paused, his slight grin spreading into a shark's smile. "Yes sir, I wouldn't mind seeing that tight-assed warden eat some crow, myself."

He motioned the specialist aside and followed the doctor through the mesh door leading into the rear cage. They settled into the broad seat as the bus threaded slowly through the afternoon shadows.

The inmates rested dreamily in their seats while Robenthral and the Colonel watched idly from the rear cage. The drive back to Marquette proved unusually quiet as the lifers drifted off into a peaceful snooze, most still wearing grins now strangely set in their faces. Some twitched and jerked like puppies lost in dreams.

Johnson and Eli snored loudly, looking like two drunks in the throws of sleeping off an all-day binge. But deep within their slumbering bodies, their adrenal systems churned like refineries running out of control. Unlike the others who had only inhaled the drug, their glands were processing the yellow dust they had ingested. Within their overdeveloped adrenal systems that rivaled that of any wild beast, a new generation of synaptic accelerators began building in the medullary portion of their adrenal glands. A dam of great power was mounting, waiting to burst at the next calling of their sympathetic nervous systems.

The bus left the gravel road and pulled onto the highway. Snowflakes began flecking the windshield, swirling from a darkening bank of clouds. By the time the bus approached the outskirts of Marquette, the snow covered the highway in a greasy film. Stretching from his seat, Robenthral smiled at the sleeping inmates then turned to the Colonel.

"Just think," he said, hands propped on his hips, "wars, riots, violent crime, will all soon be a thing of the past. Not many men get the opportunity to alter their destiny, let alone the destiny of so many. God, this a great day for mankind."

He stared out the window into the grayness, watching the dancing snowflakes pass by, apparently contemplating the depth of his words. As the bus approached the last intersection before the prison drive, a pickup suddenly appeared from the crossroad, sliding across the greasy pavement and through the stop sign. Instinctively, the bus driver jerked the wheel sharply and floored the brakes. Tires hissed in the wet snow. The bus jumped the curb, smashing a road sign and plowing into a parked car.

The great mass of the bus helped absorb most of the impact, but only the driver stayed in his seat. Everyone else was thrown forward, their relaxed bodies scattering like rag dolls among the seats and aisle. Most of the inmates still groggy from their catnap, appeared only slightly dazed. No one appeared seriously hurt. Some laughed. Others simply looked surprised — all except Eli and Johnson.

Inside Eli the dam burst. His adrenal glands dumped their powerful new load into his bloodstream. It surged through his body. His mind flashed in wild spasms as the new adrenaline in his system opened long dead pathways to the brain and never-used corridors lit up in blinding flashes. He squinted his eyes and pressed his palms to his temples. Gripped by mounting tremors, he managed to pull himself from the floor, quivering uncontrollably. His muscles jerked as if molten lead was coursing through his veins. The spasms rose into his brain. Though he clenched his eyes against the sensation, searing bursts of light erupted in his head like exploding fireworks.

"Hey! look you guys," Laragy snickered. "Eli had too much dandelion dust. No more playing in the flowers for you. No more for the big guy. Nah, nah nah, nah nah, nah."

All the inmates began to laugh. All except Eli and Johnson.

Robenthral pulled himself from the floor, watching with a clinical detachment as he noticed Eli's quivering. The doctor pressed his face against the mesh door. A series of shivers rippled through the hulk wavering in the aisle.

Laragy moved closer. He poked Eli in the stomach with a finger. "Look, he's turning to Jello. A big old fat tub of Jello."

He poked again.

Eli quivered more.

Laragy poked a third and final time.

Eli growled as his hand engulfed Laragy's face, his talon grip sinking deep into the man's features. Laragy tried to scream but only a muffled whine trickled from behind the crushing hand. The other inmates began laughing all the more.

Two stunned RCS in the front fumbled with the cage latch. In the rear, reaction overtook thought. Robenthral scrambled from the protective confine and bolted toward the quivering mountain of denim. The Colonel, still rubbing a welt on his forehead, lunged after the doctor.

Just as one of the specialists in the front shouted a warning, Johnson rose from between the seats. He grabbed Robenthral and the Colonel in tentaclelike arms, drawing them near his face. His eyes danced with wild fascination while his features convulsed in short tick-like bursts. He squeezed their necks in the crooks of his arms. Faces went white then blue.

Eli dropped Laragy in the aisle and moved toward Johnson. The big black leaned back and tightened his grip on his prize catch,

Robenthral. Eli reached for the Colonel, his hand locking fast to a chunk of the man's shoulder. Johnson yanked the Colonel back. Eli yanked harder. A tremendous quiver pulsated down the Goliath arm as Eli ripped the Colonel free from Johnson's arm. The Colonel's clavicle splintered under the force of Eli's thumb, fingers pulverizing the muscles over the scapula. Only the Colonel's fingertips twitched as he passed out from the pain.

Eli dropped his limp catch and wheeled to meet two charging specialists. The first met the full force of a double-fisted backhand, sending him unconscious into the seats. The second side-stepped Eli's swing and jabbed the hulk hard under the ribs with a stun gun, giving Eli the full charge. He convulsed anew into a massive spasm that withered him to the floor. More laughter erupted from the other inmates, followed by a flood of RCS pouring through the bus doors. They swarmed over Eli, locking his cuff chains around the steel bracing of a seat.

Another team of specialists leaped for Johnson. He was still clenching Robenthral in a forearm stranglehold while the fingers of his free hand gouged deeply at the carotid arteries in the frail neck. Robenthral's suspended feet fluttered weakly. Locked in astonishment, his eyes started to roll back into a bluish face.

Two RCS frantically pried at Johnson's arms while another grabbed a handful of coarse hair and tried to bull-dog him into submission. But the black tightened the hold on his prize. Suddenly, a muffled blast from a specialist's .45 ripped through Johnson's face. He collapsed to the floor in a quivering heap. But his grip on Robenthral remained locked.

Later that evening, the correction officers' locker room rattled with chatter.

"What jerks," Simmons said, shaking his head. "That doctor and Colonel caused their own grief. Whoever heard of transporting inmates without shackling them to the seats? And why in hell didn't they stay in the rear cage? Now we'll be filling out reports most of the night to cover our butts. I told the deputy warden I didn't like this thing. None of us did. Now look what happened."

"Don't take it so personal, Sarge," offered another officer. "We were ordered to stand clear of this one. We didn't have a choice. Just that simple. Your record is still spotless within these walls. That's the only thing that really counts. You can't save the world, Sarge. Only your little part of it."

Simmons turned and looked at the man. "Maybe you're right. Still, there might have been something I could have done to prevent it, if only they would have let me go along."

"Look at the bright side, Sarge. At least no one got killed."

"Bright side? Hell, did you see Laragy's face? It's going to take them a week just to figure out which parts go where. And those other two are messed up royally."

"Yeah, but from the sounds of it, things could have been a lot worse. Eli might have saved the day."

Simmons turned toward his locker. Eli a savior? Doesn't quite fit. Was he trying to save the Colonel from Johnson, or kill him himself? Who will ever know. He recalled the Colonel's sprawled body, the shoulder crumpled like aluminum foil. Simmons lowered his head. Maybe I couldn't have helped. Maybe it was destiny. Maybe it could have been me instead of Laragy or the Colonel. Simmons shivered.

"The big question," the other man said, "is what did they give those lifers to make most of them turn into lambs yet made Eli and Johnson go bonkers after they curbed the bus?"

"They're still trying to sort that one out," Simmons said. "The Army has a lid clamped on this thing tighter than solitary. I also heard that Robenthral was secretive as hell. Had some special contract with the military and went to extremes to conceal his work. Most of it's locked in his brain, or what's left of it. Johnson's death-grip shut the blood off to it for so long it put him into a coma. No telling if he'll come out of it. Even if he does, he might have the IQ of a cabbage now."

"Well," the other officer said, "at least all our lab rats are back in their cages where they belong. Maybe next time Washington and the Governor's office will listen to the warden when the military comes up with some hair-brained idea involving our residents."

"Let's hope so," Simmons said, "for everyone's sake."

He adjusted his belt then slammed his locker door.

"Like you said, the important thing is that our rats are back behind bars. I can't imagine the havoc they'd cause out there in the real world somewhere."

Deep in the forest, the nighttime parade of wildlife browsed and foraged across a meadow, seemingly unconcerned that their diet was lightly frosted with snow covering sparkling yellow dust. Most of the small game fed briefly and moved on. But the deer lingered.

With November's snow-flecked wind buffeting their fur, they ate with the frenzy of carnivores. Shortening days had sounded their internal alarm clocks. Winter's deathly grip was quickly closing in. Instinct drove them to gorge, build fat, thicken marrow. Eat more, now, hurry. Soon piling snows would cover nature's table and winter's long battle would begin. Only the strong would survive the days to come.

CHAPTER 5 — THE TRIP

A hundred miles north of Detroit, the Friday night stream of traffic on Interstate 75 labored northward in a pulsating necklace of lights and steel endlessly stretching into the darkness. The seasonal migration grew each year, now swelling to a million redcoats packed into vehicles, jockeying for position on their dash to deer camp. The visceral magnet of weekend's eve, promising a brief reprieve, pulled them in hordes from the nooks and cubby-holes of their metropolitan lives, drawing them like bunched lemmings to escape a daily existence they professed to hate yet thrived in; pushing them onward toward the uncertainty of a beckoning woods. Their onslaught comprised the largest single body of armed men in the world — men driven to greet the anticipation of opening day.

Swept in the flow like a mayfly on a June stream, Al Mercer's brown Suburban clung to the right lane. From the safety of the slower caravan, the Suburban plowed steadily through the night while road warriors in the faster lanes weaved and darted through the tight lines of traffic. Al seemed oblivious to the rushing traffic as he listened to another story from his longtime hunting partner and friend, Vern Larsen.

Vern sat sandwiched between Al and Warren Crane, Al's boss, who was listening from the far side. Crane's robust frame consumed more than his third of the front seat. Vern took another pull from a can of beer warming between his legs then cleared his throat.

"Yep," he said, "I can still see the old man like it was yesterday; half-dressed, half-awake, and halfway to the outhouse in the dark by the time he spotted the silhouette of that buck in the orchard. The three-quarter moon and that snow made that deer stand out like a sore thumb, even the old man couldn't miss spotting it. Sure struck him dumb. He tip-toed back inside the cabin without a word, snuck back out, and emptied his gun at the thing."

Vern broke into a series of high whinnied snickers, trailing off with several nasal snorts. Crane joined in with his own rattling chuckle.

Brad tightened his grip on his knees, thinking they sounded more like jackasses than men.

"The old man was so shook," Vern continued, "that he even pulled the trigger on an empty chamber when I tried to get him to stop blasting. Then it took another ten minutes to convince him that it wasn't a live buck at all. It was only the 4-point I'd shot opening day. The weather was so cold that year the deer froze solid in the shed so I propped it up against the tree to see if the old 'deer master' here still had it in him. Cripes, he couldn't hit diddly. Sure showed his colors!"

Brad shook his head in the darkness, his eyes staring holes in the back of Vern's neck. You drunken fool. You don't know anything, Vern. You sure don't know about Pa. I can't believe you shared camp with him all those years and still don't know that he wouldn't shoot a deer in the dark or shoot next to the cabin. Jerk, if you knew the truth you'd probably puke.

Vern turned his head, giving Pa a sneering grin and a wink. Pa just grinned back, his ice blue eyes shining from behind his glasses even in the darkness of the back seat.

Briefly bathed in the flicker of passing headlights, Brad and Corey exchanged winks, nodding for effect. Pa had told them the real story.

Pa had seen the 'frozen buck' prank pulled on others over the years but didn't let on that night. When he realized it was Vern's buck, he took careful aim at just the tines of the rack. Even in death he respected the animal too much to further violate its body or waste nature's gift of good venison, even if it was Vern's deer. He did however take great delight using open sights to trim the tips off a few antler tines. Vern didn't notice it until the trip home. That's when Pa was rewarded with the final laugh as he overheard Vern cussing himself out for chipping the tines with his own rough handling of the carcass. Pa knew Vern was too pig-headed to believe the truth if anybody told him anyway, so he only shared the secret with his genuine deer hunting friends, Brad and Corey included.

As the conversation in the front seat trailed off, Vern sucked the last swallows from his can. He dropped the empty into the bag between his feet then eyed the other half of the six-pack. After a moment, he reached down and popped the tab on another can.

"Trusty little soldiers," he said, sucking loudly on the suds rising to the top. "They always stand at attention, ready to do battle against the dullness in life." He snickered and tipped the can.

Brad watched as Vern sucked at the can like a baby at a breast. The sides of his mouth drew in with each gulp, although he appeared to be pouring the beer down his gullet rather than swallowing it. Looks like your little soldiers have more than a battle on their hands, Vern. Looks more like a war to me.

"I can't wait to get up north and do some serious deer drinking," Vern continued. "Wait, no, I mean beer hunting. No, that's not it, deer hunting, yeah, that's right, deer hunting." He ended with one of his whinnies like it was the first time he'd ever sprung the tired joke.

Besides beer, Vern's only other escape was his annual trip to hunting camp. Unlike his vices, however, hunting offered a complete escape, both in body and spirit. He'd discovered it twenty-five years ago, sitting in a duck blind with Al Mercer on opening day of waterfowl season. Together they had shared the thrills, guns readied, watching the smoke-stream waves of ducks rising from the marshes skylining Harsen's Island. After the hey-days of duck hunting withered from the northern reaches of Lake Saint Clair, their guns turned to rabbits. But soon the passion of that chase was replaced with a siren that has drawn more men into the wilderness than any other animal — the lure of the white-tail deer. Although duck and rabbit populations rose and fell, the ever-adaptable whitetail continued to flourish, and with it so did Al and Vern's fever for hunting them. Their thirst for the sport seemed unquenchable.

One remote trip led to another and eventually they pooled their savings and bought a small swatch of land in the tangles of Michigan's Upper Peninsula. Using packratted odds and ends they built a ramshackle hunting camp that grew each summer when they could steal away time to add on to the thing. And though it looked mostly like something from a tar-paper and slab wood urban ghetto, the place had a magical lure that had drawn them northward into the November night for the past twenty years.

"Hey Dad," Brad said, leaning forward, "how about some chow? Corey and I are half-starved back here. Can we pull off soon and maybe get something to eat. Besides, you've been driving non-stop since we left and could probably use a break."

"Yeah, please Mr. Mercer," Corey harped in. "If I'm going to shoot a buck, I'd better keep my strength up or Brad will have to help me drag it out of the woods. And I'd sure hate to interfere with his hunting. Might spoil his chances."

Teeth flashing, Corey mimed a silent laugh then nudged Brad in the ribs with an elbow. Brad responded with an elbow in turn.

In the front seat, Al adjusted the rearview mirror, giving Brad a faint smile. "I guess it might not be a bad idea."

Al didn't commit though. He glanced in Crane's direction as if looking for approval.

Brad sighed when he saw the all too familiar exchange. It's his car, his vacation, his hunting camp and he's still looking to Crane for what to do next.

Brad tugged at his collar. The back seat had suddenly grown warm. He turned and looked out the side window.

A design engineer by training, Al had started working for Crane's Custom Container Corporation on Detroit's north side during the boom days of cardboard containers. There, under the tight-fisted control of Crane, he designed everything from pint milk cartons to refrigerator cases. Because of Al's functionally acceptable designs, Crane had allowed him to work his way up in the company, to vice president in charge of design. There, he was allowed to think much but manage little. Managing people and making important decisions was Crane's arena, and he made it a point to surround himself with people who dared not enter it.

Once Al had suggested switching to different packaging materials but Crane had squashed the ideal like a miserable cockroach of a thought and swept it under the table. Now, after a lifetime of building only cardboard cartons, Al was trapped in his neatly folded and glued cubical in life. The new generation of plastic and foam packaging sweeping the market had stagnated the cardboard packing industry, forcing Al Mercer to cling desperately to the only two things he knew — serving Crane and collecting paychecks.

"The boy's got a point, Mercer," Crane said, his gravelly voice gnawing the silence like a rasp. Al visibly flinched. Vern even jerked from his stupor. "This damnable traffic is a nightmare anyway," he continued. "Pull off on the Old State Road exit up ahead. We'll grab a bite, gas up, and take the Old highway north for a while. We'll probably make better time and get back on the Interstate later after this logjam of idiots thins out."

Al nodded and turned off at the State Road exit heading for the glow of service stations and fast-food shops.

"Turn here, into Arby's," ordered Crane, rubbing the red flannel straining to contain his midsection. "I can't stand choking down the grease bombs at those other places. I've got to have some halfway decent food. You've got to watch what you eat nowadays you know."

No one commented. Corey rolled his eyes and pretended to be choking on the cap stuffed into his mouth. Brad threw his hands over his face to stifle the laughter welling up.

After ordering from the drive-in window, they gassed up at the Shell station near the Interstate. Vern was in no condition to drive and Crane remained engrossed in his three bags of food, so Al stayed behind the wheel. Nibbling fries from the sack on the seat, he pulled onto the two-lane Old State Highway and continued into the night.

Crane's attempts to maintain an upper class demeanor grew thin whenever food passed in front of his face. His hanging jowls quivered and his eyes peered over cream puff cheeks as he pawed through bags like a kid at Christmas. He unwrapped each sandwich with delight only to gobble it down as if it were some valuable gem that had to be hurriedly stuffed into the protection of his digestive safe before a food thief snatched it. Gulping fistfuls of fries, Crane looked like he was loading a big-bored muzzle loader, his hand ram-roding in another overcharge of powder and shot into the tongued barrel. His mouth continually made hollow sucking sounds as he swallowed more than he chewed.

Brad watched in disgust and hoped the trapped gulps of air would at least come up as belches. He thought it the lesser of two evils considering the long drive ahead to Marquette. I don't how he gets invited back to deer camp each year. Just look at him, he doesn't even fit in. Dad must feel he owes it to him. Maybe it's a small price to pay once a year for job security. A boss wouldn't lay off a hunting buddy, would he?

As they drove northward, the roadside flicker of corn stubble eventually gave way to forests of leaf-bare oaks and maples. Stark trunks hugged the roadside, jutting up in the wash of the headlights like spindly sentries, their drooping arms gently waving at the hunters driving past.

The land also began to change. The undulating rich farmlands of central Michigan rose into an expanse of rolling hills; glacial moraines formed along ice fronts when mastodons roamed the land. The occasional silhouette of a deserted homestead stood in gloom testament to the sterility of the barren soils, its clays and nutrient long ago scrubbed free by the melt-waters of mile-high ice flows. But the trees didn't seem to care. Their roots plunged downward. They crowded for space. Their leafy crowns pushed upward to embrace summer's sun while their spindly young spilled across meadows and swales. Despite the sterile sand, the forest grew thick. And with it, wildlife flourished, especially whitetails.

"Watch it!" Vern hollered, pointing ahead with his beer can. "Coming from the ditch. A buck!"

Brad bolted out of a half-sleep, straining at his seat belt for a better look. Corey gripped Vern's shoulder and pulled himself forward to peer through the windshield. Only Pa, a veteran of nighttime northern roads, braced himself for an impact.

The Suburban's oversized tires chattered along pavement for a second before gripping the cold surface with a whine that quickly rose into a screech. The vehicle skidded then lurched, throwing a loose sleeping bag forward, thumping Brad squarely between the shoulders. The skid had taken away most of his breath. The sleeping bag knocked out what little remained. The Suburban shuddered to a halt just as a spikehorn buck leaped from the ditch.

"Look at that sonofabitch go," Vern said, his voice drowning out Brad's gasp.

The deer shadow-danced past the headlights at arm's length, legs flying, hair bristled. It spun to a stop in the gravel of the shoulder and stared back at the vehicle. The buck lowered its head to avoid the blinding glare of the headlights, but the beams only dazed it more, the yellow reflection in its eyes lighting up the night.

"Man, look at those eyes," Corey said. "How come they glow like that?"

"He's mad, that's why," Vern blurted. "Mad, he don't got a date."

"Vern's just kidding, son," Pa said. "Deer are creatures of the night and can see in the dark as good as we can at dusk. The back of their eyes are designed to reflect and capture light even in the dark. And what you see is that reflective lining shining back the car lights. I don't think deer get mad."

Vern grunted and tipped his can.

Brad stared into the glowing eyes. They appeared on fire, and with steam pouring from its nostrils, the spike looked more like a demon than a deer. His throat grew tight as he looked into its eyes. They seemed to probe into his very soul as if they knew his secret weakness. His heart began to hammer in his throat just as it had a year ago on the trail. Why now? I'm safe here in the car. Nothing's going to happen. It's only a scared spike. Why should I care? I don't have to shoot this thing. He struggled to control his breathing. His palms grew damp. He sat back in the darkness. Maybe no one will notice.

"Would you look at that," Al said, "That little guy's taunting us like he knows who we are and where we're headed."

"Bullcrap," Vern snorted. "He's just another horny teenager in the deer world with a pencil full of lead but no one to write to. He figures if he runs hard and long enough he'll eventually bump into some hot doe all by her lonesome. Kinda reminds me of some young deer hunters I know."

Vern turned and smiled at the boys. Brad looked away. Vern's glazed eyes passed over him but he noticed that Vern's smile appeared genuinely warm.

As other cars approached, the buck regained its senses and bounded into the darkness. Filled with renewed talk about rutting bucks and the coming hunt, the Suburban continued on.

Brad turned toward the window. The image of the spikehorn's glowing eyes remained etched in his mind like a glossy photo. Geez, how can I get buck fever sitting safely in a car? It just doesn't make any sense. Crap, I'm not some scared little kid anymore. I'm supposed to be grown up, a deer hunter. If this happens to me now, here, surrounded by everyone, what will happen when I'm alone opening day?

Brad shook his head. He looked down at his hands gripping his knees. Crap, this was supposed to be a fun trip. Some fun.

CHAPTER 6 — ROAD TIME

As the hunters drove northward into the darkness, Brad drifted in and out of a fretful sleep. His dreams hung on the fringe of consciousness, the blazing glow of the spike's eyes following him in the darkness. Every time he drifted off, the vision of the demon deer appeared, sometimes only feet away, threatening to impale him with those daggerlike spikes. His rifle had melted like soft licorice in his hands. He dropped it and tried to run from the deer but buck fever gripped him so tightly that he couldn't wiggle a muscle, like his feet were cast in cement.

Somewhere north of the town of Grayling Brad bolted upright at the start of a even more paralyzing dream; a buck too immense to be real, its saber tines coated with fresh blood and with eyes of yellow fire. Brad shook his head and ran a hand across his chest to check for punctures. Had it been his blood? He sighed and slumped back in the seat when he found none. He swallowed to rid the tightness in his throat and forced his eyes to stay open, keeping both his dreams and fears at bay. Now, for the first time, he regretted his overactive imagination.

Here the Old State Highway ran as straight as a rifle shot for miles. It cut through clusters of red oak and past alder swamps. Groves of aspen rimmed clearings dappled with broom grass that crowded the roadside, the pale bark of aspens shining in the side glare of the headlights. Brad stared out at the highway, watching the hood of the Suburban gobble up the hatch marks along the centerline. Grittiness wore down his eyes. His lids grew heavy. His vision began to fog. He blinked to clear his eyes but the fog grew thicker.

"Turn on your wipers, Mercer," Crane groaned. "You're passing a swamp or something with open water. That AuSable River probably runs close to the highway here. Looks like convection fog to me. We'll pass through it shortly."

As Al reached for the wipers, a billow of steam erupted from the seam between the hood and the windshield wipers, completely fogging the windshield. He quickly braked, pulled to a stop on the shoulder and popped the hood release. Everyone got out.

"Looks like a mighty localized ground fog to me," Pa said, shining a flashlight on the leaking radiator hose, its hissing spray clouding instantly in the cold air. Crane peeked over his shoulder and grunted.

"It looks like maybe it's only a small split," Al said. "I think I might be able to patch it up enough for us to make it to a service station."

He fished under the front seat and emerged with a rag and a roll of electrical tape. In a few minutes he finished make-shift repairs and slammed the hood.

"There," he said, brushing his hands together, "that should keep us going for a while if we don't push it. I think we'll just have to be careful and watch the temperature gauge."

Al pulled into the sparse traffic. Brad noticed that his dad drove with his shoulders straighter, head more erect. Maybe the cold air had refreshed him. Or maybe it was handling the minor crisis without Crane's input. Either way, his dad's glow was short lived. They made less than a mile before Crane began expounding on the virtues of proper vehicle maintenance, especially before long trips. Listening to Crane made it seem longer, but it was less than fifteen miles before they spotted a cluster of small buildings, including a small service station still flashing a partial neon sign overhead that read, "CHANIC".

"Looks like we lucked out," Pa said. "You don't often find small stations along the Old Highway open at this hour, let alone one with a mechanic on duty. Must be they're counting on the rush of all us deer hunters."

Lights in the office section and the mechanic bay shined through a milky film of condensation on the windows. Al pulled up to the single bay door. The stall appeared empty so he tapped the horn once. Through the fogged windows a blurred figure flickered past and paused near the door. The old panelled door shuddered then opened slowly as a whining chain drive labored it upward. When it stopped, an arm near the door frame waved them in. Then the door ground back down behind them, banging as it hit the concrete.

The hunters emerged from the vehicle and Brad wondered if they had indeed lucked out. The inside of the station looked more like a junk parts warehouse than a mechanic's area. Rusted piles of amputated exhaust systems lay in tangled heaps on the floors. Under the web-work of iron and grease lay a potpourri of grungy car parts, long ago succumbed to an unknown fate, severed by a torch or wrench. The blackness of the oil-stained floor crept up the walls at least three feet where patches of dulled white peaked through the curtain of grime. But as he turned, the place suddenly took on an unexpected shine.

"Hi. I'm Becky," said a pretty face peeking around the doorway.

Her soft eyes drifted across the group of hunters, lingering on Brad and Corey.

"I know it doesn't look like much with all this mess," she said, her curly hair bouncing as she shrugged her shoulders. "My dad's a total slob sometimes. Don't worry though, he also happens to be the best mechanic around, these parts anyway. Just went next door to get some coffee."

She stepped into the room and looked around the men at the steam rising from under the Suburban's hood.

Brad's eyes followed her every move. He stood dumbstruck, unblinking. This is a good place to be stuck for repairs, yeah, real good. Wonder how old she is? Looks my age, maybe a year or so more at most. So hard to tell with girls. They always look older, especially knockouts in tight jeans.

He felt cool air passing across his palate. Come on dummy, shut your flap before everyone sees. And stand up straight, you're short enough. That's better. I wonder if I should stick my chin out to make me look older. Naw, I'm stuck with a plain face, no sense having a plain jaw drawing attention to it. Why do pretty girls always make me think of the dumbest things?

"Radiator, gasket or hose?" she asked, looking up to Al.

Brad and Corey exchanged a surprised glance. City girls didn't know much about cars. Then Brad realized he didn't know much about country girls either.

"Pretty sure it's just the hose," Al said. "With all the water and steam in the dark it was hard to tell for sure."

"Well, whatever. My dad can probably have you back on the road in no time. He's been fixing flats and patching exhaust systems all evening. Happens every year. That's why he's got me here at this hour helping take care of the register and gas sales." She ended with a sigh and rolled her eyes.

Brad and Corey nodded as if they understood the workings of a remote service station on the highway during opening weekend of deer season. The way she rolled her blue eyes, Brad thought he would have nodded if she told them they looked like aliens.

"You guys must be deer hunters," she said, turning her eyes back on the boys.

Brad noticed they had suddenly turned a cooler shade.

Still nodding, the boys looked at each other, trying their best to wear nonchalant deer-hunter faces.

"Oh yeah," Brad said looking at Corey. "Sure, we're deer hunters."

"Naturally," Corey said. "Of course we are."

An old cow bell clanked from over the front door in the office as it swung open. A wiry man wearing greasy coveralls and a Tiger's baseball cap walked in.

"What's up, babe?"

"These guys got a leak in their cooling system. Told them you could fix it."

"Sure," the man said, his face lighting up at the prospect of helping troubled motorists or taking their money, maybe both. He walked over to the Suburban and threw up the hood. Waving a trouble light between the radiator and the engine he prodded with a greasy hand then quickly nodded.

"Yup, bad radiator hose, all right. Only take fifteen minutes or so to fix. Got spares on the rack here. You can wait in the office there if you want or they're serving fresh coffee next door at the donut shop. Staying open late for hunters."

"Sure, coffee sounds great to me," Al said, rubbing the long miles from his eyes.

He looked to Crane who was already tugging at his belt line at the mention of donuts. Pa nodded. Vern drifted with the flow. They headed for the door. Brad and Corey shuffled after them, stealing a quick glance at Becky standing behind the cash register.

"If you're not coffee drinkers," she offered as they reached the door, "we've got a good selection of snacks and soft drinks right here."

Brad pulled his eyes from her and looked to his dad. Al shrugged his shoulders. Pa peered over the rims of his glasses.

"You know," Brad said, thumbing his chin, "with all our guns and gear in the car maybe Corey and I should hang around and keep an eye on things."

"Sure, fine," Al said. "We'll be back in a while."

Pa, bringing up the rear, glanced over his shoulder and smiled. Brad noticed the old eyes twinkle as if they still belonged to a fifteen-year-old. Pa shook his head as he closed the door behind him. The cow bell clanked, leaving the office in an awkward silence. Brad stood for a moment before stuffing his hands into his pockets, feeling for change. He walked over to the pop machine. Corey followed.

"So, where you guys headed?" Becky asked.

Brad turned to speak but Corey beat him to the punch.

"We're on our way up to Marquette. My pal here's got a cabin there and we're headed up early to get ready for opening day on Sunday."

"Doesn't your pal have a name?" Becky asked, swaying like she was keeping beat to a soft tune.

Brad looked at her but quickly glanced back to the pop machine after meeting her eyes. God, she uses those eyes like lasers. And the way she moves, geez. She's got to be older, sixteen at least.

"Name's Brad. This pal of mine is Corey."

Brad dropped his change into the machine and punched the root beer button. He pulled the can from the chute and popped the tab. Corey got a Pepsi. They both sat on an old van seat propped against the wall across from the register — and Becky. She eyed them for a moment, her hands propped under her chin. Brad looked away again. God, she wants to see us squirm. She must be seventeen.

"You guys don't look much like deer hunters."

Corey peered over his tipped can.

"Really?" he said. "Just how are deer hunters supposed to look?"

"I don't know, maybe not so cute, maybe not so sweet."

Brad almost choked on his root beer. Corey's cheeks flushed.

Brad reached up and turned down the collar of his coat. Did someone turn the heat up in here? Man, it's getting warm. She's teasing us for sure, this has to be a tease. Girls don't talk to guys like us unless we're wearing varsity jackets. Corey leaned toward Brad and turned his head as if pretending to stretch. "Probably carloads of hunters down the road," he whispered, "run off into the ditches after they gassed up here and had their guts turned into jelly."

Brad gazed at Becky then to the rack of snack foods on the counter.

"I just figured deer hunters would look more like, well, those older guys with you. They look like they don't care if they kill something — something as beautiful as a deer."

Brad's eyes focused back on Becky. Uh oh, change in plans. Time to shift into neutral.

"Well we haven't actually killed any deer yet," he said.

"True," Corey quickly followed. "You don't have to kill a deer to enjoy going up hunting."

"Oh really?" Becky said, her eyes lighting up like a cat leading a pair of canaries into her jaws. "Then why don't you just leave your guns at home and enjoy being in the woods without trying to kill a deer. You don't have to kill something to prove you're men do you?"

"Well, of course not," Brad countered, realizing too late he'd just fallen into the trap.

His collar grew warmer. Crap, I should have seen it coming. She's one of *them.*

Brad had talked to enough kids at school who had never set foot outside the plastic-wrapped urban world and couldn't understand the concept of hunting. Despite his attempts to explain how hunters served a vital role in game management and funded all kinds of wildlife programs, many of the kids at school had turned away, screwing up their faces at the idea of shooting an innocent deer. As he looked up at Becky, he wondered if a rational explanation on all the positive aspects of hunting would phase her.

"Living in the country here," he finally said, "it seems like you would know lots of hunters."

Becky leveled her eyes on him.

"Yes, I do," she said, crossing her arms. "And they're mostly jerks. What conquest they can't make out in the woods with their guns they try to make up for in the back seat of a car."

Brad suddenly sensed something deeper here, something that had happened involving a hunter maybe, something he didn't want to know about. She didn't look so much older anymore. The flash in her eyes couldn't have come from casual contact with hunters. He decided to tiptoe ahead.

"You see, we don't hunt to prove anything. It's not like we have to kill a deer to show we're men."

He knew his words made sense, but still, something deep inside challenged the logic, something primal.

"Okay," she said, "why do you hunt then?"

"Lots of reasons," Brad said. "Gives me a chance to spend a good time with my family and friends." He glanced toward Corey. "It also puts me in closer touch with nature." He looked into her eyes, still hard as sapphires. "I know that sounds lame, but it's true. It gives me a better understanding and appreciation for the environment. Lets me see the big picture of things. And as a hunter, I'm part of that big picture. It's the natural way."

"Natural? Natural for who? Some self-appointed group with guns who think they have the right to go and kill animals that belong to all of us? Those deer out there are just as much mine as they are yours. What makes it right for a few hunters to kill what most of us enjoy without killing? I want to watch the deer run free. Let nature take them back in due time. That's what puts me in touch with nature, not having some jerk blasting them to bits. How would you like it if deer hunted you?"

Brad held the disturbing thought for a second. It stirred his earlier dreams and made his collar grow hotter yet. No, I guess I wouldn't like it much. But does that mean that her reasoning makes some kind of bizarre sense? Maybe in her eyes. Now what do I say? I can't think straight when I look at her. He pulled his attention from Becky and glanced toward Corey. I need help here, pal, and quick.

Corey drew in a long breath and shrugged his shoulders.

"I guess what's natural is different for all of us," Corey said. "I don't think it's natural to artificially inseminate livestock, pump them full of steroids, feed them all kinds of chemicals and strip land so they can graze, truck them across the country to fatten them in stockyards, ship them back to have them mechanically slaughtered, pollute rivers with their wastes, have them chopped, slabbed, plastic wrapped and finally ground into fast food. Nope, to me that ain't natural, not at all. It's an incredible waste of so many resources. And I want to do my part to help reduce that waste by hunting."

Corey paused for a moment. His voice softened. "But I also respect your right to enjoy looking at deer. I think we all do. It may not be pleasant, but hunters help preserve the future of deer for all of us to enjoy."

Brad looked at Corey, then Becky. For the first time her porcelain features began to soften into doubt as her control of the conversation began to slip. Brad picked up the slack reins.

"Maybe we kinda need one another. In the long run, wildlife management involves hunters helping people like you enjoy seeing good numbers of healthy deer. And ideas like yours maybe helps serve as the conscience for game managers and hunters."

Brad held his chin up. There, that wasn't so bad. Even sounded good to me. Didn't have to stretch the truth to make the point either. Neat, I scored points with logic instead of lies. He noticed her chewing her lip. Ha, now she's back peddling. Or at least she isn't throwing something new in our faces yet.

"If you think about it naturally," Corey said, leaning on the edge of the seat. "It makes a lot of sense."

Becky turned her head and looked at him from the corner of her eye but said nothing.

"You see," Corey continued, "the thing that separated man from the rest of the critters on earth a skillion years ago was his instinct to hunt, and like it or not, the ability to kill."

She tightened her lips. Corey went on.

"Without that one little hunter label stamped in our chromosome library, we would probably be sheep or goats or something. Hey, I don't know about you, but I'd rather not be a goat."

Brad noticed the tension ease around the corners of her mouth. She wasn't about to smile yet, but he figured she was beginning at least to enjoy the lighter air where all this was leading.

Corey stood and began reading a meat stick package hanging from the snack display on the counter. He twisted his face.

"No thanks," he said, shaking his head, "I'd rather not be a pig or a cow either. I think all that monosodium glutamate might give me a rash. I like being human, and a hunter."

Becky's eyes dropped for a second. Brad noticed her foot push a waste can under the counter. He saw the remains of a fast-food burger wrapping inside. He grinned. She suddenly looked less intimidating. She pressed her lips tight as if searching for the final counter.

"Okay Mr. Naturals," she said, her eyes flashing mostly at Brad. "Just what do you intend to do with your deer once you get them, strap them to your car roof and drive around town like these puffed up heroes from the city showing how they conquered a furry piece of the wilds?"

A tightness formed in Brad's belly. It wasn't from the root beer. Naw, there was no way of winning this conversation or changing her mind. Not now. Other men who had called themselves hunters had seen to that.

With his enthusiasm now replaced with a genuine tenderness, Brad answered. "No, if we're fortunate enough to harvest a deer, we won't tie it to the roof. My dad and grandfather will help process it in camp and we'll take it home in a cooler."

Brad suddenly sensed something deeper in her stare and knew he'd won a point.

"I haven't taken a deer yet and I might not," he went on. "But I've been taught to respect them, both in life and in death. If we get one, we'll respect it and use it as a gift from nature, the same as generations of hunters have before us. Maybe the same as your father or grandfather."

Becky looked over into the bay area where the clicking of a ratchet came from under the hood of the Suburban. Her face softened with understanding or maybe a tinge of guilt. Brad couldn't tell for sure.

"Well," she said after a moment. "Maybe you guys don't look like some of the other hunters who come in here because you're not."

Maybe not, Brad thought. Time would tell.

He drained the last of his pop. The three of them sat in silence.

The cow bell clanked as the others stomped back through the door. Everyone but Vern held a foam cup, steam drifting out the small sip openings in the tops. Crane clutched a bag of donuts. From the repair bay the hood slammed and Becky's dad stepped into the office.

"Finished," he said, stuffing a rag into his hip pocket. "That'll be thirty bucks, including the price of the new hose. Threw in a little fresh antifreeze for free. Figured you might need it with this cold front coming."

Al paid Becky as the others started toward the vehicle. Her father went to the bay door and hit the open switch. Brad paused near the Suburban, waiting for his dad. Al stepped from the office. Brad's gaze went past him. Becky stood in the doorway.

"Watch yourself up there city boy," she said, somehow pressing her hands into the rear pockets of her jeans. "Sometimes the woods can be a dangerous place."

Brad nodded. He wanted to smile but Becky still wore that distant look. He sank into the seat and reached for the door. His dad started the vehicle.

"Stop in next time you're through," she said over the noise of the engine, a hint of a smile touching the corner of her lips.

The others didn't hear. But Brad didn't miss a word.

Al backed the Suburban from the bay then pulled toward the highway. Brad looked back at Becky still standing at the edge of the big doorway, its panels unfolding downward, turning her into a hazy form behind the fogged glass.

CHAPTER 7 — AN INTRUDER

Darkness filled the window when Brad woke to the chatter of the Suburban skipping down a washboard road. He rubbed his eyes and squinted into night. Somehow the roadside looked different. A broken curtain of clouds revealed a star-dusted backdrop, pinhole beams drifting past the outlines of trees, reflecting faintly off a new blanket of snow.

Brad shot up in the seat. Snow! Fresh snow. A deer hunter's blessing. Must be at least five inches of the stuff.

He looked over to find Pa and Corey sitting slumped together like two teddy bears, sleeping soundly, their bodies loosely shaking to the rhythm of each bump in the road. In front, Crane's head drooped backward across the seat. Mouth agape, a grating snore slowly rose and fell from his nostrils. Brad's father sat with arms folded, head propped up with a pillow. He too, slept through the bumps. Behind the wheel, Vern lazily guided the vehicle through the turns, one hand on the wheel, the other tipping a large foam cup. Brad smelled the fresh coffee. The remains of a donut sat on the dashboard, awash in the glow of the dash lights.

"Did we stop somewhere?" Brad whispered, sensing the hollowness in his stomach.

Vern turned his head slightly. His eyes shone clearly from the dash lights, his face and voice crisp.

"We filled up on gas and coffee hours ago at that all-night place near Shingleton. I didn't want to wake you guys. You were all sleeping like lumberjacks. I got half of one of Crane's donuts here if you're hungry. But we'll be at the cabin in less than twenty minutes and sunup is only an hour away. I'm sure your granddad will whip us up a quick batch of his famous pancakes after we get settled."

"Yeah, that sounds okay. I can wait."

Brad sat back watching the shadows of trees flicker past. He smiled to himself as Vern turned off the gravel road down the familiar two-track. The cabin lay at the trail's end, over three miles into the forest.

Brad noticed how well Vern handled the narrow, twisting trail. Seeing him mostly in the evenings, Brad had forgotten the man's morning brightness. Despite his evening bouts with beer and the sour side of life, he usually woke fresh and cheerful. Then, he was surprisingly pleasant, friendly, and even quick humored. Now I see the man dad likes. Maybe Dad overlooks his drinking. Maybe that's what friends do, mostly see your good side.

"It's daylight in the swamp!" Vern said as he turned off the engine. "A hunter's day cracks early, boys. Let's get a crackin'. I didn't want to tell you before, but I heard a buck laughing at you sleepy-heads just a mile back down the trail. No kidding, right, Brad?"

Brad grinned and nodded. "True story."

"Right," Corey groaned, rubbing his neck. "Just like all your stories, Brad. Why do you think they call you B.S. Mercer at school?"

"Because those are my initials, that's why."

Brad had stopped grinning.

"Hey, it's okay by me. I think it's cool to be a professional story teller. And it doesn't hurt to have initials that match."

Brad shook his head and opened the car door. Sleepy-eyed, everyone stepped from the vehicle and stood stretching, making guttural sounds. Steam rose from their breath in the calm air. The black shapes of spruce surrounded them like a pack of giant wolves in waiting. They listened for a moment at the stillness of the forest. The only sound was the hiss of Vern emptying his bladder in the snow.

Al fumbled with a six-volt flashlight at the side of the cabin near two large propane tanks. A narrow beam clicked on, piercing the darkness like a sword. After opening the regulator valve, he unlocked the door leading into the shed attached to the cabin and stepped inside. Brad followed with a box of groceries.

The shed held the aroma of split oak and worn leather. It served as a combination woodshed and storage area for extra hunting clothes and boots. Along one wall stood stacks of firewood. Along the other hung a few old jackets and hats, long retired from days afield, resting under a layer of dust. A row of pegs hung nearby to hold heavy hunting coats and coveralls to keep them free of cooking odors and wood smoke from inside the cabin. They all knew a whitetail's nose was its biggest asset, and did their best to keep their outerwear from smelling like careless predators from the city.

The others crowded inside with arms full of gear and supplies while Al unlocked the inner door leading into the cabin. It swung open into blackness. They went inside.

To Brad the cabin seemed unusually stale and damp. A musty odor filled his head. The flashlight beam bounced across the rafters overhead. A deer mouse scampered over one of the cedar cross-posts then disappeared in a crack near the wall. Al steadied the beam on the overhead globed fixture then reached up and lit the single mantle gas light, bathing the room in a pulsating glow. As he stepped back under the soft light, his feet crunched something on the floor.

"What the —"

As the gas light hissed to life, the others came through the doorway, anxious to set down their arm loads. But they stopped just inside, looking at the floor.

"Man, what's been going on here?" Corey asked. "Looks like somebody had a food fight."

Across the floor lay the tattered remains of boxes and paper, contents strewn in every corner. Elbow macaroni, rice, and corn flakes crunched underfoot as Al turned around, flashlight beam surveying shadowed spots under tables and in corners.

"You've got a serious mouse problem here, Mercer," Crane said. "You'd better get some traps set before these things take over this shack. Goddamn, you're overrun with them. This is disgusting."

Pa reached down and picked up a shredded cereal box. Tony the Tiger's face was chewed completely out.

"This doesn't look like the work of any mouse I've ever seen," Pa said, fingering the ragged hole. "Whatever ripped this apart has a lot bigger teeth than a mouse. This wasn't gnawed by a rodent. See? Bite marks, something with pointed teeth."

"You could be right, old man," Vern said from the far corner. "Whatever got in here had enough strength to pry open the spring latches on these cupboards. Look."

Vern stepped back, revealing opened plywood doors on the three floor cabinets. He took Al's flashlight from the table in the center of the room and stooped near the cupboards for a closer look.

"Whatever got into these," Vern continued, "had sharp claws too. Look at these scratches on the door. This thing wasn't casually pawing around. It intentionally pried them open."

"Must have been ugly too," Brad said, staring into the large porcelain sink near the kitchen counter. Fragmented shards of mirror lay scattered in the sink. "Probably didn't like what it saw in the mirror."

"Save your imagination, kid," Crane snorted. "It's getting the best of you. Like I said, mice. One of them just knocked the mirror off the nail, that's all."

"Uh, I don't think it's his imagination," Corey said, running his fingers over the slab lumber wall near the nail. "Claw marks over here too. Whatever did this looked pissed off. I mean angry. Sorry, Mr. Mercer."

The pale overhead light softly illuminated the table and the center of the room, but to Brad, the heavy shadows in the corners, behind the stove, and under the counters looked darker, deeper, more haunting than before.

"Do you think it might still be in here somewhere?" he asked.

Brad backed away from the sink toward the middle of the room. His boot snapped some macaroni. Corey flinched at the noise. They stood quietly and listened. Then, the sound of crunching glass came from the other room. Everyone froze. Brad held his breath to hear better. Corey's eyes widened.

Vern's voice made them jump.

"Hey, in here," he called from the darkness of the other room. "Come and take a look. Whatever it was is long gone."

Cautiously stepping from the glow of the kitchen, the group peered into the other room. There, flashlight in hand, Vern stood stretching upward, lighting the gas light on the center log rafter. The mantle sputtered several times then hissed steadily, filling the large room with a soft glow.

The long room was the cabin's living room. Near the middle of the inner wall sat a blackened pot-bellied stove, complete with large side racks for drying boots and socks. Its heat-blued stovepipe disappeared straight up through the roof. On either side of the stove, large cedar posts dotted with nail coat-hooks stood from floor to rafters. Between the posts and the walls stretched four lines of bailing wire for drying hunting clothes.

Like the rest of the cabin's interior, the living room walls were covered with rough-sawn pine, long ago bleached by time into a dull gray. Assorted pegs and hooks sprung from every corner, half of them holding old clothing and empty coat hangers. Near the corner hung a walnut gun rack with eight pairs of upward deer feet for holding rifles. High on the walls near the open rafters hung sets of deer antlers. Draped in cobwebs, they cast spindly shadows across the slabwood like gnarled skeleton hands reaching toward the hunters.

Below the antlers hung rows of faded photographs. Most showed happy hunters posing with downed bucks. They stood as chapters of Mercer deer hunting history, each with its own story of how luck and skill had combined to down the buck. In many, a much younger Pa stood proudly behind fallen whitetails. Brad's favorite showed Pa kneeling behind the buck of '49; a huge non-typical with thirty-some points sprouting in every direction. Legend was that Pa had hunted that buck for three seasons before finally slipping up on it in the depths of Deadman's Swamp, a place few hunters risked venturing into. Brad wondered where his first deer photo would hang, what it would look like.

Against the far wall was a large blue couch that folded out into a double bed. Near it, set at a right angle, rested a ragged brown sofa with big rounded arms. Two pine log end tables and matching rockers faced the outer wall and the room's biggest attraction — a five-foot picture window. It overlooked a sloping meadow to the west. Whether if offered a glimpse of deer at the salt lick, a mink hunting along the swamp, a grouse drumming on a log, or just a sunset; the large window was the cabin's eyepiece to the world. And now that eyepiece lay shattered on the floor.

Vern knelt near the broken window inspecting the wreckage. Fresh snow covered the shards of glass and a few dried leaves on the floor in front of the window opening.

"Whatever came through this window wanted to get in here awfully bad. Look, it even left us a calling card."

He reached out and pulled free one of the jagged pieces of glass still rimming the lower sill. Caught on the pointed end was a tuft of fur. Dried blood smeared both. Vern stood and held the shard under the pulsating light.

"Don't quite look like mouse fur to me," Pa said.

Crane grunted and stepped forward for a closer look. "Probably just a stupid skunk," he said. "They're always getting into things."

Pa pulled Vern's hand close and rubbed the dark fur between his fingers. It was long and coarse. Then he drew it near his nose. "It's got a musky odor alright, but it doesn't smell like skunk. I think we can rule out a polecat. Besides, the base of that window is a good three feet off the ground. It'd take a four-foot skunk to come charging through there. That, or one with four times the determination to break in."

Everyone eyed the fur for a moment except Brad who peered out the broken window.

"Maybe it climbed up on the wood pile first," he said.

He remembered stacking extra wood outside next to the window in September during partridge season. Now the logs lay scattered in a heap in front of the broken pane.

"The pile of logs outside," he continued, "might be high enough for a coon or badger to reach the window. Maybe that's what it was."

He squinted into the darkness. The black shapes of the spruces could be hiding anything. Maybe it was a pack of coyotes, wolves, or a whole cluster of bears? How about a deranged grizzly that had somehow wandered down from the Yukon. No, no one would ever buy that. Just a coon probably. Reality is always so dull.

Vern stepped next to Brad and looked out at the pile of wood. "Maybe so," he said. "But a five-foot pane of glass is pretty darn tough. It would take one heck of a coon to smash it in. That or it would have to leap at it."

"You mean knowingly leap at the window?" Corey said. "It would have to be crazy."

"Not necessarily," Pa said. "It ain't unheard of for animals to break glass when they see their reflection. They think it's another critter challenging or threatening them. Their reflection glares back with no fear, bares its teeth like them, and lunges at the same time. It's only natural for them to strike back in defense or charge in aggression."

"Yeah, but what animal up here would be fierce enough to leap at its reflection," Al asked, "and be strong enough to break in that window?"

"Must be a bear," Crane said. He snorted and tugged at the waist of his pants somewhere below the shadow of his gut. "Probably a big dumb bear. And I hope it's stupid enough to show its worthless hide around here again. Then I'll show you guys how to make a bear rug in a hurry."

Brad looked at Crane. And this is the man accusing me of having too much imagination?

"You know it ain't legal to shoot bears now," Pa said flatly, "And how in the world did you make the leap from a mouse to a bear?" Pa glanced back at Brad and Corey.

"What else could it be? Anyway, I'll just say I shot in self-defense. I mean look what it's already done. I've got good reason to blast it. Those Natural Resources people won't know the difference. I'll just tell them it was coming after us."

Brad glanced at Pa. The old man's brow drew into a knot.

"Your bear idea doesn't hold water," Pa said, wagging his head. "Most of them are in hibernation now. It's more likely a coyote or a coon. They're more abundant around here and that fur has gray tips. Besides, bears are clean smelling animals, have an odor more like a beaver. Like I said, this fur smells."

"Probably was a bear with gray-flecked fur that just finished eating some musky carcass before it broke in here," Crane said. He withdrew his hands from his pockets and set them on his hips.

Pa ran his fingers through his hair and pressed his lips.

"How about a wolf?" Corey asked. He hunched his shoulders and shivered. His eyes glimmered in the pale light.

"Now that's a possibility," Al said. "They've been re-introduced up here. Maybe it was a big alpha wolf that felt challenged by the dominant posture of its reflection."

"Right," Vern said, "and once he broke in, he decided to snack up on raw macaroni and Frosted Flakes. Probably made him feel grrreat!"

Vern slapped his knee and laughed. Crane joined in. Al and Pa just smiled.

Looking out into the darkness again, Brad found little humor in the possibility of lurking wolves. I've got to go out there soon, walking in and out of the woods by myself in the dark. No, wolves aren't funny at all.

"Do you think it might come back?" Corey asked, standing next to Brad and gazing out through the broken pane.

"Not likely," Pa said. "There ain't no fresh tracks in the snow and that blood stain looks old. Whatever it was, it didn't find much here to eat. I think we can just write it off as a freak accident, nothing to lose any sleep over."

"Enough stories," Crane said. "Let's get this show on the road. It'll be daylight soon and we've got lots to do today. You boys bring in the gear. I'll build a fire and Vern and Al can patch the window and clean up this mess. After that, everybody will be ready for a batch of the old man's pancakes."

No one commented. Brad didn't care for the way Crane dictated orders but the man made sense and matched the people to the tasks. Besides, everyone was still groggy from the drive and too hungry to argue.

The boys, staying close together, headed out the door. Pa began putting groceries away while Vern and Al rummaged in the shed for something to patch the window. Crane stuffed the old stove with crumpled newspapers and kindling.

Before long, the stove's warmth and the smell of fresh griddle cakes permeated the cabin. Al had just finished stapling down the last corner of the makeshift Visqueen window when Pa hollered from the kitchen. "Cakes are ready, boys. Come and get 'em while they're hot."

As the hunters attacked stacks of steaming cakes smothered in real maple syrup, gray fingers of light crept through the clouded eastern sky. It cast a bluish haze through the frail plastic covering the window.

Somewhere in the distance, the wailing cry of an animal met the dawn. It carried a musical yet urgent ring of anticipation. It too belonged to a hunter.

CHAPTER 8 – FOXFIRE EYES

Little Eli woke to the distant buzz-click of the outer cell block lock-out door. He turned his head. Was it opening or closing?

Sleep clung too heavily to his senses to tell for sure. He cracked an eyelid. Ouch, damn that hurts!

Gray curtains of light filtered through the high row of windows on the eastern wall across from his cell. Dull as it was, he still squinted and retreated into the darkness of his thoughts. Like a waking bear, they began to stir within a dim cavern in his mind.

Eli reached up and massaged the back of his neck. Eastern light, hmmm, must be early morning. How long have I been out? Probably sedated me. That's a sure bet after the thing on the bus.

He pushed massive fingers into his eyelids. Ahh, must have been a strong dose, whatever it was. Probably been out eight hours, maybe more. Don't matter none. The only thing that does is that I'm still alive. And that means hope, hope to be free.

Eli shook his head at the thought. Free? Why think of that now after all these years? Well, why not? Yeah, free, sure, why not?

The once dull eyes flicked wide as new synaptic corridors to primeval chambers of his mind began to clear even more, the new altered epinephrine in his body blasting away the cobwebs from untapped senses.

The clatter of heels on concrete approached from the far end of the cell block. Eli cocked an ear to the sound. God, it's so loud, like having a hangover. Must be the sedation, or maybe, maybe that stuff from —

His ears picked up more sounds now. Heavy-heeled steps, leather soles tapping that rhythm, must be Simmons leading the way. Someone with a scuffing gate following him. Rolland, you fat fart, still trying to act tougher than yesterday's porkchops. What? The right foot landing crisper, heavier. Okay, swinging your night-stick, the big one, in your right hand.

Eli raised up on one elbow. Hmmm? How come I never heard that before? Why hadn't I ever realized what all those sounds meant?

As they neared, Eli's senses prickled. More pathways deep in his subconscious sparked to life. He sat up, rubbed his eyes and bared his teeth, flashing them his best impression of a smile.

"Mornin' boss," he said even before the guards reached his cell.

Simmons and Rolland stopped and reared back as if they had been doused with ice water. After a moment they edged closer to the cell.

"Thought for a second we had the wrong house," Simmons said. "First time I ever heard a good morning from you." He eyed Eli, especially the smile, its drawn corners resembling a grimace, exposing powerful teeth that appeared more fitting for a horse. Simmons gave a suspicious glance toward Rolland who took a meaty grip on his stick. Rolland nodded.

Eli's mind raced. His senses reached out. Yeah, morning all right. He inhaled. Simmons is wearing that spiced aftershave again. Not a trace of whisker stubble either, a slight razor nick near his ear. Must be nice to have a hot shower all your own.

He drew in another long breath, his awakening instincts sorting out an incoming tide of data. His eyes shifted to Rolland. Ahh, fresh sausage grease in his mustache. A lingering tinge of orange marmalade and coffee on his breath too. Musta been some breakfast.

Eli's gaze dropped to Rolland's gut hanging full over his belt. Eli's tongue brushed the roof of his mouth. He could suddenly taste the sausage, the zesty kind he realized, and his mouth began to water. He slurped back an unexpected drool.

"Sorry about that thing on the bus," he said, lowering his face, fading his smile. "Musta been that stuff they gave me." Eli shrugged his mountainous shoulders and continued to stare at the floor.

Simmons shook his head as he removed a pair of handcuffs from his belt and Rolland readied his stick.

"The warden got reports that Laragy was picking on you," Simmons said. "Still isn't much of a reason to do what you did. Anyway, warden also thinks you may have helped things by pulling that army guy from J.J."

Simmons paused and cocked his head to look for any reaction on Eli's face. Eli still started at the floor.

"Were you helping? Or did you want a piece of the ground-pounder for yourself?"

"Just trying to help keep the peace, boss, that's all."

"Right," Simmons said. "Just like you did with Laragy's face?"

"Was that stuff they gave me, boss. Really, I was half out of it."

"Right, whatever you say. I don't know what your game is this morning with this sorry chatter but I'm not buying it. Not for a second. Now turn around and back up to the door. You know the drill."

Eli nodded without glancing up. He stood, placed both hands behind his back, and stepped backward toward the small horizontal opening in the bars. Though coated with countless layers of bone-white paint, the coolness of the steel touching Eli's hands raised gooseflesh along his arms. Simmons quickly snapped the cuffs on Eli's wrists. Even though it took only seconds, Eli's mind absorbed every sound, each move, the slightest sensations.

"Suppose you're taking me to solitary for what I did," Eli said. "Can't blame you. But honest, boss, it wasn't my fault. Didn't mean no one no harm."

"Save it," Simmons said as he stepped away toward Rolland. "You're not going to The Hole."

"I haven't heard him talk this much in my eight years here," Simmons whispered. "A few profanities but never complete sentences. It's weird. Stay sharp."

"Maybe they jarred something loose in that oversized noggan of his on the bus," Rolland whispered back. "Who knows, who cares. You worry too much. Just open the door, I can handle him."

Despite their turned faces and hushed tones, Eli's ears picked up every word. Damn, he could be right. Why didn't I realize that? Maybe I have changed, hell, probably changing by the minute. Okay, be cool. Don't blow it. Don't let on. Play the game. Cut the chat. You guys expect a dummy, you get a dummy. Eli let his lower jaw sag, his head droop.

Simmons pulled a large key ring from a clip on his belt and inserted a key into the latch. The lock and old-fashion keys looked as if they belonged in a cowboy movie. Nonetheless the old locks and cell door designs, built by master locksmiths in 1887, had proven unpickable. For over a hundred years they had securely held some of Michigan's worst criminals, Eli included. A few of the other blocks had been revamped over the years with newer electric lock systems, but Block F, the Dead Zone as some called it, remained cloaked in the past.

Simmons swung the door open. Rolland tightened the grip on his big stick. They tensed as Eli stepped forward.

"You're lucky," Simmons said, his eyes locked on Eli's every move. "The warden doesn't see any sense putting you in solitary. He's more interested in answers about what went wrong on the bus two days ago. So we're taking you back down to the infirmary for a checkup. Got doctors waiting for you."

Eli repressed his urge to look up in surprise. He continued staring at the floor. Back to the infirmary? I don't remember the first time. Musta carted me. Two days ago? Man, no wonder I'm hungry enough to eat a side of beef, hide and all.

His stomach grumbled at the idea while his adrenal glands responded to the thought. Stimulated by more of the drug-altered epinephrine entering his bloodstream, new nerve pathways began processing incoming data. As each new pulse flickered and jumped the synaptic link, the flow become steadier like a locomotive building steam. Each spark of an idea etched its trail through the gray network of folds and grooves into the far reaches of the frontal lobes of his cerebrum, unlocking a vault of repressed primitive instincts. His mind roared on.

The officers ushered Eli down the cell block. He snuck quick looks into the cells and faces of other lifers. A few returned brief stares. They quickly turned under the weight of Eli's probing gaze. His usually blank eyes staring into a dull infinity now held an unsettling depth that cut to their marrow. Turning away from their weight, most didn't notice the change in his step. He no longer plodded past like a giant sloth. Eli now moved with the stealth of a 300-pound cat.

Three doctors stood waiting in the prison infirmary as Simmons lead Eli through the doors. The morning glare shined brightly off the white linoleum floor and pastel walls, making Eli squint. Eli looked past the blinding light to Dr. Nolstrum, the prison's head physician, and his new intern Dr. Reed. He eyed the stranger.

Dr. Nolstrum tapped the white paper covering a padded examining bench and motioned Eli to sit.

"You know Dr. Reed here," Nolstrum said, forcing a comforting smile. "And this is Dr. Pratt. We just want to have a look at you to make sure everything's all right."

Eli nodded and moved toward the bench. The physicians drew back in unison, giving him wide berth. He sat on the bench. The paper crackled. The vinyl squeaked. The stainless steel supports groaned under his mass. After he quit shifting, the doctors inched closer. And finally, sensing they were reasonably safe, began examining Little Eli.

Eli watched Dr. Pratt with special interest. *Something about this guy reminds me of that squirt in charge of that test outside. Probably another government prick. Where's that short one anyway? Oh yeah, J.J. had him on the bus. Must be hurt. This guy wears the same look as him, yeah, Robenthral. Probably with the same outfit.*

For the next hour while the officers stood nearby, the doctors probed, pricked, and prodded Eli like hens preening a newborn chick. While they went about their task, Eli watched the details of every procedure, memorizing each inch of the infirmary. His eyes traced the lines of all the doors, windows and locks. He reached out with his tactile senses, feeling the coolness of the steel doors, testing the sureness of their latches.

Eli watched in fascination as they drew blood from his arm, needles biting flesh and probing veins. He noticed bruised spots where other needles had taken or given fluids during the past few days. As they attached suction cups strung on wires to his chest or head, he digested every motion, absorbed every word; BP, rate, sinus rhythm. He repressed his surprise as he suddenly realized what a circulatory system was, what it was capable of. *Ahh, what a beautiful thing. Full of so much life, so much blood.*

He let his mind wander like an English setter working grouse cover, darting and searching thickets, looking for a tell-tale scent to unfold. *Yeah, doctoring, it had such a discipline and order about it. Life should be like that. Think I'll play doctor someday. Maybe someday soon.*

Near the end of the exam Dr. Pratt nodded at the intern who then drew the vinyl-backed curtains across the bank of windows and turned off the overhead lights.

Eli sighed with relief as the darkness bathed his eyes. *Man, I been inside too long. Can't even stand a little of the outside.* His eyes quickly adjusted to the grayness of the infirmary. Even in the darkness, everything in the room appeared in surprising clarity, his eyes penetrating the gloom of even the darkest corners.

The doctors crowded near Eli's face. Pratt pressed closer as he peered through a steel saucer fastened to a forehead strap. He flicked on a pinhole flashlight beam that lit the corners of Eli's eyes.

Eli winced but managed to stay quiet. Ouch, you sonofa— I should tear your arm off. Easy, easy now; now isn't the time. Stay calm, they're almost done.

A moment later Pratt clicked off the light. "It's still there, brighter than ever," he said. "It appears to mirror the localized conjunctivitis of the medial canthus. Strange how it resembles the glow of fluorescein stain under ultraviolet light, even stranger still that it glows without UV light. Kind of like the glow of two crescent moons rising from his lower lids. Must be some kind of fungus he picked up."

"How would he get that in his cell?" the intern asked.

Nolstrum turned to Pratt. "Likely a strain of cellulose fungi that has attacked the irritated area," Pratt offered, avoiding the intern's question.

"Something he could pick up out in the forest?" Nolstrum asked.

Pratt paused, his eyes shifting from the intern to Nolstrum. "Who knows. His eyes offer a good moist environment for it, wherever he got it. Still, it's the first time I've seen it in someone's eyes. Better take a smear."

The intern swabbed the corner of Eli's eye then busied himself over a table near the far wall. A moment later he drew open the curtains and turned on the lights.

"That's all," Dr. Nolstrum said, stuffing his stethoscope back in his coat pocket. "We're finished today. We appreciate your cooperation." Nolstrum forced another curt smile and patted Eli's back.

Eli nodded, his mouth hanging open. Better stick to doctoring, Doc. Acting ain't your strong suit.

Dr. Pratt nodded good-bye as he finished scribbling on a clipboard chart. Simmons motioned with a wave of the hand.

Eli stood and moved toward the door. As he passed Dr. Pratt, his eyes fixed briefly on the last line of the chart; FOXFIRE EYES.

Hmmm? Have to find out what that means. Other things first, though.

From down a distant corridor, the pungent aroma of fried potatoes and fresh biscuits reached his nostrils. Eli's mouth watered, his jaws began to pulse. It was time for breakfast. A fierce new hunger stirred within — a hunger like never before.

CHAPTER 9 – STICKUPS

Woodsmoke curled from the cabin's stovepipe, drifting southeast. Its smudge quickly blended with the gray backdrop of the sky. Heavy clouds pushed in from the northwest, sweeping across Lake Superior like immense flocks of billowy birds. With wispy wings intertwined, they blocked any sign of the sun hanging somewhere around mid-morning. Fluffed bellies hung full with winter's promise.

Inside the cabin, the hunters had finished breakfast and unpacked the boxes of groceries, duffles and gear. Corey and Brad hung some of their clothes on pegs in the cabin's loft. It was built over the two bedrooms at the far end of the cabin and overlooked the living room. A rough cedar post ladder and railing added the air of a tree fort, creating a cozy sleeping area for the younger guests. The boys unrolled their sleeping bags on canvas cots set up near the center of the loft. Under the cots they laid out their heavy socks, longjohns, and flannel shirts.

Brad arranged his gear in neat rows, underwear at one end ascending to heavier outer layers at the other. He took care to fold and space the garments as if the order in his little nook over the hodge-podge life in camp might increase his chances of getting a buck. Lastly, he unpacked his turtleneck sweater. Most hunters found luck in a special hat or coat. For Brad it was the green army surplus sweater. He had worn it two years ago when shotgunning his first rabbit, a fat cottontail that had bounded from a brush pile.

He smoothed out its folds, letting his fingers linger in the thick woolen weave. It's not that I'm superstitious. It's just like having a friend near, that's all. And who knows, maybe it will bring a little luck.

"Can you guys snap it up a little?" Al called from below. "Mr. Crane and Vern are already waiting in the car. We'd better hit the trail if we're going to find some good spots and still build our stickups before dusk."

"Be right there, Dad, soon as we pull on our boots and grab our packs."

Moments later, Brad and Corey piled into the Suburban, poking and shoving each other. Crane glanced at them over his shoulder and shook his head.

"Kids," Crane snorted, "worse than having goddamn dogs in camp. I don't know how you tolerate it, Mercer. Things would be different around here if I took charge of them. Just one day and I'd shape them up."

Brad watched the folds in Crane's second chin creep up his cheek as he turned. Right, Mr. Crane, just like you've shaped my dad over the years. Thanks, but no thanks.

Al didn't comment. He dropped the vehicle in gear, pulling away toward an old logging trail that headed north from the cabin.

"Wait, Dad!" Brad said, bolting forward. "Where's Pa?"

Al looked at his son through the rearview mirror and continued driving. "Your granddad said he was too tuckered from the trip and wanted to rest up today. It'll do him good to putter around the cabin and take it easy."

"But he promised to help me and Corey find good buck crossings and show us how to make stickups."

"Sorry, son, his doctor ordered him to take it easy this year. Try to remember, he can't keep up with you boys forever. But don't worry, he told me where to put you."

Brad gazed back at the cabin. Doctor's orders? What doctor's orders? Why hadn't Pa told me? What was wrong? Brad saw the faded image of Pa peering out the kitchen window. His eyes, why those dark circles again? Brad ground his fist into his thigh and looked away. Some grandson you are, worrying about your stickup and not even thinking about Pa. You saw how he looked this morning, but no, all you could think about was getting a stupid deer. He ground his fist harder.

Corey poked him in the shoulder.

"It's okay, Buwana. Cheer up. We'll find some awesome spots and build killer blinds. Pa will still be with us, kind of. We'll use what he taught us about rubs, trails, building stickups, the whole works. You'll see, those bucks only have a day to live. Man, if they knew we were coming, they'd surrender right now and come walking out of the brush holding up their front hooves."

Brad's pressed lips slowly spread into the hint of a grin.

"Yeah, you're probably right."

He turned and looked out the window. His sigh fogged the glass. And to think I was even going to ask Pa to sit with me tomorrow.

With him by my side maybe I would have been okay seeing a buck coming, even shot straight. But now? Crap.

As the Suburban lurched down the trail, snow began speckling the windshield. The clouds had carried their burden far enough. From the northwest, clustered flakes the size of hornets swirled through the damp air.

Two miles from the cabin, Al stopped the vehicle and led the boys west on foot toward Deadman's Swamp; a nasty tangle of dense cedars and alders interlaced with sinkholes, beaver dams, and bottomless bogs.

Brad knew that hunting near the huge swamp was safe enough as long as a hunter stayed out of it. Pa had warned him plenty about its dangers. Pa's stories included the legends of many a deer hunter who ventured into the swamp after wounded game and never returned, swallowed by the swamp's depths without a trace. Oh, a few had been eventually found, still clutching their rifles, their bones picked clean by coyotes and crows.

But Pa had also told Brad that big bucks found haven in the swamps where most hunters feared to tread. The Mercers knew that hunting along the edge of Deadman's Swamp was one of the secrets of tagging big whitetails on opening day. When the first shots cracked among the oak ridges and aspen thickets where most hunters roamed, bucks tucked their tails and headed for the safety of the big swamp. And when they did, hunters from the Mercer camp would be there waiting — Brad and Corey included.

Three hundred yards from the trail, rolling stands of oaks and aspen ended abruptly at the crest of a fifteen-foot embankment. Al and the boys stopped on the crest and stared for a moment at the dark tangle before them. The ground plunged toward the swamp, marking the forest's change from upland hardwoods to a thick matting of muck-lovers; cedar, tamarack, black spruce and alder.

"Your granddad thought this part of the swamp would be a good bet," Al said. "This ridge winds around a neck of the swamp like a giant horseshoe." He motioned a gloved hand in a sweeping arc toward the north. Brad and Corey followed the gesture, blinking away big snowflakes from eyelashes.

"If you set up on opposite sides of this horseshoe ridge, you can cover almost anything leaving or entering the swamp. Scout around the edge and you'll find some trails along the heavier cover; like over there along that brush." Al pointed toward several thickets of aspens hugging low areas connecting the swamp with higher ground and oak ridges to the east.

"You guys have your lunches and packs so just hike back to the cabin when you're done. You should have plenty of time before dusk. Just head east until you hit the trail, then walk south back to the cabin. You know the way, Brad. I've got to help set up Mr. Crane somewhere between here and the cabin. You know how he is. He doesn't really know his way around the woods like you two sourdoughs."

Al winked then turned back toward the car. He held his hand in front of his face to ward off the thickening flakes. For a moment Brad thought his dad's smile and wink reminded him of Pa. Watching him walk away hunched under the heavy wool coat and cap, he even looked like Pa. Maybe time would someday season his father into a strong-willed Pa Mercer. He shook off the notion. His dad would forever be Al Mercer, a chipmunk in the big woods of life. And besides, there was only one Pa.

"Thanks, Dad," Brad said flatly. "We'll see you around dinner time. Good luck finding a spot."

Brad's words didn't fully penetrate the heavy ear flaps on his dad's cap. Al turned briefly, smiled, and gave them a thumbs up.

"Don't forget," he hollered, "no poking around in that swamp. The last thing we need is you guys getting lost. And there's no need to go spooking those deer from their beds in there."

Brad signaled back with a wave. He knew his dad's caution also included staying clear of the National Guard training grounds on the far side of the swamp. Though much of its lands remained open to public hunting, Brad knew it was strictly off limits for him and Corey. The four-year-old newspaper clipping tacked on the cabin wall told of two local teenagers who had found a phosphorous grenade lost there during summer maneuvers. Somehow they had set the thing off. Both died agonizing deaths. Rumor spread how their bodies smoldered for a full day while the white-hot phosphorous imbedded in the flesh burned itself out. Brad shuddered at the thought. The clipping had served its purpose. Even if they could safely cross the swamp, they had no intention of going near the place.

The boys stood on the timbered ridge looking toward the swamp. Bordering it, a hundred-yard swath of aspen and alders graded into a thick maze of conifers. The tangle seemed to swallow all sound and light. Even the settling snowflakes had little effect on the darkness of the place. The swamp appeared to gobble them as quickly and completely as they fell. The greenish black wall of trees stood like a fortress protecting the secrets of Deadman's Swamp.

Brad shivered. What untold legends lay buried in there? How big were the bucks hiding in that mess?

The second question made his stomach lurch. Part of him wanted to find out, to see old mossy-horns through his scope, but part of him didn't, want to face one all alone, unsure if he would turn into Jello again.

He lifted his eyes from the heaviness of the swamp toward the tree line. There, looking like captives in the maze, stood several yellow birches, leaf-bare limbs reaching desperately, as if for help, to the snow-dusted sky.

Corey tapped Brad on the shoulder and nodded toward the north. The boys snapped off two small aspens for walking sticks and began scouting along the ridge.

Rotten stumps littered the place, old reminders of logging operations decades before. Like the small spruce trees dotting the ridge, they quickly lost their identity under the piling snow, becoming crystalline creatures in frozen poses. The snow pelted harder, its sticky wetness clinging to everything it touched.

The boys shuffled through the snow looking for the telltale signs of deer. They checked saplings for buck rubs and scanned for fresh tracks or faint trails in the snow. It didn't take long to find them all.

"Look at those runways," Brad said, aiming his stick like a gun. "They kinda disappear into the swamp. Pa said that mean's they lead to a bedding area, right? Maybe we should make a stickup here somewhere?"

Corey didn't fully understand the sign either. "Sounds okay to me," he said, bunching his shoulders and looking around. "How about that stump over there?"

He pointed to a fire-charred stump just below the crest of the ridge next to a young spruce.

"Yeah," Brad said, "why not? It's south of these trails. At least the deer won't smell you with this north wind."

"Me? Just because I picked the stump doesn't mean it's my spot. Maybe you want to set up here? I don't want to hog it for myself. We can toss for it."

Brad wagged his head. "Naw, not me. I see that look in your eye. You love it. I can already picture you posing in front of that stump with your buck, probably a big 8-point. Why don't you start clearing a hideaway between the stump and spruce while I trim a few shooting lanes."

"Are you sure you're not waiting to find something better?"

Brad shook his head. No, just waiting. Stalling.

Using a folding Sierra saw, Corey sawed off the lower branches on the spruce and arranged them in front in a semi-circle. Brad walked straight lines from the blind to the runways, trimming branches with a pair of hand pruners. An hour later, they finished building Corey's stickup using more spruce boughs stuck in the ground, criss-crossed branches, and pieces of rotten stumps. Corey placed a section of log inside the small fort and straddled the makeshift seat.

"Man oh man," he said, bringing his arms up in an imaginary aim. "I've got the drop on them from here. They'll never see me until it's too late. It's all over but the shouting and pictures."

"Come on, Mr. Buck Buster," Brad said, stuffing his pruners back into his pack. "Let's go. I don't want you wrenching your arm by patting yourself on the back so much that you can't shoot straight tomorrow."

Corey stood, rose his arms in victory then bowed. Brad shook his head and laughed. He nodded toward the north. They gathered up their packs and continued along the ridge. Over two hundred yards away they discovered another series of deer runs leading from a neck of dense brush into the swamp.

"Check out this rub, Buwana. It's awesome."

Brad stepped over to a three-inch cedar shredded to pulp. As he picked at the twisted remains of the tree, he tried to imagine a buck that could have done such a thing. He swallowed.

"Looks like someone took a chain saw to it," he said. "Naw, this can't be a deer. It's gotta be an elk or moose or something."

"Come on, Buwana, don't start with the bull. There aren't any elk around here. I'm no expert but I don't think a moose has antlers sharp enough to make those kind of marks. Had to be a buck."

Brad pulled off his glove and ran a finger down one of the deep gouges cut into the cedar. It still looked like the work of a chain saw maniac from one of those horror flicks.

"If it was a deer," he said, pulling his glove on and glancing toward the swamp, "it must think it's as big and bad as an elk."

He paused for a moment. "Or maybe it really is," he finished mostly to himself.

"Hey, if you're scared of facing something this big, I'll trade places. Man, I don't want you wetting your pants when it comes out."

Brad stood, his face pressing close to Corey's.

"Look, I'm not scared. I was just wondering, that's all. If you don't like your spot and think this is better, then say so. You can have it and I'll go find my own. Well?"

"Geez, Brad, chill out. I was only kidding."

Corey looked away and crossed his arms.

Brad fiddled with his walking stick. Snowflakes burned his cheeks.

"Sorry, Corey. I guess I'm a little worked up over Pa and everything."

Corey looked at him out of the corner of his eye. "Hey, I was just trying to be funny," he said, "that's all. It's just that sometimes I can't tell if you're feeding me bull or being straight."

"Well, which do you want?"

Corey turned, a devilish grin finally lighting up his face. "Why, the bullcrap, of course. It's tons funner."

"Fair enough," Brad said, holding out his hand. "Still friends?"

"Always, Buwana," Corey said, slapping Brad's palm. "I can stand you as long as you can stand me. Now come on, I'll help you build your stickup for this chain saw thing."

Brad scanned the area and spotted two storm-fallen aspens fifty yards south of the trails. God sent trees, Pa would say. One had fallen over the other, forming a natural blind. It overlooked a wide section of swamp and offered a clear view of the main trails. A ten-foot rise in the land between here and Corey's blind also added a margin of safety from stray fire. An exceptionally safe stickup Brad thought. He doubted if Corey's shotgun slugs could reach this far anyway, and by facing north Brad's shots would enter the swamp if he missed.

He looked from the deadfalls to the swamp. If I miss? It's barely fifty yards, I shouldn't. But like Pa says, bucks don't stand still like targets stapled to back stops and anything can happen. Great, anything.

He pushed the thought to the back of his mind. It was time to concentrate on building his stickup.

They went to work, this time Corey trimming shooting lanes through the brush while Brad rearranged dead branches and sections of logs. As Brad looked back at the shredded cedar, he was tempted to fetch and pile more logs around him, hoping to fortify his position, maybe make it safer. But he remembered Pa's words: A buck will spot a new fortress in its living room, but it won't notice the same log with just another bump on it. So Brad made one last check to be sure he had a clear line of fire to the runways. He would settle for being just another bump.

Finished, Brad stood near Corey in the falling snow, hands on hips.

"Not a bad stickup, huh?" he said. "You think Pa would approve?"

"Approve heck, he'd be proud. Now all you have to do is shoot the chain saw when it comes by."

"Yeah," Brad said, his eyes drifting back to the darkness of the swamp. "That's all I have to do."

Blind building complete, their stomachs finally came alive. They dusted the snow from a large aspen log, sat, and fished sandwiches from their packs. In the cold air, the flavor of baloney and mustard on rye tasted more intense than Brad had ever remembered. He savored each bite, its sticky tang lingering on his tongue and the roof of his mouth. Corey gobbled his sandwich down like a half-starved coyote. Then he attacked his Snickers bar, almost eating a piece of the wrapper with it.

As Brad looked up at the grayness of the sky, he realized how time in the woods had a way of creeping past without noticing it. Evening was approaching fast. The sky hung lower and the wind had abated. The clouds hung heavy like gray flannel pillow cases stuffed with popcorn. Snow fell in increasing waves, swirling down like swarms of insect ghosts. It clung to their stocking caps in wet globs and christened their shoulders with the fluffy insignia of north country hunters.

"Listen Brad," whispered Corey, cocking his head. "Do you hear that?"

Brad stopped chewing a mouthful of half-frozen banana. He listened tensely, only detecting the faint ticks of snowflakes brushing his cheeks and collar.

"What?" Brad whispered. "I don't hear anything."

"That's what you're supposed to hear. Ain't it great, Buwana? Beautiful, empty, soundless nothing. It's electrifying. Can't you feel it? It's a void, a hole in our perception. No jets, no cars, no school bells, nobody telling us what to do, where to go, what time to be in; nothing."

Brad sat listening to nothing.

"And the more I listen," Corey continued, "the more I think I'm in love with all this nothingness."

"I think you've been out in the cold too long. Next I suppose you'll be in love with the solitude of all these trees. Maybe you'll get lucky and find one with a teeny-weeny knot hole just your size."

Brad reached down and pulled a branch from the snow. He hooked it around Corey's shoulder. "Oh Corey," he mimicked in a high voice, "you're such a hunk, we love you too."

At that, he yanked hard on the branch, pulling Corey backwards into the snow. Corey threw out an arm as he fell and sent Brad tumbling off the log with him. For a moment they lay there laughing, sucking in snowflakes spiraling into their mouths. But the coldness quickly sobered their mood.

Brad stood, brushed the snow from his coat and shouldered his pack. "Fun's over tree-hugger. Time to head back. Must be getting close to dark. Guess we took more time than we should have."

Corey adjusted his cap and pulled on his pack. As they turned to leave, Brad caught a flicker out of the corner of his eye. It was only a small flash of gray quickly vanishing in the maze of cedars. Brad stopped in mid stride and cupped a hand over his brow. He peered through the wavering curtains of snow, staring into the swamp. Nothing moved. Nothing looked out of place. His eyes told him nothing was there, yet a sudden tightness in the back of his throat told him something was there alright — more than a partridge or squirrel. He could feel the stare of intense eyes reaching out as if to touch him, probing, eager, flush with excitement. They held him. They dared him to run.

"See something?"

Brad swallowed hard and shrugged his shoulders, damning his imagination. "Uhh, it's nothing," he lied, his voice distant. "Just wanted one last look at the swamp here before tomorrow. We'll be walking back here in the dark and I want to remember what this spot looks like, that's all."

Brad pried his eyes from the swamp and picked up his walking stick. He turned and began trudging through the snow, the weight of the thing's stare now on his neck. Part of him wanted to break and run like a frightened fawn. A bigger part held him to a deliberate walk; one foot in front of the other, each step taking him further from it.

Without glancing back he walked to the trail road that led back to the cabin. Corey shuffled along at his side. The Suburban's tire tracks were completely covered by four inches of fresh snow. It fell in clustered globs the size of dandelion puffs. They plodded along, stopping to inspect every faint track dimpling the snow. Some revealed the travels of deer coming from the swamp for their evening forages, others looked like the trails of pine squirrels hopping through the fluff.

Halfway back to the cabin, the boys crossed a fresh track. The sticky snow made it difficult to identify but clearly it wasn't a deer's. It looked more like a fox or small predator with a short, meandering stride. They followed it down the trail for a hundred yards before it wandered off east into a stand of aspen.

"Let's follow it a while and practice our tracking," Corey said. "Maybe we'll see what made it?"

Brad hesitated. It was getting late and he knew they should return to the cabin. But like Corey had said, here they were free from adults telling them what to do. Freedom and adventure beckoned. Besides, a half-hour diversion shouldn't matter.

"Sure," Brad said, "let's do it. We'll find out what varmint braves this kind of weather."

Picking up their pace, they followed the track deeper into the timber. The track-maker seemed to wander without purpose, digging under logs and prying bark off dead trees. After dogging the tracks for twenty minutes, Brad was ready to abandon the trail and turn back. Then they spotted something new. Up ahead, the snow wore a crimson stain of fresh blood.

"Wow, check it out," said Corey, rushing ahead. "It killed something."

Brad eased forward and joined Corey's side. A rotten stump lay overturned and its humus covered the surrounding snow like coffee grounds sprinkled on a bed sheet. Next to the stump, a few orange-red droplets of blood spattered the packed snow.

"Maybe it chowed down a rabbit," Corey said.

"Don't think so. No rabbit hair. A rabbit would have struggled and there'd be lots of hair. More blood too. Unless it got eaten in one gulp."

Brad leaned nearer to the carnage. "Maybe it was some kind of
—"

Suddenly he spotted eyes staring at him from the snow. They
shined with an odd black gaze; the blank stare of recent death.

Brad reached down and gently brushed away the snow.

"I'll be darned," Corey said. "It's the friggin' head of a mouse,
isn't it? Whatever dug if from under that stump didn't want mouse
eyes for dessert."

Brad turned over the small head with his finger. "Whatever ate
this knows enough about furry snacks to avoid eating the head."

"What do you mean? Too much cholesterol in the brains?"

"No dummy. It's a short-tailed shrew. It's bite is poisonous
because of some toxin in its saliva. Maybe that's why whatever
killed it ate everything except the head."

"Is this more bull?"

"No, honest. Pa told me about it after our cat brought one of
these home last summer."

"Yucko," Corey said, twisting his face. "Never heard of that
before. Remind me never to snack on any. Hey, look, the blood's
still sticky. This musta happened just a few minutes ago. Come on.
We can catch up to it."

The boys trotted along the fresh tracks heading for thicker
timber. They had barely covered a hundred yards when they
spotted it. At first the thing looked like a porcupine with its dark
rump waddling through the snow. But Brad knew that was impossible. Porkies didn't eat meat and surely weren't fast enough to
catch a shrew. Closing the distance to forty yards, they spotted the
ringed tail dusted with snow — a coon. It was only a large raccoon
plodding along, its oversized haunches swaying back and forth.
Plowing through deep snow, it was oblivious to the boy's approach.

"Let's run it up a tree," Corey whispered. "We'll teach this dude
to watch its butt."

Brad nodded. They rushed the raccoon, wielding their sticks
and barking like mad hounds. Corey snarled between his high-
pitched bellows, his teeth bared. The raccoon snapped its head
around at the commotion then immediately flared its hackles and
tucked its tail. In a short choppy burst it leaped for a dead aspen
and clawed its way upward, frantically pulling away loose bark as
it climbed. In a flash it reached the broken off top fifteen feet up.
With no more tree to climb, it nervously jerked its head around
looking for safer refuge.

"Man, look at that," hollered Corey. "We scared the piss out of it. Hope it doesn't puke shrew guts on us."

Clinging to the dead tree, drawing its body tight with squat legs, the raccoon stared with wild, darting eyes.

But then a new emotion seemed to hit as the fear in its eyes suddenly blinked out of focus and its face contorted into a series of ticks. Its body twitched, quivering uncontrollably. Its eyes squinted shut as if blinking back the flashes of fireworks.

"Heck," Brad said, "poor thing's scared half to death. Look at the way it's shaking. Let's leave it alone. It'll probably have nightmares about us the rest of the winter as it is."

Corey lowered his stick and nodded. "You're right. It's getting late anyway and we'd better make some tracks of our own."

As they turned to leave, another wave of shivers reeled through the raccoon. Each tremor grew stronger until even the snag shook. But the boys didn't notice. Retracing their tracks, they also didn't hear the guttural snarl rising from deep in its throat.

A scant twenty yards from the tree, with caps pulled tight over their ears, the boys didn't hear claws scraping soft bark as the raccoon descended. Its silent rush through the snow gave little warning. Only the faint clicking of its jaws made Brad turn at the last moment.

He whirled at the sound, hairs on his neck prickling to life. For an instant his feet seemed fused in the snow. Another flash jolted his senses like a poke from an electrical fence. He bolted.

"Run, Corey, run!"

In two strides Brad passed Corey who stood confused watching him shoot past.

"Behind you. The coon, the coon!"

Corey spun as the raccoon bounded over a log, snow spraying its muzzle, half filling the gaping mouth. Only ten feet separated them, but Corey didn't run. He turned slightly, cocking his walking stick like Babe Ruth readying for a fast ball. The raccoon leaped. Corey swung hard, connecting with a glancing blow just above the frenzied eyes. It tumbled with a snarl, landing in a spray of snow. It rolled over twice then righted itself, head swaying back and forth, eyes blinking out of focus.

Then incredibly it lunged again, jaws snapping with the distinct popping of canines. Spittle flew. This time Corey ran. With an exhilarating sprint, he skimmed over the snow. Brad led the way, bursting through small clusters of branches and hurdling fallen logs.

The raccoon followed but its short legs floundered in the snow. It quickly fell behind. The boys dashed for over two hundred yards before slowing to watch their backtrail. Nothing followed. Only the growing darkness surrounded them.

Somewhere back in the gloom, two small eyes shimmered with the glowing crescents of new moons.

"What was that all about?" Brad gasped. "And why in the world did you try to bean it? Geez Corey, that thing wanted to chew your butt off."

"I don't know. Caught me off guard. Didn't have time to think. Seemed like the thing to do. Musta seen it in a movie somewhere. Was almost fun until I saw how pissed it was. Man, it was pissed big time. Musta decided to teach us to watch our butts. Sure worked for me." He nervously fingered his stick while scanning their backtrail.

"I don't think it was trying to teach us anything. Something was wrong. Didn't you see that weird look in its eyes?"

"I don't know. Maybe. All I know is that I don't want to see it again. Let's get outta here. Your dad's going to be steaming by the time we get back."

They trotted into the evening grayness. Prodded by the excitement of the encounter, they ran, unsure in the failing light which direction led to the trail. The snow fell heavier, obscuring their vision like seeing through a spattered shower curtain. Everywhere they turned, the forest looked the same; a clouded milky dreamscape.

A half-hour later, Brad's stomach began knotting. Crap, we're lost. And it's my fault. I didn't even bring my compass. I'm supposed to know the woods up here. Now which way?

With dropping temperatures and snow-damp clothes, he knew they couldn't survive the night out. He had no choice but to press on.

As darkness claimed the forest, Brad and Corey stumbled into a long opening in the trees.

"Look, Brad, it's the old logging trail. Which way?"

Brad looked for some sign of earlier tracks. The piling snow covered any sign. He squinted into the gloom then turned in the other direction.

"This way, I guess," he said, walking down the trail.

"You guess? That doesn't sound very encouraging."
"Sorry, it's the best I can do."
"Well, for our sake I hope it's the right way."
Brad paused and looked into Corey's eyes.
"For our sake I pray it's the right trail."

CHAPTER 10 — TEST RESULTS

Dr. Nolstrum stared out a window of the prison infirmary at the falling snow. Flakes poured from the sky in billows, their dark flecks blooming into pearly globs as they danced beneath the glow of the vapor lamps ringing the prison walls. He shook his head. It was bad enough to be working overtime on a Saturday evening. The prospect of driving home through the snowy mess added to his irritation. He combed his fingers through his hair, pausing near the balding spot on the crown of his scalp. He turned and gulped the last of his coffee, wincing at the bitterness of the overbrewed dredges that should have been tossed hours ago.

Behind him, Dr. Pratt, the Army physician investigating the incident, sat in the darkness near the yellow wash of a desk lamp. The stark light made his bristly eyebrows look like baby porcupines perched on his brow. In front of him lay a pile of notes and several pages of Little Eli's test results. He rubbed his eyes then leaned forward into the glow of the light. Tapping a few of the scribbles with his finger, he rechecked the partial results for the umpteenth time.

After a long sigh Dr. Pratt pushed the papers aside and fixed his gaze on the fax machine sitting across the desk. He propped his elbows, interlaced his fingers, and rested his chin on his knuckles. A moment later his eyes fluttered shut. Dr. Pratt's breathing no sooner slowed into a husky rasp when the machine beeped and buzzed to life. He jumped at the start.

Dr. Nolstrum moved along side him and leaned over his shoulder. With their eyes straining on each line of the emerging report, the doctors appeared to be drawing the paper from the machine by telekinesis. The fax's humming finally stopped and Pratt ripped the scrolled paper from the holder. Together, they studied it in silence for almost two minutes. Finally, Pratt spoke.

"If your lab buddy at County General didn't come with such high credentials, I'd question these results." Pratt's face hardened as his eyes moved down the page. "Just look at this," he continued, rapping a finger on a line. "We never would have found this in the SMAC-23 blood tests run in your lab here. Damn good thing you suggested that extended urine analysis. I've never seen anything quite like this. According to these catecholamine and metanephrine levels, your Little Eli fellow should be wearing fur and claws. How did you figure?"

Dr. Nolstrum rechecked the numbers. He wasn't about to admit it to this governmental watchdog, but the new test results surprised him too.

"Maybe it was the sweaty palms or the slightly increased heart rate and blood pressure. Don't know for sure. Just had a hunch," Nolstrum lied, bunching his shoulders, "that's all."

He was reluctant to divulge the overall change he had noticed in Eli's character; the complete sentences reported by the officers, the heightened awareness, the new look in his eyes — nothing he could put a clinical finger on, subtle things that an outsider such as Pratt wouldn't have noticed.

"So if it is phiochromocytoma related to a tumor," Pratt said, "what do you intent to do, operate?"

"Whoa, that's jumping the gun. We can't be certain this is even related to a tumor. Hell, your friend's experimental drug may have caused Eli's hyper-active adrenal system for we know." Nolstrum paused for a moment, glancing at Pratt, looking for some hint of a crack in the stiff features. "And maybe the drug caused Eli's violent reaction on the bus too."

Pratt looked at Dr. Nolstrum, a strained confusion coming to his face. Nolstrum couldn't tell if his ignorance was genuine or if he was covering up. These Army types were pros at that. And if that was the case, two could play that game.

"I'm just looking for logical answers here, doctor," Nolstrum said. "And I was hoping you could fill in some of the blanks about how this experimental drug might have affected the inmates. Too much of Eli's test data just doesn't fit. Look here. If this increased adrenaline output and elevated EEG are tied to a physiological response or a tumor of the adrenal system, why aren't we seeing any external evidence of it? Hell, he barely blinked throughout the whole exam. I've known Eli for eleven years and he's not one to hide his emotions. That's why he's in this place for life. He responds to the slightest agitation, in spades."

"Well," Pratt said raising his eyebrows, "he doesn't appear to respond in spades anymore. Like I already told you, we haven't been able to uncover the content of Robenthral's drug yet. Too many synthetic compounds. We're still working on it. Who knows, maybe the drug helped repress Eli's external responses. If so, then be thankful for the blessing. We'll figure this out. It just may take a few days more, that's all. One piece at a time, Doctor. Be patient. We'll find out sooner or later. We're lucky we've uncovered this much so far."

Dr. Nolstrum looked back toward the windows. Lucky my butt. And I thought State government was lackadaisical. This guy could wait until Christmas for all he cares. All the answers won't come any too soon for me. The last thing I need is him poking around disrupting things. He probably doesn't even know it's the start of flu season.

Nolstrum stuffed his hands into his pockets and turned back to Pratt. "Well, do you suppose your friend Dr. Robenthral might be able to help clear this up?" he asked.

"Don't think so," Pratt said, his eyes void of emotion. "Stopped by County General this morning. It doesn't look promising. His brain waves look flatter than the big lake out there. And we can't keep him on life support forever."

Although they couldn't see it, both men gazed out the window; somewhere beyond the swirling snow, a black line of seemingly endless water stretched to the northeastern horizon.

"Who knows," Pratt said, stuffing the test results and notes into his briefcase. "Maybe we'll get lucky next week and solve some more of this little mystery. We'll start fresh sometime next week. I'm taking a few days off to go deer hunting. Got a camp over by Iron Mountain. Great place, sauna, big screen TV, wine cellar, the works. Rarely see a deer, but who cares, it's great fun. How about you? Everybody up here takes deer season off."

Dr. Nolstrum unconsciously raised his empty cup to his lips, taking an idle sip of coffee-scented air. "Nope, don't hunt deer anymore. Used to when I first moved up here, lost my taste for it though. Maybe being around felons everyday gives me my fill of the wilds." His voice trailed off from fatigue or the words melting into his thoughts. A moment later he snapped up his head and blinked. "You want me to continue to get blood and urine samples from Eli until you return?"

"Daily on both. But I don't want him sitting around his cell. Have the warden get him back into his standard routine so his system can burn off some of that adrenaline. Maybe he'll settle back to normal levels by the time I get back. Then we'll see if we can pin a label on this mystery. We've got plenty of time. Our little lab rat isn't about to go anywhere."

Pratt pulled on his overcoat, grabbed his briefcase and headed for the door. He paused at the doorway and adjusted his scarf.

"Oh yeah, you might ask the cook to give Eli some extra meat for the next few days. The way his adrenal system is pumping it's no doubt gobbling up the complex proteins in his body. If he's a man that gives in to his urges, he's probably already eating like a lion." Pratt snickered and waved off as he headed down the corridor.

Dr. Nolstrum found little humor in the situation. Fate had dealt him a set of unknowns with this Eli mess. And uncertainty only added stress to his job. He had enough to worry about for one day. Time to head home. His wife would likely be as cold as the pot roast by now. The only bright thought was that he didn't have to return until Monday. Seemed like the whole state was taking off for opening day. No sense in busting his butt while the rest of the world played in the woods.

He turned out the lights and locked the infirmary door. Walking down the corridor, he looked out into the courtyard. The snow continued to fall, heavier than before. Down near the side gate he saw Pratt's car pull from the security lot. He noticed how the snow formed rings of pale light as it drifted across Pratt's headlights. His thoughts immediately shifted to the image of other glowing crescents — Little Eli's strange eyes ringed with foxfire.

CHAPTER 11 – STORY TIME

An hour after dark, Brad and Corey stumbled through the cabin door, cheeks scoured red, lips pale blue.

Pa turned from the kitchen stove, a dripping ladle in one hand, the other propped on his hip, ermine-white eyebrows bunching at the sight of them. He shook his head and turned back to his brew.

Brad stomped crusted snow from his boots. *Crap, why doesn't he ask me why we're late? At least that would gimme a chance to explain — or try to, if any of them will believe me. God, I hardly believe it myself. Well, maybe with Corey backing me up they won't accuse me of telling another whopper anyway.*

Brad's father and the others rushed from the cabin's living room to get a look.

"You had us awfully worried, son," Al said, stepping into the kitchen. "Why don't you give me your coats so I can hang them to dry. You look half frozen. I think you should grab a bowl of Pa's stew and come in and sit near the pot-bellied stove. After you get some hot food in you, then maybe you can explain why you were out so late."

Without a word the boys obliged. Hunched like old men, they shuffled into the living room. With steaming bowls cradled in their laps, they huddled together on a split pine bench near the stove and propped their feet on a log. Their teeth chattered. Steam rose from their pant legs. The smell of wet wool soon mixed with the aroma of venison stew.

Brad slurped from a spoon. *Okay, so where do I begin? Should I first tell them about what I saw in Deadman's Swamp? Heck, I'm not even sure what I saw. It wasn't a coon, I'm sure of that. It was way too big, whatever it was — Naw, I better just stick to what Corey saw too. That's the only way they'll believe me.*

He peeked up from his bowl. Warren Crane stood nearby sipping scotch and water. He too wore flushed cheeks, peppered with the purple streaks of minute blood vessels like tiny red worms working their way to the surface. But he didn't look cold. The upper half of his wool shirt gaped open and the hair that usually carefully covered most of his bald spot stood fluffed in a tousle — probably a new hairdo courtesy of his hunting hat.

Brad almost snickered between gulps. He looks more like a circus clown tiring in the third act than my dad's boss. If he doesn't watch it, he might start acting normal like a regular guy. The almighty Mr. Crane, a mere mortal? He'd probably puke at the thought.

Brad glanced toward Vern who slumped in a nearby rocker as if halfway to a coma. Beer cans littered the small table next to him, a fresh one clasped in his hand. He seemed locked in a trance, staring at the small icing-glass plate in the stove door. A flickering reflection danced in his watery eyes like flashes of thought going nowhere. In his other hand hung a cigarette, its long ash drooping from neglect, smoke slithering up between his fingers.

Brad gulped the last of his stew, wiped the corner of his mouth with the back of his hand, and set the bowl aside. He squirmed on the bench trying to find a comfortable position. He reached down and rolled up his drying pant legs to expose the damp socks and longjohns underneath. He glanced around. All the eyes in the room had settled on him, silent, waiting. Uh oh, story time. I mean, time for the truth. I could always make a story sound real enough to be true; but how do I deal with the impossible truth? Brad fingered his lip as if searching for the right words to begin.

Before he could start, Pa broke the ice.

"You two must have found a buck crossing better than any I've seen in forty years to keep you out after dark," he said, the pale blue of his eyes glacial behind his glasses.

Fiddling with his cuffs, Brad started softly.

"Yeah, we found some good buck crossings alright, but none that kept us out so late. That's not what happened." Brad looked to Corey for support and found him hiding behind the rim of his tipped bowl. Great, some best friend. Where's that motor-mouth when I need it?

Al leaned against one of the upright beams near the stove, cradling a mug of coffee. "Come on, son, let's get to the point. Why don't you tell us what happened, exactly what happened."

Brad glanced over at him. Geez, why can't he yell at me like a real father? Doesn't he care? Isn't he pissed? I mean, crap, I could have been killed or lost or something. At least he could raise his voice. Or is he too afraid to show a little backbone in front of Crane?

Brad dug his fingers into the wool of his pants and continued.

"We found some spots with rubs along that part of ridge near the swamp where you took us, Dad. Built two stickups there too, just like Pa showed us. And with this fresh snow it ought to be perfect there tomorrow."

Brad's face brightened at the prospect.

"Enough about your stickups," Pa said. "We want to know why you foolishly stayed out so late in this kind of weather. If you two don't have any more sense than to stay out after dark in the middle of a snowstorm, maybe you can't be trusted to go hunting at all. You want to be grown up enough to hunt deer in the big woods, yet you pull some childish stunt like this. What are we supposed to think?"

"I think we ought to make 'em chop wood all day and keep camp clean," Vern slurred, breaking his stupor long enough to fuel the fire.

Brad bolted forward. What? Stay in camp opening day? That's not fair.

Corey sputtered a mouthful of stew back into his bowl. His cheeks puffed and eyes widened. He finally found his tongue.

"Wa-wa-wait a minute, Mr. Mercer. We can explain, honest. It wasn't our fault. We got attacked. Had to run for our lives, well, kind of. Then we got mixed up in the snowstorm. A little lost, that's all. No big deal."

"Attacked?" Al said, his voice reaching tenor. "Who? Where? What happened?"

Crane and Vern scooted to the edge of their seats. Granddad canted his neck like a heron ready to strike.

"No, not that," Brad said. "Nobody attacked us. Not a person. It was nothing like that. It was a coon, a big crazy raccoon."

"Right," Vern snickered and slapped his knee. "You'd better check what these punks been smoking out in the woods. Sounds like they got a bad batch making them see charging coons. What a crock." He drowned his whinny laugh with a gulp of beer.

Brad's jaw bunched. Damn, I knew it. I knew this would happen. Now they'll never believe about the other thing I saw in the swamp.

"We're not burnouts," Corey said, green eyes glaring, more redness rising into already fiery cheeks. "If we were wasteoids, we wouldn't be here having a straight good time — or at least trying to."

Vern shrugged off the comment, finding refuge in another slug of suds.

"Come on, Dad. You know better than that. Corey and I got chased by this crazy raccoon. It was either sick or really mad at us. Maybe both."

"Look, son," Al said, stepping closer, his eyes softening as he knelt before Brad. "I know you like to glamorize your little adventures. That's okay sometimes, we've kind of grown to expect it. But you have to understand, this isn't the time for it. We have to know the truth."

Brad nodded. He cleared his throat and began, and without interruption, he recounted the entire episode, every detail in place. Corey nodded stiffly at each point in the story. Vern even managed to sit on the edge of his chair without butting in.

"...and by the time we finally found the trail road again, it was dark. We somehow ended up near the far end of the trail down by the swamp. It took a while to walk back in this heavy snow. Must be knee-deep out there by now. But we're all right. Nothing serious happened."

"Sounds like you kids pushed that coon too far," Crane said, snorting and scratching his belly. "Maybe you forgot whose home you were in? It doesn't surprise me that it wanted to sink its teeth into you. Not a very bright trick, I'd say. But then again, I'm not surprised." Crane turned and glanced toward Al.

Brad looked into his lap. Thanks, Mr. Crane, you're just what I needed, more gas on the fire. The way my dad follows your every lead, I'll be lucky to see my rifle again. Yeah, thanks a lot.

"All we did was run it up a tree," Corey said, holding his palms up. "It's not like we were out there trying to hurt it. Why would that have made it go bonkers?"

Brad's eyes drifted to Pa. He propped his elbows on his knees and leaned forward.

"Coons are dang ornery," Pa said. "And they can be mean-tempered scrappers for their size. But they don't normally go around chasing people through the woods, even if they are mighty irritated. Just ain't natural."

"If I had brats chasing me like mad dogs wielding sticks, I'd try for a chunka-their-asses-too," Vern offered, his words bunching into a slur at the end. He tossed another empty into the bag near his feet.

"Natural or not," Brad said quickly to cut off Vern's venom, "it's true, all of it. And if Corey hadn't dazed it with his stick, it might still be after us. That thing was crazy like I've never seen."

"Was it drooling or foaming around the mouth?" Al asked.

"Couldn't see," Corey said. "Had so much snow on its face it was hard to tell. All I know is that its eyes looked weird. Like it was stoned," he flashed Vern a look, "or had too many beers."

The stab went unheard as Vern clattered in the bottom of his carton for a full can.

Pa rubbed his chin, his silver stubble making a slight hiss under his thumb. "Maybe it had rabies," he said. "Coons carry it. That would account for it wandering around in this heavy snow. Rabies, yep, it's the only thing that makes any sense."

"Rabies?" Crane said, wagging his face. "You're kidding? I thought only dogs got rabies. Come on."

"Nope," Pa said. "Most domestic animals like dogs get rabies vaccines. They can't get it then. It's usually wild animals like bats, skunks and coons that get it; predators and omnivores. They say the virus is transmitted through the saliva of a carrier from either its bite or from eating saliva-infected carrion."

"Carrion?" Vern asked, screwing his face up and sticking his tongue out. "You mean like some kind of rotten crap along the roadside. I thought coons were clean, always washing their food first."

"Only on nature shows," Pa said. "Sure, they wash scavenged food around water, but they're opportunists mostly, like miniature bears. In the wild they'll eat whatever handout comes along. And they don't much care how or where they get it — carrion included."

"Sounds to me like half the lazy-asses on welfare nowadays," Crane said, tossing down the last of his scotch. "A bunch of good-for-nothing opportunists, the whole lot of them. I guess it's no wonder they call them, 'coons'."

His jowls shook as he chuckled at his wit. No one else joined in, not even Vern. Al pushed his hands into his pockets and looked away.

Brad was pleasantly surprised by the embarrassment in his dad's eyes. Maybe Dad can't stand the fat toad any more than the rest of us? Hmmm, maybe he puts up with him because of us?

"But rabies, this far north?" Al finally asked, breaking the tension.

"Only logical answer," Pa said. "Makes sense too. I remember seeing mad dogs when I was a kid, long before they developed rabies vaccine. Pain drove them loco. It attacks their nervous system and works into the spinal area, eventually the whole brain. Drives them crazy. They'll tear into anything in their path."

"Sounds awful," Corey said, drawing his legs up close to his chest. "If that coon got rabies around here, do you suppose other animals like wolves or coyotes could get it? Or a deer or bear? That'd be awesome!"

Pa pushed his glasses back up the bridge of his nose and bunched his eyebrows.

"Guess it's possible," he said after a moment. "I've even heard of cows getting it after being bitten by infected foxes, but, whoa, that's really stretching things, even for a story-teller." His eyes drifted over to Brad.

Brad looked away from Pa toward the flicker in the stove. Why do they always look at me? So I stretched a few fish when I was a kid, cried wolf now and then. Big deal. It was just for fun, I didn't know any better then. Can't they see I've changed? Heck, I'm grown up now. Can't they tell the difference?

"Never heard of a bear getting rabies," Pa continued. "Then again, maybe nobody ever lived to tell about meeting up with one. Just to be safe we better report this coon thing to the Natural Resources people. They'll want to know about a possible outbreak of rabies. Have to wait until we can make it into town though. And no telling when that will be with this snow storm."

Vern stood from his chair, swaying a little in front of the makeshift window where the scavenger had broken in. Outside, the storm worsened. Waves of snow pushed against the plastic like a heavy hand.

"Probably a whole pack of them rabid wolves out there right now," he said, gazing in the boys' direction, as if looking for something to focus on, "just frothing at the mouth at the thought of you juicy smurfs. Yep, I'd sure hate to be you guys come morning in the swamp."

He took another long draw from his can and edged closer to the boys. "That's right," he continued, "them wolves probably realize we're the only easy food anywhere around this big old swamp. They're probably planning right now — making some horrible trap for first light when they can lay in hiding behind the outhouse, wait for you to get busy trying to find yourselves... Then sneak up behind you and... MAKE BREAKFAST OUTTA YA!" He leaped at the boys, snarling, his sour breath causing them to draw back.

Vern broke into his whinnying laugh. Crane joined him. Brad scowled. His eyes met Corey's. Corey glanced sideways at Vern, as if to say: Can you believe this guy?

"Don't try to scare us," Corey said, his green eyes flashing back at Vern. "We're not that green. A pack of wolves up here? Get real."

"I've heard that rabies can spread pretty fast through an area," Pa said, "but it ain't likely there's a whole pack of rabid wolves running around the swamp. They'd be too sick to run in a pack. Besides, I doubt if there's enough wolves around here to make up a pack."

"But it could happen!" Vern shouted as he shook his finger at Pa. The turn in the conversation had somehow stirred his senses to life. "If it happens to wild dogs then it can happen to wolves. Admit it, old man. Admit it!"

"On second thought," Pa said, turning slightly and winking at the boys, "you could be right, Vern. Matter of fact, that frothing pack might decide to pick us off one at a time as we head to the outhouse in the morning. And for their sake, I hope they know which one of us is full of horsecrap!"

The room filled with laughter. Vern frowned for a moment, then, unsure of who to sneer at, slipped into laughter despite himself. Corey and Brad rocked back and forth slapping their knees. Pa wore a smile prouder than if he'd just landed a three-pound trout.

Just as the laughing began to ebb into giggles and snorts, Brad glimpsed something flicker outside past the plastic window. A swirl of snow?

A dark shape neared the window then was gone. Brad gasped and gripped Corey's leg. Corey had seen it too. They stiffened, eyes flaring. The others saw their reaction and turned toward the window. The room fell deathly silent.

Outside the window, a low moan rose and fell. Gasps hissed inside the room like the sounds of ladies sipping tea. The moan lasted only a moment, almost blending with the snow and wind. But it was there nonetheless. Everyone heard it and held their breath. Vern dropped his beer can, its clank splitting the thin silence. Al glared at him.

The moaning rose again, this time more clearly. Vern shuffled away from the window until the heat of the stove stopped him. Crane pushed himself back on the sofa, his mouth agape, eyes fixed on the plastic.

As the moan died, a faint scratching grated the outside of the wall, like a branch swaying in the wind. But unlike a branch, the sound moved along the outside wall, inching closer to the door, like long claws searching for a way in.

"For God's sake, Mercer," Crane hissed, "do something, damn it. And do it quick."

Pa nodded toward the gun rack. Al scurried across the floor and jerked his .30-06 Remington from the pegs. He grabbed a full clip from the rack's shelf and jammed it into the magazine. With a jerk of the hand, he pulled back the bolt, chambering a soft-nosed shell, the bolt clacking sharply in the stilled room. He leveled the rifle at his waist.

The scratching stopped.

Everyone listened.

Nothing.

"It heard you, Dad," Brad finally whispered. "Maybe you scared it away. Maybe it —"

Brad gulped air as the scratching resumed. This time it grew louder and had moved to the kitchen door leading to the shed. Claws, big claws for sure now. The boys crowded together. Pa stood firm, head cocked. He cupped his ear and listened.

The scratching grew into a clattering at the door, then a pounding. The rusty hinges creaked and the door knob began to rattle.

"It's that goddamn bear that broke your window," Crane said, his droopy features drawn tight like he had lost fifty pounds. "It came back and now it's coming in here. Shoot the sonofabitch through the door! Shoot, Mercer, before it gets in here again."

Al shouldered his rifle and pressed his cheek against the stock. Despite Crane's orders, his finger stayed clear of the safety and trigger.

"Wait!" Pa said, a slight smile forming, grabbing the barrel of rifle and pushing the muzzle down. "Don't shoot, I think we know this bear."

Puzzled faces turned.

The pounding stopped.

The boys let out held breaths.

But they sucked them back in as the door knob shuddered anew then began turning slowly. The boys jumped as a gust of wind ripped open the door, snow billowing into the kitchen like a ghost from the night. Vern staggered back into the stove, cursing as he singed his arm. Crane pressed himself back to the top of the sofa.

For a moment only silence and cold air engulfed the room. Then the moaning began again from the darkness of the shed.

"Yoooo, yoo, yoo hoo. Yoo-hoo, is anybody in there?"

Al sighed and almost dropped the rifle.

"Come on in you nasty ol' bear," he hollered, "before I change my mind and shoot you anyway. You're letting in the cold. Fun's over. Get your crazy butt in here."

Pa chuckled and shook his head.

From the darkness stepped Larry Mercer, Al's younger brother. Looking like a bear, he moved though the doorway with a blend of power and grace, his bulky sloping shoulders leading the way ahead of a long torso that appeared oversized for his narrow hips and squat legs. He kicked the door shut behind him and stepped into the light of the overhead gas lamp. He yanked off a wool lumberman's hat and shook his head. Wet snow sprayed from his beard and mane of hair, both thick and shining like the prime fur of a bear rug.

"Howdy, slicks. Good to see ya."

His broad face lit up like neon, undersized chestnut eyes glistening like those of a wild creature. He reached up and yanked at the icicles hanging from his handlebar moustache.

"Holy crow, it's cold out there. If I didn't know better, I'd say it was January instead of mid-November."

He stomped snow from his full-laced logging boots, shiny slick with bear grease. He fingered the buttons on his long plaid wool jacket and laid back its oversized collar.

"Man," whispered Corey, "he looks like he stepped out of a time machine. Right from an 1890's lumber camp."

Brad nodded and smiled. "Uncle Larry! You scared the pants off us."

Larry grinned and nodded toward Brad's rolled up cuffs. His eyes shined even brighter.

"Well, by God it looks like I did a little. Must be getting better at these pranks in my old age." He ended with a laugh that would have shamed Santa as he plopped down two bulky rucksacks. But he tenderly set a long deer-skin case in the corner. He turned and winked at Corey. "It's my job to scare these city slickers. Somebody's got to keep them on their toes, sharpen city-fied senses."

Larry paused, suddenly sensing the concern still fresh in everyone's face. He nodded to the cabin's regulars, Crane and Vern.

"Gee, sorry, guys. I didn't mean to scare you that much. I figured you'd know better, especially you, Dad." He strode over and wrapped a big arm around Pa. Pa reached up and patted him on the shoulder.

"It's just that we didn't expect you until early tomorrow morning," he said. "You caught us off guard, that's all."

Larry nodded toward the rippling plastic across the window.

"No way I could wait until morning. There's a nasty northwester blowing in and I figured I better get back in here tonight or I wouldn't make it at all. Took me nearly two hours just to drive the fifty miles from Munising. The snow is already belly deep to a coyote in the woods. I parked my Jeep three miles down the trail near the gravel road. The snow drifted across that first hollow in the trail. Even with four-wheel drive I didn't want to risk getting stuck there so I played it safe and parked off to the side. If it snows all night at least I can walk out to my Jeep and four-wheel it back to town. No sense me being stranded here after I get my buck. Let's hope it melts some by the time you slicks try and get out with that two-wheel tank of yours."

He shook more wet snow from his jacket and hung it on one of the posts. He held his hands near the stove. He looked back at the window.

"Grouse fly through the window?"

No one answered at first.

"Something broke it," Al finally said. "Got into the cupboards looking for food. Something small we figured."

"Probably an oversized pack rat stocking up on supplies before this storm hit," Larry said with a chuckle. "Boy, the way it's coming down out there it should make for a grand opener. Those bucks along the swamp ought to be bunched up in there like spawning salmon." He looked at the boys and bobbed his eyebrows.

"Uncle Larry, this is my friend, Corey Stiles."

Larry stepped over and extended a hand to Corey.

"Uncle Larry is a park interpreter at Pictured Rocks for the National Park Service. He's a geologist. Leads groups of tourists along Lake Superior. Served two tours in Vietnam too. Was a kick-butt Ranger in the Army."

The brightness in Larry's smile faded and his eyes lowered slightly.

"Come on, Brad," he said as he wrapped his big paw around Corey's hand. "Let's forget that kind of stuff in camp. We're all just deer hunters here. Right?"

Larry's fingers enveloped Corey's hand like a baseball mitt. Corey managed a faint smile then withdrew his hand, wiping his palm on his pants.

Larry turned back to the stove. He held his hands over the flat iron top and rubbed his palms together. His eyes gazed at nothing in particular as he stood in silence.

Brad watched him. There he goes, withdrawing into that part he doesn't want anybody to know. Crap, must have been my big mouth again that sent him there. I know Uncle Larry doesn't like talking much about the past, the war. But it's all so exciting. Figure he's got to have a ton of cool stories about it. Why does it bother him so much? What happened then? Oh well, I know what he does like to talk about anyway.

"Why don't you show Corey your gun, Uncle Larry."

Larry turned slightly and paused. He finally blinked, his eyes focusing again, the ghost of a smile returning.

"Sure. Sure, Brad. Got it right here in the case."

From the long leather case fringed with buckskin, Larry withdrew a wooden longbow. He placed the lower end on the instep of his foot, and with a quick push-pull of his hands, bent the bow and slipped the bowstring into place. He plucked the string as he handed the bow to Corey. It was still humming a musical note when Corey gently took the bow.

"Man, I've never seen anything like this. It looks like something from a Robin Hood movie," he said, his eyebrows jumping high enough to touch the red hair draping his forehead. "Where in the world did you get it, an archery museum?"

Larry grinned.

"No, Corey, I made it."

"You really made this thing?"

"Sure. Used a piece of osage orange, hedge apple some people call it. The settlers used to plant it for hedge rows. Makes great bows. That rough side there is backed with deer sinew from leg tendons. The tips are made from the antlers of a buck I shot several years ago. That same deer provided the buckskin wrap on the handle and over the arrow plate. Even used his brains to tan the leather. Made the Flemish twist bowstring too, but I had to use Dacron, modern stuff. Sinew bowstrings don't last worth a darn.

Even the Ojibways who lived up here centuries ago switched to more modern strings after the whites started trading in the north. But everything else on that bow is as primitive as the hills."

Corey's mouth hung open as he glided his fingertips up and down the bow. He held it toward the light, revealing the reddish-orange grain patterns along the limbs. He slowly shook his head.

"Man, this thing's awesome. Can you really kill something with this? I mean a deer or something big?"

Larry chuckled and tipped his head. "Sure can. I've taken deer with self-wood longbows like this for the past eleven years. This is a new one, a lucky one at that. I've been fortunate enough to harvest an 8-pointer and a bear with it so far this season. Lots of small game too. It's a sweet shooter."

"Fortunate, heck," Pa said, stepping next to Larry. "This bear here hunts more like an Injun or a cougar than a man. Only white man I've even seen that could slip up on a sleeping deer and slit its throat if he wanted."

"Come on, Dad that's a bit much. You're starting to sound like Brad here. I'm just a little lucky, that's all."

"Horsefeathers," Pa continued. "Don't let him soft-sell you, Corey. He's a deer hunting fool, a predator from the old days."

He reached up and draped an arm around Larry's shoulder. Larry shrugged and smiled at Pa, suddenly looking like a shy boy.

"Well, I suppose we ought to be hitting the hay," Al said. "Daylight in the swamp will come mighty early tomorrow."

Crane stood from the couch and stretched. He rubbed his ample belly and yawned. Vern picked up his empty can from the floor and dropped it into the bag with the others.

"Larry's going to have to sleep on the sofa," he said, avoiding Larry's eyes and glancing toward the window. "That's the only empty spot in the cabin. He'll have to make do. This ain't a hotel."

Brad watched Larry withdraw again into himself, stepping back into a shadowed corner of his mind. Heck, Uncle Larry could make do out in the snow if he had to. Just because Vern owns half this place doesn't give him the right to be such a prick all the time. Why can't Dad at least stand up for his own brother? If I was Uncle Larry I'd break Vern in half, just for starters.

"Sofa will be just fine, thanks," Larry said after a moment. He cast Vern an empty look — no smile, no scowl, no nothing, just a blank wolf stare, a probing wild void that could mask any realm of emotion. Vern quickly looked away as if icy claws were reaching out for him. He turned toward the back bedroom.

"Like your dad said, Brad, daylight in the swamp comes early," Pa said. "Off to bed with you boys. It's been a long day for you both and tomorrow will be even longer. Guarantee it. Opening day has a way of becoming one of the longest in your life. Now go on, scurry up in that loft like pine squirrels."

Brad and Corey climbed into the loft and crawled inside their sleeping bags. Their cots creaked as they squirmed inside their bags. Below, others settled into bedrooms.

"Your Uncle Larry is really cool," Corey whispered. "It's like he came from some other place and time. Like some guy right out of some mountain man movie."

"Yeah, he's one of kind alright. Hunts, traps and fishes most of the year. Lives alone in a cabin near the big lake. Always says he was born two hundred years too late."

"What are those little beads around his neck?"

Brad glanced through the rungs of the railing. "Indian beads of some kind," he said. "Uncle Larry's really into old Indian ways. Sometimes I wonder if Pa didn't adopt him from an Indian tribe."

Corey raised up on his elbow.

"Lay back down, I'm just kidding. He's a loner that's all. I guess people who live alone seem a bit strange to the rest of us. Maybe that's why Vern doesn't like him. Too much of a lone wolf to be trusted. Who knows?"

"Well, I still think he's neater than hell," Corey said, burrowing into his bag.

Corey quickly drifted off, his breathing measured slowly against the faint ticking of the alarm clock under Brad's cot. Brad sighed and laced fingers behind his head. He stared at the ceiling. How can tomorrow be longer than today? Geez, building stickups, getting chased by that coon, getting lost, wading through all that snow.

He closed his eyes but sleep wouldn't come. The cabin grew quiet except for the hushed conversation of his dad and Larry still sitting near the stove. Brad's breathing began to slow. His muscles relaxed. The warmth of the bag started to draw him into the darkness of sleep. He faintly overheard his dad telling Larry about their incident with the coon. Larry's calm voice suddenly grew strained as he spoke words Brad didn't understand. Brad's ears prickled. His eyes flicked open.

"Matchi Manitou," Larry said, as if an icy hand had squeezed the words from his stomach.

"What?" Al asked.

Brad sat up and cocked his head.

"Matchi Manitou, the evil one. The Ojibways had other names for him, Winabijou and Manabozho. Each swamp held one, an evil spirit that dwells there for all time. You know the Indian legend of Deadman's Swamp? There's a reason so many hunters have vanished there over the years."

"And you think it's this Matchi whatever? Are you kidding?"

Brad cupped a hand to his ear.

Only a drawn silence filled the room below.

"Please, Larry," Al whispered. "You know how Vern gets all worked up over this Indian legend stuff. So let's keep this just between us. And for God sakes, with Brad's imagination, the last thing we need is to plant that seed in his mind. Let's just forget it, okay?"

"Yeah, sure," Larry replied. His voice distant.

Al stood and turned down the gas lamp. Larry unrolled his sleeping bag on the couch.

"What's the Indian meaning of this Manabozho thing," Al asked, curious in spite of himself.

"He's a bad one. Specializes in luring young hunters to their deaths; hunters trying to make their first kill to show they're worthy to become braves."

"How does it do that?"

"Manabozho is a shape-shifter."

Brad's eyes flicked wide as he suddenly recalled the strange shape in the swamp; and the feeling that whatever it was out there somehow wanted him.

Al stood in silence as the gas lamp faded to a dull orange then flickered out. He turned and went to bed, the floor boards creaking under his weight like the grinding of old bones.

CHAPTER 12 – A HUNGER

Eli awoke with a start. Sweat stung the corners of his eyes, his T-shirt clung damp to his chest. His powerful jaws bunched, his teeth whining under the pressure. His heartbeat hammered in his veins.

Like a grey moth, the trail of a dream fluttered away from his senses, winging into the subconscious to be forever buried in the folds of his mind. Eli stilled his consciousness and reached across the chasm toward the darkness. It was like a great door cracked ajar, waiting to be pushed aside. Without knowing exactly how, he nudged his mind past it. Inside hung a foggy realm filled with the hiss of static and the smell of fresh rain. There it was, up ahead, hovering for an instant before crossing over into the din. With one sure swipe, Eli reached out with his mind and snatched the dream. Something deep in his subconscious cried out, told him to let go of it, but an overpowering curiosity made him hold fast to the thread, drawing it slowly back to conscious thought.

At first it came as translucent sequins strung along a thread that threatened to break apart in too strong a grasp. He eased his tension, drawing it slowly like pulling an earthworm from its hole. More shards came, sprinkling about him like confetti. Two pieces fell into place; a section of a picture. Then more joined in; fragments of sound, a rush of wind. Suddenly a torrent of pieces swept into his conscious mind, a river of thoughts that quickly formed into scenes, unfolding action. Finally, it came as a great flood, sweeping Eli into the thick of the dream. His recall came as if from a primal past, flickering through pathways opened since the test. The new generation of adrenaline in his system had opened a dormant chamber deep within his brain; a place of power shrouded for decades — the graveyard of dreams.

Eli swam into the dream. He sprang down the hillside in a great leap. He met the ground with his front hands as if to fall but found his balance as he drew his feet up past his shoulders, planting them solidly, surging again with another great stride. He realized he was running on all fours, hugging the ground, bringing his front feet tight under his chest as his hinds dug into the earth and uncoiled anew.

The wind laid back his ears and tugged at the corners of his mouth. A single tear flew from his right eye as tall grass stung his face. He gained more speed and his testicles drew tight into his crotch, tingling like the muscles in his jaws. Fresh scent filled his nostrils. New strength burst into his legs. He leaped high into the air and came down, claws unfolded. He buried his face into the warmth. The sweetness of blood quenched his thirst.

But wait, another scent. He snapped his head from side to side. A low growl rumbled in his chest. Another predator, younger, quicker, coming to steal his precious blood. Run, hide, hurry. No, it's yours. Stay and fight for it. Hair bristled along his neck. In a blinding flash it was upon him. He gasped.

Eli bolted up and shook his head. A salty warmth filled his mouth. He reached up and touched his lower lip. Blood streamed from a bite clean through. He stood and tried to shake the odd tingle the dream had left under his skin. But now like a caterpillar, it clung to his senses, gnawing the foliage in the back of his mind.

He reached up and grabbed the bars of his cell. The chilled steel cooled his palms. He stared into the darkness. Even in the shadows of midnight his eyes reached out into the cell block. Dim light entering the high bank of windows reflected off the stark walls and concrete floor, bathing his world in a greenish glow. The light pulsated like the flicker of a distant fire. A snowstorm Eli realized, blankets of it settling in the night.

God, I can almost taste the freshness of the flakes, feel their coolness on my lips. How is that possible? Why now? Why not before? His thoughts burrowed deeper into his awakening mind. Yes, I remember now, as a boy in the school yard. Snow everywhere. Kids playing in it. Christmas coming. But wait. It's them again. All of them against me. Run. Let go. Clubs, a knife. Cutting. You bastards. Blood everywhere.

Eli reached up and touched the oldest scar on his face, just a faded patch of leathery skin, but a scar that reached all the way to his soul. And that wasn't the only place they had cut him. Payback is coming, soon. All of them I can get my hands on. I'll do worse than this. They think they can hurt me? They don't know what hurt is. Now that I have this, this, power, this thing in me, nothing will stop me. The world will find out in time. But for now I must guard my secret. Play the lumbering oaf a bit longer. Maybe Simmons suspects already. I can deal with him when the time comes.

Eli stuck his tongue into the nasty bite, brushing away a clot of blood. He swished it across his palate, savoring its richness. He swallowed it slowly. His stomach lurched at the morsel then growled for more. A great hunger stirred within him. He thought of breakfast still hours away; eggs and bacon. No, steak and eggs. No, just the steak, heaps of it, rare, quivering.

Drool filled his mouth. Eli swallowed, his hunger rising into frustration. He turned his thoughts toward more pressing matters; the prison cafeteria, tomorrow's dinner, the pain, the blood, the panic, running wild with the wind in his face.

Eli stood staring into the darkness for almost an hour, his mind leaping uncharted chasms, spurred by the strange new essence surging through his veins. Finally, his plan complete, he smiled and turned back to his bunk. He took a half step before he stopped at the image facing him. There, staring back from the darkness of a mirror on the far wall, hovered a face he had never seen before. He inched closer to the reflection. With intrigue he peered deep into strange eyes that held the glow of new moons rimming the lower eyelids, a yellow phosphorescence he realized.

His smile widened as he recalled what the doctors had said.

He whispered hoarsely.

"Foxfire eyes. How nice."

CHAPTER 13 — WINTER'S HAND

Throughout the night banks of clouds swept in from the northwest. Rushing low across the big lake they picked up more moisture, becoming swollen and finally bursting their bellies as they neared the shoreline. Over the land they dumped the full weight of their load. In swirling sheets the snow covered the prison grounds. In heavy waves it piled high in the forest near Deadman's Swamp.

The storm pressed on, as mini-storms within the main mass smothered the western half of the Upper Peninsula. The mini-fronts alternated between waves of driving crystalline snow and torrents of sticky-wet globs. The wet snow clung to everything in its path. The colder, crystalline fronts froze it in place then dusted it with spicules of ice. Nothing escaped its heavy sculpting hand.

The barren branches of maples, oaks, aspens and alders fought off the onslaught at first. But eventually they succumbed. The layers of wet flakes and ice crystals coated their spindly branches and smooth trunks. The branches grew heavy with the stuff, drooping wearily as the storm wore on. Some bent to the point of breaking. Others touched the ground with relief. Branches bent to the earth formed a labyrinth of archways. They hung like tentacles of giant ghostly squids, intertwining with a thousand others into an endless maze of white.

Across the open meadows, ferns and goldenrods dipped their faces away from the wind. Their heads soon grew heavy. Slender stems bowed, never to stand straight again. Meadow grasses became pencil-thick sheaths of white before collapsing in heaps of icy straw. Even the resilient bramble berries bent under the clinging strain.

Along the swamps the conifers suffered the worst. They quickly became skeletons of abstract snow creatures. Their networks of needles strained the snow from the air like sieves. The branches of spruce, cedars and jack pine grew clogged with flakes. They hung heavy from the load, intertwined, gathered more snow, and finally fused into puffy frozen statues.

Deep within the confines of the swamp, animals found little refuge. A great-horned owl perched among the branches of a black spruce ruffled its feathers to dislodge yet another coating of snow. Its head swiveled as if mounted on finely meshed gears. It squinted into the wind.

Below it in the hollow snag of a yellow birch, a family of raccoons shuffled for position. The mother burrowed deep beneath her yearlings, drawing from their musky warmth. The runt of the litter, pushed to the top, blinked as snow sprayed into the opening above. It buried its face under its tail and shivered.

Below the coons lay a group of deer huddled under a dense canopy of cedars. They tucked their tails and heads, ears pressed flat. The yearlings crowded near the bellies of their mothers. The does drew their legs in tight, backs hunched against the driving snow.

Nearby, catching the occasional scent of the does, several bucks lay covered with snow. It coated their antlers and piled heavy upon rug-thick foreheads. They too tucked their tails and noses — all except one that laid some distance from the others. It raised its nose to test the air, searching for a stronger hint of estrus from one of the does upwind. It knew the time was near. Ten long tines marked it as a veteran of the swamps, a huge buck destined to soon lay seed to another generation of whitetails.

It lowered its nose into the crook of its front leg. It sighed. Like the tingle of stretched muscles, an impatience stirred deep in its loins. Five seasons among the forest had taught it that the does would soon accept its advances. The approach of five winters had taught it that the lesser bucks nearby would give it wide berth.

Another sense churned deeper within the buck. Five seasons had also taught it fear; the fear of humans and the mayhem of gunfire on opening day. The stench of anxious hunters had filled the swamp for the past two days. Soon they would come.

In a primal nook within the buck's brain, a newer sense also began to stir; a sense of loathing for men on the prowl. Its mind began to race. Repressed instincts surfaced. Fear melted into a growing tide of buried hate as new links to pathways sparked to life from a forgotten time when bucks had used their dagger tines to rid two-legged predators from the land.

Somewhere nearby a branch cracked from the weight of the snow. The big 10-point lifted its head, eyes wide. Into the night it stared, the cold fire of new moons rimming the lower lids of its eyes.

CHAPTER 14 – OPENING DAY

Like Christmas mornings of years past, Brad lay awake in the darkness filled with anticipation. With hands laced behind his head, he lay lost in thought, waiting for the others to waken. Beside him Corey breathed soundly from under the cover of his sleeping bag.

The only other sound filling the loft was the metronome tick-tock of Brad's alarm clock. Sitting on the floor under his cot, it sounded unusually loud, much louder than it had last night during the snow storm. Outside, the branches of the old spruce no longer brushed against the cabin wall. The tar paper sides and plastic window no longer rippled in the wind. The insectlike ticking of snow pecking the tin roof now lay hushed, as if a great sleeping bag covered the cabin. It was an unsettling quiet, like the quiet within a coffin, buried under mounds of earth. Brad wondered how quiet death sounded with all its eternity. The notion raised gooseflesh along his arms. He burrowed deeper into his sleeping bag. The penetrating tick-tock of the clock followed him. He listened to the seconds of his life ticking away, precious seconds gone forever.

Brad reached down to cover the clock's grating sound with a shirt, but just as his hand touched it, the alarm sounded. The brass clanging made him jump. He swatted the alarm into silence as if he were slapping an oversized mosquito.

Minutes later, the buzz of his dad's alarm sounded from below. Soon, muffled coughs and thick-tongued mumblings of waking hunters replaced the silence. Pa began rattling pots and pans in the kitchen. By the time Brad and Corey climbed down from the loft, the smells of coffee and bacon filled the cabin.

"Keeerhrist almighty," Vern said, stomping snow from his boots as he came through the shed door into the kitchen. "There must be three feet of snow out there. Couldn't even make it to the outhouse. Had to piss by the propane tanks. Colder than a witch's butt too. We'll have to wear everything we own."

Pa looked up from the huge griddle of hot cakes he was tending.

"Mornin' boys, I mean, men. Looks like you got that tracking snow you were praying for, and an extra couple of feet to boot.

Should be a dandy opener. Now belly up to the table. Better eat plenty too. Going to be a long day in the swamp."

Brad noticed how Pa's eyes and yesterday's tired face now looked fresh. Pa even moved with a brisk air of excitement, like he too would be playing a part in the thrill of the coming day. He shoved a heaping platter of hot cakes and bacon in front of the boys.

"Now dig in. Got more coming."

From all sides of the table the hunters attacked the stacks, washing them down with steaming coffee and cocoa. They filled the gaps between bites and slurps with opening day chatter.

"You boys might want to save one of the old man's pancakes there to take into the woods," Vern said, wearing an unusually cheery face.

"I think we'll be plenty full after all this," Brad said, nodding toward his plate. "Pa's cakes have a way of swelling in your stomach after awhile." He grinned at Pa.

"I didn't mean for eating, boy," Vern said. "The old man's flapjacks are so tough they're noted far and wide for making the best sittin' pads in the woods, especially in deep snow. They'll keep your butt warm, dry and comfortable all day. Best dual-purpose hot cakes anyone ever made. Fact is, I've got one from two years ago that I still use. And the best part is that the squirrels and porkies won't even touch it."

Everyone laughed behind mouthfuls of food. Even Pa lowered his coffee cup, chuckling. Vern was such a contradiction, Brad thought; morning's brightest star, evening's darkest cloud. He found it odd that both characters could be trapped within the same person. Which one showed the true Vern Larsen?

After breakfast the tension of the unfolding day began to build as everyone except Pa donned their hunting outfits. Up in the loft, Brad and Corey pulled on heavy pants and flannel shirts. While pawing through his garments, Brad looked at the heavy frost creeping between the slats of lumber in the roof above his head. He held his lucky wool sweater in one hand, his new down vest in the other, measuring their bulk, wondering which to wear. He glanced over at Corey pulling on a tattered sweat shirt. Brad lowered the garments. He bunched the thick sweater in his hand for a moment then tossed it at Corey.

"Here, wear this. You'll need it today. I've got too much on as it is. Besides you could use the luck."

Corey hesitated for a moment, tentatively reaching for the sweater.

"Man, I can't take your lucky sweater."

"Why not?" Brad said, pulling on the vest. "I'm not going to wear it. Won't fit under this fluffy vest."

Corey picked up the sweater. "Thanks, Buwana. Thanks tons. But I'll only need its luck today. After that you can have it back. I promise not to get too much blood on it."

Down near the couch Larry dressed in his turn-of-the-century outfit, topping it off with a blaze orange vest stippled with a black camo pattern.

"Your Uncle Larry looks odd wearing that blaze vest," Corey said, peering under the railing.

"Yeah, but it's the law, even for bowhunters during gun season. And he knows it's safer too, especially the way he goes creeping through the swamp. He's different alright, but he's a lot like Pa too; he respects the law as much as he does deer."

Corey bobbed his head, his eyes following Larry as he uncased and strung his bow.

The hunters finished lacing heavy boots, shouldered day packs and grabbed weapons from the gun rack. They headed out the kitchen door into the shed where most had hung their heavy outerwear to keep them free of odors. The men climbed into blaze orange coveralls while the boys put on heavy coats and blaze stocking caps.

"Good luck men," Pa said, patting Brad and Corey on the backs. "Now don't go shooting any puny deer. Make them good; the kind you'll remember the rest of your lives."

Brad forced a confident smile. I hope I don't let Pa down. Hope the fever doesn't get me.

"Don't worry Pa," he said, his voice tight, "whatever I shoot I'll remember the rest of my life."

"Double ditto for me," Corey said. "Because I'm going to shoot one twice as big as Buwana's." His freckled face beamed and his rusty eyebrows danced under the brim of his stocking cap.

Pa smiled. "Don't forget," he said, "if you see your old friend the coon, leave it alone this time. No sense provoking another incident."

"Sure," Corey said, "But what if it comes after us for no reason?"

"Then shoot it. And bring back the carcass. The DNR will want to examine it."

"Will it be okay to touch it?" Corey asked.

"Yep, just don't kiss it or stick your hand in its mouth."

Corey made a face. Pa laughed.

Brad didn't smile. He looked at Larry again who appeared engrossed in checking his quiver full of arrows. What if it wasn't a coon, but that Manitou thing? Naw, it couldn't be. That's even too much for me to swallow.

"Don't fret boys," Pa added. "With this heavy snow that coon's probably deep in some hollow log sleeping until spring."

"Time to move on men," Al said, shouldering his way out the door. "With this cloudless sky, dawn will be showing her face in less than an hour. You don't want to be caught with your britches down when that old buck comes trotting down the runway."

Guns cradled, the troop headed out the door into the frigid air. Larry, bow in hand, lingered at the doorway while Pa whispered in his ear.

Steam clouded from their breath in plumes as the hunters met the cold. A stable weather front from the northwest had cleared the skies during the night, bringing with it temperatures in the teens. As Brad's eyes adjusted to the darkness, he soon became entranced with the majesty of the woods around him. Even in the faint glow of a new moon and a spray of starlight, the snow reflected the heavens in a sea of shimmering crystals. It appeared as if the forest had been oversprayed with the reflective paint used on highway centerlines.

"I'll be hunting the south end of the swamp with Vern," Al said. "You boys be careful and keep an eye out for one another. If you can take the cold, try and stay in your blind most of the day. Just get back to the cabin well before dark, and together. Understand?" He leveled an eye at Brad.

The boys nodded like two puppets being operated by the same hand.

"I'll be back this evening," Al continued. "If you hit a buck and it goes into the swamp, don't trail it by yourselves more than fifty yards. If it goes past that, come back here and wait for help. Your grandfather will be here. Bring him some good news for a change."

With that, Al, Crane and Vern shuffled off through the snow. The air-light dusting on top fluffed in small rooster tails around their legs as they walked. They disappeared west toward the big swamp, gliding silently through the stuff, looking like short-legged angels floating on clouds.

"You men mind if I walk with you a ways?" Larry asked. "I'll be hunting the north end of the swamp where it thins into aspens."

"Heck no," Corey said. "Glad to have you along."

Even in the moonlight Brad saw the gleam in Corey's eyes as he looked at Larry. He tried to read Larry's face too, but saw only a distant look. *Is he walking in with us because he really believes there's a shape-shifter out there somewhere?*

With moonlight on their shoulders, the three plodded north along the trail road through the snow. At first Brad and Corey waded the snow as if trudging through fluffed sand, wallowing and struggling with each step. They began to sweat and heavy billows of steam spewed from their mouths.

Larry held up a hand, stopped and turned to them. "Ease up men. We're not in a race. Unzip your coats and let some of that heat out. The last thing you need is to get sweated up before sitting in this kind of cold. That's a good way to get hypothermia."

Under the blaze vest, Larry's heavy wool jacket hung open with only the leather belt around his waist and the strap from his otter skin back quiver snugging it together.

"Also, don't fight the snow. It's your friend today. Just flow with it. It's okay to feel its weight on your legs but don't bull through it or try to raise your legs from it with every step. You won't last long that way. Glide through it like a deer. Pretend you're wading through shallow water. I'll lead the way and show you how."

Larry walked ahead while leaning his stout frame into the snow as if he were leaning into a strong wind. His legs moved effortlessly through the snow, his stride powerful yet measured. Brad and Corey followed in his wake. They soon walked without their hearts hammering in their ears, the cold air refreshing their faces.

To Brad the trail road no longer resembled the path he had walked only the day before. With the entire forest sprayed in a thick layer of snow it looked like a winter dreamscape where everything appeared as a panoramic negative; the once dark trees now white, the once bright sky now dark. The land looked like a frozen ocean of milk with hilltops of crested waves and sprawling meadows of gentle swells. Rising from the sea, schools of obscure creatures broke the surface. Stumps and logs rose as albino killer whales and white fur seals. Clusters of bushes became flocks of penguins huddled on ice flows.

Trees towering above the white sea no longer looked like trees, but like deformed skeletons, branches drooping from the weight of snow, giant arms waiting to snatch unsuspecting prey. Dappling the scene along the trail was the contrast of small red oaks that still held clutches of fawn-brown leafs. Oversprayed with snow, they looked like marbled clumps of butterscotch ripple ice cream.

More entrancing to Brad was the quietness. Countless fluffy baffles consumed every breath of sound. The occasional cough or clink of gun steel against zipper was swallowed by the fluffy maze. The only trace of sound was the muffled swish of boots sifting through the snow.

After walking down the trail for a half-hour, Brad stopped and motioned toward Deadman's Swamp. "This is where we head back to our stickups, Uncle Larry," he whispered.

Larry lifted his nose and tested the air. He blew out a cloud of steam that drifted southeast.

"Good wind for hunting that horseshoe, men. With this fresh snow the bucks will be traveling the edge of the swamp, south to north probably. But don't be too anxious. With all this snow, deer probably won't move until midmorning or later. So sit tight and be patient. This weather will put some of those does into heat and the old bucks will be chasing them by noon. Not enough hunters in this section to really get them moving. Still, you better keep a sharp eye. Bucks have a way of sneaking up on you when you least expect them. Be safe. Be careful."

He said the last with a shade of tension and Brad wondered if he was really warning them of something else.

Larry gave them a thumbs up and headed northwest off the trail into the snowy maze. In a few seconds the white fingers swallowed his shadowy flicker.

Brad watched him disappear. Were Larry's final words a warning about the shape-shifter? If so, then why didn't he just come out and say it? Crap, it was so hard to tell with Uncle Larry. A spirit in the shape of a coon, what next? Brad looked over his shoulder at Corey. Naw, no way, this Manabozho couldn't take on the form of Corey or even Larry, could it? How would I know until it was too late? Brad took several deep breaths. Look, get real here, I'm not an Indian, not even close. And I sure as heck don't have to kill a deer to prove I'm an Ojibwa brave. So even if that thing is real, which it can't be, the spirit probably doesn't even care about me. Brad swallowed and headed for the timber.

Walking through the first stand of oaks and aspens, the boys discovered that the pristine snowscape held a few of winter's booby traps. Their first reminder came as Corey reached out to steady himself on a small tree. A slight tug broke loose snow clinging to the branches, causing a mini-avalanche. They gasped as cold snow pounded their heads and shoulders, handfuls of the icy stuff washing down the back of their necks.

Cursing, they dug the stinging snow from their collars. They pulled their caps down further and plodded on. The next trap revealed itself as Brad began crossing a small ravine. Drifted snow had filled in a deep wash in the center of the ravine. One moment he was walking along with the snow at his knees, the next he sank into it past his waist. After floundering for a moment, he wallowed out of the fluff and they continued. By the time they reached Corey's stickup, a thin line of pale blue had slit the horizon.

"Wanta get together for lunch, Buwana?"

"Yeah, but hold out until one o'clock. I'll come here and we'll chow."

"Okay, but if you hear shooting before then, come over and I'll let you take pictures of me with my buck."

"You're on," Brad whispered. "Shots fired or one o'clock, whichever comes first. Good luck."

"Got that," Corey said, reaching up to the collar of the sweater.

Brad held Corey's stare for a moment before turning and heading toward his blind. He located it as the pale skyline melted into the orange glow of a cloudless dawn. The fallen aspens that formed his blind looked like the walls of a snow fortress. He cleared snow off the logs and dusted a stump to sit on. He unrolled his sitting pad and settled in. Looking down at the foam pad, he grinned at the thought of Pa's fried cakes and Vern's joke. It struck him how Vern's humor was similar to Corey's. Only Vern's disappeared after a few beers. Corey would never be like that. But maybe that's what Dad had thought of Vern twenty years ago.

Brad raised his rifle and sighted down the shooting lanes Corey had cleared the day before. He was surprised to see not much remained of the lanes but a criss-crossing network of snowy branches drooping across the openings. He couldn't see clearly thirty yards through the maze, let alone a hundred. Corey's 12-gauge would be better suited for blasting through this stuff.

As first light spread across the setting before him, the snow made everything look two-dimensional. Without much in the way of contrast or shadows the white-on-white landscape looked like giant paper cutouts pasted together with globs of Elmer's glue.

The snow also smothered the forest's odors. The aromas of pines, sweet ferns, and musty logs remained locked beneath the blanket of crystals. The only smells Brad could detect were the lingering scent of chocolate on his breath and the faint odor of moth balls from the collar of his plaid wool coat.

The morning wore on slowly. Brad busied himself by wiggling warmth back into his toes and by keeping a sharp eye open for any movement; deer, coons, shape-shifters. He squinted as the sun set the snowscape ablaze into a million specks of light, each flake a tiny diamond reflecting facets of brilliance. But even when the sun rose higher into the trees and lanced the long shadows, nothing moved. Not even the flutter of a chic-a-dee or a bluejay broke the stillness. It appeared as if every living thing had been frozen or buried.

By noon, bored and hungry, Brad began to fidget. His stomach grumbled for sandwiches and his butt ached for a break. At 12:45, as he stood to leave and shouldered his pack, a thunderous boom split the air from Corey's direction. Brad flinched. He recognized the roar of Corey's blunder-bust. He gripped his rifle. Maybe the blast would scare a buck in his direction. He waited, looking, listening, the first hint of a tremble coming to his hands.

Another boom ripped through the woods. On the heels of its echo rose an odd noise. Brad cocked his head and listened. It sounded like Corey had wounded a coyote. Brad pulled the cap away from his ears. A faint wail grew into a cry; suddenly a desperate cry for help that clutched at Brad's soul. It was the cry of a friend.

Brad stood rooted, paralyzed at the sound. What's happening? Did his gun backfire? Is he hurt or just excited? Corey, what's the matter? Should I go help, or go for help?

He lifted a trembling hand to his mouth and yanked off his right glove with his teeth. He jammed it in his pocket and gripped the rifle, his finger testing the feel of the trigger. As the sound trailed off, Brad finally broke free of himself and ran toward it. Snow spraying, he ran, cursing at the fluff clinging to his legs. His day pack pulled on his shoulders. The gun sagged heavily in his arms. He grunted and rushed on, running with a desperation he had never known.

CHAPTER 15 — BAD LUCK

Brad sprinted the two hundred yards to Corey's blind, his legs and lungs burning as he finally slowed. Ahead sat the stickup, as barren as the surrounding snow; no Corey, no deer, no sounds, no more yelling, no nothing. Brad tried to call out but his breath came in wheezing gasps. He tried to swallow but a thick phlegm clung to his throat. He eased forward with his rifle ready. There, in the blind, sat Corey's day pack. Next to the stump Corey had used for a seat lay an empty shell casing. A set of tracks showing the long stride of a run, headed into Deadman's Swamp.

Muscles tense, Brad followed the tracks. They descended the slope and disappeared into a tangle of alders. The heavy coating of snow had bowed the softwood alders over like wet hair. Brad eased into the maze. Corey's path was easy to follow. He had bulldozed a swath through the stuff, either in excitement or panic. As he neared the wall of cedars he stopped suddenly. There in the snow, barrel jammed into the ground, stuck Corey's gun. A few feet ahead the snow turned red.

Brad approached the bloodied snow, hands trembling, heart lodged in his throat. He again tried to call out. This time a faint croak spilled out. The sparse blood mixed with Corey's tracks soon turned into a confusion of sign; long smears of blood, deer hair, Corey's mitten, his hat, deer tracks over Corey's, the snowy imprints of — a struggle?

He jumped as the branches of a cedar moved only yards away. He jerked his rifle to his shoulder and drew back the hammer. His arms quivered. His aim wavered. His eyes caught a slight movement under branches draped to the ground. A boot. Corey's boot. It moved.

Brad lowered the hammer and rushed forward. He knelt and parted the branches. There lay Corey, face down, blood-stained snow speckled around him. Brad touched him gently. A faint whimper drifted up from the snow. Brad slowly tugged at Corey's shoulder and rolled him over.

Corey's face wore a crystalline mask of crusted snow tinged with blood. He winced in pain, spitting out bloodied snow and gasping for air.

"Is it gone?" he wheezed between gasps. "Is it dead? Did you see it?"

He wiped snow from his face and Brad sighed when he saw Corey's eyes and nose still in place and only shallow scratches on his cheeks and chin. Most of the blood was coming from a badly split lip that was already swelling into a deep blue.

"See what?" Brad asked. "I didn't see a thing. What happened? How bad are you hurt?"

Corey moaned and shook his head. "Don't know. Hurt all over but I don't think anything's broken. Mostly got the wind knocked out of me."

He sat up and gently touched his side. Brad's eyes followed the movement and saw a huge tear in Corey's coat rimmed with blood. A hot prickle squirmed up Brad's neck.

"Yeeeouch," Corey said, drawing his hand away. "It got me good. Probably would have kept it up too, but I played dead, just like those guys in the bear stories we read, remember? After pushing me face-first through all this brush it finally gave up. Man, I thought it was going to tear my chin off. Probably figured it had finished the job."

Corey reached up and felt his chin.

"Didn't you shoot it?," Brad said, nervously looking around. "I heard you shoot. Was there more than one?"

Corey looked down and brushed snow from his pants. "Rushed my shot. Got so excited I almost forgot to pull the hammer back. I just pulled up and shot. What a dummy. Didn't even take good aim. Don't tell Paw, or Larry either. I don't want them to think I'm a jerk." He spit out more blood strung out with saliva.

"I won't. But they wouldn't think that."

"Man, I don't know why I got so rattled. It was only a 4-point with long tines. I hadn't seen a thing all morning and I automatically pulled up and shot. It was so close I figured I couldn't miss. Musta hit a branch or something. Thought I maybe got it at first because it flinched then just loped a ways and stopped. Started trembling all over. Figured it was going to drop right there. I ran over to finish it off. That's when it turned and came for me."

"It charged you? You mean it just turned and came after you for no reason? Come on, you must have wounded it or something. I heard you shoot twice."

"Yeah, but the second shot didn't hurt it either. I didn't even have time to get my gun up. Had to shoot from the hip. It was on me so fast. All I did was punch a hole in its ear. It was only ten feet and I thought the blast from Ol' Killer would blind it, but it kept on coming. I turned to run. That's when it hit me. Man, it felt worse than the time I got blind-sided in football by Billy McDermit. Everything started to go black. I landed face down in the snow and the cold must of brought me to. I got up on my hands and knees and started sucking air. Then from nowhere it hit me again and began pushing me through the snow like a mad bull. I think I even sheared off the top of a stump somewhere with my face." Corey reached up and gingerly tested the size of his lip.

It looked ugly but Brad was more concerned about the blood on Corey's side. It wasn't bleeding badly but he was still afraid to look at the wound more closely. Besides, he knew that prodding around and looking now wouldn't do either of them any good. It would have to wait.

"Can you stand? We've got to get back to the cabin. Pa will take care of you. We also have to tell Dad and the others about this."

"Do you think it had rabies?" Corey asked, standing and testing his weight on wobbly legs. "Maybe it got bit by that coon and that's why it came for me. And now maybe I'm going to get rabies. Do you think that can happen?"

Brad looked at the lines under Corey's eyes. He suddenly looked much older.

"Don't know, Corey. We'll have to ask Pa. I don't think you can get rabies from antlers. But Pa will know. He'll know what to do. Come on."

Brad turned quickly so Corey wouldn't see the fear in his eyes. God, what did this, a rabid buck or a shape-shifter? Maybe I should tell Corey about it? Tell him what? Some crazy story. Don't be stupid. He's got enough to worry about.

Brad retrieved Corey's hat, mittens and gun then helped him climb the slope out of the swamp. He gathered up the gear from Corey's stickup, then with his rifle and senses at ready, Brad led the way back to the trail road. Corey shuffled behind, clutching his shotgun in one hand, holding his side with the other.

They trudged slowly as Brad retraced their morning path through the snow. Though the walking was easier than breaking new trail, Corey still lagged behind. Brad slowed his pace and looked back. Part of him wanted to leave Corey behind and run for help. He wanted to run to burn off the mounting tension chewing on his insides. He wanted to run away from Deadman's Swamp and the fear of encountering whatever had charged Corey. Each time Brad looked over his shoulder, he expected to see the buck charging from the snow, eyes crazed like the coon's, hair bristled in rage.

By the time they reached the trail road, midday thermals began stirring the treetops. Brad had just looked back at Corey when a muffled thump-thump came from beside him.

He wheeled to meet the oncoming charge. He whipped his gun up frantically. Slowed by the snow and heavy clothes, he knew he was too late. Crap, why are my reflexes so slow? He blinked his eyes against the blinding reflection. Damn it, where is it? Brace yourself, this is going to hurt. Those tines will tear flesh, not pierce it.

He gasped.

Brad stood dumbly for a moment then sighed to see nothing but clumps of snow tumbling to the ground from a large spruce. His shoulders sagged. More sounds pounding through the snow made him tense and spin anew. Again, more snow cascaded from the treetops. The wind and temperature increased, sending snow tumbling from the trees all around them. Brad flinched at each blur of movement, snapping his head at each sound. Sweat began to sting his eyes. His neck grew stiff. His mind buzzed.

The farther they walked, the farther Corey lagged behind. Halfway back to the cabin Brad waited again for him to catch up. Brad watched him struggling along. The wound in his side and the beating from the thing were overcoming his strength. As Corey neared, Brad noticed haggard shadows under his eyes.

"Sorry, Buwana," Corey moaned. "Gotta take a rest. Just for a minute."

Brad nodded. A minute wouldn't help, not even a handful. Instinctively, he looked toward the swamp, and unexpectedly, his eyes grabbed a thread of hope. There lay a line of tracks snaking through the trees; the fresh boot prints of a hunter.

"Look, Corey, someone still-hunted through here. Probably Uncle Larry or my dad coming to check on us. Sure, it has to be one of them."

Brad saw a glimmer brighten Corey's eyes. "They can't be far," Corey said, waving his hand. "Go find them. Bring help. I'll wait."

Corey brushed the snow off a stump next to the trail and eased himself down. He let out a moan and held his side. Brad noticed a fresh trickle wetting the frozen blood that rimmed the tear in

Corey's coat. Brad fought off another prickle of nausea. He had to find help, soon.

"Okay, but stay alert. And keep Ol' Killer there ready. Your buck may be following us, waiting to charge again. Might even give you a chance to settle the score."

"Really? Man, that sounds crazy."

"Yeah, but that thing's gotta be to have charged in the first place."

Even through Corey's haggard and bloodied features, Brad saw a flicker of excitement. Corey tightened his grip on the old shotgun. He had cleared the snow from the barrel with a stick and dropped a live shell in the chamber.

"I'll be alright," Corey said, patting his 12-gauge. "I won't miss again."

Brad turned toward the line of tracks. "Be back as soon as I can."

He trotted after the boot prints, wondering whether they belonged to his uncle or his father. In a hundred yards, the tracks disappeared into the maze of Deadman's Swamp. Brad slowed to a walk, and as he neared the edge of the swamp a fresh tightness gripped his throat — the home of Manabozho? He wondered if he dared enter the place. He pictured Corey and knew he had no choice.

He gripped his rifle, wondering what good it might be against a spirit.

He entered the swamp.

CHAPTER 16 — WORSE LUCK

Brad followed the footprints into the tangles of Deadman's Swamp. He leveled his rifle at his waist. I've got to find Uncle Larry or Dad or whoever made these tracks — if I can keep from stumbling into that crazed buck that attacked Corey. And crap, if there's one, maybe there's more.

The idea made him slow his pace, his eyes darting quicker from the tracks to the surrounding shadows. Up ahead the swamp opened into a small cranberry meadow. He stepped from some stunted cedars into the sunlight and raised his hand to shield his eyes.

There, on the far side of the meadow, stood a figure in full blaze orange. Brad bolted upright. Finally, help. Orange coveralls, can't be Uncle Larry. Must be Dad or Vern. He rushed ahead but within three strides recognized the paunchy profile of Mr. Crane. Brad's shoulders sagged. Well, any help was better than none.

He cupped his hands to his mouth but before he could yell, Crane raised his rifle and jerked off a shot. Brad's eye followed the line of fire to the north edge of the meadow. The crack of Crane's big gun was still ringing in Brad's ears when he spotted a buck slide belly-first into the snow near a cedar. Crane rushed ahead. Brad's eyes flicked back to the buck. Tremors ripped along its flanks. As Crane neared the deer, it coiled its legs tight under its body. The hair along its mane bristled like a guard dog. It stretched its neck out flat in the snow and laid its ears back alongside a 4-point rack. Red, blood red. Brad squinted against the brightness of the snow. One ear wore a bloodied hole. Brad cried out.

Crane spun at the sound. He spotted Brad and waved, a smile tugging at his jowls. He threw his arms up in victory and continued his rush toward the buck.

Brad yelled again.

"No, Mr. Crane. Stop!"

Brad ran forward, waving his arms. It's alive. Get away.

Crane gave him an odd glance as he bent over and spread the branches of the cedar to reveal his trophy.

Crane's smile froze for an instant before drawing into a grimace. In a spray of snow and fur, the buck launched forward.

Brad's legs slowed then faltered at the scene before him. In the bright sunlight the details unfolded in surreal vividness.

Crane let out a childlike shriek as the buck's horns buried deep into his belly. His rifle flew end over end as if it were a plastic toy. His arms windmilled backwards, his legs floundered, the buck twisted and drove its head deeper as a dull tearing mixed with his cry for help.

The buck bunched its legs and bucked anew, toppling Crane backwards in a wash of snow. Spittle sprayed from Crane's lips as his shriek rose into a scream. The buck hunched its back and drove its head downward. The buck's muffled grunts blended with Crane's. A plume of red steam filled the air.

Brad shouldered his rifle. He squinted through the scope, its lens crowded full of blaze orange and buck brown. I can't shoot, I'll hit him. Crap, I've got to shoot. No. Yes. No. Damn it, do something!

Brad hollered and waved his arms. The buck pressed its attack. Crane's arms flailed weakly. His cries drained into whimpers. Brad drew back the hammer of his rifle and fired a shot over the mayhem. The buck jerked its head up. Crane laid limp in the snow.

The buck stood staring at Brad, eyes wild, blood glistening on its tines. Its legs trembled. Quivers wavered down its back. The hairs along its mane stood stiff. Brad shuffled backward. The buck stepped toward him, legs rigid, steam jetting from its nose. Brad worked the lever action. The spent shell spun into the snow. He pulled it back and a new shell slid halfway into the chamber. The deer lowered its head. Brad tugged harder on the lever. It wouldn't close. He risked taking his eyes off the deer and looked down at the gun. The shell had jammed. He jerked harder on the lever but the brass casing only wedged tighter. His knees sagged. His mouth gaped.

When Brad looked back up, the buck was bounding through the snow toward him. It's eyes held the same hate as the coon's.

Brad dropped his rifle. He ran.

Behind him the buck grunted with each bound, its legs kicking up a spray. Hooves pounded through the snow, biting frozen ground, gobbling up the distance. A heavy breathing rose into a hiss just over Brad's shoulder. He expected to feel the hot sting of horns driving into his back as he burst through a curtain of cedar branches. The sun blinded him. He gasped. A sudden flash roared past his face. His ears rang. The buck plowed into the back of his legs, driving him deep into the snow.

Something sharp dug into his hip. He tried to scramble away but his hands and legs sifted helplessly through the snow. The weight of the buck held him fast. He tensed for a second then laid still. Just play dead. It worked for Corey.

As Brad settled in the snow, so did the buck on top of him. He laid still for a moment and felt the buck's legs twitch then sag limp. Something hot wetted his legs. He tried to squirm away from it but the buck began twitching again then jerked, tugging at his legs.

"Buwana, Buwana? Are you okay?"

Brad wiggled free as Corey pulled the deer off him. He wiped stinging snow from his eyes and gasped. He stood staring at the dead buck near his feet and at Corey, shotgun cradled in the crook of his arm, a faint wisp of blue smoke still rising from the muzzle.

"You shot it? You shot it!"

Brad steadied himself on Corey's shoulder.

"Yep. Heard the ruckus and came fast as I could. Told you I wouldn't miss again. Check out that shot. Running too." The sun danced in Corey's eyes. The rosiness had returned full to his cheeks.

Mouth still agape and panting, Brad looked down at the buck. A single thread of blood trickled from a thumb-size hole in the center of its brisket. A jagged tear along its flank showed where Corey's slug had exited wildly from its body. A furrow across the buck's back barely slicing the skin marked Crane's grazing shot. Brad knelt near the deer and stared into the depths of its eye. He saw his reflection, Corey's over his shoulder, the sun gleaming behind them with a sapphire glint like a miniature photo taken with a wide angle lens printed on black glass.

Brad looked closer, noticing a puffy redness rimming the buck's lower eyelids. It looked haggard as if driven by an unrelenting force. Madness from rabies? Or possessed by an evil spirit? He touched the hole. Can Manitous bleed? Be killed by bullets? If so, where was the spirit now? A distant moan made him spin around.

"Mr. Crane, oh my God. Come on, Corey."

"Where? Why?"

"It's Mr. Crane. Your buck got him before it came after me."

Brad turned and rushed toward the sounds, scooping his rifle from the snow as he trotted. He eased up to Crane and knelt beside him.

"It's okay, Mr. Crane. We're here. Just take it easy."

Crane responded with a faint moan, his eyes knotted. Brad looked at the nasty tear in Crane's coveralls. Brad's heart skipped a beat. His breath locked in his throat. Oh no, this isn't going to be all right. Not at all.

A long section of pink intestine hung from the wound like too much sausage spilling from an overstuffed bag of groceries. Blood ran from torn vessels straining to hold the mess together. Bits of bacon in a tan soup of spent pancakes and coffee dribbled from several punctures. It steamed as it dripped into the snow, its sour stench filling the air. Brad gagged and finally looked away. Corey shuffled up beside them.

"Holy crap," Corey hissed. He knelt next to Brad, closely inspecting Crane's insides laying out with an odd gleam in his eye.

Brad choked down the bile welling in his throat.

"What do we do?" he whispered to Corey.

Corey started to chew his lip then winced. "Ouch," he said, then looked around.

"Man, all I ever learned in Boy Scouts was how to make a tourniquet. And we can't put one on that," he said, his eyes flicking wide back to Crane's midsection. "Guess all we can do is try to make him as comfortable as possible, then go for help. Maybe we should lean him against that log and at least get him out of the snow. We can't leave him laying here freezing."

Brad shook his head then nodded. He propped his gun against a sapling and began scuffing snow away from a nearby log with his boots. He finished clearing the snow with his mittens and dusted off the log. He leaned over Crane.

"Mr. Crane. We have to sit you up against this log or you'll freeze in the snow. We'll try to be careful, but you'll have to help because Corey's hurt too."

Crane's eyelids cracked slightly as if that was all the strength he could manage. He shifted his eyes toward Brad. They wore the same pitiful stare as a grouse Brad had wounded once; a glaze of terror and helplessness clouding any glimmer of hope. Brad turned and nodded to Corey. They each gently took Crane by the upper arm and pulled. Crane didn't budge.

"Come on, Mr. Crane," Brad said. "Sooner we get you propped up, the sooner we can go for help."

The logic of Brad's words broke Crane's stupor. He nodded and began drawing in his legs and arms.

"Okay, Mr. Crane, on the count of three we'll slide you back and sit you up. Work with us as much as you can. Here we go. One, two, three —"

The boys heaved on Crane's upper arms while Crane pushed with his legs. Crane let out a powerful groan as he slid backwards, blood vessels rippling across his forehead. His groan quickly faded as a tearing sound poured from the wound. Brad looked down in time to see a tangle of intestines spill into Crane's lap. Crane gasped in surprise and grabbed at the mess, feebly trying to push it back into the bloodied hole. The boys stumbled backward.

Sitting upright with his back against the log, Crane began crying as he tried to tuck his insides back where they belonged. But with each handful he pushed in, another handful squirted out. Soon he had the mess packed with sticks, snow and leaves. Unable to stem the tide of abdominal pressure forcing his guts into his lap, he gave up, raised bloodied hands to his face, and began sobbing.

Brad looked away. He desperately wanted to run from the horror of the scene, to leave it behind like a terrible dream. He wanted to erase the pitiful sight from his mind, yet knew it would always loom in his memory. Part of him even wanted to unjam his rifle and shoot Crane in the temple, ending the suffering that would only grow worse.

"Come on," Corey said, tugging on Brad's sleeve. "Nothing more we can do here. Let's get back to the cabin. We've got to bring help, fast."

Brad picked up his rifle and turned to leave. Crane's words stopped him.

"Don't leave. Please don't leave me like this." Crane sobbed. His words slurred past a thick drool of slobber and bile.

"We have to get help," Brad said. "Corey's hurt too. I have to take him back. We'll bring the others back as soon as we can. I promise. Don't worry."

Brad realized how foolish his last words sounded; telling a man with a bleeding lap full of guts not to worry. Why not tell him to enjoy the afternoon while they were gone?

Crane reached out. "Bring me my rifle. What if it comes back?"

"It can't come back," Corey said flatly. "It's dead, over there. I shot it."

The knot in Crane's brow softened. More tears welled into his eyes. "Good boy, Corey. You're such a good boy." He began sobbing heavily again.

Brad walked over and retrieved Crane's custom built Model 98 Mauser. With its stainless steel barrel, fancy stock and variable scope, it was a gaudy thing compared to his lever action. He dusted the snow off the big 30.06 and chambered a live shell.

"Here, Mr. Crane," Brad said, propping the gun next to him. New worry lines creased Crane's forehead as he looked at the gun then toward the dead buck.

"It's only in case you see someone and need to fire a signal shot. We'll be back soon as we can."

Crane nodded, crossed his arms and gently lowered them across his wound. He let out a long moan and closed his eyes. A billow of steam drifted up from between his legs.

Brad and Corey turned and began retracing their tracks in the snow back to the logging road.

"You set the pace, Brad. Go as fast as you can. We've got to get help quick. I won't be far behind."

Brad turned and looked at Corey.

"You gave him that gun," Corey said, " because you think there might be more crazy deer out here, didn't you?"

"I don't know. It just seemed like the right thing to do. That's probably the first and last crazed buck we'll ever see."

He turned away before Corey could see the doubt on his face.

"Hope so, Buwana. I sure hope so."

Corey drew his shotgun close to his waist and looked over his shoulder.

Brad pressed on. He forced his eyes to scan the woods around him for any sign of more danger or someone to help, but try as he might, his eyes kept drifting down to the jammed shell in the open breach of his rifle.

"I hope so too, Corey," he mumbled.

CHAPTER 17 — PREOP

Little Eli spent part of the morning in the prison library reading several intriguing books, an unlikely visit but few seemed to notice. He spent the rest of the morning in laundry detail, a job he found revolting now for the first time — handling the filth and sweat of others, animals that didn't deserve sheets to soil. But he went through the motions nevertheless, his mind racing ahead to the details of a plan already set into play.

He made several trips to the supply room; two more than he needed to finish the laundry chores. No one noticed the extra bulges under his shirt.

Matter of fact, most, residents and officers alike, now avoided looking at him altogether. They turned away under the new weight of his stare; once flat eyes that now held the unsettling depths of a serpent.

An inmate's ability to deliver a chilling stare was almost as important to survival inside the joint as physical prowess. Eli's size and strength had never required him to develop much of a stare. With his build, a blank uncomprehending look had always been enough to turn away any threats. But since his recent ordeal, his eyes seized each passerby, boring deep into the marrow of the man.

It was little surprise then, that when he fixed his new stare on another resident during lunch, the man shrank into his seat.

"Say, Echolm," Eli grunted, "let's switch duties today."

The man flinched as if the words were birdshot peppering his backside.

"I'd like kitchen detail. You get my laundry duties. Okay?"

The man bobbed his head, a mouthful of sandwich lodged in the back of his throat.

Eli smiled broadly and slapped him once on the back, causing him to choke. Eli scooped up his tray and headed toward the kitchen. The man spit spent tuna on his plate and gagged. He finally cleared his throat.

"Damn, you see the way he looked at me, that smile and all?"

"Yeh, I seen it alright," said an old black sitting next to him. "Friggin' creepy, that's what it is. Never seen that oaf smile in ten years, never had the brain for it."

"Man, those crooked, yellow teeth look like a horse's."

"No, don't think so, chum. Spent some time poaching in the bayous years back. That's the smile of an alligator, a big gator that's cornered its prey and is waitin' for the kill."

The two men watched as Eli swung the kitchen door wide and stepped in.

He squinted against the bright glare of banks of fluorescent lights, the white enamel paint, and the glitter of all the stainless steel; oven doors, stoves, sinks, overhead vents, rows of dangling pots and pans. He grimaced. Damn light. Soon the night will come, and it will belong to me.

He drew quick glances from a few of the inmates going about their jobs. He paid them little attention and pulled a full-length white coat from a hook near the door. The fabric groaned as he forced his muscled arms into sleeves too small. A few seams began to split as he tugged the front shut and fingered the buttons into place. Eli turned to the blurred reflection on the steel door of the walk-in cooler and paused. He swayed from side to side, admiring himself, smiling all the while. Quite like a doctor, a master physician with an important operation waiting.

"What goes," barked Nick Stone, the head cook approaching Eli. "You ain't supposed to have kitchen detail today. I got Echolm on my roster."

He had heard Eli was back on line but hadn't seen him yet.

"Echolm asked me to fill in," Eli said, turning and grasping Stone in his stare.

Stone stopped in midstride and fell silent. Eli swaggered up to him, causing the man's blood to drain from his face. Eli spread his lips in a wide smile and dropped it to within an inch of Stone's nose.

"Glad to help today, Stoney. Sorry your helper took ill, but we wouldn't want him contaminating the food with all his nasty germs, would we?"

Somehow, Stone managed to wag his head but the "no" struggling to rise in his throat refused to come out.

"Used to be quite a cook when I was younger," Eli said, still holding the man with his eyes. "Figured I'd let you take it easy today while I pinch-hit for you."

Stone nodded, his head jerking up and down as if it were a bobber on a line tugged by a perch.

"Good," Eli continued. "What's on the menu for dinner?"

"Ma-ma-meatloaf," Stone sputtered. "And scalloped potatoes."

"Ma-ma-meatloaf?" Eli said. "That sounds like some kind of soul food for the brothers. I was thinking more along the lines of something hot and spicy to help ward off this cold-ass weather we're having." Eli glanced over to the window and Stone let out a long breath.

"Meatloaf is what we have scheduled, Eli. Got all the hamburg thawed and everything. I was just getting ready to mix it up."

"I think we'd all rather have something spicy like chili," Eli said resting a heavy hand on Stone's shoulder near his neck.

Stone swallowed hard.

"I can make the meatloaf spicy, real spicy."

Eli drew his thumb and index finger together until he had a sensitive chunk of Stone firmly in his grip.

"Chili," Eli said, tightening his grip, Stone's face twisted.

Again Stone's head bobbed frantically, eyes watering. Eli released his grip as if letting go of a fly held by the wing.

"Sure," Stone said, rubbing the side of his neck, "chili sounds fine to me, make it however you want. I can even get you some —"

Stone held his breath as Eli reached for his head with both massive hands. Eli smiled as he plucked the white hat from Stone's head. It wasn't really a chef's hat, just an oversized, white hair retainer. But it was Stoney's and to Eli it meant he was king of the kitchen. He placed it on his head, looking much like a grotesquely huge white-capped mushroom. With a rattling of two giant forty-gallon kettles he began making his chili.

"How 'bout baking up a bunch of corn bread," Eli called from over the hiss of hamburger browning in the kettles.

Stone, who had crept back toward the sinks, stuck his head around the corner.

"I love corn bread with my chili," Eli said, smacking his lips and smiling.

Stone nodded and even managed a thin smile himself. "Huh, corn bread with chili," he mumbled. "Not a half bad combination. Maybe this won't be too bad after all."

Stone began mixing a giant bowl of corn bread batter in the huge power beater while one of the helpers nearby greased rows of baking trays.

"Look at that," Stone said to the man. "I taught my share of residents over the years in the rehab food service program, but hell, none of them took to it like that. See how he moves around the stove? How come he never got on kitchen detail before?"

The helper shrugged.

"Well, what the hell. At least he's helping now. This might just turn out to be the cat's ass, the baddest boy in this joint in my kitchen. Let's see them hard asses complain about my food now."

Billows of steam hissed from the kettles as Eli tossed in more handfuls of hamburger. He reached deep into the plastic-lined carton, scraping the last of the burger from the bottom. As he withdrew his hands full of red meat, he paused.

The burger at the bottom had become soaked with blood draining from the rest of the carton. Blood ran freely between Eli's fingers and he watched each drip of the thick purplish goo with fascination, the plop-plopping adding to the small pool forming in the bottom of the carton. A smile crept across his face, his huge teeth emerging slowly from behind rough lips. Drool formed in the corners of his mouth. Unconsciously, he let it spill down his chin where it ran to his chest.

After a moment, Eli lifted his hands from the carton and held them over one of the kettles. He watched unblinking as he let the hamburger sift between his fingers, bit by bit, the blood dripping with elongated drops. More steam rose. Sweat beaded his brow. He smiled even wider. With blood-soaked globs clinging to his hands Eli glanced around. The other inmates remained busy at their tasks. Keeping an eye on them, he licked the mess from his hands, sucking each finger clean like a blood-coated popsicle.

Eli wiped his hands on his whites and added heaps of chopped onions to the browning meat.

After mixing the corn bread, Stone glanced at Eli who appeared to be having the time of his life stirring his concoction and tasting the early stages with delight. Eli collected arm loads of spices from the cupboard and arranged them around the kettles. As he added a dash of this and a handful of that, he hummed merrily. None heard the soft words mixed in with the tune.

"...ta-da, dot, dot, dot, da-da, dot, dot, dot, there'll be a hot time in the old town tonight."

CHAPTER 18 — TOO LATE

Brad stumbled over the legs of the buck laying in the snow near the shed as he rounded the corner. He didn't give it a second glance before bursting through the shed door and into the cabin. He slid halfway across the kitchen floor on rubbery legs then fell to his knees, wheezing.

"Whoa. Looks like maybe someone got their first buck," Pa said as he rose from his chair in the living room and walked over to the doorway.

Larry, sitting on a stool near the stove, looked up from mid-stroke of drawing his knife across a sharpening stone.

"Better learn to take it easy, Brad," he said, smiling and shaking his head. "You shouldn't get so worked up in front of your hunting buddies. The mark of a sage hunter is how nonchalant he can act after taking his buck."

Larry laughed and winked at Pa.

"No," Brad said between gulps of air. "Not me, it's Crane. No, I mean Corey. Both of them, they need help."

"They both got bucks and you didn't?" Larry continued. "If you get this excited when someone else gets a deer, what will happen when you shoot your own?"

He started to chuckle but was cut short.

"No! Listen!" Brad shouted, finally finding his wind. "Corey and Crane were attacked by a buck. They're hurt and need help."

Larry's playful bear features set to stone as he sheathed his knife and rose in one motion. "Where are they and what happened?" he demanded, his voice suddenly as sharp as his blade.

While Brad explained, Larry laced his boots and threw some things into his day pack. He grabbed a wool blanket from the couch and lashed it to his pack. He snatched the rifle still clutched in Brad's hands, and with a powerful snap of the wrist, ejected the jammed cartridge. He jerked the lever action closed, chambering a live round.

Brad watched the ejected shell roll across the kitchen floor. The flush on his cheeks spread across his face. He lowered his gaze to his boots caked with snow that was beginning to melt about him;

melting like his nerve had in the swamp. He had failed to save Crane. He had failed to save himself. He had failed as a deer hunter.

Larry tucked the rifle under his big arm, shouldered his pack, and pulled on his cap.

"Let's go, Brad," he said as he headed for the door. "Dad, tell the others what happened. We'll be back before dark."

Outside, Larry handed Brad the rifle then pulled an old toboggan from behind the wood pile. He shook snow from it, plopped it down and checked the pull rope. Without a wasted movement or word, he grabbed the rifle back from Brad, held fast to the pull rope and began trotting down the trail road in long powerful strides. Brad struggled to keep up.

Just past the first bend north of the cabin they encountered Corey. Despite his mauling, he was walking at a strong pace, holding his head high.

"Heard you had quite a time getting your first buck," Larry said as he approached Corey. "Brad told us the whole story."

Corey still appeared badly shaken from the ordeal, but he responded with a puffy-lipped grin and shrugged his shoulders.

"Now that's cool," Larry said as he gently took Corey's shotgun and laid it on the toboggan. "Sorry, pal, but I've got to take a quick look. I'll try to be careful."

Before Corey could reply, Larry unzipped the boy's coat and tenderly lifted the layers of bloodied and ripped clothing. Corey sucked in at the sting and the cold air. Larry prodded careful with a finger for a moment then slowly pulled the layers back down.

"You're awfully lucky you were wearing that sweater," Larry said, giving Corey a reassuring smile. "Looks as if that thick wool tangled in the buck's horns and softened the worst of its blows. You're still bruised pretty bad and there's a nasty gash that laid the skin back a few inches. You'll need some mending. Nothing I can do now. Just get back to the cabin and have Pa wash and dress the wound. I'll butterfly it when I get back."

Larry picked up the shotgun and handed it back to Corey. He put a hand on the boy's shoulder and held him in the clear gaze of his eyes.

"Here's your gun, deerslayer. Any man that can pull off a pressure shot like that and claim his first buck while saving a friend's life is a man I'm proud to call a hunting partner."

Corey's eyes flashed in the afternoon light. He smiled, his split lip drooping to one side.

"Off with you now," Larry said. "And watch your backtrail. No telling what we're dealing with out here."

Larry grabbed the toboggan rope and took off down the trail. Brad lingered.

"Forgot to say thanks, Corey."

"For what?"

"For saving my life."

"No sweat, Buwana. You'd have done the same. From what your uncle says, sounds like lending me your lucky sweater saved mine."

Brad's eyes slid away. Yeah, some hero I am. Lending the sweater hadn't taken any courage. And I sure didn't save Crane when I had the chance. Could I have saved you, Corey, if the tables were turned? No time to explain now.

"Gotta run."

"Be safe, Buwana."

Brad trotted after Larry who was already disappearing around the next bend in the trail. By the time he caught up, his sides heaved and sweat trickled from under his cap. After a while Larry slowed his pace and turned toward Brad.

"How much farther?" he asked.

"About another quarter mile before we turn off the trail and head for the swamp. Yeah," Brad continued as he pointed ahead, "just over that next rise a few hundred yards, that's where we —"

A rifle shot split the cool air. Larry halted so abruptly that Brad almost ran into him. Larry cupped a hand to his ear just in time to catch a faint cry drifting up from somewhere in the swamp ahead. Brad heard it too.

"I think that's Mr. Crane," Brad whispered, turning his head toward the sound. "We left him his gun to signal in case he —"

Another blast cut Brad's words off again. The ring of its echo had barely faded when a terrible shriek rose and ended quickly as if chopped off by an axe. Larry grabbed Brad by the shoulder and charged toward the sound.

"Let's move," he growled, "and stay close behind me."

Brad stayed plenty close. The shriek sent a hot flash down the back of his neck that settled into his legs, making them pump with new vigor. As he ran, he noticed an intensity in Larry's face he had never seen. Those bear eyes were filled with a wildness, the face drawn unusually taut.

Larry's heels kicked snow over the toboggan as he lunged ahead. Brad followed in the spray. They retraced the boy's tracks as they turned from the trail and headed toward the swamp. As they neared the thick matting of cedars and spruce, Larry slowed to a walk. He raised his hand for Brad to halt and dropped the toboggan rope. He drew back the hammer of the rifle. He leveled the gun at his hip. Slightly hunched in a combat stance, Larry edged forward, eyes dissecting each quadrant. He paused as he passed the dead 4-point, eyes briefly darting downward and clicking a snapshot of the scene before leveling back on the surrounding brush. Brad eased up to his side.

"We left Mr. Crane sitting against a log behind those tamaracks," he whispered, pointing to the far side of the cranberry meadow.

Larry nodded and advanced. Brad stayed in his shadow. As they rounded the tamaracks, Brad gasped. There in the cleared patch of snow next to the log laid Crane's rifle, bolt open, empty of shells. Crane was nowhere in sight.

Brad tugged at Larry's sleeve. "He couldn't have left," he said. "He was hurt bad, real bad, too bad to get up and wander off."

Larry didn't reply, he just edged closer to the rifle laying on the ground and knelt next to the cleared patch. The snow around the area showed a jumble of sign; the frantic, blood speckled imprints of Crane's earlier struggle with the dead 4-point, the boy's boot prints circling the scene, the piled snow where Brad had scuffed it to one side. Finally, Larry's eyes swept to a dense wall of cedars twenty yards away and locked onto something. He rose and shouldered the rifle.

"Crane didn't walk anywhere," Larry said, nodding toward a trail in the snow. "Something drug him, no, pushed him through the snow. See? Deep tracks in the center. The blood there is still deep red and hasn't faded to orange yet. This just happened."

Brad peered around Larry to a deeply furrowed swath in the snow tinged with blood. It disappeared under the branches of some cedars. They crept closer.

"Yep, it pushed him," Larry said, his words choppy, his eyes snatching glimpses of the trail before locking back on the wall of cedars in front of him. "See how its tracks are spread wide with toes flared biting deep into the snow? Big buck, pushing one hell of a load. Look, random arm prints. Crane struggled."

Brad pictured the scene and his stomach knotted. His breath grew heavy as if the cold air had suddenly lost its oxygen. He could hear his heart drumming in his ears. He sucked gulps of air. His legs trembled and threatened to collapse altogether. He shuffled closer to Larry.

"Another crazed buck?" Brad managed between shallow breaths. "Uncle Larry, what's going on here, an outbreak of rabies?"

Unblinking, Larry pressed his finger to his lips and shook his head. He scanned the cedars in front of them. The gun remained rock-steady in his arms. Brad looked at his uncle's eyes and noticed something that wasn't there moments ago.

"Hush now," Larry whispered, his words kitten soft. "Don't want to give away any edge we might have on this thing."

Brad blinked. Thing? What do you mean, thing? A Manitou, the shape-shifter? Brad held his thoughts.

Larry moved forward in measured steps and pushed aside a large cedar branch using the muzzle of the rifle, his finger ready at the trigger. On the other side of the cedars in a small opening lay a heap of blaze orange rippled with red. Face up, eyes glazed wide in an unbelieving stare, Crane lay motionless at the base of a large birch.

In silence, Larry and Brad eased up next to him. A foam of pink bubbles filled his mouth. Steam rose from a neat row of holes spread across his chest like the burst from an Uzi. Blood rimming the wounds had already started to congeal or freeze around the edges. Below the series of holes, Crane's abdomen lay gaping wide, his entrails tangled in a snow-crusted mess around his legs.

Brad stared. Crane looked so unreal, like an oversized rag doll with all the fluffy stuffing pulled from it, its sides draped in, sunken in the cavity that once held so much of the man. At last Brad blinked and his mouth filled with a bitter wetness. He turned and retched. He gagged then retched some more.

Brad reached down and scooped a handful of snow and washed out his mouth. Larry had moved close to the large birch bark tree, stained with blood four feet up. Larry pulled off his glove and picked at a hole pierced deep in the bark.

"No ordinary whitetail did this," he whispered, pulling several orange threads from the hole, still clinging to bits of flesh. "Impaled Crane square in the chest. Drove him into this tree, pinning him through with its tines. Must have one hell of a rack to skewer him completely through the chest and out his back. Plus, it lifted him several feet before driving him into this tree. Crane must weigh over 250, even with his insides spilled. Took an incredibly powerful animal to do that."

He turned his head. His eyes retraced the bloody swath through the snow.

"What bothers me more," he continued, eyes darting quicker to the surrounding cedars, "is that it's a smart one, too damned smart. This was no berserk mauling. That thing purposefully pushed him over here so it could use this tree to drive home its tines. The other trees around here are too small. No, it purposefully picked this one to deliver its death blow." Larry paused and slid his feet backward, inching away from the scene while focusing on the tangle in front of him. "This is one bad-ass critter we're dealing with. Evil —"

Surrounded by the thick cedars, Brad's eyes darted from shadow to shadow. More sweat ran down his brow. Come on Uncle Larry, let's beat feet outta here. We're like flies stuck in a spider's web standing here. That thing can hop out any second. Please, let's go. I don't want to become another legend of Deadman's Swamp.

"Maybe one of Mr. Crane's shots hit it," Brad dared to whisper. "Maybe he wounded or killed it."

Brad looked for some sign on Larry's face. But his uncle's eyes were busy sorting out more sign; a lone set of tracks departing the scene. Larry followed them. Brad followed in his boot prints.

"Only a few flecks of blood here," Larry whispered, pointing with the barrel of the rifle. "Could be Crane's blood dripping from its antlers as it left." He reached down and fingered a few of the swatches.

"Can't tell," he continued, "if he did hit it, I doubt it's lethal. Not enough blood. Nothing pumping fresh. It's already getting sparse. No, in his condition, Crane probably couldn't even shoulder his rifle. Slim chance he hit anything."

Brad clenched his hands at his sides. I have to know, Uncle Larry. He took a deep breath.

"Do you think it was Manabozho?" he asked.

Larry gasped as if Brad had shoved a handful of cold snow down his neck. His eyes flared. His upper lip drew back in a half-snarl, exposing teeth. Brad shrank back as Larry grabbed him by the arm and jerked him close.

"Don't ever," he hissed, "mention that name out here."

Larry dropped Brad's arm and snapped the barrel of the gun around as if he expected the shape-shifter to come bursting through the wall of brush at any second. His eyes swept around, pausing only long enough to give Brad a fiery stab.

"By acknowledging it," he whispered, "you make us vulnerable, especially here in the swamp. It preys upon the weak. The more you show that you believe, the stronger its evil powers. If it heard you here, we're dead men."

"But Uncle Larry, we're not Indians. Why would —"

"Do you see any Indians running around this swamp? Wake up. It's just us. It can't afford to be picky nowadays."

"I'm sorry," Brad whispered. "I overheard you last night and only wanted to know if —"

Larry held his finger to his lips and hissed. "No more, not now." He snapped the rifle up as some snow fell from a nearby cedar. Brad jumped. They both stood frozen for a long moment, staring into the maze of cedars. Finally, Larry eased backwards, keeping the rifle pointed at the spot.

"We're not doing any good here," he whispered over his shoulder. "Sooner we get Crane and ourselves out of this place, the better."

When they reached Crane, Larry nodded toward the meadow. "Run over and fetch the toboggan. We need it to get him out."

Brad looked to the far side of the clearing then back to Larry. I know you're not asking, but, but, crap it's a hundred yards over there. How far will I get before it pounces on me from somewhere, drive those tines through my back? He pictured his own mouth rimmed with pink bubbles. He shivered at the thought and looked up at Larry.

"Don't worry," Larry whispered, hoisting the rifle. "I'll cover you. Just make it snappy and keep as quiet as possible."

Brad swallowed at the film clinging in his throat. He turned toward the clearing. He began to trot but almost fell at the start on wobbly legs. After several strides his muscles eased, his knees grew solid. Soon his legs were skimming through the snow, eating up the distance. He grabbed the toboggan's rope and began running back. He made it halfway before a flash of brown brought him skidding to a halt.

Even in the growing afternoon shadows, Brad spotted the unmistakable flicker of deer legs in the swamp. They flashed through a small patch of alders on the south end of the meadow then disappeared just as quickly. He stood rooted staring at the spot.

Larry waved him on, the arm flicking with the force of a backhand karate chop. Brad responded to the command and intensity in Larry's eyes. He started trotting again, holding his gaze on the south end of the clearing. Running made all the shadows move, made a hundred branches look like deadly waving tines. Finally, he reached Larry's side.

"Saw a deer," Brad gasped. "Over there," nodding toward the alders. "Now what?"

"If that was Crane's killer, it probably would have made its move for you when you were in the open. Maybe it was just some deer you spooked. A crazed deer wouldn't slink off." Larry paused at his own words, his eyes again scanning the surrounding brush. "But maybe a crazy smart one would."

Brad noticed a new glint in his stare, something from long ago beginning to glow like an ember unearthed from a smoldering fire.

"Come on Brad, no sense standing here. If that thing really wants us, it will try to take us out on its terms. And that's not when we're ready for it with this rifle."

Larry took the rope and slid the toboggan next to Crane's body. He unshouldered his day pack with one arm and knelt in the snow.

"Here, take this," he said, handing Brad the rifle. "Keep a sharp eye while I take care of this... this mess."

Brad tucked the gun under his arm and pointed the muzzle toward the south end of the clearing. He jerked his head from side to side, trying to keep an eye on the surrounding net of brush while stealing quick glances at his uncle's progress.

From the corner of his eye, Brad saw that Larry had probably taken care of other men in Crane's condition. Without hesitation or a crack of expression, he tucked Crane's insides into the vacant cavity and rolled him in the blanket he'd taken from the pack. He then lashed the bundled body to the toboggan using several lengths of rope. He finished up the job by cinching the ropes tight like packaging an oversized Thanksgiving turkey for delivery.

Larry stood and quickly rigged a harness with another length of rope. He tied the toboggan rope to the harness and slipped the rigging over his wide shoulders. He pulled his cap tight over his ears and turned to Brad.

"I'll take point, pulling our load here. It's the only way we'll make it back to the cabin before dark. We can't be caught out here after dark. If it's after us, we wouldn't stand a chance in hell then. Bring up the rear and cover us."

Brad looked down at the rifle then at Larry. Me? Cover us? You're kidding. Do you want us both to die? I can't, what if I? Crap, wait for me.

Before Brad could protest, Larry broke into the clearing, trudging ahead, the heavy toboggan hissing behind him across the snow. He slowed only long enough to grab Crane's empty gun jammed with frozen snow and stuff it under the ropes along side the body.

Brad wanted to yell out that he couldn't save their lives, that he couldn't shoot a deer or a Manitou that looked like one, that he would only fall apart if he tried. But he stood silent, afraid to yell, afraid the swamp's killer might hear them, afraid that it would all come true. His fear, growing dangerously dark like the late afternoon shadows, closed its icy fingers around him.

Brad broke into a run, his legs pounding the frozen earth as if he was running for his life.

CHAPTER 19 — MOUNTING HUNGER

Eli lifted the ladle to his mouth for the eleventh time. His lips slurped loudly as he sucked in another steaming mouthful of chili. He drew in a breath and let it slowly escape between his teeth as his eyes fluttered upward, finally disappearing under heavy eyelids. He pressed his lips for a second before popping them wide with a smacking sound. His eyes flicked open at the same instant.

"Perfecto!" he growled, raising the ladle high into the air and spilling the last few drops on his badly stained whites.

Stone glanced up from the tray of hot corn bread he was pulling from the oven to see his new helper posing like the Statue of Liberty. "Crazy bastard's really getting into it," he mumbled.

A greasy blend of sweat and chili glistened across Eli's face. His whites read like a cookbook. They wore splashes of tomato sauce, bits of fried onion, smears of grease and flecks of hamburger, all dusted with layers of spices; red cayenne, bone white garlic powder, the black grey specks of pepper and several indistinguishable shades of pastels — odd colors for chili but no doubt some spices Eli had dredged up from the bottom of the cabinet.

Eli pivoted his head and motioned to Stone. His gator smile flashed.

"Come over and taste this delight," he commanded. "And bring one of those loafs of corn bread."

His hands protected with heavy cooking mitts, Stone flipped a tin of corn bread upside down on the counter and tapped the pan smartly, dumping the steaming loaf into his mitt. He walked over to Eli, eyes lowered, looking at the white floor spattered red.

Eli studied Stone's face. Why, that old fart's pissed off 'cause I trashed his kitchen. Well, that's some thanks I get for helpin' him. Eli reached up and stroked his iron jaw. You shouldn't fret so much Stoney, ain't good for your heath.

The prison kitchen hadn't seen such havoc since the 1950 incident when a handful of inmates took visiting Governor G. Mennen Williams hostage in the kitchen. The Governor's bodyguard surprised everyone though when he drew a revolver he had concealed from prison officials and quickly made one of the inmates a permanent short order by spicing his chest with a lethal dose of hot lead.

Eli's mess didn't quite match the carnage of that day. Nonetheless, the stove top, nearby counters and floor were covered in a half-dried coating of spilled chili and strewn ingredients.

Stone peered into the massive pots and saw the reddish brew bubbling near the tops. He looked back to the floor.

"I know what you're thinking," Eli said. "It's a miracle I got any left in the pots by the looks of your floor. Don't fret, you'll forget about the mess when you taste it." Eli dipped the ladle in the nearest pot and skimmed some of the broth. "Here," he said, lowering the ladle in front of Stone's face. "Wrap your lips around this and see if it doesn't remind you of Mama."

Stone took the ladle and blew on the broth before sipping just enough to flavor his tongue and palate.

"Holy jumpin' catfish," he gasped sucking in air and fanning his mouth. "That crap's hotter than a New Orleans whorehouse. Goddamn Eli, you're one hell of a cook."

Eli's smile broadened even more, exposing puffy pink gums above the teeth. A chuckle rumbled in the back of his throat as he grabbed the hot loaf of corn bread from Stone and jammed half in his mouth.

Stone rose a hand. "Wait, it's too h—"

Eli gobbled the steaming loaf, large bits of corn bread crumbling from the corners of his mouth. Another guttural laugh rose in his throat, spraying Stone's whites with a sticky mess of spittle and corn bread.

Stone turned from the spray and peeked into the other pot. He noticed it had a deeper tinge of red, almost blood-like, and he dipped the ladle curiously. He drew it near his mouth and blew on the steaming stuff. He parted his lips when a powerful blow rocked him. Hot chili spilled across his chest and the ladle flew from his fingers. A vise-like hand clamped on the back of his neck. He instinctively lurched to struggle free but found his feet flailing in midair. Eli held him fast by the neck at arm's length like a cat caught stealing milk.

"That pot ain't for tastin'," Eli growled as he drew Stone close to his face. More corn bread spittle spattered in Stone's face and he winced.

"That's my special batch for us lifers, so don't go messin' with it."

Eli shook him by the neck to add effect to the words. Stone's eyes bulged and a wet spot began yellowing the front of his pants.

The other residents in the kitchen stopped working and stood staring at the helpless head cook. Eli laid wild eyes on them then again shook Stone like a doll.

"If I catch any of you messin' with my main brew here," he said, nodding toward the rear kettle, "you'll be meat loaf for tomorrow's dinner. Understand?"

A half dozen heads bobbed in unison and the men quickly resumed their tasks. Eli finally released his grip on Stone who staggered back against the sink and grabbed the edge to keep from collapsing. Eli snatched him by the collar and held him upright until Stone managed to stand on his own and his eyes flicked back into focus. Then Eli spun him back toward the bread ovens and released his collar.

"You just stick to bakin' your corn bread. I'll tend to my chili. We'll make quite a team that way. Who knows, Stoney, if we ever get outta here, maybe we can open a restaurant together."

Stone started to look back, shook his head, then rubbed the back of his neck as he shuffled toward the ovens. Eli reached up and adjusted his white hat off to one side and slightly over his brow. He looked over at the window and noticed how his pale reflection resembled the chef on a box of Cream Of Wheat. What a perfect disguise for a doctor. No one will ever guess, not even that wise-ass Simmons — until it's too late.

He looked past the reflection out into the fading light. An arctic high had cleared the sky and the thin air had turned brittle cold. Plumes of steam poured from the mouths of two officers talking on the far wall. They stomped their feet and flapped their arms. Eli grinned. Yep, it's going to be a crunchy one tonight. The kind of cold men don't linger in, the kind where they hurry about their business or freeze, the kind where they make hasty decisions. Perfect.

As Eli gazed into the evening air, his pupils widened, his nostrils flared. He reached out with his new senses into the night. He shivered. And suddenly he could feel the cold air beyond the window brushing his cheeks. It made them tingle. Color rose into his face. His jaws flexed. The inside of his nose prickled. His eyes watered. He sucked in a long breath, swishing the clear air across his palate and swallowing it slowly like an exotic dessert. It tasted so unlike prison, so sweet and incredibly pure. His hunger mounted, his mouth watered for more — the pristine taste of freedom. Soon he would gorge himself on it.

CHAPTER 20 – CLOSING IN

When Larry and Brad finally rounded the last turn in the trail, nightfall had closed its dark hand on the forest. Trees lining the trail stood raven black against the blued reflection of the snow. Criss-crossing shadows spread wide and dark, creating a labyrinth of hideaways for a killer to lurk, to come dashing into the twilight at any second, catching them off guard.

Sweat trickling from under Brad's cap watered his eyes as he snatched his head from side to side, looking into the failing light for the charge he was sure would come before they could reach the safety of the cabin. He hadn't seen a thing since leaving the cranberry meadow, but sensed a presence following them, waiting for the right moment when darkness would give it full advantage. Brad's legs pumped onward, long since knotted, long ago drained of their energy. But still he ran, the image of Crane's body driving him beyond his limits. The increasing bite of the evening air clawed at his lungs with each breath. It chilled his teeth until they ached. It pricked his nostrils like needles of ice. It scoured his cheeks raw. The plummeting cold made the snow crunch loudly under his feet, whining with the squeaky wails of distant voices.

Up ahead, Larry pushed on. Despite the towed burden of Crane's body, his long strides ate up the trail. His arms pumped in harmony with his legs, the wide shoulders swaying in time with the hips. Plumes of steam puffed from his mouth, frosting his beard, coating his collar. His leather boots groaned against the cold, throwing behind a spray of snow that had dusted Crane's wrapped body in a solemn blanket of white. The dropping temperature crystallized the snow, making the toboggan glide more easily as he ran.

Larry increased his stride. Brad noticed him pulling ahead and reached out an arm as if to drag him back. He opened his mouth. No, don't speak, it will hear you. Wait, wait up, Uncle Larry. Don't leave me behind. Why are you running faster? Is something coming?

Brad looked back and stumbled, almost losing his balance on feet that floundered like snowshoes. He regained his footing, turned and slowed. "Yes," he hissed between breaths. "Finally, safety."

A hundred and fifty yards ahead, a glow filtered through the windows of the cabin. Woodsmoke billowed from the stovepipe, rising far into the evening calm. His tense shoulders sagged. A hundred yards from the cabin his legs slowed more and his heels dragged in the snow. He let the rifle droop in his hands.

Larry pulled farther ahead. Brad sighed at last, his eyes now glimpsing a figure in the window, probably Pa. Brad started to raise an arm but it dropped limply at his side. Larry was almost there now, figures rushing from the cabin door to meet him.

A branch snapped nearby in the darkness.

Brad spun at the sound.

A rustling now, the dull crunch of hooves pounding closer.

Brad gasped and squinted into the shadows, trying desperately to rid his eyes of the ghost images of the cabin lights. The crunching stopped, only yards away. His eyes squinted. His throat tightened. His breath came in short pants. He listened. Only the hammering of his heart filled his ears. At last his eyes settled on a shape, a horizontal form mixed with the vertical patterns of the trees. And as his eyes finally adjusted to the dark again and opened wide, Brad stopped breathing altogether.

Out of the darkness, only one powerful lunge away, two pale crescents glowed with the yellow aura of new moons. As they blinked off and on, Brad realized they weren't moons at all, but eyes, glowing eyes, eyes centered in the head of the dark shape beneath a glistening crown of tines.

Brad's entire body sagged as if a lead blanket had been draped over him. His eyes bulged, unblinking. His knees trembled. His mouth hung wide. His arms drooped. The rifle slipped from his hands. He stood rooted, waiting for the piercing tines he knew would steal his life before his next heartbeat.

In the distance, the cabin door slammed with a clap that echoed through the still air. The glowing rimmed eyes blinked and turned toward the sound. Over the ringing in his ears, Brad heard the thudding of boots approaching in the snow. He managed to turn his head. Corey, Oh God, no. Run, it's here! Brad opened his mouth to yell, but the warning clung deep in his chest as if held back by the thundering of his heart. No Corey, get back!

"Buwana, Buwana!" Corey hollered as he neared. "Come on, man, you're going to freeze your doddle-berries off out here. Let's hurry to the cabin, everybody's going bonkers."

Brad's eyes flicked back toward the buck-thing. What? Where is it? I didn't hear it leave. But it's... it's, gone. Brad squinted into the darkness. Nothing... nothing but trees. Did it shape-shift into a tree?

"Boy, you must be one tired puppy," Corey said, tenderly holding his side while he bent down and picked up the rifle. He took Brad by the arm and turned him toward the cabin. "You look half-frozen too. Come on, Buwana, let's get you thawed out. Your dad's got a zillion questions."

Brad shuffled along side Corey, mouth still agape. He shook his head and tried to swallow the knot in his throat. He looked at Corey. The knot tightened.

"Corey, that's the second time you... you saved my life today."

"Come on, you're not that bad. Just cold and tired, that's all."

"No, not me, it —"

Brad glanced back over his shoulder into the darkness but saw only the glow of a new moon reflecting off the snow in a thousand sparkling crescents. Was that what I saw?

"Corey, is that what I saw?"

The lights from the cabin began to spin like moths flying into the night.

Brad never felt the cold slap of the snowy ground hitting his face.

CHAPTER 21 – NIGHT EYES

Brad leaned into the steepness of the hillside and ran with all his might. Behind him came a thunderclap of hooves from the darkness below. This time it would catch him for sure. This time he would die in great pain.

There was no escaping it but still he ran, his feet sinking helplessly into the pale ground, more like soft flesh he realized as he struggled to gain speed. He cursed as his moccasins sank into the mush, his strides lagging in pitiful slow-motion.

From the darkness behind him, it bounded in long leaps, closer and closer until its breath became hot on his neck, its stench making him scream. But the only sound to come out was a faint whimper. He struggled onward. In one desperate effort before it fell upon him, sinking its wickedness deep into his soul and draining away his life, Brad lurched toward the light at the top of the hill.

He clawed at the hillside but it came away in gooey clumps. He cried out and turned, kicking at the thing. And as his feet pounded in frustration at the darkness, his fear began to swell into anger. In his struggle, the sticky hillside smeared his eyes, blurring his vision into shades of gray. Unsure where to strike, Brad flailed wildly, the helplessness of the situation driving his anger to rage. His hands tangled with the feathers in his long hair. He stiffened, waiting for the beast to spring upon him. He held his breath. But nothing came. He looked about in the grayness. There was no sign of the beast, just the pounding of his heart, the hotness of his anger still fresh in his veins.

He gently reached out, feeling for it in the darkness. Something brushed his hand and he snatched it back to his chest. And suddenly there it was, under the breastwork of beads and buckskin shirt, inside him, pounding. He gasped at the thought. Then the realization began to surface. The creature wasn't out there in the dark. It lived within his fear. With his primary senses blurred and forced to reach out with a deeper sense, Brad recognized the real demon. And he also saw a way to conquer it.

The more his anger grew, the smaller his fear became. And the more he focused his anger upon the fear, the quicker it turned from an ominous shadow into an insignificant veil. As he at last focused his anger like the tip of an arrow, fear vanished altogether. He cried out in joy and turned to the hilltop. The light there had grown brighter and voices from above beckoned him — other Ojibwa braves who had conquered the Manitou.

"Brad, Brad, wake up. Come on, son, please."

Brad squinted against the glow of the overhead gas light as his vision cleared. Huddled around him, the clouded faces of the Indians on the hill focused into Pa and his father. Uncle Larry, Corey and Vern hovered in the background.

The memory of the dream vanished as Brad blinked.

"Sorry if I pushed you too hard," Larry said, leaning over. His usual happy-bear eyes wore bluish circles. "All I could think of was getting back here before dark. I didn't consider what you'd been through all day. Sorry, pal."

Brad started to sit up but a dull ache behind his eyes like sharp fingers forced him back down on the couch. He moaned and laid back. Pa leaned over and wrapped Brad's hands around a mug of steaming cocoa.

"Here, try sipping this. After you thaw, I'll bring you some deer heart stew, complements of your uncle here." Pa stroked a hand across Brad's forehead and turned to the kitchen.

Al knelt near the couch and looked into his son's eyes. He leaned forward and tentatively pulled the wool blanket across Brad's chest, tucking it tight around his neck — something he hadn't done since Brad was a child. Brad smiled. His dad smiled back.

"You just lay there and rest, son. You deserve it. We'll talk when you're feeling better."

Brad nodded. His dad rose and turned to the pot-bellied stove. Al grabbed the iron poker, swung the door wide and began prodding at the coals. Sparks danced inside the stove's cherry-red belly. The flames growled with new vigor. The stovepipe popped and pinged.

In the red glow, Brad noticed new creases on his dad's face. How's he going to tell Mrs. Crane? Brad wondered. And what will happen to his job with Mr. Crane gone? Crap, the plant will surely fail with the old bastard and all his arrogance now laying out there in a pile of frozen meat. No wonder Dad looks worried.

Brad looked from his dad's face into the flames. 'You just lay there and rest, son. You deserve it.' What a joke. I don't deserve anything. Nobody even knows that I failed to save Crane and Corey.

I don't deserve to be alive, yet here I am, *deserving* while Corey's hurt and Crane's dead. Maybe fate has a different ending planned for spineless cowards. Maybe something fitting?

After drinking his cocoa, Brad slurped a steaming bowl of stew as he watched Larry tend to Corey's wounds. Larry gently unbuttoned Corey's shirt and lifted the blood-stained undershirt. Corey twitched between a grin and grimace as Larry removed the gauze Pa had taped on earlier after washing the wound.

Brad stopped eating and straightened for a better look. With most of the blood gone from Corey's side it didn't appear half as bad as Brad expected. It still looked plenty bad though.

The skin wore bruised shades of purple where three ragged gouges wept a watery blood. Below them a swollen crescent tear the size of a silver dollar had peeled the skin back, exposing pink flesh.

"This may sting a bit, partner," Larry said, soaking a gauze pad with disinfectant. "Need a bullet to bite?"

Corey just shook his head and looked up at the ceiling. His nervous smile tightened into a wince as Larry wiped the wounds. Orange disinfectant ran down his side, raising goose flesh as it went. Larry patted the wounds gently then bandaged the three long gouges using gauze and tape. Using four butterflied strips of tape, he drew the peeled flap of skin tight and taped it neatly in place.

"There, that ought to do it," Larry said, his big hands gently pulling Corey's T-shirt back down. "A deer hunter as tough as you shouldn't take long to mend."

The sparkle returned to Corey's eyes as he looked up at Larry. Brad saw how Larry's stoic features melted in front of Corey. Quite a pair they make; opposites attracted by each other's qualities. It's funny how Corey quiets down in Larry's shadow and how that hard shell of Larry's softens when he's near Corey. I wish Corey brought the best out in me. Seems like all I can do is fail him though. Crap, I couldn't even dredge up enough courage to call out a warning earlier. Can't even save my best friend. I just stood there.

Chills rippled up the back of Brad's neck as he recalled the eyes, their blackness rimmed on the lower half with phosphorescent crescents. He pulled the blanket tight around his ears. The more he tried to recall the image, the fuzzier it became. Was there really a killer buck out there somewhere? If it was real, why didn't it charge? I dropped the rifle. It had plenty of chance before Corey came. And how did it vanish without a sound? Corey didn't even see or hear it. He shook his head. Maybe I was so exhausted I imagined the whole thing. I never fainted before. Who knows what the mind thinks before shutting down, especially after everything that happened today. Rising voices drew him from his thoughts.

"Hogwash," Vern hollered from in front of the plastic-covered window. "I might swallow the story of a wounded buck goring a reckless hunter, even two in one day. But this crazy killer buck crap is too much. Crane probably just screwed up like those kids."

He looked at Al through glazed eyes and pointed a near-empty beer can in Brad's direction. "You're starting to sound like that story-telling kid of yours. And I thought you knew better," he went on, waving his beer can in Al's face.

Vern shook his head and tipped the last of the beer. Al clasped his hands on his hips and stuck his jaw out. Brad clenched the blanket. Al lifted his hands from his hips, palms up. As the jaw tipped down, the eyes followed.

"Come on Vern," he pleaded, "don't be so hard on the boys. They've been through a lot today and seen more than most adults ever do. Give them a break."

"A break!" Vern blurted. "What they need is a good strap of leather across their lying little butts. First they get everyone shook up with that loco coon story. Then they come running back here, spoiling everybody's hunt with this killer deer crap. When's it going to end? When are you going to realize that your kid has too much imagination for his own good?"

Larry rose from beside Corey and moved toward Vern. Vern dropped his empty can and shuffled back against the window.

"Tell Crane out there it's all someone's imagination," Larry said, his voice as solid as the set in his chin. "You've seen this boy's wounds. They're real, just like the buck he shot that was going for Brad. You're the one who better wake up to reality before you end up like Crane."

Vern blinked as if his mind was trying to focus enough to counter. Finally, his eyes widened and his mouth twisted into a sneer.

"Right. Just look at the facts for God's sake," he said, nodding as he gained momentum. "Did YOU see any attacking deer? No, of course not. None of US did because there weren't ANY. The only ONE'S who think they saw killer deer are these kids here, and who knows what they been smoking out in the woods."

Pa slammed his coffee mug down on the stove and stabbed a finger in Vern's direction. But Vern continued with his rapid fire babble before Pa could interrupt.

"Sure, sure, I know what you're going to say old man. Oh God forbid, not our boys here, they're too sweet," Vern snorted. "Come on, wake up. Kids everywhere are into drugs nowadays. These smurfs are too young to get girls or handle booze so what else can they do for kicks? It's a wonder they're not telling us they're seeing ghosts."

Larry's eyes shifted darkly to Brad then back to Vern. Al caught the brief exchange. He too turned back toward Vern. He bunched a loose fist and shook it in Vern's face.

"I don't think these boys would lie, well, not intentionally," he said, his tone as unsure as his fist. "No matter how you look at it, I think we have to get out tomorrow and contact the authorities. According to the boys, and Larry verified it with the sign he saw, that 4-pointer didn't kill Crane. It was already dead. Something else did."

Vern reached into the bottom of a nearby six-pack and pulled out another beer. "Think whatever you want," he said, popping the top and taking a long pull. "Go ahead, waste tomorrow, see if I care. I'm going hunting. Crane was your boss, not mine. He's not wrecking my vacation. I waited all year for this. We're all going to die some day. His number just came up. And what's the big rush? It ain't like he's going to spoil out there."

He waved his hand as if swishing away a gnat near his nose then tipped his can. The room grew unnaturally quiet, only the sounds of beer gurgling down Vern's throat and the roar of logs in the stove filling the stillness. As Vern lowered his can, Pa tugged on his suspenders and stepped forward.

"I can't believe you. You're as pitifully ignorant as you are a drunk," he said.

Vern snapped his head around and tried to throw Pa an angry stare but his eyes watered out of focus. He drew his upper lip into a snarl.

"You're also a poor judge of character," Pa continued. "Certainly of these two boys. Your notion of them on drugs is plumb crazy. Never seen two fellas more entranced with the pure spectacle of nature. You don't need drugs for that, not even a six-pack."

"I'm crazy?" Vern blasted, spittle flying from his lips. "You want to talk about crazy. Crazy is this cock'n'bull story of a killer deer that came back and finished off Crane — a killer deer no one saw. If that doesn't sound like the most —"

"I saw it," Brad said, standing near the stove with the blanket wrapped around his shoulders like an Indian. "I saw it close up just before Larry and I made it back to the cabin, right before I passed out. It ran up to me only yards away. Right out there." Brad pointed toward the meadow beyond Vern and the plastic window.

"And you better pray you never see it," he continued. "It's huge with tines as long as spears." He paused for a second and finally spit out the rest. "And its eyes glow in the dark. I think it might be a Manitou."

All faces turned to him. Everyone stood staring.

Brad looked around, his eyes red. There, I said it, okay? I know you won't believe me. But I just had to say it. I couldn't keep it in any longer.

"Manitou? Ha! See! What did I tell you," Vern hollered. "The kid's gone off the deep end. A Manitou with eyes that glow. Where do you suppose he got that idea?" Several heads turned toward Larry. "When will all this lying stop?" Vern continued. "Hell, what kind of fools do you take us for, kid? I suppose next you're going to tell us that it's going to come rushing in here and gobble us all up like gingerbread men."

Brad looked to Larry for support. His Uncle pressed his lips and glanced away. Brad looked to Pa, the old eyes suddenly heavy with disappointment. Brad looked down at his feet. Tell them lies and they believe me, tell them the truth and they call me a liar. Maybe a lie would have sounded more like the truth. What can I say to make them believe?

"Hey, killer buck," Vern taunted, turning toward the Visquene-covered window. He began waving his beer can over his head. "Yeah, we're in here. Come on in and join the party. We'd like to see your shining eyes. Come on you big old nasty son-of-a-bitch. Come and get us!"

Still waving his arms in front of the window, Vern howled in triumph like a coyote then broke into his whinnying laughter as he tipped back his can.

Brad looked at him through narrowed eyes.

Larry grabbed for Vern.

Pa gripped Brad's shoulder.

Al stepped back.

Brad gasped as a dark shadow flashed outside the window.

"WATCH OUT!" he cried.

Had it been in time to do any good, most wouldn't have believed him anyway.

CHAPTER 22 – CHOW TIME

Eli stood at the front of the line wearing a smile. He rested his hands on his hips and spread his massive chest like a proud father about to show off a new baby.

He had finished his cooking creations hours ago, leaving the kitchen only after giving Stone and his crew explicit instructions about serving dinner, including lots of shredded cheese and chopped onions. He had showered and donned clean duds for his grandest of prison meals. Now he waited behind the lockout door leading into the mess.

Behind him in the corridor, the lifers took their place near the front of the seemingly endless chow line that disappeared around the corner. Decades ago prison officials learned that feeding the worst trouble makers first headed off much of the trouble before it started, which it too often did in the mess hall. That's where most of the stickings occurred. Even though the inmates were only allowed plastic forks and spoons for eating, laughable weapons at best, some still found ways to make shanks for ventilating their foes. And with all the confusion and bodies in the mess hall, it made an ideal killing ground for driving an ice pick between someone's shoulder blades before melting into the masses.

Painted slate gray, the sprawling hall held just over a third of the several hundred maximum security inmates. They chowed in three shifts, short timers pulling the final dogbone shift. Ten long rows of sterile tables with stainless steel tops spread across the room, interrupted in the middle by a single aisle. Like the tables, shiny benches lining each side were securely bolted to the floor to keep them from being flung through the air when squabbles erupted. The lifeless glow of fluorescent lights made milky reflections on the matching gray floor.

Near the long string of waiting inmates, a lone unarmed officer stood next to the lockout door leading from the corridor into the mess. He glanced at Eli then quickly turned his gaze toward the clanking of the kitchen help making ready for the hungry horde.

"Hear you been helping Stoney with tonight's menu," he said.

Eli's grin widened. "Sure did," he replied, tugging up on the waist of his pants. Residents weren't aloud to wear belts but Eli had little trouble keeping his blues in place. "Got tired of choking down the same old crap every day and figured the boys would appreciate some real home cookin'."

The officer nodded in passive agreement. "Well, smells good, whatever it is." He checked his watch then craned his neck, looking at the helpers loading the last of the stainless steel tubs behind the serving line.

Eli eyed the officer with contempt. Ah, such an eager little watch dog, always looking for a way to score kiss-ass points with the shift supervisor. Okay, just do your job, Fido.

"I only tried to help," Eli said, sliding his hands into his pockets and looking at his shoes. "Just wanted to keep the boys happy with some variety, you know, the spice of life. That's all."

He leaned over slightly toward the officer. "But I think Stoney got pissed," he continued in a whisper, "you know, at me for meddling in his kitchen. The man's got a mean streak in him about that sort of thing. Thought I even saw him put something in the food. Hope it wasn't more chili powder to make me look bad."

Eli watched the officer's attention perk and he leaned even closer.

"But please, don't say nothin' to no one. I don't want anybody hassling the old fart. He probably don't mean no harm. It's just that he don't want no one showing him up." Eli ended with a sigh then began rocking back and forth on his heels waiting for the door to open.

The officer shifted his attention to Stone. A moment later the officer caught the nod from the old cook and slid back the barred door. He watched the inmates as they grabbed trays and hustled over to the serving counter. He eyed Stone, standing behind the servers.

Eli looked at the officer watching Stone. See Fido? See Stoney fidget? Not right for Stoney to twist his apron like that. Must be something's wrong. Good boy, make your neck stiff, go on point. That's a good little watchdog.

Eli swaggered to the front of the line. He fanned his face with the plastic mess tray and fingered his collar. Sweat beaded his forehead. His heartbeat rose. He turned around to the anxious line.

"Hope you guys like it hot," he said wearing his best imitation of a friendly smile. "Cause this chili will keep your chestnuts roasting near the fire all night long. It's my mama's secret recipe.

And naturally I don't want none of you offendin' my mama. So you boys eat up good, ya hear?"

Grinning, he turned to one of the servers in front of the big stainless tubs. He looked at the man then raised his eyebrows as if about to ask a question.

On cue, the server asked, "What'll it be. The hard-ass chili or the wussy stuff?"

Eli frowned. The man flinched.

"Sorry, friend," Eli said, cocking his head sideways and raising his voice. "Didn't hear you with all that shuffling going on behind me."

The inmates behind him became still. They looked quickly at one another then back to Eli and the server.

"A little louder please," Eli growled.

The server cleared his throat, swallowing hard. "What'll it be? The hard-ass chili or the wussy stuff?"

Eli jumped back in mock surprise. "Well I sure as hell ain't no wussy!" he bellowed. "Give me a heap of that man's chili."

As the server filled a bowl with Eli's superhot batch, Eli turned and nodded to the inmates behind him.

"Wussy?" he said to no one in particular. "I don't think we got any wussies around here. But just the same I think I'll keep my eye open." His eyebrows arched near the outer edges in a devilish pose. "'Cause I sure could use a wussy in the showers."

He grinned again and turned, sliding his tray down the serving counter, steam rising from his bowl of chili. Even before he stopped at the big trays of chopped onions and shredded cheddar, a chorus of voices behind him made him grin all the more.

"I ain't no wussy."

"I sure as hell ain't no wussy."

"Hey, not me either, gimme the hot stuff."

Eli heaped on a mound of cheddar cheese over his chili and sprinkled on some onions. He took a seat near the end of the chow line and began spooning in dinner, stopping between bites long enough to smile and nod to any inmate who dared cast him a look.

Thoroughly astonished at a smile from Eli, none noticed that he had swallowed heaps of the cheddar topping and washed it down with gulps of milk without touching the chili. Before downing his reddish brew, he paused, rubbing his massive gut and belching. He leaned over toward a few of the inmates who had ventured close at his table.

"Man, ain't this the best stuff you guys had in ages?"

They nodded between fanning their mouths and gulping water. Eli snickered. He noticed others down the table using crackers or corn bread to help quench the flames.

He took one last gulp of milk then raised the bowl to his mouth. In a long slurp, he sucked the chili from his bowl.

"Man, this stuff's good," he said, wiping the corner of his mouth and rising. "But it sure heads south on me in a hurry."

He strolled over to the lockout door.

"Hey, boss-man. Open up the can before I crap my pants."

The officer turned, brow rumpled that someone was bothering him so soon. "Oh, you, Eli. What's the problem, Mama's cooking giving you the runs?"

Eli quenched the impulse to reach through the bars and crush the man's face. Instead he smiled shyly. "Sad truth is I ain't so tough. Man, chili rips me up, especially this batch for some reason. Feels like my guts are on fire. Gotta go bad."

"Okay, okay, spare me the details. Just get on with it."

The officer pressed the electronic latch that opened the lone bathroom door across the corridor.

Once inside, Eli wasted no time jamming a finger down his throat. He gagged twice before the swell of vomit rose in his throat. His eyes watered. In a spasm, his gut contracted and expelled the chili, onions, cheese, and already curdled milk. Eli flushed the mess down the toilet then washed his face and mouth with cold water.

Moments later he was back in the chow line, eagerly looking forward to a second helping.

Only the server heard him whisper, "Wussy stuff, please."

Eli slowly slurped his second bowl full, nibbling corn bread and daintily patting his lower lip while enjoying immensely his last prison meal.

CHAPTER 23 – EVICTION

Brad's warning echoed inside the cabin like a siren. Everyone spun at the wail of his voice, their pirouettes flickering in time-stop frames before his eyes.

As Corey's head turned, his mouth dropped open. He bunched his shoulders tight around his ears like a turtle drawing its head in for safety.

Pa's hand slipped from Brad's shoulder, his fingers trailing down the folds in the blanket. Behind the rimmed glasses, old eyes widened, exposing milky patches of cataracts around the speckled blue-grey irises.

Off to the side of the window, near the corner, Al wheeled like the instant replay of a wide receiver completing a button-hook. His arms flew awkwardly, a puppet turned too quickly on limp strings. Eyebrows climbed up a forehead wrinkled in surprise.

One of Larry's big hands had just reached for a shirt-full of Vern. His fingers stiffened at the sound, his shaggy mane of hair and beard lagging behind the turning head. His eyes still held a wild glimmer of anger. His lower lip dropped in confusion.

Despite Larry's advance, Vern continued laughing as he jerked back from Larry's reach. His back pressed against the makeshift Visquene window. He still held the beer can over his head like a victory cup. His eyes shuttered closed, the wrinkles of his years squeezing out bleary-eyed tears. His mouth spread anew, another fit of laughter beginning to erupt from his lungs. It never made it.

For a split second, the shadow outside filled the window, blocking the reflection of snow in the meadow. An instant later the Visquene imploded, a sharp crown of tines leading the way over glowing crescents rimmed with white fur grading to brown, buck brown, big buck brown.

Vern's eyes flew wide as driving tines lifted him off the floor. The dull rip of antlers piercing tissue mixed with the hiss of escaping breath before being drowned out by his rising scream. His boots flailed in the air as the force of the blow threw him across the room, the buck's head firmly planted in the square of his back. The beer can fell from his grip, spraying beer and clattering to the floor.

The force of the impact knocked Larry aside. He fell hard on his knees and spun across the floor.

Held fast by the spectacle of the unfolding scene, Brad watched with a queer fascination. He saw a magnificent creature, bigger than his wildest imagination. Its winter coat, each hair seemingly glued in place, glistened under the glow of the gas lamp. Its powerful neck muscles bunched under the weight of its new load. Shoulders and flanks rippled as legs churned on the wooden floor, its hooves splaying wide to gain footing. The dark hair along its mane bristled. Its black nostrils flared. The mesmerizing eyes had somehow lost their glow under the cabin lights. They appeared to squint. But to Brad they also took on a depth that made his heart go numb. It was as if the eyes were reaching out for him, as if they wanted to seize his soul. He blinked to break the spell. To his surprise the buck blinked too. And as the buck sped past at arm's length, he felt the weight of those eyes press upon his chest, like a icy hand trying to grab his heart.

Brad jumped back from the stove, almost too late, as the buck drove Vern solidly into the stove's iron belly. The big stove rattled off its legs and spun sideways, the door flying open, flaming coals scattering across the floor. Vern's scream rose to new heights as his hands pressed against the searing iron and the tines drove deeper, several pushing through the front of his shirt. The buck lunged again, dislodging the stovepipe in a hail of smoke and sparks. The pipe struck the gas lamp, bursting the globe and snuffing the room's only light. In the dark and confusion, Vern's cries quickly died to a faint gurgle.

Brad spun from the sparks and tumbled backwards over a chair. He found himself tangled with the blanket around his head, feet in the air, struggling to right himself — like his struggle in his dream he suddenly remembered. In the dream it came for me!

He scrambled to his feet and threw off the blanket. He held up his arms to brace himself for the impact. He squinted into the darkness and smoke, looking for the onrush of glowing eyes. He stepped back. His stocking foot landed on a hot ember and he danced from one foot to the other. He jumped further back and fell again among the confusion of overturned furniture, grunting, hollering, thumping of bodies and increasing smoke. Crap, we'll all be killed in this mess.

Brad spotted an orange light through the smoke and charged toward it. But instead of the kitchen doorway, he found a patch of flames climbing a slabwood wall, crackling as it fed on the tinder dry wood. He reared back. Fire! God, we've got to put it out. He spun. Wait, we can't. The buck's still here somewhere. Forget the fire, save yourself. Run. Where?

He spun again, realizing he had stumbled the wrong way in the confusion. He threw up his hands as more flames leaped the walls around him, the fire quickly devouring the volatile resins in the pine and spruce slabwood with a hungry roar. He scrambled toward the kitchen doorway.

Brad's hand had just touched the doorway when someone grabbed his arm and pulled him into the kitchen. Under the smoke-dimmed light he made out the figures of Pa, Corey and his dad, all three hunched over, gasping for breath.

"You okay, son?"

Brad coughed and nodded. "Think so."

"Gotta get out of here," his dad said. "No way to stop it now. Go into the shed. That will give us some time."

"Wait, where's Larry," Pa wheezed, squinting into the smoke.

"What about the buck?" Brad said.

"Thought I saw it leap back out through the window," Al said. "Now get outta here. I'll get Larry."

Al pushed Brad and Corey toward the outer door leading to the shed. He grabbed a towel from the counter and threw it over his head. He disappeared into the smoke. The boys grabbed Pa by the arms. He gasped for breath in the thickening smoke. Without his glasses, he stumbled in the darkness. The boys pulled him toward the shed. Brad swung the door open. Behind him the flames growled stronger. They rushed into the shed's cool darkness, pulling the door shut behind.

Brad fumbled in the shadows near a small window until he found a flashlight. It was the big yellow plastic six-volter they used during nighttime trips to the outhouse. His thumb clicked on the beam. Though the shed was temporarily safe from the smoke and spreading flames, its numbing temperature seeped through Brad's wool shirt like ice water. Fortunately, the hunters had hung their heavy outerwear in the shed to keep it free of cabin odors. Brad grabbed his coat off a nearby hook and pulled it on. He handed Corey and Pa their coats and turned back toward the kitchen door.

"I'll be right back."

Still wheezing badly, Pa held up a hand in protest. Brad didn't see it in the darkness, not that it would have mattered anyway.

He flung the door open but staggered backwards as a blast of heat hit him. Across the kitchen, flames rimmed the doorway leading into the living room. His flashlight beam lanced the smoke as his dad burst from the doorway, Larry clutched tightly to his side. Brad held the door open as they staggered into the shed. He slammed it shut. Behind the closed door the flames hissed and growled louder like an enraged beast, consuming and growing at an astonishing rate.

Al and Larry sank to their knees, coughing out smoke. The stench of burnt hair quickly filled the small confines of the shed. Brad moved the flashlight beam across his father to the still-smoldering form of Uncle Larry. His Uncle's once great mane of hair was now burned within an inch of his head. His proud beard had been nibbled back by the flames to a short stubble. He held his stomach and retched.

"You okay, Uncle Larry?"

"Yeah," he paused, sputtering between coughs. "Toasted a bit on the outside, probably looks worse than it is." Larry coughed hard and spit up a mouthful of black phlegm. He looked up into the light.

"Tried to help Vern but he was too far gone. Nothing I could do. Tried mouth-to-mouth, but, God, it just wheezed out the holes. Tried to drag him out when the smoke got the best of me. That's when your dad found me."

He cupped one hand over his mouth as he began coughing again while slapping the other hand on Al's shoulder. Brad reached out and handed them their coats, even though the heat from the fire was quickly warming the inside of the shed.

"Can't stay in here," Pa said. "This whole place is going up in minutes."

Brad shined the light against the wall of the cabin. Near the bottom boards, smoke began streaming between the cracks.

"Grab anything to keep warm," Larry said, rising slowly to his feet. Still hunched over, he took the light from Brad and swept the beam around the shed.

It settled on their extra boots lined against the wall. They rushed over and yanked them on.

"And over there," Larry said, the light now shining on some old hats and a long scarf hanging on the hooks, "take those too."

The fire's flicker now reflected off the snow outside and its dancing light came through the window. Brad and Corey snatched

Vern's coat, two old stocking caps, the scarf and a tattered pair of coveralls. Brad turned to look for anything else that might keep them warm, when gunfire erupted from within the cabin, the ping of bullets ricochetting inside. Instinctively, Larry flattened to the floor. The others flinched.

"Everybody out!" Larry hollered, scrambling for the door on all fours.

Brad rushed ahead and tugged on Larry's coat as his hand reached for the door.

"Wait, Uncle Larry. What if it's waiting for us?"

Larry turned the flashlight toward Brad's face. "What if it is? We sure can't stay here. And with all the guns and ammunition burning in the cabin we sure can't shoot our way out."

"Maybe we can make a break for the car," Al said.

Several more bullets exploded inside the cabin. Larry turned the door knob.

"Roasted, shot in the ass, or facing that thing ain't much of a choice, but it's all we got. Like your dad said, run for the Suburban."

Larry grabbed an axe near the door and lunged outside, most of the others close on his heels.

Brad lingered.

More bullets exploded.

He clutched the clothes to his chest, took a breath, and rushed into the night.

CHAPTER 24 – DOCTOR CALL

Eli laid on his bunk waiting patiently. He belched for the umpteenth time, the flavor of digesting chili and onions filling his nose. He rubbed his massive stomach and sighed. Soon, very soon now.

His serpent eyes probed the darkness around him. Even with the cell block lights doused a half-hour ago, he clearly saw the shadows of restless inmates shifting on their bunks. His ears twitched at each sound, reaching into distant cells for the first hints of what was to come.

It began with the faint grumbling of stomachs. Some burped, others passed wind. Eli grinned as he overheard strained voices cussing his chili and insulting his heritage. Then came faint gasps as the first stabs of pain began knotting guts. The lifers instinctively repressed the short burst of pain, squirming on their bunks, waiting for the discomfort to pass. And for many it did while the unseen damage spread throughout their bodies, looking for weak points to escape like millions of gnawing maggots about to swarm free as flies. For others the pain grew worse, much worse.

Within an hour after the lights-out the cussing had trailed off. The inmates sank into their own worlds of suffering. Though some drifted off into a fretful sleep, most just laid coiled in fetal positions. Others moaned, rocking back and forth. A few simply whimpered. In the darkness, no one realized that the running noses and uncontrolled drooling wasn't mucus or saliva. And despite the discomfort and odd tingling in their veins, none dared to show their weakness by calling out for help. None wanted to be labeled a wussy, not in Eli's block.

Eli sat up on the edge of his bunk and listened. Faint twinkles of light reflected off his teeth as his alligator smile spread wide. Playing doctor is such fun. So much power over so many. Too bad it will end so soon with so many captive patients at hand. Oh, the possibilities are endless. What a shame I can't stay to become Dr. Nolstrum's assistant. Oh well, at least I got to give most of these animals their final prescription. But I suppose none of the ungrateful bastards will ever thank me for giving them an early parole.

He rose and walked to the sink. He unbuttoned his shirt and splashed his face and chest with water, soaking his T-shirt and denims. He ran wet hands through his hair. It bristled on end. He returned to his bunk.

The first gags of retching echoed from the far end of the block now. Even before the faint smell of vomit tinged with blood reached Eli's nose, other inmates began coughing uncontrollably in the dark, gurgling sprays rising in their throats. Within minutes a mass wave of hysteria spread throughout the prison as some of the inmates realized their plight. Finally, they screamed into the shadows. They begged for help.

Lights blinked on. Officers ran down cell blocks. Feet slapped concrete in confused circles. Voices rose. Panic swept through each block like the growing stench of vomit and feces mixed with blood.

Phones rang in the night.

The Warden grumbled as he buttoned his heavy coat and headed for the door. In the near-zero weather, his boot soles squeaked in the snow like shrews underfoot.

Doctor Nolstrum cradled the phone and cast off his covers. He reached over on the bed stand and fingered the remote control. The TV blinked out. He wouldn't catch the late movie tonight, an old John Wayne western too, True Grit, too bad. He paused for a second and thought maybe it would be more enjoyable if he could fast forward through the commercials anyway. Sure why not? He took a moment and programed his VCR. He got all the settings right on the third try. You'd think they could make these things so at least a doctor could program them. He shook his head. Must be designed by astronauts.

He swung his legs off the bed. His feet touched the cold floor. He jerked them back. Sometimes I hate this job, especially being on twenty-four-hour call, and especially when it's so blasted cold.

He shivered as he began dressing. But he had taken the oath, signed on the dotted line. And now duty called. As he buttoned his shirt he wondered what in blazes the assistant warden meant by a mass outbreak of some kind. Hell, the plague went out with the dark ages. Maybe it was some virulent strain of flu. Jamming bodies into packed cages would certainly spread the stuff. Who knows?

He shrugged his shoulders and stepped into his pants. He figured he'd know soon enough.

CHAPTER 25 — FLIGHT NIGHT

Brad lunged from the shed door into the night. As he burst outside, he squinted at the brightness and threw his hands in front of his face. In a flickering halo surrounding the cabin the night burned brighter than day, flames shooting high out the windows and spiraling out holes in the roof.

He spotted the others a hundred feet away, standing outside the Suburban with the doors open. He rushed toward them. The cluster of spruce trees behind the vehicle stood like morbid spectators, their shadows wavering curiously from side to side as flames surged out opposite ends of the cabin.

In front of the spruces, the hunters stood on the edge of the glow and the heat, the fire's reflection lighting their faces. As Brad neared, he noticed Corey's mouth still hung agape, his head wagging. Pa wore a distant gaze, his pale eyes following the billows of smoke rising high into the night. The circles under his eyes sagged as if the fire had softened the flesh like wax. The stark light caused his withered face to look like parchment stretched over a skull.

At the driver's side of the wagon, Brad's father leaned heavily on the door frame, his chin propped up on folded hands. His face held a blank expression, mesmerized by the inferno. His eyes drifted to the corpse of his boss lashed to the toboggan just beyond the fire's reach. After a moment, his eyes flicked back to the large picture window, pupils narrowing against flames leaping from the sill, flames feeding greedily inside on Vern's bubbling flesh.

Larry sat hunched over in the back seat with his legs hanging out the door. He clutched the axe in one hand, his midsection with the other. Shadows hid most of his face. But as Brad neared, he noticed the mouth clenched, the drawn, stoic face. Was Uncle Larry bothered that much by not being able to save Vern? Yeah, that could be expected, even from a rock like Uncle Larry. But what if... what if he somehow knows our fate now, knows what the buck or shape-shifter can do? Why can't he tell the others? At least let them know what we're up against.

Brad moved closer and looked into Larry's face. Larry appeared to stare through him. Brad leaned in front of his uncle but Larry still ignored him, eyes fixed on the flames.

Brad looked back at the fire, now a beast gone wild. The flames leapt and merged with great bursts of joy, dancing in frenzied spirals of reds and yellows as they went about their hurried business, gutting the cabin, gobbling it inside out. Their bursts hissed and growled like anxious wolves tearing down a deer, their mounting chorus growing into a roar that filled the night.

With an effort, Brad pulled his eyes from the inferno and swept them to the surrounding woods. Inside the glowing halo of light the woods appeared lit by a giant street lamp, flickering from voltage surges. Beyond the glow, the woods stood blacker that the darkest of nights — an ideal haven for a killer to lurk, to watch, to attack.

His eyes shifted to the dancing shadows. It could be anywhere out there, and we're standing around like clay pigeons just waiting to be picked off. He edged closer to Pa.

"Come on," he hollered over the growl of the fire, his voice cracking, "let's get inside the car. It's not safe out here."

Al slowly turned his head as if pulling his gaze from the fire took all his strength. He stared at Brad for a moment with an uncomprehending look. He finally blinked and nodded. He slumped behind the steering wheel and closed the door. The others climbed inside. Brad slammed the door behind him, shutting out the heat, the roar, and whatever else the night held.

Inside the Suburban the hunters sat in silence, clinging to private thoughts, watching the flames quickly reduce the remains of the cabin to a skeleton of glowing embers. At last, only threads of white smoke drifted from the rubble. The darkness of the night closed tightly around them.

"Now what?" Corey asked, pulling his collar up as the chill began to reclaim the night and creep inside the wagon.

"Guess maybe we should wait for help," Al said. "The car keys are in there somewhere," he continued, his eyes shifting to the charred outline in the snow. "Probably melted. Even if we had them, I don't think we could drive out with all this snow. What do you think, Pop?"

Al swung his arm over the seat and looked at Pa. Brad glanced over, waiting for an answer. Pa shrugged his shoulders and sighed. His grandfather looked tired and frail in the shadows, a few strands of wispy hair mussed on end, exposing much of the balding head. At last he cleared his throat.

"Suppose we can't expect help from anyone else," Pa offered. "The fire looked big this close but the woods hides a lot. No clouds to reflect the fire's glow. Other camps were probably in bed. But we may as well wait awhile and see if anyone shows up."

Brad looked over to Larry. Larry however, stayed huddled inside his coat, arms drawn tight to his sides, chin buried against his chest.

"What do you think we should do, Larry?" Corey asked, following Brad's gaze, "hold tight or go for help?"

Larry shifted glassy eyes without turning his head. "Guess we wait," he mumbled from beneath what remained of his beard. He coughed and closed his eyes. "An hour," he whispered under his breath, "then we have to —" He appeared to drift off within his thoughts or maybe even to sleep.

For the next hour they huddled in the darkness as the cold seeped into the Suburban. Despite their warm jackets, the steel of the vehicle seemed to absorb the numbing temperatures, drawing the frigid outside inside their small refuge. Their breath steamed. It fogged the windows and quickly crystallized into frost. Brad kept rubbing a small patch of frost off the side window and peering out.

Al flicked on the flashlight and checked his watch again.

"Hour's up," he said. "Doesn't look as if we can expect any help. I guess we'll have to huddle for warmth and wait until morning."

"Man, Mr. Mercer," Corey said, his teeth chattering behind his swollen lip. "We'll be frozen turds by morning. Can't we hot-wire this buggy and at least get some heat cranking?"

Larry cracked an eyelid at Corey's words. He groaned and sat upright. He drew in a long breath then shook his head.

"Sorry men," he said. "Can't wait for the cavalry or morning. Gotta take my chances tonight. You stay. It's probably safest. But I gotta go."

Before anyone could ask why, Larry pulled the door handle, leaned into the door and fell out into the snow.

By the time he rolled to his knees and struggled to stand, Brad and Al had him by the arms and ushered him back into the wagon. Larry simply followed their nudges like a blind man behind his seeing-eye dog.

"What the hell's going on?" Pa demanded, voice strained, eyes wide.

Al scurried back behind the steering wheel and grabbed the flashlight. He flicked on the beam and pointed it in Larry's face.

Corey gasped.

Despite the near-zero temperatures, sweat trickled down Larry's forehead, matting his scorched hair and casting a sheen on his deeply reddened skin. His eyes wore a heavy glaze.

"Is he sick from the fire?" Corey asked.

Pa took the flashlight from Al and slowly moved the beam down across Larry's chest, finally settling it on the seat between Larry's legs on a smudge of blood. Without his glasses he had to lean close to see.

"It wasn't," Pa finally said, "just the fire."

He gently unfolded Larry's arms and opened his coat. The beam found a small bloodied tear in Larry's shirt just above the belt line near the lowermost button. With the coat open and the wound agitated from his tumble out the door, a pasty trickle joined the small flow of blood. A bittersweet smell filled the confines of the vehicle.

Al and Pa exchanged unblinking stares. They had smelled enough gut-shot deer over the years. They had also recovered enough of them to know the wound was always fatal, given time.

"What in God's name happened, son?" Pa asked, his voice now quivering. "A stray bullet from the fire?"

"Naw, I've been shot before. Hurts worse than this." Larry tried to crack a smile to ease the worry on their faces, but it drew tight at the effort.

"I couldn't just sit there and let the poor bastard get it in the back," he continued in a shallow voice forced between his teeth, "no one should have to get it like that. By the time I got to my feet and rushed toward him, I couldn't see a thing in the dark and smoke. Next thing I knew I was flying back across the room. Took an antler tine in the belly somehow. Guess the buck was charging back toward the window. Didn't hurt that much then so I figured it hadn't punched anything important. But damn, it's sure on fire now."

Larry dragged the back of his hand across his lips. Thick whitish spittle smeared his cheek. "Sorry, gotta go. Gotta get a drink."

Pa held him fast by the sleeve. "Don't worry, son," he said, gently pressing his folded handkerchief under Larry's shirt. "We'll get you a drink. And we'll get you out of here — tonight."

He took the scarf from the bundle of clothes tossed on the floor and wrapped it around Larry's mid-section. He fumbled with a loose knot over the wound as his hands trembled, finally tying it snugly before rebuttoning Larry's coat.

"We can't leave!" Brad said. His eyes flashed in the dim light as he looked from his dad to Pa.

"We don't even have a gun," he continued. "They burned. If we go out there, that, that thing will get us. You've seen it. Why can't we wait for morning?"

Brad looked to Larry, his eyes pleading. Come on Uncle Larry, tell them about the Manitou, the shape-shifter. It can't hear you in here. Tell them it might be that instead of just a killer buck. Brad blinked at the thought. Just a killer buck? Hell, what's the difference? Does it really matter now? If it is a shape-shifter, it's not about to turn into a harmless mouse. No, it's a buck, real thing or Manitou, a killer buck just the same, and it's out there. It wants us, all, dead. Brad glanced from Pa to Corey, then lowered his eyes to the floor. You know that I'm scared, don't you. I can see the way you're all looking at me. And you probably think that I'm a coward too.

Al reached over the seat and lifted Brad's chin and looked into his son's eyes.

"Brad, listen. We're all scared here. We'd be fools not to be with that deer or whatever it is out there. But your Uncle Larry doesn't have much time. He won't make it until morning. And he can't make it out of here alone."

Al looked at Pa and Corey then back to Brad.

"I don't think we have many options here either," he continued. "I'm afraid you and I are the only ones who can get him out. Corey and your grandfather aren't up to it."

"Bull, Mr. Mercer," Corey said, bolting upright and grabbing the back of the seat. "My side hurts some but my legs aren't broken. I can still help. I'm not staying behind." Corey looked at Larry.

Brad dropped his chin. His cheeks prickled.

"I sure as hell ain't spending the night here either," Pa said, unconsciously spitting the remains of some chewing tobacco on the floor. "I bet that damn thing can ram through one of these car windows almost as easily as it did that plastic. And I sure ain't going to be sitting here twiddling my thumbs watching my boy die when it does."

Brad's jaw tightened. His face flushed.

"I'm going too," he finally said, his chin protruding like a bulldog about to bite. His voice wavered at first then grew steady as he turned toward Larry. "I didn't know how bad Uncle Larry was hurt. I didn't know we couldn't stay. I'm sorry if I sounded like I was only thinking of myself." Brad looked back to his dad. "But I'll help, and we'll get him out of here tonight, together."

Brad turned toward the window and unconsciously rubbed the frost clear again and looked out.

The night had never looked blacker.

CHAPTER 26 — LONE SENTRY

"Maybe we won't have to walk out," Al said, drawing his folding knife from his coat pocket and flicking the blade open. "What do you say we try hot-wiring this thing like Corey suggested. It's only two-wheel drive, but who knows, this old Suburban still has lots of push in deep snow."

Al gave the boys a reassuring grin as he reached under the dash. Corey held the light.

Brad saw past the thin smile and noticed worried lines creasing his dad's face. But as he looked past the worry, he also saw something new — a fresh resolve. He watched as his dad fumbled with the wires under the dash. Just look at you, Dad. You've taken charge of a situation without direction from Vern, Crane, Larry, Pa, or anybody. Maybe you've always been capable of managing things in your own way, using subtle silence, gentle nudging, letting others appear to lead the way. As Brad watched his father's hands grip the wires, it looked as if Al Mercer, emerging wagon master in the night, was solidly taking hold of the reins of their fate.

"No," Corey said, shining the light on Al's face then moving it up toward the ignition. "You first have to bust out the steering column lock, Mr. Mercer."

Eyebrows knotted, Al paused and looked at Corey.

Brad handed his dad the double-bladed axe.

"Here Dad, try this."

Al narrowed an eye at Corey as he put his knife on the dash and tentatively took the axe.

"Hey, I remember some guy in auto-shop class showing me how to do it. I never hot-wired one myself, honest. But I know those wires under there won't help if we can't steer the car, right? So you've got to break out the ignition-steering lock. The wires you need to start it are in there anyway."

"Okay, okay," Al said, nodding his head. "Sounds like it makes sense. Thanks."

Al wedged the sharp axe behind the flange of the steering column lock and twisted it to the side. Brad could see from the way his dad awkwardly handled the axe that he was still a man of computer keyboards and slide rules. But he stifled the impulse to ask if he could help and watched in fascination.

Al grunted as he pulled the handle. The metal flange had just begun to groan when the axe slipped. Al cursed as his knuckles banged against the inside of the steering wheel. He propped the axe blade on his knee and rubbed his hands together.

"Blasted cold," he said, cupping his hands and puffing into them. "Can hardly feel a thing with these fingers."

After flexing his fingers a few times, Al used his right hand to hold the axe blade in place while he pried on the handle with his left. The metal started to groan again. Al began to whisper a slow "yessss" when the steering lock ignition tumbler broke free, bits of metal hitting the dash. The axe lurched then clattered to the floor. Al jerked back his right hand. He tucked it under his armpit. His eyes winced. He sucked in, making a serpentine sound.

"You okay, Dad?"

Al didn't respond. Eyes still closed tight, he began rocking back and forth.

Pa pulled his attention away from Larry and leaned forward on the back of the seat.

"Let's see," he said, reaching over and gently drawing Al's hand from under his arm.

Brad sipped cold air as the flashlight beam settled on his dad's bloodied hand. It drip-dripped onto the cold vinyl seat with the beat of a clock. Al turned his hand palm up to catch the flow of blood and exposed a nasty gash across the webbing between his thumb and index finger. Streaming blood covered most of the gaping wound, but the dangling thumb clearly hung in an unnatural position.

Brad pulled out his handkerchief and offered it to Pa. Without a word, Pa gingerly tucked Al's lolling thumb back in place as best he could then wrapped the whole mess tightly. The bleeding stopped almost immediately. At last, Al let out a heavy breath.

"Damn, I'm a klutz. Can't even hot-wire a stupid car." He hung his head.

"It's okay, Mr. Mercer. Look, you popped out the ignition and steering lock."

Corey slid across the front seat and lifted the mechanism hanging from a series of wires.

"You hit the accelerator, Mr. Mercer, while I spark the wires. I think it's the white one and the yellow one. Or is it that black one?"

Corey continued to mumble to himself as he took Al's knife off the dash and stripped the wires. He held his elbows tight to his sides as he worked and winced each time the jerk of his hand stripped a wire clean. He touched the exposed ends together.

A blue spark snapped across two wires and the engine jumped. Corey touched the wires again. With a low moan that soon ground into a growl, the engine turned over against the cold. It sputtered twice, threatening to die altogether as Al pumped the pedal. Then finally it roared to life. Al flicked on the headlights, the beams slashing holes in the night like sabers. Cheers erupted within the station wagon. Pa clapped. Corey pounded the dash. Brad leaned over the seat and patted his dad on the shoulder.

"Great job, Dad. Great job, Corey."

Al turned and embraced Brad with a smile that appeared to momentarily push away the pain in his hand. His head straightened. Corey folded the knife and slipped it back into Al's jacket pocket.

"Now, let's see if I can drive us out of here."

Hooking his injured hand over the gear lever, Al dropped the car into drive. The transmission whined helplessly in icy-thick fluid for an instant before the clutch caught and the Suburban lurched forward. Cheers rose again. Al began to shout.

"Go-go-go-go—"

The others joined in the chorus.

"GO-GO-GO-GO-GO—"

Inch by inch, the wheels churned and shuddered. The rear tires sifted through the snow, grabbing bits of leaves and twigs, lurching the car forward, spitting out a rooster tail of white. The momentum grew into a steady pace, barely more than that of a slow walk, but a continued pace nonetheless.

The cheering grew. Even Larry cracked an eyelid and grinned. Al began to gently nudge the wheel around with his good hand, nosing the vehicle into the clearing where he could turn around. The vehicle slowed as wheels began pushing sideways through the snow. The back tires spun. The cheering died. Al gave it more gas. Instead of going forward, the Suburban slowed and seemed to slowly sink as if in quicksand.

Al pounded the brakes and threw the vehicle into reverse. It lurched backward a few inches before the rear wheels churned in the snow. He threw it in forward and it bucked again. As it rocked back and forth from gear to gear, the tires dug deeper and deeper, like two workers digging narrow graves.

At last Al thumped his good hand against the steering wheel. They sat in silence for a long moment, only the mixing of their sighs filling the vehicle.

"Maybe I can help by pushing," Brad offered.

"Thanks, but it's no use, son." Al lifted his head and looked at Brad through the dark of the rearview mirror. "If we can't even turn around, we'll never make it up some of the grades on the way out or through the drifts in the low spots. No, we'll have to walk out."

Larry moaned as he shifted his weight. Al flicked on the dome light. Even under the sheen of Larry's sweat-glistened face, his rosy cheeks had faded to a pasty white, resembling a mannequin or a soon-to-be corpse.

"Let's get a move on," Al said, tugging at his collar and grabbing the axe with his good hand. "Brad, you take the light and come with me. The rest of you stay here until we get the toboggan."

Al flicked on the bright lights and stepped out the door. The headlights jumped farther into the night, illuminating a cluster of aspens that looked like skeletons huddled against the cold. Brad hesitated for a second then snatched the light from Corey and followed his dad into the night.

Outside the car, Brad fingered the flashlight switch and swung the beam around back toward the remains of the cabin. Exhaust fumes billowed around the vehicle like a churning Loch Ness fog, swallowing the beam. Beyond the reflection of the exhaust, the night stood black and vacant. Brad stepped along side his dad.

"Here Dad, let's trade. I can swing an axe better with two good hands."

He handed his father the flashlight and took the axe from his dad's grip. He laid it over his shoulder like a batter stepping to the plate and gripped the worn hickory handle until his knuckles ached. Even wearing the light Jersey gloves he had found in his coat pockets, the cold from the handle seeped into his hands. Together they walked through the exhaust curtain and down the tire tracks toward the faint black patch, the sooty outline of the cabin's remains.

Al swung the beam from side to side. Brad's eyes followed every sweep of the light but he saw nothing lurking in the shadows of the timber. Maybe the fire and all the commotion drove it deep into the forest? Yeah, maybe it would stay there long enough for them to make it to safety. Maybe it had filled whatever need made it kill. He sighed. Maybe you're kidding yourself, Brad. Maybe it's time to start dealing with reality.

They slowed as they approached Crane's form stretched out on the toboggan. Brad knelt in the snow and tugged at the knots on the ropes that held the body fast. Fingers stiff, Brad clawed at them to no avail. The fire had melted the snow on the ropes into a wet glaze that had refrozen solid. He took the axe and hacked at the knots with short chops, each one popping under the slice of the sharp blade.

After freeing the ropes, Brad and Al each grabbed an end of the toboggan, tipped it sideways and unceremoniously dumped Crane into the snow. Neither noticed Crane's Mauser tucked in the shadow along the far side of the body. It fell off first and the weight of the bundled corpse pushed it into the snow. Al reached down and grabbed a handful of the blanket wrapping Crane. He pulled on it and the frozen body rolled out like a carnival corndog from a paper wrapper.

Crane landed face up, his glazed eyes staring toward the heavens. Al swung the flashlight beam to the rounded face. Brad glanced down at the mask of death. He wondered if it enraged the old bastard to have some lesser-minded creature seal his fate. Brad stared at the eyes, bulged and distorted from freezing. No, don't see any anger there, just kind of a helpless terror like when something knows it's going to die, feels it's dying, unable to stop it. No wonder his eyes are bugged.

Brad turned away and tried to shake the thought. Well, at least you're no longer guiding every minute of my dad's working life. Who knows, maybe you'll do him more good now than you did in life. Can't be much worse. At least he has a chance to think for himself, us too, now.

Brad gazed skyward. His dad tugged at his arm. He blinked and turned. He nodded. He towed the toboggan as they returned to the car.

Back at the wagon, Al opened the car door to the back seat.

"Okay, Larry on the toboggan first. Brad and I will help him. Corey, bring the blanket after we get Larry settled. Pop, hold the toboggan steady while Brad and I set him down."

Brad listened to the sound of his dad giving orders, orders based on logic and reason, silent traits that must run deep in his dad. They moved about their tasks without comment. Brad and Al moved Larry to the toboggan while Pa kept it from sliding. Corey began to wrap Larry in the blanket.

"Wait," Al said. "Pop, better sit behind him to give him support during the ride. Otherwise, it will be too hard on him."

Pa opened his mouth to protest, but couldn't counter the sense in Al's words. Brad noticed that his dad hadn't pointed out the obvious facts that Pa's heart was probably too frail to make the strenuous walk out through deep snow, or that his aging body couldn't stand the strain.

"Besides," Al continued, "by wrapping both of you in the blanket your body heat will help keep him from going into shock." Pa nodded and huddled behind Larry on the toboggan. He wrapped his arms around Larry's slumped shoulders.

Brad helped Corey bundle the two in the blanket. He tucked part of it tight over Pa's head like a hood and over Larry's big shoulders. What a contrast, father and son; Uncle Larry injured, yet so big and strong, Pa apparently healthy yet so much smaller and helpless now. I guess time has worn away at Pa. Suppose it will make us all smaller and frail someday.

In the stark beam of the flashlight, Brad looked at the husk of a man he too might one day become, if he lived long enough. His eyes shifted to Larry and he saw how much of a man he might become, if he lived long enough to become a man at all.

Al slipped the rope towing harness across his shoulders and tested its fit by leaning into it. The toboggan glided forward a foot. He stopped and turned.

"Brad, you handle the axe and take up the rear. Corey, take the flashlight and make one last check of the wagon to see if there's anything else that might keep us warm or we can use for a weapon. May as well turn the engine off too. Then follow behind the toboggan."

Corey quickly rummaged through the car then turned off the lights and ignition. He stepped out holding Vern's jacket.

"This is all that's left," he said, shaking the jacket.

A muffled tinkle of brass sounded like distant sleigh bells in the night. Corey fished a hand into the pockets. From a large front pocket he withdrew three shells, live rounds for Vern's .270 Model 70 Winchester.

"Only bullets for Vern's rifle," Corey said, cocking his arm to toss them. "Won't do us any good."

He whipped his arm forward.

A hoarse "NO" split the night.

Corey almost released his grip on the shells when the force of that single word made him flinch and clutch his hand. He spun to the sound and was surprised to see Larry sitting fully upright, reaching out.

"No," he said, his words ragged. "Keep them. Crane's gun. Get it. They might work."

"Crap, I forgot," Brad said. "Larry put Crane's custom Mauser along side him on the toboggan. We musta dumped it in the snow."

With Al towing the toboggan and leading the way, they shuffled back to Crane laying in the snow. There, barely showing in the imprint where they had rolled him, glistened the end of the stainless steel barrel of Crane's 30.06.

Brad pulled it from the snow. He brushed it off, revealing the shimmer of ice coating the weapon. Like the knotted ropes, the fire's heat and winter's night had also glazed the rifle.

"Will it work?" Corey asked.

Brad shrugged his shoulders as he scraped away at the ice around the chamber then threw back the bolt. Particles of ice broke free.

"I don't think they would have given you that hunter's ed card," Corey said, handing Brad the three shells, "if they knew you were going to try .270 shells in this big gun."

Without comment, Brad dropped one into the empty chamber. It rattled in loosely and he racked the bolt shut. He turned and extended the rifle looking for someone to hand it to. As he met his father's gaze, the realization struck him.

"You're the only one who can shoot it, son."

Brad looked at the gun then to his dad and back to the gun.

"I can't shoot with this hand," Al continued. "I couldn't even grip it if I wanted to. And Corey couldn't handle that heavy gun even if he could raise it to his shoulder with both arms. He's hurt too bad. Pa can't see without his glasses, especially at night. And Larry — no, you're the only one."

Brad swallowed at something deep in his throat like a giant millipede clawing its way up. I'm the only one? Great, just great. You people are in trouble.

His eyes went from face to face. Dad, I know you're only trying to do what's best for everyone, but, crap, I don't know if I can do it. You don't understand what happens to me when I see a buck.

Hell, I don't even understand. If I only had your logic. His mind began to churn.

He looked to Corey. Best friend, life saver, if I could only be the same for you. I wish I could, really. Wish I had your balls too. His stomach tightened.

Brad made a noise under his breath and looked to Pa who had done so much to make him ready for a moment like this. If only I had your experience, Pa.

He glanced down at Larry. Nothing would scare you, not even a Manitou, I bet. Imagine what I could do with some of your courage.

At last Brad looked back to the gun. He gripped it tighter. A new hotness flushed his face. He looked up at his father and nodded.

"Let's do it, Dad," he said, his voice uncertain at first, gaining force as the words flowed. "With three miles to go we better make some tracks."

Even in the darkness, Brad saw an odd gleam in his dad's eyes before Al turned and leaned into the harness. Clutching the axe in his good hand, Al lunged forward and the toboggan followed, hissing like a bobcat as it skimmed over the snow.

Corey shuffled after it, the beam of his flashlight dancing across the ground. His boots squeaked in the bitter air, each step crunching loudly in the calm.

Cradling the big rifle, finger on the safety, Brad brought up the rear. He looked over his shoulder. It's so quiet, that thing has to hear all this commotion. And it's sure to smell us; this many humans in this pure air, Larry's burnt hair, the blood. Well, with all this noise, at least it won't hear my heart hammering.

Brad trotted onward. The cold air splashed his face. It filled his lungs. It tingled his senses. He drank in another sweet lung full. God, I've never felt so alive before, so important. Is this how men feel going into battle? I'll have to ask Uncle Larry someday — if someday ever comes. Maybe this is how men feel before they die? Guess dawn will answer that one.

CHAPTER 27 — OUTBREAK

As Dr. Nolstrum pulled into his parking space near the Personnel entrance, he noticed lights shining from most of the cell block windows. Odd, it was well past lights-out and the shadowy flickers of officers running down corridors made his stomach churn. The scene looked more like a full-scale prison riot than a medical problem he had been summoned to solve. He paused halfway out of his car, poised on the open door, looking in disbelief, wishing he could slip back behind the wheel and simply drive off into the night. Whatever outbreak the deputy warden had been babbling about, it seemed to be spreading like a jackpine fire.

He slammed the door and ran toward the security entrance. The posted officer inside the entrance window was waving him on like the sole cheering section at the finish line of a marathon. As Nostrum neared, he noticed panic in the man's face. Damn, he thought, shouldering his way through the doors, this is going to be more than I can handle, more than I signed up for.

Once an overworked general practitioner without enough free time to enjoy his beloved trout fishing, Nolstrum had thought that taking the job as prison physician would be the answer to his prayers. At first it seemed the ideal blend of soft hours and the cushy benefits of State employment. Treating wards of the State, he no longer had to worry about the burdensome cost of malpractice insurance, and without the expense of a staff or offices, he looked forward to a financially comfortable retirement. But like everything else in life that often looked too good to be true, it was.

Nolstrum left private practice to rid himself of the constant parade of whining kids with runny noses and overwrought parents. In an odd way he thought treating inmates forty hours a week would be a fresh yet easy-paced challenge. But behind the gray walls he soon discovered another constant parade — one of clever hypochondriacs looking for free handouts of drugs or a waiver from work detail. Even the legitimate cases quickly became a drudgery, treating the foulest of diseases in the foulest of men. In time, the drudgery led to a depression that followed him beyond the stone walls. He even carried it to the secluded trout streams where he retreated to forget work. In the end he realized he was only patching up caged piles of garbage so they could rot behind bars in good health while devouring taxpayer's dollars. Human parasites till the end, once preying on society outside the walls, now living freely off them from within.

Now it looked as if his infirmary would soon be packed with them. If not for the oath, he would have turned back into the night. But he had taken it once; and even though it was many years ago, he still believed in its ideals. So he pushed through the next lockout door, wearing a scowl, and ran down the long hall that led to the infirmary. One way or another he would try to clean up whatever mess awaited him.

The doctor had just hung up his coat when the warden came charging through the infirmary's swinging doors. Noted for a stoic demeanor as solid as the prison's granite walls, the warden's face looked unusually pale, his mouth hung agape.

"God almighty," he said, more to himself than the doctor, "I never imagined it could get this bad. How could I have let it happen? I'm finished here, washed up for good. I'll be lucky if they don't incarcerate me after this."

He rubbed weary eyes and looked at the doctor. He drew in a long breath as if he were about to explain all he knew of the outbreak but decided against it and simply lifted his trembling palms as if begging for help.

"Come," he said, "please come, now."

The doctor quickly slid into his white jacket, pockets perpetually stuffed with his standard examining fare. He began buttoning it as he took off after the warden. Trotting along, he pulled the stethoscope from one of the large pockets and clipped it behind his neck. Their feet slapped the concrete as they made their way down the corridor toward the central prison. The warden slowed for the doctor to catch up then grabbed him by the arm. He resumed his pace, pulling the doctor along as if the older man needed either physical or inspirational help to keep up.

"Looks like a case of mass poisoning," the warden explained. "Shortly after all the confusion started, an officer found the head cook, Stone, hanging dead from the bars of his cell. Said he found some kind of suicide note too. Haven't seen it yet though. The deputy warden said there was nothing out of order logged on the mess shift but I've got him checking with the head officer on duty then. Also sent a detail to see if they could find out what Stone may have used."

"Any idea how many have been affected?" The doctor's voice trailed off weakly.

"Looks like about a third so far," the warden said, "most of them are lifers. Tough to tell for sure. Some are howling like hell while others are just sitting there, draining out slowly."

The doctor skidded to a halt, dragging the warden to a stop with him.

"Draining out? What do you mean, draining out?"

The warden swallowed as if about to clear his throat then shook his head.

"No, I'm no medical man. It's better if you see for yourself."

The officer buzzed open the double security gates to the first cell block. The warden led the way. Standing in front of the nearest cell the shift commander and another officer turned and snapped to attention.

"Sorry to let him sit there like that sir," the commander said, glancing back at the cell. He wiped his palms on his black pants, leaving a sweaty sheen. "Couldn't let the nurses in either. Everyone's screaming for them. Only two on duty tonight, and... well, there's just too many like this — " The man shook his head and looked into the cell again.

The warden nodded without comment then motioned to the officer and pointed to the cell. The officer fumbled with the key ring then turned the lock. The warden swung the door open. The doctor stepped inside. The warden followed. There in the corner of the cell, head hung and sobbing, sat a small-time thug named Jersey who once had big ideas about armed robbery. Dr. Nolstrum approached the man and stooped in front of him.

"What seems to be the—" the doctor began as he reached out and lifted Jersey's chin. Nolstrum gasped and reared back.

"Oh my God," he hissed.

Although the doctor had seen his share of gore inside the joint, the sight of the weeping man still caught him by surprise. It wasn't that he hadn't seen men cry before or seen plenty of blood. But it sure as hell was the first time he had seen one crying blood.

Streaming from the corners of Jersey's eyes and flowing down his cheeks like red ribbons of lava, blood soaked his shirt and lap. He reached up to wipe away the tears, smearing his face with red. He blinked several times, as if trying to clear his vision, spilling more blood from the corners of his eyes. He finally looked up toward the doc, seemingly blind, the once whites of his eyes a purple mess of bleeding vessels. The doctor lowered his stare and noticed a watery flow of blood also draining from the nose and mixing with the growing pool. He shuffled back from the man. Jersey's sobbing increased, the tick-tick of blood dripping from his chin adding to the puddle between his legs.

Nolstrum spun and took a step. He rubbed his hand across his forehead and took several deep breaths. He paused for a moment then shook his head. This time he grabbed the warden by the arm. He pulled him out and toward the next cell. The officer opened the door. They stepped inside.

Draped over the rim of the lone sink at the rear of the cell, a large black man gagged and spit. Nolstrum approached him. The man turned and coughed. Blood sprayed from his lips, spattering the doctor's whites.

"Damn, I'm sorry, Doc," the inmate said, tentatively reaching out to wipe off Nolstrum's jacket then pulling his hand back to cover his mouth.

"Thought I brushed my teeth too hard when my friggin' gums started bleeding and wouldn't stop. Then I heard the talk about poison or somthin'. What's goin' on, Doc.? How bad is it? Can you help me?"

Nolstrum looked into the man's eyes and saw the confusion and fear of a child.

"Sure, sure we can help you," Nolstrum said, painting his best calm doctor face. "We just need you to take it easy while I get a few things ready to treat you. We'll have you in the infirmary and feeling better soon."

Dr. Nolstrum didn't like lying to his patients but considered it better than the widespread panic the truth would surely bring. Again, he led the warden by the arm. They walked through the outer lockout doors to an isolated section of corridor.

"Appears to be some kind of poison all right. Probably a blood thinner, possibly a derivative of coumadin."

"Couma-what?" the warden asked.

"Coumadin. It's a blood thinner I prescribe for patients with arterial or heart problems. It thins the blood and dissolves clots. I don't stock enough to have caused anything as widespread as this. Besides, my stores are accounted for. It was used in rodent poison years ago. But it was so damned lethal they stopped using it. Maybe Stone somehow got his hands on an old carton of rat poison."

"The supply rooms!" the warden said.

"What?"

"The supply rooms have shelves full of outdated stuff used for maintenance and prison programs. The system requires three times more paperwork to get rid of the junk rather than store it. Must be several administration's of garbage jammed in there. No telling what Stone found in that chamber of horrors."

"But aren't the supply rooms limited access?"

"Not to a head cook with the stroke Stone has. Hell, he could probably get into any place in here expect for the administration offices." The warden paused, staring at the brick wall. "If Stone used poison from those supply rooms —"

He fingered his lower lip. The repercussions of the thought appeared too much to contemplate for the moment. The doctor's grip on his arm tightened.

"If we're going to save lives, then we have to pull out all the stops. Are you with me?" The doctor shook the warden by the arm, attempting to reel his wandering thoughts back in like a hooked trout running downstream.

"Yes, of course. Whatever you say. What should I do?"

"I'll call in our intern and the emergency backup staff and get them down here, stat. We'll also need four details of officers to start shuttling patients to the infirmary. But even stacking them between beds it will be overflowing in no time. We'll have to pull in County General on this one."

The warden shook his head. His eyes cleared and widened.

"No way! My residents stay here. Whatever you need to treat them — people, supplies, whatever — have it brought in. No one leaves these gates."

Color flushed the doctor's cheeks. He yanked the stethoscope from his neck and shook it in the warden's face.

"If you force me to attempt mass transfusions on hundreds of men who all need immediate attention, you'll be taking them out the gate by the truckload — in body bags. This isn't the flu we're dealing with here. These men are bleeding to death one way or another. And the only way to save their lives, is with mass action, now."

The doctor paused. He saw wheels of doubt churning behind the warden's shifting eyes.

"Listen," Nolstrum continued, "Country General can quickly put together a half-dozen trauma teams. They've got stockpiles of whole blood, the support people, and the facilities to handle this type of situation. What they don't have is bars and officers. And you can supply the officers. But believe me, none of these poisoned residents are in any condition to go running off."

The warden scratched an ear lobe. He looked over his shoulder toward the sounds of moans rising from the cell block then back to Nolstrum.

"Okay, but under strict conditions. You only send the most critical patients; the ones who physically couldn't cause problems if they wanted to. The rest stay here under your care. Sorry, that's the best I can do. I can't afford any more screw ups."

The doctor squeezed his stethoscope as if he were strangling a massasauga rattler about to strike. He wondered if the warden was more concerned about his civil service butt than the welfare of the inmates under his care. Still, Nolstrum knew there was no use in arguing. He had worked with the man long enough to know when to shut up and get to the task at hand. Besides, he could always stretch a diagnosis if need be. He nodded.

"Fine," the warden said, a sense of control returning to his face. "You get on the horn to Country General and tell them what you need and what to expect from this end. I'll arrange the officer details for the hospital and the transportation. But no one leaves here without my personal approval. You understand?"

"You're the warden."

"Good. Let's get to it."

The two men turned in opposite directions, the warden hurrying to his office, the doctor heading for the infirmary.

As the doctor rushed down the corridor, an old sense of exhilaration swept through him. He wasn't thrilled with the misery scores of inmates would be suffering in the coming hours or the vital importance his role would play. Ironically, for the first time in years he would be fighting an identifiable evil that could kill his patients. And he wanted to help them. Not only for the oath, but for the inmates who had suddenly been reduced to a constant parade of children with runny noses — draining their life's blood maybe, but with runny noses just the same.

CHAPTER 28 – THE TREK

The only pair of snow-shoes had burned along with the cabin. They had hung on the wall mostly for decoration Brad figured. He had never seen them used. But surely the way his feet now slipped and sank through the knee-deep snow, they would have helped. He wondered if the others were having as much trouble.

A black shadow leading their way, his father leaned into the rope harness pulling the toboggan and pushed on into the darkness. Al's leather boots plowed into the snow, disrupting the intricate lace work of snowflakes recrystalized by the frigid temperatures. The dry arctic air had refrozen the white blanket into countless spicules of ice that sifted like sugar around his feet. For each step Al took, he lost a quarter step. But for a middle-aged desk jockey he still kept up a fair gait, especially considering the load he was towing.

Huddled under the blanket on the toboggan, Pa held Larry as best he could. Still, the swaying of the ride caused them to shift about, bringing grunts from both. Pa's eyes watered against the spray of snow kicked up from Al's feet. He squinted and hung on.

Behind the toboggan, Corey managed to keep up. He clutched his injured side with one hand. He held the six-volt flashlight with the other. Its beam bounced off the backs of Al and Pa, casting willowy shadows that lurched across the sparkling snow. The beam also flicked from side to side as he trudged along. It made the flat silhouettes of oaks and aspens lining the trail jump to life in three dimensional forms that appeared to leap out toward the hunters, only to retreat as dark shadows when the beam danced away. The snow churned under his feet. For each step he took, he lost a third.

Close on Corey's heels, Brad brought up the rear. He cradled Crane's Mauser in the crook of his arm, his thumb poised near the safety, his index finger riding lightly on the trigger. The heat from his hand had melted the glaze of ice from around the grip, wetting the fingers of his Jersey gloves. And despite the cold that seeped from the rifle through his gloves and into his hands, he held the weapon like the girl of his dreams, tender yet firm. His head swept from side to side like radar as he walked briskly, his eyes straining for any sign of the buck. They had made over two hundred yards so far without a glimpse of it. Maybe they would make it out without an encounter. But then again they still had nearly three miles to go. Maybe he was hoping for too much. Brad tried to step into Corey's boot prints for easier walking, but the smooth soles of his boots slid and floundered. For each step he took, he seemed to lose a half. The snow washed around his feet like the fine sand of an hourglass.

Brad glanced down at the heavy rifle for an instant then looked back into the shadows. With its stainless barrel and big scope, it weighed considerably more than his old Winchester, but its heft balanced delicately in his hands. The rifle was equipped with a variable power scope, not that it would do him much good in the dark. But the over-under scope mount allowed him to peer through the oval opening under the scope and view the sights beyond. In the darkness the sights weren't much more than gray shapes but at least sighting through the oval rings created a natural field of fire for any close-range target. As he slowed and shouldered the rifle, pretending to take aim in the dark, Brad recalled Larry's last comment — maybe it will work.

The word, *maybe* caused a gentle ripple of doubt to begin chewing at his thoughts. He remembered the sound of Vern's .270 shell rattling in the chamber of the big gun before he slid the bolt closed. Would it fire? Or would it misfire and cause the breech to explode in his face, brass shrapnel tearing out his eyes a split second before the searing flash of gunpowder scorched his shredded face like a burger on a grill?

Another doubt hit as he realized that he hadn't checked the barrel for obstructions. If the melting snow and refreezing had coated the outside with ice, how much coated the inside of the barrel? Could the bullet tear it free or might that also cause a misfire? He tried to shake the thought, his mind probing the possibilities. And as his eyes lowered back to the gun, it dredged up the final scenario. Maybe the shell wouldn't fire at all, the firing pin striking short because of the mismatched bullet in the chamber. Maybe he would raise the gun, take careful aim at the killer buck bearing down on him, only to "click" softly before the charge toppled him backwards, the long tines robbing his life in the night.

Brad glanced up just in time to keep from running into Corey, who had stopped behind the toboggan. The faint outline of his father stood frozen on the crest of a rise, his arm held rigidly back with his palm up. He eased toward his father, gun poised. Corey joined his side and shined the light down the trail.

Ahead, the two-track dropped down a gentle slope toward the east branch of Deadman's Creek and the swamp that bordered it. The dark shapes of spruce and cedar crowded near the trail there, begrudging space to the oaks and aspens that lined the higher ground. The black figures of conifers appeared furry in the probing light, as if a tight pack of beasts lay crouched, patiently waiting for prey to draw near.

"See something?" Brad whispered.

"No, just a feeling, that's all."

Brad knew his father as a man of logic and reason, and hearing the word *feeling*, as if were some sixth sense, caused him to pull his eyes from the trail and look at his father. Al turned his head slightly and cupped a hand to his ear. In the faint side wash of the flashlight, Brad saw the taut muscles in his dad's face and the keen glare in his eyes. It appeared as if a deeper sense had sprung to life in his father, nudging aside the plodding man from the city, freeing the able woodsman that lurked within. They stood in silence for a moment listening. Only the sound of their heavy breathing filled the emptiness.

"Maybe it's nothing," Al said. "But it's probably a good idea if we rest here a minute before pushing on. We may have to hurry through the section along the swamp. I don't like the looks of the place."

They stood listening, waiting, unsure.

"That's why you haven't seen it yet," Pa said, his voice hoarse from the cold.

"What do you mean?" Brad asked. He huddled close to the toboggan, afraid that somewhere in the dark tuned ears were listening.

"We're not dealing with a stupid animal like Crane or Vern thought. Why do you think it waited until Crane was alone and out of ammo to strike? And what better place and time to kill a hunter than at night inside his own cabin where the rifles would be unloaded and safely tucked away in the gun rack?"

"You mean this thing thinks and plans how it's going to attack?" Corey asked, his whisper coming in puffs of steam.

"That's what I mean. I don't know if it's a Manitou or what. I'm not much for Indian legends. But it sure as hell ain't no ordinary buck crazy with rabies. No telling what we're dealing with."

"You think it will attack us down there?" Brad asked, nodding toward the swamp.

"Can't say," Pa said. "If I was a wise buck and had my mind set on finishing you off, I'd strike where you had the least warning, the worst defense."

"Like down there along the dense cover of the swamp," Al said.

"Yep," Pa said, turning his head. "Or maybe it's waiting until we're tired or let our guard down — like now."

Brad snapped around looking for movement or the faint glow of crescent eyes in the dark. Corey flashed the beam through the sparse timber. Nothing stirred.

"No matter where or when it strikes," Pa continued, his eyes falling heavily on Brad, "it will try to take out the one with the gun first. It knows where the major threat lies."

Brad shifted his grip on the rifle as if it had suddenly taken on an unbearable weight. God, I wish someone else could shoot this thing. He glanced at the others. No, don't be dumb. It's up to me, even if this gun marks me as its next victim. I couldn't pass that sentence on to Dad, Pa, Larry, or Corey. Brad hafted the gun tighter in the crook of his arm. Maybe I could toss it into the snow, be rid of its curse altogether. No, that's stupid too. Then the buck would just go after the guy with the axe. He looked at his dad. Nope, no way out. I guess if wishes were wings, frogs wouldn't bump their butts when they hopped.

Larry poked his head out from underneath the blanket.

"Stick close," he said weakly. "Don't let it draw you apart. Safety in numbers. Vary your pace. Don't become predictable. Move together like a single deer. Watch for —"

Quivering from cold or pain, possibly both, Larry's words trailed off and he drew the blanket back over his head, snuggling deep within his cocoon.

Despite the glazed, almost crazy look in Larry's eyes as he rambled, Brad digested his every word. Uncle Larry had said *it* again. Did he mean a buck or Manabozho? He said the shape-shifter lives in the swamp. Hmmm. Safety in numbers. Does that mean it might charge a lone man if it thought it could stab quick and retreat? But maybe not five. Yeah, stick together.

The others pondered Larry's meaning as well. And under the sprinkling of star beams, they huddled around the toboggan forming a plan, their voices mixed whispers that sounded like an errant wind in the trees.

CHAPTER 29 — ENCOUNTER

Brad took a deep breath as they headed down the trail toward the swamp. They walked in tight unison now, Al's pull rope shortened so his heels almost brushed the front of the toboggan. One step behind the toboggan's spray, Corey swung the flashlight beam back and forth in measured sweeps like a stalag guard behind a spot light. Brad walked a yard behind him, his head tracking the probing light, his rifle swinging side to side in a combat stance. As they neared the first bunch of cedars hugging the trail, Al stopped. Corey froze. Brad stiffened.

They stood in silence, each one canting his head, listening in the deathly calm for any sound of an approaching deer. Although the darkness cast an inky curtain over their ability to see the buck coming, their collective hearing still reached far into the night. Though the snow might muffle hooves biting earth, the buck couldn't move through the tangle of the swamp without creating a betraying sound. If it came, they should hear it.

Moments later, Al resumed his pace. His legs glided through the snow in long strides. Corey and Brad followed in tight formation, their boots swish-swishing through the snow. The toboggan made a muffled sizzling sound like bacon frying in a covered skillet.

Approaching a small opening in the tangle, Al stopped abruptly. Again, Corey and Brad rooted in their tracks. For an instant, Brad thought he heard a clipped noise, a faint brushing sound that stopped a split second after he did. He hadn't heard it long enough to get a fix on its position or even be sure it was real. Still, his pulse quickened. He held his breath to hear better. Only the drum roll of his heart and the slight rasp of his neck turning against his coat collar filled his ears. His eyes followed the narrow beam knifing the darkness, slitting such a small niche in the vastness of the night. So many shadows for the buck to hide in, the beam touching so few. Steam rose from his resumed breathing, clouding his view. He bobbed his head to the side to see better and blew his breath downward. But the probing light, penetrating the dark, only illuminated the stiff forms of trees.

Like a cautious whitetail moving through timber, Al hurried past the small opening. Nearly-grown yearlings hugging his flank, Corey and Brad scampered behind the toboggan in tow. They repeated the stop-and-go pattern again and again, eating up dangerous sections of the swamp. Al had been timing his pauses near natural openings to give them the advantage of a clear field of fire if a shot presented itself, but now the black fingers of the swamp closed in around them, crowded branches reaching from the trail's edge like gnarled fingers, grabbing at coat sleeves. A wall of cedars and spruces packed each side of the trail, thick and black against the night. The long silvery ribbon of road disappeared into the gloom. The needles of the conifers stripped away the faint aura of starlight leaving them standing in a hollow blackness.

Without another opening to stop near, Al was forced to pause and listen in the thick of it. Brad's boots crunched to a stop when he heard the snap of a twig behind him. He spun at the sound. Corey heard it too and swung the light beam toward the noise. A wall of branches blocked the beam. But somewhere beyond in the tangle of trees an antler scraped against a branch. Brad flicked off the safety as he brought the rifle to his shoulder. His finger touched the trigger. He peered through the scope mount. His heart raced. He began panting. The rifle started bobbing with the rhythm of his ragged breaths.

Brad stood aiming into the maze of trees, looking for a glimpse of a target to shoot at. The rifle sagged. It's so heavy, I can't hold it forever. Damn it, where are you? He jerked toward another faint sound in the dark. Maybe if I fire in that direction, I might hit the thing or scare it away. He touched the trigger. No, wait! What if the gun misfires? Don't risk it. Wait until you have to shoot. The barrel swayed lower. Just when it felt as if the sagging rifle would drop from his grasp, he heard his father take off down the trail again, this time with urgency in his pace.

The light beam bounced as Corey took off after the toboggan, still trying to illuminate the spot in the brush.

Brad whipped his head around. What's happening? He tried to turn and run but his boots seemed frozen in the snow. Wait, don't leave me. Larry said to stick together, don't let it separate us. Damn it, what's going on? Brad started to run, almost tripping as he tried to scuttle sideways while keeping an eye behind him. Finally he turned full around, sprinting after the others. The bouncing flashlight beam swept past his eyes, blinding him for a second. Branches stung his face, spruce needles raked his cheeks. He raised his arm to shield himself and was thrown sideways. Something grabbed his foot. No, let go. With a gasp, he tumbled headlong into darkness. Stabbing pain ripped along his neck and forehead. Agh, get back. He struck out at his attacker, only to discover the sharp branches of a dead cedar.

Still clutching the gun, Brad scrambled to his feet and looked about. He had stumbled only a few feet off the trail. He turned and saw the shadows of the others still trotting down the road. Crap, they didn't even seen me fall. The buck could have gored me and they wouldn't have noticed. Great, some plan. He gritted his teeth and ran after them, his legs pumping hard, the snow spraying around his boots like water. He caught up to them when they stopped where the trees thinned back from the trail.

"Why did you leave me behind?" he said. "I coulda been killed."

"If we stood there any longer you might have been," Al said, panting. "Saw a shadow through the trees. It was flanking you. Brad, you've got to stay more alert, son. When we took off it knew one of us spotted it and it sneaked back into the thick stuff."

Brad stomped his feet in the snow. How could I be so stupid to just stand there and think the buck would step into the light? What a jerk. Keep it up and I'll be a dead jerk. Then maybe Crane and Vern will let me join the dead jerk's society.

"You mean this friggin' thing is that calculating?" Corey asked.

"'Fraid so," Al said. "And we can't dally here any longer. Gotta keep it off guard. Can't do any one thing too long. Stick to the plan as best you can. It won't be giving up now. Will probably try for us again before we leave this part of the swamp. maybe within the next two hundred yards."

Al choked up his grip on the handle of the axe. He strained against the tow rope then paused. He looked over his shoulder.

"Do your best, son. God help us all."

He turned and sluffed down the trail, the toboggan skimming after him.

"Good luck, Buwana. Punch it a new belly button." Corey grinned then was off too, the light beam again sweeping the sides of the trail ahead.

Brad trotted behind him in the spray of his boots. Despite the immense burden of their words, Brad held the Mauser high with new vigor in his arms.

With less than a hundred yards to go before breaking free from the confines of the swamp, Al stopped again. Corey halted, sweeping the light on the trail ahead.

Brad readied the rifle. A voice cried out from his subconscious. Behind you, look behind you.

He glanced back over his shoulder in the opposite direction, and there, not thirty yards away, floated a pair of glowing crescents, like two errant fireflies cast out of a time warp into the dead of winter.

Brad gasped. He shouldered the rifle. But before he could draw aim on the glowing eyes, they vanished. Still pointing the rifle, he tracked the direction they had floated.

There, much closer, only twenty yards, the eyes flickered past an opening in the brush. He snapped the safety forward. He fingered the trigger. Gone too fast. Damn, no time for a clear shot. Wait, there it is. Another flicker, fireflies drawing closer. He snapped his head toward Corey.

"This way, Corey," Brad hissed, "shine your light over —"

The light swung in the direction of his barrel when a splintering of branches broke the calm. Brad flinched and pressed his cheek against the stock. Through the oval openings under the scope the buck bounded into view. Twigs flew through the air in a spray of snow. The light danced off its chest then flooded its face. The buck skidded to a halt not ten yards away.

"Shoot! Shoot! For God's sake shoot the son-of-a-bitch!"

The words became but a faint echo in Brad's ears, only registering as background static against the ringing in his head. The buck stood there, swaying its deadly rack as if to dodge the beam in its face. Dried blood coated its dagger-like tines. A thick layer of red gore covered the thick hair on its forehead.

Brad stared trancelike at the cluster of tines, struggling for breath, his mind running beyond reason. Just look at them, perfectly pointed, each one long enough to pierce a man's chest. Were they genetically designed for that? Geez, then how many hunters over the ages have felt the stab of those things? How many others like you turned the tables through time, becoming hunters to save yourselves from the likes of us?

Brad looked for some hint in the mysterious eyes. A numbness gripped the rest of his senses. They weren't the sheep-eyes of other deer he had seen. They didn't hold that flat gaze lacking emotion, comprehension. These were probing things, like deep pools of yellow oil. Even squinting against the light, they reached out for him with a hate that made his scalp tingle. Steam jetted from its nose like a fire-breathing demon. Its ears laid back. It pawed at the trail with its front hooves, snow flying back into the cedars.

Blinking away the water clouding his eyes, Brad finally broke free of their spell. He focused over the sights. He held his breath. Somehow, he managed to squeeze the trigger.

He squinted and braced himself against the kick of the big gun or the misfire. Feeling no burning flash of gunpowder, he opened his eyes. The buck still stood wavering, eyes narrowed, turning its head away from the light. No bullet hole. No blood. Just a giant deer standing unscathed. More static words broke through the ring.

"Dry-fire, dry-fire! Try another shell. Quick!"

The realization struck Brad like an antler tine into his heart; the gun hadn't fired. Major crap. He gulped cold air and yanked back on the bolt. He fumbled in his pocket for another shell. The buck advanced on stiff legs. Brad shuffled backward as his fingers drew the shell from his pocket. He jammed it into the dark chamber. It wouldn't go. He jammed harder. It clicked something. More voices came to him.

"Hurry! Shoot!"

His mind floundered for a second before unraveling the confusion. The first shell was still jammed in the barrel. The bolt had failed to eject it. Brad yanked off the cotton glove with his teeth and clawed at the shell. His fingertips had gone numb, they wouldn't respond.

He heard the swishing of boots behind him. The light stayed fixed in the buck's eyes. Must be his dad. His fingers nudged the shell. It broke free. He pulled it loose and tossed it aside. He looked up. The buck inched closer, now only yards away with its nose in the snow to avoid the light, the eyes reflecting the glow of the beam, squinted almost shut. His father nudged him aside as he swung the axe high and yelled a guttural scream, the primeval cry of a parent protecting its young.

The buck wheeled in a mighty bound. The axe sliced snow and earth. A brief flash of white tail filled the beam and was gone.

"Holy crap, Mr. Mercer. You almost got him." Corey shouted. "Man, did you see the way you scared him away with that axe. He's probably still running."

Brad looked down at the axe in his dad's hand. It didn't seem like much of a weapon. Maybe the buck had fled because of the scream instead. Brad looked at his dad's trembling hands.

"The light," Pa said.

They turned to him. His face was drawn and pale in the wash of the flashlight. His eyes appeared to stare far into the darkness.

"What about the light?" Al asked.

"It ran from the light, not the axe. Blinded by it. More than a deer should. Never seen one squint like that. Must be something wrong with its eyes, if it's a deer. Its eyes —"

"Cool," Corey said. He swept the light around in a full circle, probing the shadows. "I'm like Luke Skywalker with a light saber. Ha, when the buck gets near, I'll just zap him in the eyes with the beam. That'll take the fight out of him."

Brad let the rifle sag in his arms. He sighed. Damn, the dry-fire round caused me to miss that perfect chance. I'm sure I had it square in my sights. We would have been rid of it. But now? It's still out there somewhere, probably already planning its next move. Brad looked at Corey waving the light. Crap, with this gun useless, that flashlight is its biggest threat. Maybe it will try to take out Corey next. Luke Skywalker or not, he's injured. He might not be able to dodge the buck's lunge.

"Let me have the flashlight," Brad said, reaching out. "This gun's a waste. The buck knows that now."

Corey yanked back the light.

"Forget it. I'm doing just fine with my light saber."

Brad grabbed for it.

"No." rose a weak voice from under the blanket.

Brad stopped and turned. The blanket shifted and Larry moved with a groan.

"Gun might be okay," he managed, his voice cracking. "Didn't hear the pin click."

"The firing pin?" Brad asked.

"All it's been through, might be iced up," Larry said, his head barely sticking out from under the blanket. "Try pulling the trigger on an empty chamber."

Brad pocketed the shell still in his hand and racked the bolt closed. He pulled the trigger. The gun made a dull tunk.

"No, still froze," Larry said. "Try again."

Brad racked open the bolt and scraped at the pin opening with his finger. It was too dark to tell if any ice came off. He closed the bolt and pulled the trigger again. This time he felt the sharp "tink" of the pin breaking free.

"Think I got it."

"Sounds like it," Larry said, covering his head. "You'll know next time you squeeze her." His words faded from under the blanket.

"Good, 'cause we gotta go," Al said. "We've lingered here too long. More than halfway to go yet. Load the gun, Brad. Corey, stay alert with that light. Let's hit the trail."

Brad noticed the crumpled brow and brief flash in Corey's eyes as he turned after the toboggan. Brad reached out to grab him by the arm but let him go. Geez Corey, the one time I try to maybe save your life and you won't even let me. Maybe you'll understand later after I explain, or maybe if you think about it long enough I won't have to explain at all.

As Brad rushed after the others, he noticed that his eyes had grown more accustomed to the darkness. The shadows between the tangled trees no longer held a sooty blackness. He could now distinguish the gray web work of branches against the shadowed snow. Away from the flashlight beam, the trail glimmered in silken shades of blue. Maybe the shifting stars shown brighter. Or possibly northern lights shimmered from above. Then, as he looked at the light beam again, he realized with a pang that the night had brightened not from a heavenly force, but because the flashlight beam had started to fade and his eyes had adjusted more to the darkness.

The cold, the constant draw on the battery, and the jostling had all taken their toll on the light. Their saber of safety was fading quickly.

With so far to go, he knew the light would never make it.

He wondered if they would either.

CHAPTER 30 — FADING FAST

Brad nervously glanced over his shoulder into the darkness. No glowing eyes appeared in the trail. No dark shadows slinked through the timber. Good, maybe it gave up, got tired of the chase or feared the light. Or maybe it realized how close it came to Dad giving it a permanent part down its forehead. Wow, that was close. Or maybe it was Dad's scream that's keeping it away. God, I never imagined he had it in him. It was like he was a madman for a moment. Even scared me and I was already scared. Well, whatever the reason, I hope it stays away.

Brad shook his head at the irony of the thought. Here I've been daydreaming for the past year of getting a buck in my sights. Heck, any buck would do, even a spike would have been enough, maybe more than enough. And now this, this thing with its magnificent rack. But with bloodied tines and those eyes, now it's the last thing I want to see. Ever.

He picked up his pace and neared Corey. He noticed the flashlight beam was now lighting the dark more like a candle in the fog. Can't Corey see it's dying. Maybe he should turn it off, save what's left in case it charges again. But maybe it's been keeping it at bay all along and has already saved us from other ambushes. No, rather than put us in greater danger with my big mouth, I better just keep quiet. Besides, Dad and Corey have to see it's growing dimmer, if they haven't already. He looked over his shoulder again. I hope we're the only ones that see it's fading. He gripped the rifle tighter.

At last they distanced themselves from the oppressing confines of the swamp. The tangle of conifers in the low ground thinned to scattered groves of aspen and clusters of oaks. A few giant red pines towered in the night like lofty sentries standing in silent watch over the rest of the forest. Star beams filtered brightly past the leafless branches of the aspens along the trail, lighting the snow with glittering facets of pale blue.

Ahead near the trail the silhouette of the ancient burned out pine stump stood like a hunched black bear and marked the halfway point. Only one more thick section of swamp, The Narrows, separated them from the final aspen flats leading to the main road,

Larry's Jeep, and safety. Up ahead Brad's father must also have felt safer in the open timber. Al slowed the pace.

Brad lowered the gun into the crook of his arm and reached up and massaged his neck. The sifting snow, the cold, and endless trudging through the night after the longest day of his life had drained him completely. His legs shuffled on with the jerky strides of a puppet rather than the flow of flesh and bone. As the party slowed even more, Brad's thigh muscles stiffened. He reached down to rub them. The dampness of perspiration in his longjohns drew in the numb air. Goose bumps raised on his legs. His calves knotted. At last Al stopped on a small rise.

"How much farther, Mr. Mercer?" Corey asked between breaths, still clutching his injured side.

"Less than a mile, I suppose. Mostly open country." Al braced his hands on his thighs and leaned forward, breathing heavily. Sweat matted a few strands of hair sticking out from under his cap. Plumes of steam rose into the air as he fought to catch his breath.

"Sorry I can't go any faster," he said, wiping condensation away from the stubble around his mouth. "Too many years behind a desk I guess."

Brad reached out and touched his shoulder. "Hey, you're doing great, Dad, just great. Even with the load you're pulling, you're almost leaving Corey and me behind."

Al straightened and starlight reflected a faint twinkle in the corners of his eyes. He spread his shoulders wide and adjusted the rope harness.

"Oh no," Corey grunted as he tapped the flashlight then shook it. "Awh man, my light saber is giving out." He turned to the others, holding out the light. "Now what?"

"Turn it off and tuck it under your coat." Al said flatly, as if he had known it was fading for some time. "Maybe giving it a rest and warming it up with your body heat will make the battery last a bit longer. I think we're safe in the open here for now. Just save what juice it's got left until we near the swamp along The Narrows."

"Maybe we won't need it, Dad. Looked like you scared it away back there in the swamp. We might not —"

"You'll need it," Pa interrupted, his words as bleak as the night.

Everyone stared at him in the darkness. Pa looked into the night without blinking, his face slack and haggard.

Brad saw him as the spent shrunken form of a man who once had stood so tall in his eyes. Was he giving up? Or did he know something else, something worse about this thing he wasn't telling? Or is it that he's just exhausted like the rest of us, old and sick with something, sick of holding his dying son?

Pa finally blinked and shifted his gaze toward Al.

"It will be waiting for us at The Narrows."

Brad pushed his cap back and stepped forward.

"How can you be so sure?" he asked. "If the thing is crazy, who knows what it will do. Heck, it may be miles from here by now off chasing another deer for all we know. Besides, it's dark and we've come a long way. How does it know to ambush us there?"

Pa's eyes settled on Brad.

"How many trail roads out of here?"

Brad thought for a moment.

"Just one, I guess. This one."

"Who lives in these woods all year, that buck or us?"

"The buck of course, but —"

"No buts about it. It knows we use this road to get in and out. And it knows we're trying to get out." Pa's brow furrowed even more. "You saw it. That look in its eyes wasn't loco crazy. Crazy with hate maybe, but not out of its mind crazy with rabies. It's something else. And it knows what it's doing. Has all along. It ain't about to quit until it's finished what it started. It'll be waiting at The Narrows all right, waiting to finish us."

"If it's really that smart," Brad said, lowering is voice, "then it can't be just a deer. It's got to be a Manitou, the shape-shifter, that Manabozho thing Uncle Larry talked about."

Under the blanket Larry stirred.

"I don't think it matters," Al said, "if it's this Manitou thing or an incredibly smart deer that's decided to hunt us. The bottom line is that we're committed to getting out of here, and it seems committed to stopping us."

Brad scanned the darkness for a moment. He turned back to his dad and Pa. "Well, we don't have any Indian magic to help us, but at least Pa thinks he knows when and where it's going to try something. Can't we use that somehow, I mean come up with some kind of plan anyway?"

Pa stared down the trail for a moment before his eyes widened. He blinked then looked back at Brad.

"Ahh, maybe you are learning. That buck knows how smart it is. In one way that's bad for us, real bad. But on the other hand, we just might be able to use its smarts to our advantage. Like I've always said; the way to kill a smart buck is to use its smarts against it, let it think it's getting the drop on you. It may be our only chance."

Pa motioned them closer with his hand. Brad squatted near the toboggan. Corey huddled next to him. Al leaned over. Pa whispered. A moment later Al looked at the axe in his hand. His shoulders slumped. Corey peeked inside his jacket at the flashlight. Brad shook his head and let the rifle sag in one hand. After a bit they nodded and rose, then resumed down the trail, each step drawing them closer to The Narrows.

With the flashlight doused and tucked under Corey's jacket, Brad's eyes quickly adjusted to the darkness. Ahead, the ground rose to the crest of a broad ridge where they had searched for Indian arrowheads during their summer visits to the cabin. It was such a peaceful place then. Brad could almost smell the aroma of ferns baking in the summer sun, the tinge of humus under his fingernails where he had been sifting through the dirt for artifacts. But now the ridge seemed like the entrance to a house of horrors at the carnival. Just over it lay The Narrows, a stream-eroded gouge in the landscape choked with cedars. The place offered spring brookies, a few fall grouse, an occasional winter mink, and now whatever else the night held.

Brad brought up the rear, using the rifle like a walking stick, jamming the shoulder plate into the snow and dragging the stock along. He limped as he walked, the brief rest causing his thighs to stiffen even more. He no longer swept his head nervously from side to side looking for danger. Instead, he barely shifted his eyes, and only while adjusting his cap or scratching an ear.

Ahead, Corey followed the toboggan, swinging one arm carefree, the other cradling his side. He glanced at the stars overhead as if thoroughly enjoying a midnight stroll.

In front of the toboggan, Al walked with measured steps, his axe poised over his shoulder, his body rigid. Leading the troop, pulling the injured and old, he was the apparent alpha wolf of the pack. And with the flashlight and rifle seemingly useless, he now presented the greatest threat to any attacker. In doing so, he presented himself as the buck's prime target. With him out of the way, the pups and sick would fall as easy prey.

Al paused as he crested the ridge. He looked down the trail toward the matting of brush that appeared to swallow the two-track. Where the trail narrowed, cedars hung next to it like rows of black velvet curtains, concealing any cast of characters, waiting to leap on stage for their performance.

He glanced over his shoulder and nodded. Pa looked back from the toboggan. Corey nodded and glanced back at Brad. He tightened his grip on the gun's barrel.

Brad looked down at the gun. Will it fire this time? Will Vern's undersized bullet fly true? He felt the last shell in his pocket. God, I hope I don't need this. If I do, who might die before I can chamber it? He tried to shake the thoughts and looked ahead to the others. At least I can swing the gun. All Corey has is a plastic flashlight — some weapon. Dad, one good hand and an axe. It's got to be numb in his grip by now. And poor Pa, he knows he's a sitting duck, can't even see clearly what's going on. I hope he's right about all this.

Al began trudging down the trail. Brad sucked in a lung full of air and hobbled after them.

For the next twenty yards everything went according to plan.

After that everything went to hell.

The crystalline snow had long since glazed the toboggan's bottom with an icy sheen. It glided across the snow with almost no effort. As the slope quickly dropped away toward The Narrows, gravity took control. Al stumbled slightly as the toboggan gently bumped into the back of one leg. He took longer steps. It nipped at his heel again. He increased his pace to jumping strides. But it surged after him, as if it had a mind of its own, hurrying, faster, hungry to rush ahead. His lope turned into a trot. Now it bit at his calves like a hungry coyote. His trot increased to a run. It chattered after him. His run burst into a sprint. Still, the loaded toboggan pursued him, threatening to pile drive him into the snow and smash Pa and Larry into the trees. Afraid of dumping his precious cargo, Al ran wildly, trying to keep the toboggan on the trail.

Clutching his side and running as best he could, Corey sprinted after the runaway toboggan.

Brad looked ahead to the noise. His father had surged forty yards in front of them and was running like a madman toward the thicket along The Narrows. Corey was following. What's wrong? Why are they running? This wasn't in the plan. Did they see something? Brad looked over his shoulder and lunged ahead in one motion, expecting the buck to be on his heels. Nothing. He turned back to the trail ahead. They were too far in front. No, this won't work. I can't even see them, just shadows.

Brad bolted ahead to catch up. He gritted his teeth as he tried to pump his legs. But loaded with lactic acid, his sapped muscles responded like limp rubber bands. He groaned as he struggled to make them move. Come on, damn it, I've got to stay with them. The snow sifted around his boots. The rifle pulled on his arms. Crap, go faster. He fell behind as if mired in the mushy hillside of his dream. In the back of his mind, flickers of that dream resurfaced, bits and pieces floating to the brink of consciousness. The dream, it's like my dream. I couldn't get away until I ... got mad.

A searing ripple of anger flashed inside him. He had suffered years waiting to discover his real father, for the two of them to find each other, and he wasn't about to let this buck end it now. Like a spreading oil fire feeding off its own heat, the spark of anger ignited more. His fear scuttled aside. Hot pulses flashed into his legs. They came alive. They pounded the frozen trail with long strides. He began to close the gap.

Almost a hundred yards ahead, his father slowed as the toboggan chattered across uneven ground. Pa and Larry bounced under the blanket, tipped sideways and almost toppled into the snow but hung on. Where the ground leveled near the bottom of The Narrows, Al finally bulldogged the toboggan to a halt. He sagged to his knees, wheezing. He lowered the axe into the snow. Corey slowed.

Seemingly from nowhere, it came.

A dark shape melted from the tangle near the trail and floated across the snow like the drifting shadow of a giant bird of prey. But unlike a shadow, a pair of glowing crescents led its charge.

Brad screamed, "NO-O-O-o-o-o-".

You damned thing. New hot flashes rippled through his body. He flew downhill.

His dad spun toward the sound, turning his back on the charging buck. Clipped words of warning came from the toboggan. Al wheeled and scrambled to get to his feet. His hand found the axe next to him as he rose. Stiff fingers gripped the handle. The buck dipped its crown of tines. Al brought the axe around. He let out a guttural cry. The buck stiffened legs and neck. The axe flashed in the starlight. Ivory tines met hickory and steel.

Despite his injured hand, Al wielded the axe savagely. But the buck fended off the strikes like an expert swordsman, each tine countering with uncanny accuracy. Tines speared forward. Al jerked back and struck again. The buck hooked its rack upward with a mighty snap of the head. Al grunted as the axe flew from his good hand, the fingers of his injured one barely clinging to the hickory handle. A new fire glared from the buck's eyes. It reared back on hind legs and dipped its head. Al fumbled with the axe. He threw up his arms as he straightened himself between the lunging buck and the toboggan. Their shadows merged as one.

A wail rose from deep within Brad's lungs. The blood vessels in his forehead and neck rippled. A burning tidal wave of hate engulfed him. His lips exposed barred teeth. His legs pounded onward.

The buck and Al tumbled backwards off the edge of the trail, sweeping Pa and Larry into the turmoil. Human grunts mixed with the buck's. Their forms became an entangled mess of flailing parts. The buck regained its legs and stood above the floundering heap. It arched its back to plunge headlong into the men sprawled before it. Tines glistened under the starlight.

From the darkness a beam of light pierced the night, dousing the buck's face in a wash. The buck paused and squinted against the light. It grunted and turned its head away from the beam. It backed off several steps, almost tripping on a deadfall under the snow.

Corey rushed in, stabbing his light saber into the buck's face. "Take that! You son-of-a-bitch!" he hollered. "I hope it hurts all the way down to your balls!"

He shuffled closer. But before he could add another insult to his bravado, the light flickered. He rattled it in his hands and it blinked out altogether.

The buck dipped its head toward Corey. It blinked. Corey took a step back. It blinked again, its widening eyes again exposing the fire near its lower lids. Corey stole two more quick steps backward. The buck bobbed its head. Its eyes flashed with a fiery hatred, the lower rims suddenly glowing brighter than ever.

"Uh, oh," Corey muttered.

The buck planted its hind legs. Corey threw the six-volt at it, spun, and ran back down the trail toward Brad. The buck swatted the dead light to the side with a dash of tines then leaped after Corey.

Brad held the gun tight to his chest as he ran. His finger flicked off the safety as his legs gobbled up the thirty yards between them. Even in the faint light he could see Corey's eyes, wide with fear, pleading for help.

The buck bunched mighty shoulders and leaped. It ate up half the ten yards separating it from Corey. It hit the ground, front hooves spraying snow, muscles rippling under its coat all the way back to its flanks. Corey pumped his arms. His legs churned. His eyes grew wider still. The buck's hind legs coiled up near its front. They exploded like giant watch springs. It sprang high into the night air. It dipped its rack. Its eyes focused on the center of Corey's back.

"DIVE!" Brad yelled as he shouldered the gun and skidded to a halt.

Corey reached out, fingers clawing at the dark, as if he could somehow pull himself closer to Brad. Brad's eye found the oval opening under the scope. Corey floated beneath it, looking like Pete Rose sliding for home plate. Brad raised the gun two inches. The airborne buck filled his sight window. Brad held his breath. The buck descended. Brad's eye followed it through the steel oval. Downward it came. Brad swung the gun with its motion. Tines filled the oval, ears laid back, glowing eyes, nose flared, mouth cracked, white throat patch, neck, and finally chest. Brad's finger pressed the icy steel of the trigger.

It clicked.

The main spring lurched.

The pin snapped forward.

Tempered steel impacted the stainless gilding of the shell primer, crushing the priming compound between the primer case and the anvil. The primer detonated, igniting 56.9 grains of 4831 Dupont powder. Shell brass expanded to the walls of the chamber. The 150 grain Spire point Hornaday bullet with lead core, metal jacket jumped from the casing. It streaked at 2900 feet per second down the barrel, its 2800 foot/pounds of energy caring less if there was ice obstructing the muzzle.

Blue flames belched into the darkness, the muzzle flash robbing Brad's night vision.

He heard the thump of the buck hitting earth followed by Corey's scream. He squinted into the darkness but could only see the ghost image of the muzzle blast still clinging to his vision. He whipped off his glove and threw back the bolt of the rifle. He clawed the spent shell from the chamber and drove his hand into his pocket. The last shell, who might die before he could use it? Who would die after?

Corey hollered louder, less frantic, but the words became jumbled with the rifle shot still echoing in Brad's ears. He jammed the last shell into the chamber and slammed the bolt closed, and as he looked up, two glowing crescents burned their way through the clearing after-image.

Brad blinked and the eyes were upon him at pointblank range. Scuttling backwards, he leveled the rifle at his waist.

His finger reached for the trigger.

Too late, the impact of the buck caused him to finger the trigger. The rifle bucked free from his hands.

Like in his dream, everything ebbed into slow motion. Brad spun in an awkward arc, dagger tines narrowly missing his face and tearing open his coat. Something slammed against his midsection, knocking the wind from him and toppling him backwards. He instinctively threw up his arms, but they wouldn't respond. He found his hands gripping coarse hair. Further backward he fell. His diaphragm stung. He spun his head as the crown of antlers jerked toward his face. Glowing eyes met his. Their hatred flickered like dying embers, fading to some deeper sense. Pity? Understanding? What was it? A breath expelled from the buck into Brad's face. It carried the pungent perfume of death, spraying him with pin-drops of blood. Snow billowed around them as Brad finally hit the ground. The smell of burnt hair and blood filled his nostrils. Turning sideways, he met the eyes only inches away. They bored deep into his soul, as if reaching out, begging for some answer as to how it had all come to this.

Brad's spirit stilled. He lay motionless, looking into the eyes, his anger melting about him in a pool of compassion. He knew now with sudden clarity who would forever reign as the supreme survivor in Deadman's Swamp, long after both their bodies had turned to dust. Not Manitou or man. A more magnificent creation. And oddly, the thought of whitetails bounding through the forests in a world where man had become extinct gave Brad immense comfort.

In a final widening, the flicker of life behind the buck's eyes blinked out, leaving Brad in a vast darkness.

CHAPTER 31 – BODY COUNT

The last flicker of life blinked from the buck's eyes, freeing Brad from their mesmerizing bond. He shook his head and pushed himself away from the deer, a real deer of flesh and blood, not some evil spirit that lurked in the minds of the overimaginative.

He stumbled to his feet and looked around in the darkness. He had fully regained his night vision, but still squinted, looking for some sign of life. Nothing moved along the trail. No one waved for help. None cried out in pain. Only a deathly calm hung over the slit of pale blue cutting through The Narrows.

Brad's hands began to tremble. Where is everyone? God, am I the only one left? A fear greater than he had even known gripped his heart like the icy talons of a loathsome vulture. The fear of losing the ones he loved towered darker than any fear he could possibly have imagined for himself. He opened his mouth to call out to his father but the words wouldn't budge from his throat. He tried to rush forward yet his legs shook with such force they wouldn't hold him. He dropped to his knees. No, Oh God, please no.

A muffled groan from the snow arose only yards away. Brad turned toward the sound. The faint outline of a body dusted with snow stirred. Brad managed to stand and took a step toward it. His knee buckled but he braced it with his hand. He took another step. His leg held the weight. Then, before he knew it, he was rushing ahead, diving toward the figure. Brad skidded on his knees as he reached out, grabbed a handful of coat, and righted Corey. Brad stared at his friend, unable to speak. A whimper trickled past his lips as he saw the crusted bloodied mess where Corey's face used to be.

Corey moved in Brad's arms. Brad gasped and reared back as Corey reached up and wiped away the bloody snow coating his features, filling his eyes. Brad sucked another breath, expecting to see eyes stabbed from their sockets, jagged punctures exposing shattered skull and brains. Corey sputtered more snow from his mouth and sat upright.

"Holy crow, Buwana. Whew! That was close."

Brad blinked in surprise as Corey wiped the rest of the snow from his face and stood.

"You-you-you're okay?"

"Yeah, but, man, look at the mess you caused," Corey said, shaking the last of the bloodied snow from his face then grinning. "But I'm sure glad you made a bloody mess of that buck before he had a chance to make one out of me. Your shot upended it. Man, it slammed into me sideways and rolled over on me. Really knocked the crap out of me." Corey paused, realizing the look on Brad's face.

"It's okay, Buwana, honest. It's the buck's blood, not mine. See?" He reached up and patted his cheeks.

Brad reached out and hugged Corey. Corey hugged back.

"I owe you big time, Buwana, forever. You saved my hide."

Brad nodded and without a word, turned and ran toward the others. Corey rushed after him.

Off to the side of the trail, the profile of the overturned toboggan stood black against the snow. Just beyond it the blanket lay in a rumpled heap. From under one end stuck a pair of legs. Brad reached down and tugged on the blanket, exposing Pa with his arms still wrapped around Larry's shoulders. Brad leaned over them.

"Pa, are you all right?"

Pa slowly turned his head and nodded. His skin shown as pale as the snow, his lips dark like the night sky. "Yeah," he managed through chattering teeth, his voice weak. "Ju-ju-just a little cold, tha-that's all." Pa looked toward the brush. "Your father."

Brad turned and saw the short tow rope disappearing into a matting of cedars. He reached over and gently pulled on it. The harness came free from the branches, no father attached.

"Dad, Dad," he yelled as he rushed forward. He spread the branches and there lay his father, sprawled backward across a deadfall, his arms and legs limp in the snow.

Brad knelt and gently lifted his father's head. It lolled to one side, showing eyes still half open gazing skyward, skin a cold shade of blue. Dark flecks of blood speckled the snow around him.

Tears welled in Brad's eyes. He began to sob. He held the lifeless form tight to his chest. He began rocking. No, not Dad, not now, not after tonight, not after finding each other in these final hours. No, this can't be. I tried to save you, Dad. Really, I tried so hard.

A big hand gently pulled on Brad's shoulder, separating him from his father.

"Let's see," Larry said, Pa and Corey huddling close to help him stand.

Larry sank to his knees in the snow next to Al. He motioned toward Al's legs.

"Get him off this deadfall," he said, his command more hoarse grunts than words. "Lift his legs and lay him flat. Gently now, gently."

Brad and Corey lifted Al off the deadfall and laid him in the snow. Larry had already pulled open the coat from around Al's neck and lay his finger along the side of the throat. Next to Larry's hand the faint light barely revealed a broad purple welt across Al's neck near his Adam's apple.

"Got a pulse. Shallow, too slow, still a pulse. But he's not breathing. Brad get down here, now."

Brad dropped to his knees across from Larry. He wiped his eyes with the back of his hand.

"Listen, Brad. I can't blow life back into your dad," Larry said, clutching his lower abdomen, his eyes squinting back pain. "But maybe you can."

Brad looked up at Larry and blinked away the last of his tears. He nodded.

"Just do what I tell you. And for your dad's sake, don't stop."

Brad nodded again.

"Looks like a pinched trachea. Might be crushed. Gotta get some air past it. Tip back the head like this."

Larry placed one hand under the back of Al's neck and cupped the other on his forehead, tilting back the head. Brad's hands followed the motion.

"This should open the airway."

Larry prodded a finger in the corner of Al's mouth and pulled the jaw open.

"His tongue settled back. It's blocking the throat."

He reached in and pulled the tongue back in place.

"Stick your thumb over the lower teeth and hold the tongue down against the bottom of his mouth."

Brad's hands responded.

"Good, now pinch the nose with your other hand and give him a breath. A breath of life, Brad."

Brad nodded and leaned over his father's face. He paused for a second, looking at the man who had given him life. The young Brad Mercer wanted to scream, to burst into tears and run off into the night, to forget the terrible scene. An emerging Brad Mercer choked back the impulse and he cupped his mouth over his father's and blew in.

"Nothing's happening," Larry said, his voice gaining strength and a greater sense of urgency. "The chest isn't rising, blow harder!"

Brad drew in a bigger breath. He pushed back the pain in his own gut and tried to force breath into his dad's lungs. Come on, Dad. Take it. I'm giving, take it, please.

"No good, damn it. You're not blowing hard enough."

Panting now, Brad sucked in a deep breath and leaned back over his father. He blew with force but felt the air escaping past the pinched nose. Still, he kept blowing until his ears rang and white dots started drifting around the edge of his vision. At last, he drew back and began gasping for air. He looked down. His dad's skin had darkened to a deeper shade of blue, the lips almost black in the light. Larry's hand was already back on the throat.

"Barely got a pulse now," he said, a new quiver in his voice betraying his panic. "Give him another try."

He reached down further on Al's throat over the bruised area and felt the windpipe between his thumb and finger.

"Okay, Brad, a big and steady breath. But don't start until I tell you."

Brad drew in the stinging air until his lungs could hold no more. Then he placed his mouth over his dad's. He waited, looking into the eyes only an inch away. A thousand flashbacks flooded over him, all the times his father had been this close, the smiling face of Daddy, bending over to kiss him.

Larry's hand moved on Al's throat.

"Now, Brad. Steady and strong."

Brad blew. Air seeped past the pinched nose again. Brad grunted and squeezed the nose harder. Still his breath wouldn't expel. He continued to blow, harder. Veins in his neck throbbed. His throat burned. His diaphragm ached. More white spots danced between the scant space separating his face from his father's. A ringing whined in his ears. But still he kept blowing. Larry's hand shifted again, trying to reshape the collapsed trachea.

"Keep blowing. Don't stop."

"The white spots turned dark and began closing in like drapes being drawn from the sides of his eyes. His heartbeat drummed in his head, stronger, faster, pleading for oxygen. And just as Brad teetered on the rim of consciousness, breath began to leave his lungs.

"That's it," Larry said, "keep blowing, more."

Brad choked down the sourness in his throat and continued to blow. More air left his lungs. A darkness blacker than the night closed around him. His body slumped forward. Still, he blew.

"That's enough. Stop, stop!"

A hand jerked Brad back. A wash of sweet air filled his mouth and lungs. He drew in more. A dark shape materialized through the starburst of white spots in front of him. Dad, Dad wake up. Brad gulped more air.

"More. Now!" Larry commanded.

Brad dipped his head and blew again. This time the air flowed more freely into his father and he felt his dad's chest rise as he blew.

"Enough."

Brad pulled back and dared to glance down at his father's chest, his eyes expecting to see the precious breath leaking back out through bubbling tine holes.

"Again, more."

Brad blew again. Then again. Quicker. Suddenly his dad's body flinched. Brad jerked back. His dad coughed and drew in a ragged breath. Then more. Pink washed away the pasty white in Al's cheeks. The blue lips faded. And as he began steadily breathing, Brad's body also convulsed, laughing, weeping.

His dad turned and looked in his direction, his eyes clearing. He reached out to Brad. Brad took the hand and drew it to his face. He hunched over, his mix of laughing and crying giving way to crying altogether. The five of them crowded in the hushed night, huddling close, clinging to the one thing that had brought them this far — each other.

Al finally sat up. He opened his mouth to talk but a only raspy wheeze came out.

"Take it easy," Larry said. "Don't move until we check you over."

Al shook his head. He reached in the snow and pulled out the axe with one hand. He held it sideways in front of his face as if still fending off the buck's lunge, then pulled it back near his throat. He held up a bloodied forearm.

"So, that's what happened," Larry said, nodding. "Bracing that axe sideways between you and the buck's rack was pretty quick thinking. That and Brad here, saved your life. Now let's take a look at that arm."

Al waved him off and flexed the hand of his bloodied forearm. He shook his head and motioned toward the toboggan. Brad helped him stand. They righted the toboggan back on the trail then helped Larry toward it. Hunched over more than before, Larry was barely able to stand. They lowered him slowly to the toboggan. Pa huddled behind him. Corey covered them with the blanket.

Brad slipped into the tow rope harness. Corey stepped up to his side and grabbed the rope with one hand. Cradling his punctured arm inside his coat, Al drew near on Brad's other side.

Al reached up and laid a hand on Brad's shoulder. Together, they turned and looked back at the fallen buck, part of its sprawling rack sticking high above the snow, the butt of Crane's rifle exposed next to it. Al nodded and patted his son on the back. The faint light hid most the tears pooling in their eyes. Brad noticed one running down his dad's cheek.

He turned back toward the trail ahead and leaned into the harness. The rope groaned briefly. The toboggan slid forward. And as one, they walked from the darkness of The Narrows.

Up ahead, the trail opened into the aspen flats. Far above, a celestial curtain of northern lights shimmered pale shades of green and yellow, and under its glow the trail sparkled brighter than it had all night.

CHAPTER 32 – BEYOND THE GATES

Doctor Nolstrum's long white jacket looked like a vampire's rendition of snow camouflage with irregular white patches showing through the spattering of blood. He pulled off latex gloves and tossed them into the trash with dozens of bloodied pairs before them. He shook his head. Covered from head to toe with coughed, sneezed, and puked blood, yet here he was worried about getting a little on his hands. He pulled on a fresh pair nonetheless, realizing that it was for the safety of the next patient as much as for himself. He couldn't be too cautious. Inmates or not, they still deserved the best treatment he could offer, which didn't seem like much as he looked at the growing rows of corpses laid out in the far end of the corridor.

The increasing tally of dead revealed an emerging pattern. Lifers appeared hit the hardest, the smaller the man, the more devastating the effects. With less body mass and blood volume, the blood thinner, whatever it was, quickly found weak spots in the circulatory system and began draining the man's chances of survival. Some died without an outward trace, probably from massive brain hemorrhage or a leaking liver, while others were brought in bleeding from every opening in their bodies. He had sent more than enough blood samples to the lab at County General for analysis. But they were still trying to sort out what type of blood thinner and accelerator Stone must have used to cause so much devastation so quickly. And despite the mass transfusions of whole blood and heavy injections of vitamin K he was administering, Nolstrum felt like the kid with his finger in the dike holding back the sea. He couldn't hold back the growing tide forever. The infirmary had filled up over an hour ago, bodies packed so tightly on and between the beds that his aides and nurses could barely negotiate through the mess without becoming entangled in the dangling network of IV lines.

The doctor moved further down the packed hall, wading among the bodies. An assistant called out a name off a resident's shirt label. Inside the infirmary office, a nurse punched up the name on the computer and the man's medical record, complete with blood type, scrolled up on the screen. Yelling back the blood type, another nurse wrote it down on a simple adhesive tag and slapped it on the man's shirt. Another tallied the blood types and phoned ahead to County General, requisitioning more whole blood. Nolstrum hoped that he and the new intern could keep up with the rivers of red pooling around them. Hell of a way for a young man to be introduced to doctoring. The intern would probably bolt for private practice as soon as this mess was over.

Nolstrum wondered how long the hospital's blood supply would last or if they had already summoned more from other facilities. Maybe with the hospital's help they could round up a blood drive in the morning. The local university alone had enough vibrant bodies to fill the need. But most probably wouldn't roll up their sleeve and face the prick of a needle for the sake of an inmate. No doubt they would need to be enticed with an incentive. Free cookies and juice alone wouldn't do it. Nolstrum glanced up and saw the warden waving from beyond the confusion. The doctor headed his way.

"Looks like Stone was our man all right," the warden said.

Nolstrum pushed his glasses back up the bridge of is nose. He knew that inside the walls the warden didn't need a trial and jury to establish the guilty.

"Just talked to the officer on mess shift. He noticed Stone acting suspicious during dinner and said he didn't eat a thing. Also said one of the con's told him he saw Stone messing with the food."

"I thought that was his job," the doctor said, raising his eyebrows.

"Of course it was," snapped the warden. "But he didn't make the main course tonight, Eli did."

"Eli? Maybe he had a hand in it."

"No, I don't think so," the warden said. "I saw Stone's suicide note. Something about there being too many predators, a terrible imbalance in nature's proper scheme of things, or some crap like that. Seems he had some crazy notion about killing off the useless competitors. Must have figured this was a good place to start or his only chance. Whatever; the hard time must have been too much for the old coot's mind."

The doctor peered over the warden's shoulder as another bleeding inmate was escorted around the corner and joined the growing line.

"Are you sure about Eli not being in on this? Simmons mentioned that he's been acting odd since the test incident. Anybody checked his house?"

"Yeah, your intern up there says Eli's sick all right, wringing wet, cramps, moaning. Reports from some of the others is that he ate as much as anyone. Eli's no genius but he wouldn't poison himself. No, he's a survivor. Simmons is off on this one. He's a good man, he's just a bit paranoid about all the residents, especially Eli."

"Guess you're right. It'll take a healthy dose to kill that brute. He can wait until the dead make room for him or his symptoms get worse. Any lead on the poison yet?"

"No, my people are still looking. Probably rat poison though. Had a real problem with them over the decades in this hell hole, worse than a Medieval castle. But the way they filed inventory on all the junk in the store rooms, it's making it tough to track down. We don't know what's in half those unmarked cases."

The doctor nodded as if he were concerned at the last comment but his eyes had already shifted to an inmate slumping to his knees. The man was coughing up blood, adding to the mess already staining his blues.

"Gotta go," said the doc with a wave of the hand. "Keep me posted on what you find."

The warden shuffled away from the scene, drawing his hands close his body to keep from getting any of the inmate's leaking juices on his wool jacket.

In F Block, Eli's ears filtered out a conversation above the chaos of cries for help.

"Doc's backed up past the infirmary hallways," the intern said. "He's surpassed overload."

"So now what?" asked the aide.

"The warden's orders are to keep most of them locked up. The only ones we can let out are the worst cases who have to be carted away. We're sending them over to County General under guard. Advanced respiratory bleeding cases only. The simple gut bleeders have to stay and take their chances. We'll treat them as best we can in their houses."

"Nice call," said the aide, shaking his head and shoving his hands into his pockets. "Remind me never to stay here. Sure would hate to be one of these poor birds — waiting in a cell to maybe die or being carted out to die for sure."

Eli glanced out the corner of his eye to check that no one could see in his cell. Like straight folks always said, timing is everything. He reached up and grabbed the bridge of his nose between his massive thumb and forefinger. He smiled as he began slowly twisting it, cartilage and bone grinding and snapping under the pressure. A hot wash of blood burst from the ruined nose. He twisted it back in place as best he could. There, that wasn't such a tough price for a ticket outta here. He laid back on his bunk and let the blood rush down the back of his throat. The warm taste aroused his senses. He fought back the urge to drink its sweetness. Finally, when his throat was full, he began gargling. Blood foamed out his mouth and nose like a kettle boiling over with witches' brew. He gagged and fell on the floor. He laid there for a moment, making a thorough mess of himself with the foamed blood. But no one came. Damn, what do you have to do to get some decent service in this joint? He reached up and tipped over his bunk, the metal frame clanging loudly against his cell bars. Voices rose down the block. Feet began pounding in his direction. All right, escort service.

Moments later, the aides carted Eli near the corridor leading to the infirmary. They quickly labeled his blood type and called Dr. Nolstrum to his side. Eli gazed though unfocused eyes as the doctor waved a small penlight across his face. Eli saw the suspicion in the doctor's eyes. The brightness almost blinded him but he held fast to his stare, his willpower making his pupils fight their instinct to dilate. He panted like a dog on a hot day as foamed blood dribbled out the corners of his mouth.

"So, Eli, it's come to this?"

The doctor stared intently at the big face, searching for a hint of a ruse.

Eli continued to gaze at the ceiling. Okay, Doc, you need more symptoms to believe. How about this?

Eli increased his panting, sucking a large clot from the back of his throat. He swished the blood across his palate to get the most of the foaming effect as he breathed out through the mess. He gagged and spewed out a stream of frothed blood.

Nolstrum reared back and blinked. He folded his hands in a prayer pose.

"Well, Eli, I guess we'll never solve your foxfire mystery now."

He glanced over to the aide on the gurney.

"Get him on the next ambulance shuttle over to County. At least he'll be closer to pathology when the time comes to dice him up."

Eli repressed the mounting desire to leap up laughing and scare the piss out of Ol' Doc. Man, this acting stuff was tons more fun than doctor work, a real rush.

"I thought the warden had to give his personal okay before a lifer goes out?" the aide said.

Suddenly, Nolstrum had had too much; the blood, the dead, and the dying. He fired the aide a grizzly stare. "I didn't know you were the doctor here? For God's sake, look at the man. Do you think he's in any condition to do much other than die before he gets there? Or are you questioning my authority on this?"

The aide shrank back and shook his head.

"Alright. Now get your butt in gear. And stop looking so worried, they'll handcuff him before he passes the secure lockout area."

Eli's heart pounded harder, the taste of freedom blending with the sweet blood he allowed himself to swallow now. What a luscious dessert after so many years of having his spirit caged and broken by The Man. Soon the world beyond the gates would be his for the taking, and he would take plenty, not stupidly like before, but with his new powers, fulfilling the mounting hunger that boiled within him.

The aide rolled Eli down the maze of hallways toward the loading dock. Before passing final lockout, an officer wrestled a pair of stainless cuffs around Eli's huge wrists. Latches hummed. Bars slid back. The gurney rolled on. Two electronic doors swung open as the aide wheeled Eli behind another inmate waiting to be loaded onto one of three shuttling ambulances. Eli sucked at the deliciously cold air that washed over him. Above, the Milky Way stretched across the sky like a train load of spilled glitter. Oh what beauty. Eli's heart drummed harder. Oh sweet freedom. He snuck a quick glance around. Officers swarmed on the scene like hungry vultures, waiting to latch on to the next weakened victim, half repulsed by all the blood, half entranced by the gruesome uncertainty of the spectacle around them. An ambulance backed up to the dock. A crowd of officers grabbed the first gurney and folded up its legs as they slid the other man inside. A half dozen officers packed around Eli now, gloved hands hoisting at the sides of his gurney.

"Holy smoke," one muttered. "This guy's twice as big as he looks inside his house. We should have called for a goddamn crane."

"You know what they say," grunted another, "there's nothing heavier than dead meat. And Eli here looks about as close as you come to buzzard bait."

"Eli?" a ranking officer said from near the ambulance. "Let me see."

Eli didn't have to turn his head to recognize the officer. He instantly knew the voice of Simmons. Damn.

Simmons pushed his way past the other officers and looked down at Eli before flashing his eyes to the aide.

"Who in hell gave orders to clear this man?"

"The doctor," the aide replied, taken back by Simmons' glare. "Look, Sarge, I already checked twice and the doc said he probably wouldn't make it there in time. See for yourself. He's almost a goner."

Simmons glanced back at Eli. His eyes passed over the matting of frothed blood around the mouth and moved up toward the seemingly blank eyes. For an instant he felt the stab of their probing depths and his hand unconsciously went for the holstered Beretta he had been issued for transport detail. More frothed blood seeped past Eli's parted lips. He blinked and shook it off. God, it was hard to be this close to Eli and repress old habits. Once such a fearsome ape of a man, now reduced to this. There was no threat here, was there? Uncertainty held him.

"Come on Sarge," one of the officers said, "you're holding things up. We're all freezing our asses off out here. Either shoot him or load him, but let's get on with it."

Simmons nodded toward the ambulance and stepped back.

The officers surrounding Eli's gurney groaned as they struggled to slide it into the ambulance along side the other inmate.

"You stay here," Simmons ordered another officer near the rear of the ambulance. "I'll take over watching this pair. You can catch the next run. Eli and I go back a ways and I want to make sure he's in good hands. Never thought I'd see him leave like this. Who knows, maybe we can get there in time for them to help him."

Simmons climbed in the back between the inmates while another officer slammed the rear doors. He patted the side of the ambulance. "Get this wagon moving."

Red flashes danced off the granite walls as the ambulance passed the prison gates and sped into the night. The hospital was only ten minutes away.

Eli shifted his gaze to Simmons. Gee, boss, sure would be nice to enjoy our ride together, you know, savor these final moments with my brethren behind bars. But, alas, the key to any successful plan is timing. Yep, boss, timing is everything. And now it's time for someone to die.

CHAPTER 33 — FREEDOM

Brad's legs plowed through the snow. He seemed to have left his fatigued muscles in The Narrows with the dead buck. With Corey lending a hand on the tow rope, the toboggan slid gracefully along the two track cutting through the last leg of the aspen flats. The cold air washing in Al's throat caused the swelling to subside, and he could now manage to croak a few words. He brought up the rear, keeping an eye on Larry and Pa, making sure they didn't fall off.

Larry had grown worse since the incident in The Narrows and now barely had the strength to stay righted on the toboggan. Pa held onto him as best he could, but the final confrontation with the buck had also sapped what little strength remained in his aged body. Despite the cold, he too had broken into a sweat and the color in his face had faded. The purple rings that formed under his eyes matched the lifeless hue of his lips. Each time Brad glanced over his shoulder at Pa, his legs found another burst of energy and a new sense of urgency increased his pace.

As the most frigid part of the night settled over the forest, the northern lights shimmered brighter than ever. Curtains of ice crystals flickered and rippled like immense luminescent sheets swaying in a breeze. It cast pastel shades of green and blue on the snow, lighting the trail like the distant glow of mercury-vapor lamps. Brad looked up at the lights as he walked. How can the night up here be so incredibly beautiful and so horrible at the same time? So inviting yet so intimidating? He shook his head. Maybe it's that mystery that makes Dad come back here each fall. As he looked back at the trail ahead, he spotted the black outline of Larry's Cherokee, parked near a clearing in the aspens.

Brad picked up his pace even more. He skimmed over the last fifty yards with more power in his legs than he had during the first fifty yards leaving the remains of the cabin. The toboggan skidded to a halt next to the Cherokee. Brad slid the rope harness off his shoulders.

"It's locked," Corey said, jerking the door handle then throwing up his hands.

"Should have kept the axe," Al said.

"Wait," groaned Larry from under the blanket. "Here."

The others drew near.

"No need wrecking my Jeep," he continued. "Already proved you can hot-wire a rig. Got my key in a zipper pocket inside my jacket."

He tried to reach his hand inside the coat but the strain was more than he could manage. He squeezed his eyes shut as his arm dropped back into his lap.

"Sorry, It's just too —"

"It's all right," Pa said in a hushed voice. "It's all right, son."

Pa gently reached his arm around Larry and slipped his hand inside the jacket. His fingers searched for a moment before withdrawing the keys. He held them out.

Al reached for them but the pain in his arm stopped him short. He shook his head.

"Brad, you drive."

Brad took the keys and began trying them in the door. This is going to be different than driver's ed on dry parking lots. Crap, this is a ton of snow. What if I get stuck? What if Larry gets worse, or Pa, or Dad stops breathing again? He sighed and found the right key. He twisted it in the lock. Don't force it and break it, geez. It's stiff. Just be cool.

The key clicked. The power locks thumped. Brad climbed in and folded down the back seat so Larry could lay down and reduce the pressure on his abdomen. Pa and Corey crawled in the back with Larry. Al climbed in the front. Using a scraper from behind the seat, Brad cleared the heavy snow from the windshield. He climbed inside and slammed the door.

He fingered the key in the ignition. Okay, let's go, baby. Don't have a dead battery like Mom's car last year when she left it out in the cold for days. At least the dome light went on when I opened the door. The battery can't be dead, can it? He tapped the wheel. Come on, stop being such a worry-wart and get on with it. Brad held his breath and turned the key.

The starter groaned before cranking the engine over. It coughed several times as if it wanted to start but was fighting the tremendous cold that had seeped into every bolt and gasket. The starter whined slower and Brad flicked off the key. He sighed and depressed the gas peddle once, lifted his foot, and tried again. The engine groaned over slowly once, twice, then coughed to life. Brad let out a long breath and placed his hand on the gear shift. Alright, now if I can only keep from getting stuck.

He searched for a second before finding the headlight switch and turned it on. Their breath had already clouded the inside of the windows and he reached up and rubbed clear a small patch to see through. He dropped the lever into drive and noticed the four-wheel-drive light showing green. His foot pressed the accelerator. Nothing happened. He pressed it further, the engine laboring as if the tires were frozen in place. Brad was about to depress it further when the Cherokee broke free with a lurch like a horse slapped on the flanks. He eased it onto the trail and stopped. Now for the tricky part. They were pointed in the wrong direction. He would have to turn it around.

Brad swung the back end of the Jeep into a small clearing next to the trail. The rear end sagged as he stopped. He winced and shifted the Jeep into drive and tapped the accelerator. The Cherokee jerked as the wheels floundered in the deep snow. He gave it more gas. Snow flew from under the tires but the Jeep only chattered in place. Brad clenched the wheel. Please, no, don't let me be stuck.

"Try rocking it back and forth," his father offered. "You're doing fine, son, just don't turn the wheel so sharp until you get going."

Brad nodded and straightened the tires. Shifting from drive to reverse, he rocked the Jeep forward and backward in the snow. At first it didn't seem as if he were gaining an inch, but he felt the Jeep creep further with each lurch. Finally, it eased back onto the trail.

"Okay, Buwana," Corey hollered as he patted Brad on the head. "Get this buggy headed for town."

Brad let out a sigh as the Jeep gained momentum and glided down the trail. With the tires slicing through the deep snow, the Jeep handled like a power boat cruising through gently rolling waves. The Jeep slowed when it nosed through the drifts, but Brad kept up the speed and overcame the deeper snow. Soon he swung through the final turn toward the County Road. After that, they would be home free.

Brad smiled to himself as the headlights bounced off the far embankment of the main road. He slowed as he neared it. Suddenly, he jerked himself toward the wheel as he realized is wasn't the far side of the Country Road but a huge bank of snow blocking the trail. He took his foot off the gas pedal.

"No! Don't stop!" his father hollered. "Give her gas, now. Hurry."

Brad jammed his foot back on the pedal. The Jeep roared forward.

"Everybody brace yourself," Al said, pushing his good arm against the dash. "They blocked the damn trail when they plowed the main road. Keep her moving, Brad, faster."

Brad had the pedal pushed all the way to the floor now. The engine roared as the tires chewed the snow into rooster tails flying behind the Jeep. He braced his arms against the steering wheel as the bank of snow filled the headlights and engulfed them. Snow billowed over the hood and covered the windshield in darkness. The Jeep lurched almost to a stop as if grabbed by an immense hand. Larry groaned. Pa cussed. Corey thumped into the back of Brad's seat. The engine whined as Brad pumped the gas pedal and the Jeep teetered as if on the edge of a cliff, wheels spinning in mid-air. Then it tilted forward and slammed to a stop on the County Road.

"Man," Corey said, rubbing his arm where it had banged into the seat. "What demolition derby did you learn to drive in?"

Brad threw Corey a glance over his shoulder as he put the transmission in park and got out. He walked around to the front of the Jeep. The plastic grill had shattered along with one headlight. But everything else looked okay — operational anyway. He cleared the mounded snow from the hood and windshield and got back in.

"Nice job, son. Now see if you can get us to town without wrecking the rest of your uncle's car."

Al winked at Brad then reached over and turned on the heat.

Brad bunched his shoulders and looked in the rearview mirror toward Larry. Corey's and Pa's faces barely showed in the darkness. Larry remained a shape under the blanket. It's okay Uncle Larry, you can bitch at me when you're feeling better. For now, just hang on. I'll have you to the hospital in thirty minutes. I promise.

He turned on Highway 41 toward Marquette, the tires humming a fresh tune as they sped along the blacktop. The heater's warmth filled the Cherokee and added a glow beginning to stir in their voices.

"That musta been one pressure shot you made back there, son. Wished I could have seen it."

Brad looked over to his dad. "Guess I didn't have time to think about any pressure. Don't think I had time to think at all."

"That's the mark of a true Mercer," Pa said from the back. "It's pure hunting instinct. You got it or you ain't. Good thing for us you got it."

Everyone sat in silence for a moment, the impact of Pa's words seeping into their bodies like the car's heat.

"When are we going to report this to the Natural Resource people, Mr. Mercer?"

Al glanced in the back at Corey then looked at Larry. "It can wait until we get some medical attention and clearance from the hospital. Brad's buck and your's aren't going anywhere. And they'll keep fine in the cold."

Corey nodded and stared ahead out the window, green eyes shimmering, mind apparently lost back on the trail somewhere admiring his buck or Brad's.

"Well," he finally said, leaning near Brad's shoulder. "All I can say is, Man alive, am I ever glad the worst of this day is behind us."

Brad nodded and looked in the rearview mirror. No headlights behind them. No glowing crescents either. Yeah, the worst of it, so far behind.

As he looked back to the road, the image of glowing eyes appeared in his mind's eye, sending a shiver up his back. He reached over and turned up the heat, wondering if he would ever shake the chill.

CHAPTER 34 – FINAL FREEDOM

Eli turned his head towards Sergeant Simmons. The officer stiffened at the movement as if he had suddenly recognized a rattler coiled next to him on the stretcher. Eli's lips parted and a faint whisper trickled out. Simmons didn't understand the garbled words but the look in Eli's eyes begged for someone to listen.

He watched as Eli struggled to swallow then coughed up a dribble of blood. Poor bastard wasn't much of threat anymore, more like a sick kitten than a tiger.

Eli whispered again, the rustle of his voice growing fainter, the look in his eyes more desperate, squinting as if he saw a divine light from above. Simmons leaned closer. Eli strained to speak. Still, the words wouldn't come. He drew in a raspy breath then with an effort rippling the veins in his forehead, he managed to speak.

"You been a good boss, boss," he said faintly. "Gonna miss you."

For the first time Simmons saw a glint of compassion in Eli's eyes. It seemed so foreign in the grizzly features that he had difficulty matching the emotion with the face that wore it. It seemed like a piece out of place in a jigsaw puzzle. Nonetheless, Simmons forced the piece into place in his mind and patted Eli on the arm.

"It's going to be okay, Eli. We'll be there soon."

He could see beyond the narrowed eyes that Eli didn't believe him as the glint of compassion melted into a different look.

"One last thing," Eli whispered faintly, his fading words begging for attention, for someone to listen closely before they came no more.

Simmons leaned closer to hear over the road noise of the moving ambulance.

"Don't ever," Eli whispered hoarsely.

Simmons lowered his ear almost to Eli's mouth, the stench of blood almost making him pull away.

"Don't ever," Eli continued, "trust your life to a con."

Eli seized Simmons' head in both hands and pressed the man's waiting neck against his mouth. Massive jaws snapped shut. Horselike teeth sank deep and bit out a fist-sized chunk of the man's neck, tearing away the jugular vein instantly. Simmons lurched backward, frantically clawing at his holster. But Eli twisted his head with a snap of the wrists and Simmons fell limp across Eli's chest.

The officer in front heard a thump and turned to peek around the partition. He found Simmons slumped on the floor between the two cons. Both inmates appeared unconscious, only the whites showing in the nearly closed eyes, Eli looking the worst as more fresh blood covered his mouth and chest. The officer unfastened his shoulder harness and hurried into the rear of the ambulance and leaned over Simmons.

The driver didn't hear the puppy-like yelp or crunch over the sound of the engine. And by the time he turned a moment later to see what was happening, Eli jammed the 9MM muzzle of a Beretta against his temple. Though both of Eli's huge cuffed hands gripping the pistol made it appear toylike, the hollowness of the barrel looked immense.

"Ain't gonna hurt you pal. Just want to get off here. So stop this thing, now."

The driver responded like a robot, braking the ambulance less than a hundred yards from the hospital's emergency entrance and pulling off to the shoulder of the road. He put the vehicle in park and turned back toward Eli.

"Sorry pal," Eli said with a grin. "I lied."

Eli wrapped his arms over the head of the driver and dropped his cuffed wrists around the man's throat in one swift motion. Still gripping the gun, he jerked the driver into the back of the ambulance, cutting off the man's wind with the cuff's chain and ultimately squeezing the life from him. He supposed he could have shot him, but there would be the noise, and besides, this was so much more fun. He dropped the body among the rest and went about the task of finding a key for the cuffs.

Brad followed the arrows on the white-on-blue "H" signs as he neared the center of town. In the numbing cold and ungodly hour, Marquette looked like an abandoned ghost town. Not even a carload of hunters returning from last call at some local bar drove the streets. Only the Cherokee traveled through the stillness. Brad swung the Jeep onto a side street. Up ahead stood the outline of the hospital. Brad tapped the wheel and straighten himself in the seat. He slowed as he approached an ambulance along the side of the road near the hospital, its flashers still sending angry lances of light into the night. A policeman emerged from the back of the ambulance, anxiously waving him over under the yellow glow of a street light.

"What should I do, Dad?"

"Better stop. This cop isn't out here for his health."

Brad pulled over and braked under the yellow wash of the mercury-vapor lamp. The policeman rushed up to his side of the Jeep and jerked open the door. The man moved fluidly despite his immense size — more like a 300 pound cat than a man.

"Sorry pal, the entrance ahead is closed."

Eli saw the look of confusion on the young man's face. Squinting against the glow of the street light, he quickly scanned inside the back of the vehicle. Perfect; an old man, another juicy kid and some chump who looked like death. Easy pickings.

"I'm hospital security. Got a bad outbreak and this section is quarantined. I'll drive you around to the other side of the hospital. It's a bitch to get there at night if you don't know where the hell you're going."

Before Brad could turn to his dad for advice, the hulk lowered himself in the door and nudged Brad over as he tried to slide behind the wheel. But his massive torso wedged behind the steering wheel and he had to reach down and slide the seat all the way back before he could wiggle in.

"There, that's better," Eli said, adjusting the guard's cap that sat ridiculously high on his oversized head. It matched the pitifully short arms of his jacket. "I used to be a tyke like you once myself."

Brad looked up at the man. Tyke, hell, I never felt older. And I sure can't imagine you ever being a "tyke". God, what's that smell? Has he been eating rotten hamburgers? Brad noticed the guy steal quick glances out of the corner of his eye, squinting whenever his eyes shifted toward the dome light.

Eli reached out and slammed the door shut. The dome light winked out and he pulled back onto the street. Keeping his eyes locked on the road ahead, he fingered the controls until he found the dimmer switch for the panel lights.

"Nice rig you got here. Ain't driven one like this in a long time."

Eli's big fingers found the switches on the driver's side door. He toggled the power locks. The doors and lift-gate clicked as the locks engaged. The noise made Brad feel even more uneasy, wedged between the burly cop and his father. The confines of the Jeep grew stifling. Brad tugged at his collar as a warm prickle spread across his face. Eli swung the Cherokee around the corner and gunned the engine.

"Just a second, officer," Al managed hoarsely, reaching behind Brad and tapping Eli on the shoulder. "I think you turned the wrong way. Isn't the hospital back in the other direction?"

Eli grinned.

"Ah, sir, maybe we can see your ID," Al asked.

"Sure, my name's Eli," he said reaching inside his jacket. "And here's my ID."

Eli pulled his hand from inside the open jacket and back-handed Al with the Beretta. The powerful swing caught Al on the side of the head, slamming him back into the window, the back of his head cracking the glass. Eli's hand landed most of the impact, but the barrel of the gun still split a nasty gash across Al's head. A hot rush of blood began running down the side of his face. His eyes wobbled as he appeared to hang on to consciousness.

Brad reared back from the man, throwing up his hands in front of his face, expecting to get the same treatment.

"Don't worry none, tyke. Ain't gonna hurt a sweet thing like you."

Eli leaned close to Brad and smiled, the stench of his breath tainted with the smell of death. Brad saw traces of blood on the man's face and soaking his now exposed shirt. Eli's eyes widened, revealing glowing yellow crescents.

Brad pushed back against the seat until the springs groaned. *My God, what's happening? Glowing eyes in a man, how can it be? Did the shape-shifter somehow follow us into town? Is it him? No, I killed it. Or has the whole area become infected with glowing-eyed killers while we were at deer camp? Is that why the streets looked so deserted when we entered town?* He tried to sort out the answers. But only one thought broke through; they had to get away from this guy, this thing, fast. His heart hammered against his windpipe. His mind raced.

"Yeah," growled Eli, running his tongue over his lips, "It's been a long time. I think I could fall in love with a sweet tyke like you."

Eli dipped the pistol toward Brad's leg and stroked the inside of his thigh. Brad quivered and tried to squirm further away from the man but remained wedged between him and his dad. Eli laughed and flashed his glowing eyes at Brad.

"Don't be so jumpy, tyke. Like I said, ain't gonna hurt you. Ain't gonna hurt none of you."

Eli looked at the shadowed faces of the others in the rearview mirror. What pretty sheep for slaughter. The old man will die quickly, not much fun there. Probably the hurt one too, might get a twitch or two from him at best. But ahh, that other tyke's full of piss. I can see that. Yeah, that spark in his eyes. Now there's some big fun. Eli grinned wider as he saw the fear in their faces and knew they were staring at his eyes.

"Oh, don't let these scare you," he said, reaching up and pulling on his lower eyelid, exposing more of the foxfire in his eye. "It's just a little eye infection, nothing to worry about. It's the least of your problems. Believe me."

In the back, Corey, Pa, and Larry exchanged glances. They looked as if they believed him. They exchanged other looks.

Brad turned back toward his dad. Al had regained his senses and also noticed the glow in Eli's eyes. Despite the dreadful lump that had already started to swell on the side of Al's forehead, a new fire burned in his stare.

"Manitou," Al hissed, sounding more like a groggy gasp for breath than a word. All but Eli recognized it.

Seeing his Dad's battered face, a spark of anger ignited within Brad. Damn you. Damn you to hell. I didn't save my dad and the rest of us to let them fall prey to some asshole like you. If we made it out of Deadman's Swamp, we can deal with you. Brad peeked at the man out of the corner of his eye. God, but he's so big. How can we overpower him? And the gun.

Brad looked toward his father. Al's jaw tightened. He barely nodded to Brad, just as he had back at The Narrows, ready to walk into its depths. Their eyes met in the dim light of the Jeep, their bond of blood now transcending words. Time to survive another beast from the dark. Al slipped his hand into his coat pocket. Brad heard the faint but familiar click of his dad's folding knife locking open.

Turning slowly, Brad glanced over his shoulder. Corey, Pa, and Larry barely nodded in unison from the back. Their shadowed faces were drawn tight. Larry's eyes burned from dark sockets. Corey's flashed like coldfire. Pa's upper lip curled, old crooked teeth bared. Again, a pack of hunters bonded as one, ready again to switch the roles of hunter and prey.

Brad looked forward again. He shifted his eyes to the brute. Think like your foe. Use its strength against it. Right Pa. We look like a battered bunch, each of us easy victims for this guy. But it ain't gonna be like that. Not one at a time like he wants, on his terms. He won't expect resistance. Most victims think of defense, not attack.

Corey's eyes shifted to Larry, his pillar of strength in the night. They winked, magnets drawing strength from each other. With catlike quiet Larry removed the blanket and silently untied the long scarf from around his midsection. His face twisted from the effort. He handed Corey and Pa one end while he wrapped his big hands around the other. Then they waited like lions in ambush.

Brad saw they were entering the east outskirts of town. Only a few intersections separated them from the darkness of the wilderness once more. He glanced at Eli and saw him squinting each time they passed under a street lamp. His eyes! Just like the buck's! Light blinds him. A moment of reprieve, of action. Yes, Pa. Prey upon the weakness, make it our strength.

They were nearing the final stretch of lighted highway when Brad saw the red flashers of an ambulance approaching from the east. He watched the man squint each time one of the bright red beams completed its wild revolution. The man slowed the Jeep as the last traffic light on the outskirts of town turned red.

"Damn," he growled under his breath. "Keep still. Any of you move, and you won't live long enough to regret it."

He nervously fingered the pistol in his right hand as he slowed for the traffic signal and stopped. A bright wash of yellow light flooded the intersection from street lamps on three corners. The man lowered his gaze, snarling at the light, his attention now focused on the approaching ambulance, followed by a police car cruising with its flashers off, Brad realized. He glanced back to his dad. Al had also seen it and nodded again. Brad held his breath as he reached up and appeared to scratch the side of his head. His hand continued upward, his finger finding the switch on the overhead dome light.

The ambulance slowed for the red light. The police car turned on its flashers as it neared the intersection to warn any oncoming traffic. Their blue and white strobes punched through the night. The man squinted even more.

Brad flicked on the dome light.

"YOU LITTLE BASTARD!" Eli bellowed.

Brad ducked as Eli reached up with his pistol hand and blindly struck at the light as if it were an attacking bird.

Eli squinted shut as the brightness of light blinded him momentarily. He flailed at the light, hoping to smash it to bits with the gun. Suddenly something encircled his neck and jerked his head back against the head-rest. He reached up with his left hand and tried to pull the thing away from his throat. But it had already found one of the deep folds of skin around his neck and sunk into it. He clawed at the thing with his left hand. He tried to level the Beretta behind him and shoot the sneaky bastards but found the goddamn brat clinging to his right arm. What the hell? He tried shaking the kid free but the little monster hung on like an enraged bobcat.

"You're all going to die for this," he managed before the thing around his neck constricted even tighter like the coil of an enormous snake, cutting off his air altogether. He continued clawing at it with this left hand.

He bucked forward, jerking Corey, Pa and Larry into the back of the seat with a resounding thud. The force threatened to yank their arms from their sockets, but they hung on. And somewhere in the tight confines of the back end, amidst the bond they had welded, they found the collective strength to yank back. Young and old voices cried out together like a pack of snarling wolves as they pulled with a new vengeance now, again drawing Eli's neck tight against the head rest of the seat.

Near panic, Eli fingered the trigger of the Beretta, discharging a volley up through the roof of the Jeep. Still the brat hung on. Then Eli felt the searing slashes of a knife biting into his chest and abdomen like the canines of a huge mongrel chewing out his insides. What the hell was happening? These crazy bastards are insane. Something had turned the battered bunch into a seething nest of hornets stinging him from every quarter. How had a handful of frightened kids and tattered men sprung into an enraged beast with ten arms and five heads, all savagely working to spill his blood? They would pay for every drop of it with all of theirs.

Brad hung on with all his might. His dam of anger burst in a massive flood, funneling its power into his will to hang on. The man shook his arm with all the force of a bucking bull, smashing Brad into the dash and against the seat as if he were but an oversized charm bracelet. Back and forth, his head and shoulders banged the dash and seat. He caught blurred glimpses of his dad's face twisted in rage, the bloody sheen of his knife striking again and again. The man roared. Brad's head took out the rearview mirror in a shower of glass. The bones in his forearm cracked as he was again smashed into the dash. Brad pushed back the flashes of pain and clung fast. He heard another roar, deafening gunshots only inches from his ear.

Eli twisted his head to the side and opened his mouth. Enough of this. Time for someone to die. He reached over with his free hand to crush the kid's face. But only inches from it, a pair of hands, one bandaged, surged up and grabbed his wrist. He jerked back but the hands held like talons, then teeth behind a twisted face sunk deep into the tendons on the back of his hand. Eli's mouth widened more. But only a hiss escaped his pinched throat. His arm strained as he tried again to reach the kid's face. Snarling, the mad-man fought harder, biting deeper. He tore free a tendon then bit for another. Eli jerked both arms. In his other hand, he pulled the trigger again.

Outside, tires whined on the cold pavement as the prison security car following the ambulance skidded to a halt near the Jeep. The ruckus inside the lighted vehicle at the intersection had made them slow. The flash of gunshots brought them screeching to a stop. Now, recognizing Little Eli entangled in a vicious struggle with the occupants of the Jeep, they leaped from their car, weapons poised.

The lead officer leveled his shotgun at the door and ordered one of the others to open it. They found it locked. More gunfire ripped through the roof. Without another word, the man hoisted the butt of his shotgun and smashed in the window. He raised the lock and swung open the door. All three of them grabbed a piece of Eli and pulled.

Brad hung on as he watched his dad wrestle back the man's hand. Every vessel pressed against the skin of his dad's face as the eyes, bulged in the viciousness of the attack, looked as cold as a shark's. At that instant, Brad knew, that man was truly an animal; smarter than most others maybe, but an animal nonetheless.

More gunfire erupted within the Cherokee, the roar penetrating past the ringing in Brad's ears. He wasn't sure if anyone was hit, but he felt the sting of exploding glass striking his face. He squeezed his eyes shut and hung on. The shooting stopped. He felt the cold slap of the night air. Gruff voices rose above the ringing. Someone from behind tried pulling him off the brute's arm. Still he grunted and hung on.

For a moment, Eli felt as if his throat would be pinched in half by the force of the madmen pulling on the noose around his neck while the others tried to yank him from the Jeep. His vision had grown dark, either from the bright lights, the lack of air, or the loss of blood wetting his chest. His mind buzzed on the brink of unconsciousness. Let go, drop into the well. Let it be done, over for good. But then a final spurt of the altered adrenaline surged through his system, finding that primitive chamber in his mind. His senses rocked back to life. No, don't quit. Survive, whatever it takes. Flee into the dark. Run fast. Get away. Hide. Hurry-hurry. A coppery stench filled Eli's mouth. What was that taste? The playground, so many years ago. The taste of fear.

The noose loosened from around his neck. Yes, free. He sucked in a sweet breath, then another. His mind began to clear. I'm still alive. Survive, run, quick, be free forever.

The lead officer didn't wonder if the Beretta clutched in Eli's grip was empty. Any weapon in the hands of an escaped inmate was considered loaded. He touched the trigger of the 12-gauge, waiting for the moment. One of the officers finally managed to pull off the man gripping Eli's hand as another yanked free the kid clinging to Eli's other arm. The officers stepped back, pulling the men from the line of fire.

Free of his clinging attackers, Eli rolled to his knees and brought up the pistol to shield his eyes against the headlights of the patrol car. To the officer, it looked as if Eli might be pointing. He didn't much care. His 12-gauge spit a blue flame and buckshot. The impact at pointblank range would have ripped most men in half. But Eli took the buckshot like the brute he was, rising to his feet and staggering toward Brad. The officer fired again. Eli rocked backward but still kept coming. Another volley rang out. Finally, he crumpled slowly to the pavement and rolled on his back, steam escaping from his body like a draining colander.

An officer was already yanking the Beretta from Eli's limp hand as the last long breath left his body. His head lolled to the side and his eyes met Brad's. They seemed to gaze completely through him for a second then suddenly blinked back to life and focused. Their probing depths reached out to Brad as if he were some distant kin, begging him to come near at this final moment.

Brad pulled from the clutches of the officer, took a few steps closer, and looked down. He saw past the faintly glowing crescents below the irises and looked into the wide pupils of the man. And there, in the watery blackness, Brad saw not only a monster, but a glint of himself too. He saw beyond the two-dimensional reflection into the very essence of a supreme hunter. Despite the modern world they lived and died in, they were still both two-legged predators, both with the instinctual drive to chase prey, fight, survive at all costs — the inherent bond of hunters for thirty thousand years. He shivered and stepped back. The man's eyes rolled back under drooped lids.

Brad turned to the sound of footsteps as his dad reached out for him. Brad stepped into his arms and they held each other for a long moment. They moved to the Jeep and peered inside. Brad fought back warm tears as he realized none of them had been shot. They looked battered but alive. Even Larry smiled.

"You hangin' in there, Uncle Larry?"

"You bet, Brad. Corey and I were just about to make plans for him to come a visit this summer. Figured we could make him a bow too."

Even in the poor light, the green in Corey's eyes sparkled like emeralds. Brad gave him a thumb's up. Pa winked.

"Climb in you guys," the officer interrupted as he brushed glass bits from the seat and slid behind the wheel. "I better drive you to the hospital. We can't wait for an ambulance. They're all busy tonight."

He pulled the Jeep away and waved to the others still standing over Eli's body. He turned around in the intersection and headed toward the hospital.

"Good thing we'd been ordered to escort the ambulance to the hospital," the officer said. "Our last one didn't arrive. Guess we know why now."

He looked at the passengers but they said nothing. Oddly, they kept staring into his eyes. Somehow they seemed inordinately pleased with his baby blues.

The officer looked back to the road then pulled up his collar to help ward off the icy blast rushing in the shattered window.

"Sorry about this cold ride but we'll be there in a few minutes. Sorry about what happened back there, too. We'll need a full report after we get you taken care of."

They still sat there quietly. Only the wind stirred the silence. The officer squirmed in the seat and looked around at his passengers.

"Looks like you guys took a real beating tonight. You're lucky to be alive. That guy back there was an escaped man-killer from the prison. One of the worst."

"How'd he get out?" Corey asked.

"Don't know the details yet," the officer said, the tension in his voice growing slack now that someone had replied. "But when they put all the pieces together, I'm sure it's going to be one heck of a story."

The man rubbed the left side of his face with a gloved hand. He glanced back at the others.

"You guys deer hunters?"

Brad looked up at his dad.

"You bet we are," Al said, wrapping his arm around Brad.

"Maybe you heard of us," Pa offered from the back, a renewed vigor returning to his voice. "We're the Mercer's, deer slayers, every one of us to the core."

He reached up and laid a hand on Brad's shoulder.

"Yeah. Some of us like to hold out for the real bruisers," piped Corey, rubbing the top of Brad's head.

"Make fancy running shots too," Larry said, his voice weak but clear.

The officer's face softened some and he tipped back the brim of his cap.

"You guys sound like an old story teller I used to know in deer camp," he said, raising an eyebrow and grinning. "But the old guy had the big racks to back up his tales."

The officer paused, giving them a moment to begin a deer hunting tale. Brad turned to the others. No one said a word. The man noticed Brad shift in the seat and looked over at him.

"Well, son, a young hunter like you must have at least one story to tell about opening day."

Brad sighed and looked at the man.

"Yeah. But I don't think we have the time to begin it right now," he said, looking ahead again. "It's kind of a long story."

The officer nodded and smiled as if he sensed Brad was a story-teller beyond his years.

"Oh, one of *those* kind of tales," he said, as if he somehow knew.

But Brad realized only a handful ever would.

Deep in the tangle of Deadman's Swamp, a black bear the size of a grizzly stirred deep within its den. It groaned as if aggravated by the numbing cold that had seeped into its lair. It rolled over and shivered. Its eyes opened for a moment, showing a yellow glow glistening in the corners of its intelligent eyes.

High above, the northern lights cast an golden aura over the forest. But none of that glow should have reached the depths of the bear's den.

The giant bear closed its eyes and resumed its heavy breathing. Sleep and fat would hold it there until spring. Then, it would emerge, and with it, a great hunger to fill.

If you enjoyed *Opening Day*, and like bowhunting, you'll love *Bowhunting Fireside Tales* by Dan Bertalan.

This collection of Dan's 15 finest short stories takes you into the tapestry of the imagination, exploring the essence of the human spirit on its enduring adventure with the bow and arrow.

Bowhunting Fireside Tales awaits you.

But watch out for stray sparks!

WHAT ARE THE EXPERTS SAYING ABOUT THIS BOOK?

"Humorous, entertaining, chilling ...at times deeply thought-provoking, this collection of stories from Dan Bertalan is a welcomed addition to the bowhunter's library...has a way of grabbing and not letting go of the reader... will open your eyes to many things we may take for granted in our day-to-day life."
T.J. Conrads, Editor/Publisher, Traditional Bowhunter Magazine

"Dan Bertalan's latest book, a collection of bowhunting tales reflecting his intimate knowledge of our sport, demonstrates what happens when you combine an obvious talent for well written prose with a vivid imagination. The end result is a collection of sometimes funny, sometimes frightening, sometimes nostalgic and always entertaining stories that hit the mark time after time like well placed arrows. If you're looking for readable bowhunting fiction, Dan Bertalan's *Fireside Tales* is a worthy addition to any hunter's library."
M.R. James, Editor/Founder Bowhunter magazine

"A refreshingly new kind of bowhunting entertainment. Tugging on our hearts as well as our minds, the author uses short stories to remind us of the *real* values of our sport. A unique opportunity for the reader to not only look into the mirror of outdoor responsibility and respect, but a chance to see a reflection of our values as well as the shadow of our outdoor spirit. Bertalan's light footsteps in the forest have left footprints on my heart. Excellent reading!"
Gene Wensel, Bowhunting Author

Bowhunting Fireside Tales; 121 pages, softcover

Order your copy today — Send just $6.95 (plus $2 shipping) to: Envisage Unlimited Press, P.O. Box 777, East Lansing, MI 48826, or call in your credit card order now at 517-834-2276.

TRADITIONAL BOWYERS OF AMERICA

The Bowhunting and Bowmaking World of the Nation's Top Crafters of Longbows and Recurves

DAN BERTALAN

HAVE YOU READ *TRADITIONAL BOWYERS OF AMERICA* by Dan Bertalan?

If you're interested in traditional bowhunting, this book is for you!

In profiling 30 of America's top traditional bowyers, this hefty volume reveals over 700 cumulative years of bowhunting and bowmaking adventures. It details the building of recurves and longbows, offers valuable advice on selecting the perfect custom bow for you, tells how to improve your instinctive shooting, gives big game hunting tips from east to west, and serves up a potpourri of exciting bowhunting stories.

Just listen to what the experts say about this book.

"This book is so entertaining, so informative, I read it from cover to cover two times before I could get back to work! I find it to be a much used reference in my day-to-day work. The amount of history in this book cannot be found anywhere else, and no bowhunter should be without it in his or her own personal library." *T.J. Conrads, Editor/Publisher, Traditional Bowhunter magazine.*

"It's an excellent book for hunters who are considering a switch to longbows and recurves from compounds. It offers knowledge that can't be obtained anywhere else." *Dave Richey, Outdoor Editor, The Detroit News.*

"This is a must read for anyone interested in the heritage of American archery and hunting." *Dwight Schuh, Author, Bowhunting Editor for Sports Afield magazine*

"I missed two days of hunting because I got so engrossed in reading *Traditional Bowyers of America*...real down to earth style of writing...I felt I was sitting in those bowyer shops...my latent desire to build a longbow has been rekindled." *Vern Struble, Professional Bowhunter's Society Librarian.*

"The most interesting, entertaining, book I've read in years. A timely text of the life-styles and/or philosophy of some of the greatest men in our sport...the roots and seeds of bowhunting...yesterday, today and tomorrow." *Gene Wensel, Bowhunting Author and Outdoor Writer.*

Traditional Bowyers of America :528 pages, 166 photos, glossary, index, hardcover.

What more can we say? If you're a traditional bowhunter, you owe it to yourself to buy this book, today! Credit card orders accepted. Call now, 517-834-2276. Or send check or money order to; Envisage Unlimited Press, P.O. Box 777, East Lansing, MI 48826-0777. $29.95 plus $2 shipping (MI residents add $1.20 tax).

ARE YOU A WHITETAIL HUNTER? OKAY, QUIZ TIME.

Q — What costs less than a dozen broadheads yet makes the difference between consistently successful trophy hunters and the thousands who want to be?

A — *Knowledge*

So before next season, hunt with the knowledge of **Bowhunting's Whitetail Masters.** You won't believe the difference it makes having these twelve guys on your side; Bob Fratzke, Barry Wensel, Quince Hale, Noel Feather, Bill Meyer, John Hale, Roger Rothhaar, Gerald Shaffner, Russell Hull, John Kolometz, Mitch Rompola, and Gene Wensel.

Just listen to what the experts say.

"*Bowhunting's Whitetail Masters* is a winner. In a single text it serves up the experiences, tips and secrets of 12 of today's hottest whitetail hunters. It would take 12 books to replace this on...The blend of information and entertainment is excellent." *Bill Krenz, Vice President, Hoyt USA, Bowhunting Writer*

"The words that best describe this book are thorough, probing and insightful. It would be impossible to read it and not become a better deer hunter." *Patrick Durkin, Editor, Deer & Deer Hunting magazine*

"One of the best books on whitetails and the bowhunters who pursue them I've ever had the privilege to read, and I read them all. Honestly! Pure enjoyment and that's from the heart." *Alan Foster, Outdoor Writer, North American Whitetail*

"Thanks to Dan Bertalan's excellent new book, *Bowhunting's Whitetail Masters,* we have at our fingertips a collected wealth of information unselfishly provided by a dozen of this country's most successful deer hunters. It's all here, too; bowhunting techniques, success secrets, solid advice and candid comments, plus a rare glimpse at the men themselves. All told, this entertaining and informative book is the next best thing to meeting these experts and having them speak to us one-on-one. It's must reading for serious whitetail hunters." *M.R. James, Editor/Publisher, Bowhunter magazine*

If you love bowhunting whitetails, you owe it to yourself to buy this incredible collection of bowhunting techniques, secrets, and success stories of America's premier deer hunters.

BOWHUNTING'S WHITETAIL MASTERS: **344 pages, 66 photos, hardcover.**

Credit card orders accepted. Call now, 517-834-2276. Or, send check or money order to; Envisage Unlimited Press, P.O. Box 777, East Lansing, MI 48826-0777. $29.95 plus $2 shipping (MI residents add $1.20 tax).

ABOUT THE AUTHOR

A national award winning outdoor writer, Dan Bertalan's bowhunting articles appear regularly in *Bowhunter, Bowhunting World, Traditional Bowhunter,* and *Deer & Deer Hunting* magazines. His popular non-fiction books, *Traditional Bowyers Of America* and *Bowhunting's Whitetail Masters* have earned him international acclaim. With over 50 feature articles published in recent years, he is recognized as one of today's top bowhunting writers.

Exclusively a bowhunter, Dan has hunted across North America for 30 years, from the eastern barrens of Newfoundland to the western slopes of the Alaskan Peninsula, and from the far reaches of the Northwest Territories to the cactus flats near the Mexican border — and through it all, harvesting a dozen different big game species, many registered in the Pope & Young Club's record book.

An active supporter of quality, ethical bowhunting, he is a Regular Member of the Professional Bowhunter's Society, an Associate Member of the Pope & Young Club, a member of the NRA, a member of the Michigan Bow Hunters, and a member of Michigan Traditional Bowhunters. In the writing arena, he is a member of the Michigan Outdoor Writers Association and the Outdoor Writers Association of America.

He lives in rural central Michigan where he loves chasing whitetails and sharing his bowhunting adventures through writing — both real and fiction, from the heart and from the well of imagination.